RACHEL WESSON

a home for unloved orphans

Published by Bookouture in 2020

An imprint of Storyfire Ltd.
Carmelite House
50 Victoria Embankment
London EC4Y 0DZ

www.bookouture.com

ISBN: 978-1-83888-979-1
eBook ISBN: 978-1-83888-978-4

This book is dedicated to my amazing husband and our three incredible children. I should also include our dog, which arrived during the writing of this book. I was going to name her Shadow but my daughter decided Gracie was nicer.

CHAPTER 1

New York, December 1930

"Away in a manger, no crib for His bed, the little Lord…"

Lauren Greenwood blinked rapidly, not because of the snow dusting her eyelashes, but because the children's sweet voices rose over the bustle of New York's 34th Street. How she missed Nanny and everyone back at Rosehall. She screwed up her eyes, ignoring the crowds of shoppers pushing past her, as she let the singing transport her back to Delgany, Virginia. She wasn't standing on a busy New York sidewalk, surrounded by strangers, but on the grand staircase back home, watching with the children from the estate, and the servants, as Jackson, the butler, placed the dazzling angel at the top of the Christmas tree. No shop-bought tree for Rosehall, but one of the magnificent fir trees that grew high up on the Blue Ridge Mountains. She could almost taste the snickerdoodle cookies Cook would bake for the occasion.

"This is like a Christmas fairyland." Mary's eyes widened with wonder, staring at Macy's façade.

Lauren picked up on her maid's excitement. "Wait till you see the window display. People come from miles to see it. I've missed you, Mary. I wish you could have gone to Europe with me."

"A maid go to a finishing school? That would be a first, Miss Lauren."

Lauren's smile dropped as she caught sight of two little girls, barefoot, dressed in rags without a coat between them. They were holding hands, their matching bright red hair and freckles suggesting they were sisters, their gaze locked on Macy's window display. She moved closer, wanting to do something to help these poor children, but what? She was half tempted to take them by the hand into the department store, where she would buy them coats and shoes. Nobody should walk barefoot in New York, especially not in these freezing temperatures. She watched as the taller of the two girls tried to pull the other one away from the window.

"Come on, Maggie, we got to get home. Ma will have us for dinner if we don't."

"No, I want to stay. I want a Mickey Mouse doll just like that one from *Steamboat Willie*. Do you think Father Christmas will bring me one?"

"Nope. We'll be lucky to eat on Christmas Day. Come on, now. We shouldn't even be here. This is for rich folk."

"Why? Lookin' in a winda is free, ain't it?"

The small girl's protests made Lauren smile.

"Maggie, stop arguing and come on. I'll go without you."

"Na, you won't, Biddy. Ma will kill you if you lose me." Maggie returned to staring at the window display. Lauren saw fear on the older girl's face, catching her looking at a police officer who was standing further along the block.

"Biddy, can you buy me a hot roll? I ain't ever had one of them," the little girl said.

"With what?" her sister responded sharply.

"Girls, would you like something to eat?" Lauren said, unable to stay silent any longer.

"No, miss, but thank you," the older girl responded, but her younger sister immediately spoke up.

"I is so hungry. I haven't had a piece of bread in this long." She held up five fingers.

"Maggie, come on. We can't speak to strangers. They'll send us away from Ma." Biddy pulled at her arm but Maggie wasn't going anywhere.

Lauren glanced around and spotted a food cart. "Wait here, girls, for just a minute. Mary, I'll be right back." She ignored her maid's raised eyebrows and pursed lips.

Not giving Mary a chance to voice her objection, Lauren crossed the street toward the cart. She bought hot frankfurter rolls from the stall, buying four at five cents each. She added two iced sodas, thinking the girls would enjoy the sugary treat despite the winter snow. Handing the vendor a dollar, she told him to keep the change.

"Merry Christmas, lady," he said, glancing down at the dollar and back at her.

Running back across the street, Lauren handed the hot rolls and sodas to the girls.

"This is all for me, just me?" Maggie asked, her eyes wide.

The food had cost thirty cents but Lauren would have given the child a million dollars if she'd had it. She smiled. "Yes, Maggie, all for you and your sister. Do you live near here?"

"Yes, miss," she replied.

Biddy glared at Maggie. "What did you tell her that for? Now she'll want to take us home."

Lauren exchanged a look with Mary. The maid shook her head but Lauren chose to ignore her.

"I'm Lauren and this is Mary. We would like to meet your mother. Do you think we could walk you home or maybe take a streetcar?"

"We ain't got the money for no streetcar," Biddy said immediately.

"Biddy, it will be our treat. Let us take you home, please. Your mother must be hungry too."

At that the girl's shoulders slumped and she lost her attempt at bravery. "Ma's sick. She can't get out of bed. The baby is crying all the time. We were supposed to find her somethin' to eat but nobody wants to hear us sing our carols. The coppers, they keep movin' us on."

"We heard you singing 'Away in a Manger', didn't we, Mary? It was beautiful." Lauren shivered, despite her warm coat. "Come on, girls, let's get you home before you freeze."

After they'd step down onto the sidewalk, the little girl pointed to what loo like a passageway between two tall buildings. She took Lau 's hand while Biddy led the way, holding onto Mary.

As the alley grw darker, despite it being morning, Lauren wondered if shd been mad to suggest this. What if the girls led then to a denof thieves or worse? But then her beloved Nanny's voice came to mind: *Young children in need should never be ignored.* She rolled her shoulders back and followed along.

"Ma doesn't look her best. She's been sick a while." Biddy's voice sang out as she led them through a cavern of buildings until they stopped in front of one. The outside door was hanging off and Biddy just pushed it aside, leading the way. The stench brought tears to Lauren's eyes, a mixture of boiling cabbage with an underlying hint of ammonia derived from human waste. Her stomach churned as they climbed the stairs, higher and higher into this building. She wanted to put her hands over her ears to block out the screams and shouting of the residents. It would also be a good way to avoid touching the walls, which appeared to be streaming with water... or at least she hoped it was water.

Biddy finally stopped climbing just as Lauren's legs had begun to scream in protest.

"Can you wait here till I check Ma's awake?" the girl asked, her voice trembling.

"Of course," Lauren squeaked, since Mary seemed incapable of talking.

The door closed behind the children, but it wasn't heavy enough to mask the conversation.

"What d'you mean, you got ladies with ye? What type of ladies? Holy Mother, it isn't dem nuns, is it? They've come to take ye away from me. I swear I'll kill you meself, Biddy, if you let them women come near youse."

Lauren opened the door. "Excuse me, ma'am. We haven't come to take your children. We, that is myself and Mary, were outside Macy's and met your girls. We enjoyed their lovely voices…" Lauren fell silent as the woman got up out of bed, wearing a rather sheer nightgown. She turned her back to give Biddy's mother a chance to dress.

"Come in, while you're here. You can't be standing in the door. Take a seat at the table but brush it down before you sit, your fancy clothes might get stained. Biddy, put the kettle on and make these nice ladies a cuppa. It'll have to be black as we don't have no milk. We don't have anything by the way of eatin'. I'm Mrs. Sadie Cullen, by the way." As she finished speaking, the woman paled and almost fell, but for Biddy catching her.

Lauren, who had turned round to listen to her, jumped to help. "Please don't worry yourself about us, Mrs. Cullen. We didn't mean to cause you trouble."

"Ma, can we eat the rolls now? They got mustard on them and everythin'," Maggie burst out. "You can have some of mine, if you like."

"Rolls?" Their mother held her hands to her breast.

"Yeah and sodas." Biddy took a sip. "We didn't find nuthin' for the baby. Nobody gave us any money for our singin'. Them ladies bought us these."

The baby. Lauren glanced around the room but couldn't see or hear a baby. She looked back at the mother, catching her eyes as they lit upon a drawer.

"Where is the baby, Mrs. Cullen? I promise we aren't going to take any of the children away. Why would you think that?"

"They took my eldest two boys. They never told me or nuthin'. The priest, he said it was best for them, but what sort of life is it for childer to be away from their parents?"

The girls were hungry and dressed in rags, but Mrs. Cullen appeared to be a loving mother who was simply down on her luck. Wouldn't it be better to keep families together? Lauren mused.

"Where is your husband, Mrs. Cullen?" Mary asked.

If it were possible, the woman's face grew paler.

"Daddy's in jail cause he hit the copper who came to take the boys. The copper didn't like it and he put Daddy in a place where he can sing all day," Maggie told them between bites of sausage, the yellow mustard staining her face and fingers.

"He can sing?" Lauren didn't understand.

Mary moved forward. "I think the child means Sing Sing, the prison. Is that right, Mrs. Cullen?"

"Aye. Daniel was arrested for thieving. He stole a loaf of bread and some milk for the baby. It's my fault. I can't feed Cian, the little boy. Not no more. The copper let him off but then when Daniel tried to stop them takin' the boys and hit another copper, they said he was bad news."

Lauren reached for the drawer as Mary took a seat on the bed and held Mrs. Cullen as she sobbed. The baby stared back at Lauren, his dark blue eyes huge in his shrunken face above his little body. She lifted him up as gently as possible, and he didn't make a sound. But for his eyes, which were moving, she'd have thought him dead.

"I think he needs a doctor. He's so tiny." Lauren couldn't believe a baby could be so light. She handed him over to his mother.

"Three months old and only looks like a newborn. Cian's stopped cryin' now. He doesn't have the energy even though he is half-starved."

The door banged then, making them all jump. "Mother Mary and all that's holy, what are you doing, botherin' poor Sadie Cullen?" said the woman, bursting into the room. "Can't you see she's had enough help from do-gooders to last her a lifetime? Takin' her boys from her was an awful sin and now that lovely young husband of hers. What do you want?" The woman faced them with her hands on her hips, her big bosom heaving with indignation.

Mary stood up from the bed. "We didn't mean any harm. My name is Mary and this is Miss Lauren. We were on our way into Macy's and happened upon the girls. They gave us a song and we paid them in hot rolls. We should be going now. Miss Lauren?"

But Lauren couldn't walk away. She knew she should, but something was stopping her.

"Frances Murphy, will you leave these poor women alone? Sure they were only tryin' to see to my girls." Mrs. Cullen turned back to Lauren. "If it weren't for the kindness of Frances and her Seamus the whole lot of us would be ten foot under. They've been givin' us food and keeping the rent collector at bay. They bought me enough time to get past Thanksgiving. We have to be out tomorrow."

"It's almost Christmas. Where will you go?" Lauren asked, ignoring Mary's movement toward the door. "What will happen to you?"

Mrs. Cullen couldn't answer. Lauren looked to the woman introduced as Frances Murphy, but she was staring at the ground. Even the children fell silent, no longer eating.

"Mrs. Murphy, can I please impose on you?"

"What?" the woman replied, looking confused.

"I mean, will you help me, please? I want to go to the store first. This family is going to have a Christmas they won't forget."

"You mean it, lady?" Maggie grabbed Lauren's coat, tugging it to get her attention. "You is goin' to get us an angel for the tree and presents? I want a Mickey Mouse toy." The little girl jumped up and down.

"Margaret Cullen, where are your manners?"

Maggie took a step back when her mother used her given name.

"What will these ladies think of you? They'll believe I don't know how to rear childer." Mrs. Cullen turned her tear-stained face to look at Lauren. "I thank you for your kindness, miss, but I can't ask you to do that."

"You're not asking, Mrs. Cullen. I want to. Christmas is a time for children, the one moment in the year where every dream should come true." Lauren rubbed the woman's arm. "Please let me do it. For the girls?"

Biddy and Maggie both spoke at once. "Please, Mammy, let her get us Christmas. *Pleassssse.*"

Mrs. Cullen sobbed, making no attempt to hide her distress. "'Tis a miracle my girls found you."

Lauren was having trouble not breaking down herself. "Please don't cry. I was trying to make things better."

"Miss Lauren, we can't fix everything," Mary protested, at the same time as Mrs. Murphy seized Lauren's arm.

"I'll take you, lady. You'll only get cheated and charged extra lookin' like you do and soundin' all fancy like. Girls, I think you done found your mother a guardian angel." She led Lauren out the door fast, while Mary shrugged her shoulders and said she'd come along too to help carry things.

Together, the three of them walked back down the stairs, with Lauren and Mary listening to Frances Murphy explaining how it was to live in such a place.

"There should only be ten families livin' here but there are upward of twenty. It's the Depression. Them that have jobs have had to take pay cuts. They be the lucky ones. All share the same privy out the back, hence the smell. Good, honest, decent folk in this house, but there's nothing can be done to make the place fit for anythin' other than pigs. Even they'd refuse to live here." The woman laughed at her own joke, but Lauren couldn't laugh. It was simply too heartbreaking.

As they walked out the dark tenement into the alley, she could see that snow had been falling. Even the snow was gray here, not like the pristine white snow in the mountains where Lauren came from.

"New York really is a tale of two cities, isn't it? Where else would the richest and poorest of society live almost door to door?" Mary whispered to Lauren once they had reached the filthy street again. People didn't look up as they passed by. Everyone seemed to be staring at their shoes. Mary caught the look on Lauren's face as she watched them. "Miss Lauren, everywhere you look there are people in need. You can't help them all."

Lauren wished that she *could* save them all. "I know," she replied. "But I can help the Cullens. Maggie and Biddy are so brave. I have to do something, I can't just walk away." *Why don't the newspapers do more to highlight the plight of these children*, she wondered. If her heroine, the American journalist Nellie Bly, were still alive, she'd be writing about these unseen victims of the Depression, making sure they weren't forsaken by society.

Mary looked at her watch. "Miss Lauren, we need to get on our way or we will be late for your dress fitting."

"I know but... I feel responsible."

"You aren't. Just give Mrs. Murphy some money and let's get going. Your father won't like it if you don't have a new dress. He said a lot of his contacts would be at this ball."

Lauren was torn, but she saw the maid's point. Her father was something to be reckoned with. She walked back to Mrs. Murphy, who had stopped in the alley. "We have an appointment to get to, Mrs. Murphy. Would you be able to find someone to help you with the food shopping and take it back to the Cullens? Maybe in a cab?"

"No need of a cab for me, dearie, but you wait here a minute." The woman put two fingers in her mouth, and whistled.

Lauren jumped, but it worked. Out of nowhere, several boys came running. "You want us, Ma?" one of them asked.

"Charlie, you help these ladies find a cab. Mikey, get your finger out of your nose. You're to help me do some shoppin'. Seamus, Jnr., you're to go get the old pushchair and come to meet us. No lollygagging. Straight back here or you'll feel the back of my hand across your bare legs."

"Yes, Ma," the boys chorused, before running off to do what they were told.

"You get along. I'll make sure the Cullens have a nice meal. Don't you fret," she said to Lauren.

"Mrs. Murphy, how much is the rent for the Cullens' room?"

"Five dollars, that's for a week. But I think Sadie is behind."

Lauren put her hand in her purse and pulled out thirty dollars. "Will you pay her rent for her and use the rest for the food for both your families? I will try to get back to see Mrs. Cullen over the next few days, but will you please tell her not to worry. I won't see her and the children put out on the streets."

Mrs. Murphy wiped a tear from her face. "I don't know who sent you, love, but you're a Christmas angel. That's what you are. Thank you."

Lauren nodded, too choked up to speak. Mary caught her arm and pulled her to where the boy, Charlie, was waiting for them. He seemed about ten years old, skinny and dirty, just like the Cullen girls.

"Want the streetcar or a cab?" the little boy asked.

Mary had to answer as emotion stopped Lauren. "A cab please, Charlie. We're late."

Charlie came back with a cab, confiding he had to promise the driver a dollar to come and fetch them. The man took off his hat and nodded to them. "Thought the lad was telling me stories when he said two rich women were in Hell's Kitchen. You got lost?"

"No, sir, but we are late. Can you please take us to Madame Bouvier's dress shop on Fifth Avenue?" Mary's smile seemed to seal the deal because the driver agreed. Lauren handed Charlie a quarter.

"Gee whiz, thanks, lady." The boy ran off, probably to spend it before his mother got hold of it.

CHAPTER 3

"Miss Lauren, the dress is stunning. It highlights your cream skin and dark hair and the style suits your height too. You'll turn heads at the Woolworth Ball." Mary's face lit up with admiration.

Lauren barely glanced at her reflection. She moved away from the long mirror to look out the window. She almost stepped on the seamstress, who was putting the finishing touches to the hemline. Outside, pristine snow covered the roofs of the closest buildings, changing their dull gray appearance to that of a magical white carpet. Gazing down toward the street, she looked at the endless traffic and sheer number of shoppers turning the snow on the sidewalk into gray slush.

"What's wrong, Miss Lauren? Don't you like the dress? Your father has been very generous with your allowance."

Lauren tried to focus on the dress but all she could think of were Maggie's and Biddy's faces when she'd given them the hot rolls… and the place they called home. How could she get excited about a fancy new dress when families like the Cullens were going hungry? The men, on the street below, looked half-frozen as they stood in line for scraps of food, desperation etched onto their faces, each waiting their turn for the soup kitchen.

"I'm grateful, of course, but don't you think I've been to enough parties, Mary? It seems wrong to be buying a new dress for each one, when so many people have so little."

Mary turned to the seamstress. "That's perfect now. Thank you."

The woman nodded, her mouth full of pins.

"We best get back to the hotel, Miss Lauren. Your father will be waiting. You go get changed. I'll pick up some matching ribbon for your hair."

After Lauren had changed, she came downstairs to the shop area, where she found Mary pacing the floor and looking at her watch.

"What took you so long, Miss Lauren?"

"I was thinking."

Mary smiled before doing a perfect imitation of Lauren's father's voice: "That's bad for your brain. Your job is to look pretty and land a rich, successful husband."

Lauren poked her tongue out at the maid. The pair had practically grown up together, being of a similar age. Mary had been an orphan and was a distant relative of Cook at Rosehall, who had taken her in and treated her as a daughter.

*

As the cab driver that the doorman at Madame Bouvier's had hailed drove Mary and Lauren to the hotel where her father was staying, Lauren peered out the window beside her. Every building looked similar and not just because of the snow. Maybe the white dusting on the upper levels served to highlight the dirt and despair of those living on the crowded streets. Mounds of garbage littered the sidewalks. How often did cleaners come to this area?

Lauren's eyes widened as she saw a family emerge from one of the piles. The mound of discarded boxes and broken pieces of furniture appeared to be their home. It made the mean rooms where the Cullens and Murphys lived seem like castles. She shuddered. Someone had to help these people.

Lauren turned her head from the window and closed her eyes, trying to conjure the feel of the winter sun on her face as she took Prince out for a ride across the hills above Rosehall. Sam, the head groom, was looking after Prince for her while she was in New York. She secretly hoped the horse was missing her as much as she was missing him. A day's riding in the Blue Ridge Mountains, followed by some of Cook's legendary fried chicken, and last but not least a cup of hot chocolate, while sitting with Nanny, was her idea of Heaven.

She wished Nanny had been able to come to New York, but Father had said that the traveling would prove too much for the older woman. Lauren didn't know how old Nanny was. She was her mother's aunt and had looked after Lauren's mother when she was just a girl. She couldn't wait to get home to see her. She'd missed Nanny most of all.

*

Mary stood back from the dressing table in Lauren's bedroom. "Miss Lauren, you look perfect. You're the image of your mama in the portrait at Rosehall. You were right to pick out a rose-tinted material, it highlights your creamy skin. On me, it would just make my freckles stand out more."

"I love your freckles and red hair, Mary. You look so different to everyone else. I just blend in."

"Sure you do, Miss Lauren." Mary rolled her eyes. "If I wasn't your servant, I would hit you for being so ungrateful. God blessed you with such deep black hair, you can almost see your reflection in it. Most people with your coloring have brown or maybe blue eyes but you got violet ones. He didn't give you a humped back or a hideous birthmark, did He? You should be grateful for your beauty, Miss Lauren."

Lauren stood up and walked to the full-length mirror on the wardrobe. She inspected her reflection, trying to see herself through Mary's eyes. The tight-fitting bodice, studded with pearls, diamanté and crystals, was, Madame Bouvier had assured her, the height of fashion. The rose-tinted tulle skirt, beautifully embroidered with silver threads, flowed to her ankles, beneath which her feet were clad in matching silver shoes. A set of elbow-length gloves completed her look.

Mary was being kind. She wasn't as beautiful as her mama, who had been much sought after.

"Are you woolgathering about finding a man?" Mary asked, amusement making her Irish lilt softer. "You'll be the belle of the ball, Miss Lauren." The maid pushed a few loose strands of hair back into her creation, before she stood back, her head tilting to one side. "You look like you're sucking on a lemon."

"I don't want to go to this ball."

Mary's eyes widened. "Why not? I'd love to see the Astors and the Vanderbilts up close."

"Why, Mary? They are just people like you and me."

"You don't have an ounce of romance in your soul, Miss Lauren. All you think about is your books and your studies. You should dream of princes or millionaires, dancing and laughing all night, with the prospect of a ring on the horizon."

Lauren scowled. "I wish everyone wasn't in such a hurry to marry me off. I can look after myself. I don't need a husband."

"Really?" Mary's eyebrows rose as she surveyed the room, where Lauren's discarded clothes lay in piles around the floor.

"It just seems so wrong to go dancing in a dress that cost hundreds of dollars when children like Biddy and Maggie are starving."

"What of all the people employed by the hotel? The seamstress who made your dress? Those people need jobs, Miss Lauren. Especially now." Mary patted a stray hair into place. "You go on now and put a smile on your face. We all have a role to fill and tonight yours is to look beautiful and smile. And remember to notice what the birthday girl is wearing, please. You know how much I love fashion."

"You should go in my place."

Mary roared with laughter as she picked up her skirt and pretended to dance.

Lauren laughed despite herself. Mary could always make her giggle.

She was about to leave when the maid called out to her. "Miss Lauren?"

She turned.

"Don't go kissing any toads."

CHAPTER 4

Lauren was still smiling as she walked into the living area of their suite where her father stood smoking a cigar. His superbly tailored dress suit flattered his towering height and trim figure. He'd had a haircut and shave, the flecks of gray more visible in the shorter style. Lauren caught the subtle flash of diamonds in his cufflinks and noticed he was wearing his wedding ring. He stared at her as she entered the room.

"Father, when are we going home to Delgany? It's almost Christmas and we don't want to miss the fun there."

When he remained silent, Lauren prompted, "Father?"

"You look lovely, Lauren." He ignored her question and continued to stare at her. "You look like your mother."

"I wish Mama was here. Why did she have to die so young? She liked dancing, didn't she? Nanny said she always enjoyed the balls, especially at Christmas."

Her father's gaze had turned icy cold. Why didn't he like her talking about Mama? Was his heart still broken?

"Your mother would want you to find a good man to settle down with, Lauren. Now, shall we go?"

The journey from their hotel to The Ritz wasn't far, but heavy traffic delayed them. Along the way, Lauren saw several apple sellers on the route. She had heard that the desperate times were driving men to sell the fruit on street corners even in blistering, icy winds, snow and sleet. She would have given them something if she was carrying cash, even though she knew her father was disapproving.

Once they arrived at The Ritz and walked inside, all Lauren's melancholy thoughts were temporarily banished. "Oh, Father, it looks like a garden under moonlight," she said in awe, as they entered the rooms where the debutante ball for Barbara Woolworth Hutton was being held. She gazed up at the ceiling, which was covered with blue gauze and decorative stars. She memorized every detail of her surroundings, remembering her promise to Mary. Silver Birch trees competed with Eucalyptus, both imported from California for the occasion.

She lowered her eyes and gasped. "Are these real?" she asked him, bending over some decorative rose beds. "How did they get roses to bloom at this time of year?"

"Money can buy you everything, Lauren. Please stop acting like a country hick. Stand up straight and don't let me down."

Lauren straightened up, imagining Miss Caroline prodding her in the shoulders, reminding her to stand tall. She could hear her teacher's voice now, encouraging her to accept her height as she towered over her classmates.

She looked around and her eyes caught those of a man. He was very good-looking, about six feet tall, with blond hair and blue eyes. He raised his glass to her, making her blush. She glanced away, but when she snuck a look back, he was still gazing at her.

"Lauren, you look very flushed. What's the matter?"

She couldn't answer her father. Her mouth grew dry as she sensed the man was making his way toward them. She looked around for an escape route, but there was none. "Please pass us by," she muttered under her breath, but it wasn't to be.

Within moments her father was greeting the same man as if they were long-lost friends. "Justin, how are you? I thought you were still in Cuba."

"No, came back last week, sir."

"I told you to call me William, Justin."

Lauren gasped, but a glance from her father turned it into a cough. She didn't know anyone other than her father's peers who called him by his first name. She guessed he was in his late twenties. She couldn't look directly at Justin, yet she couldn't help taking quick glances at him. He was gorgeous, his eyes bluer than the Mediterranean Sea. She could lose herself in their depths.

"Lauren?"

Her father's voice came from far away.

"Lauren, this is Justin Prendergast. Justin, forgive my daughter for her lack of manners. She appears to find her surroundings overwhelming."

"I am delighted to meet you, Miss Greenwood. You are even more beautiful in person."

Lauren turned her eyes to him, not understanding.

"Your father showed me some photographs on our last business trip."

"You work with my father?"

"Yes, on occasions. So, how do you like The Ritz?"

Lauren didn't miss the rapid change of subject. She thought it would be rude to say she preferred the smaller, intimate settings of the hotels in Charlottesville or even Richmond, back down South. She wasn't a fan of crowds of strangers kissing the air and making small talk all night long. "It's very stylish," she said instead. "Miss Hutton's party planners have done a wonderful job."

Justin leaned in closer, his eyes running over her face, his gaze lingering on her lips. Butterflies danced in Lauren's stomach as she inhaled his woody-scented aftershave. Her heart raced as he took her hand, her cheeks flushing again as she darted a glance at her father. *Has he noticed? Will he disapprove?*

"Have you heard Rudy Vallee sing yet?" Justin asked, distracting her from her thoughts.

Lauren merely shook her head, as she couldn't find her voice. She didn't want to admit that she had only seen Rudy Vallee on a movie screen or listened to him on the radio.

"May I?" Justin offered his arm. Lauren hesitated, glancing at her father, wondering if he would prefer she stay by his side.

"Go on, Lauren," her father said gruffly. "You'll find me in the smoking room, hiding from fortune hunters or their mothers."

Justin laughed. Watching her father go, Lauren glanced at the other ladies in the room. Their jewels glistened at their throats, arms, and fingers. How many children would one of those bracelets feed and house if it were to be sold? Blushing as she realized she had been woolgathering again, she turned to apologize to Justin. He was staring at her, a slight smile on his lips. She looked directly into his eyes and forgot about everything else.

Justin put his hand gently on her elbow and whispered, as if afraid to break the moment between them, "Miss Greenwood, this way. Would you like some champagne?"

"No, thank you."

Lauren didn't drink. Champagne bubbles made her tongue itch so she stuck to water. The amount of alcohol at the party surprised her, given the strict Prohibition laws. She supposed that money *could* buy everything, just as her father had said.

Her elbow was tingling from Justin's touch. She didn't like the way he made her feel. All girlish, with not a serious thought in her brain. She was twenty-one, not a child. But he was good company, making her laugh and asking her questions without making her feel like she was being interrogated.

Now he was smiling at her, as if he could read her thoughts, sending more tingles down her spine. What was wrong with her? Usually men of a similar age bored her to death.

"Would you like to dance?" Justin held out his arm as they moved into the ballroom.

Lauren nodded, thankful she had practiced the Foxtrot with Mary.

"I hope I don't stand on your toes, I'm not a very accomplished dancer," he said.

"I don't believe that for one second, Mr. Prendergast."

"Can't you call me Justin?"

She could barely say anything, aware of his hand on her waist while the other held hers lightly as they moved to the music. He leaned in closer, their knees almost touching as they followed the music's rhythm. She felt like a china doll in his arms, not the lanky-legged colt she usually resembled. He was a good head taller than her, so she had to look up at him. He smiled a lot.

"Justin, you lied. You dance very well."

"Only with a good partner."

The look in his eyes brought a blush to her face and she tried to put some distance between them. They continued dancing, and if Justin realized that other men were trying to cut in, he didn't show it. Secretly she was pleased. She'd lost count of the number of men she'd danced with over the last three weeks in the endless rounds of debutante balls. She had the bruises to prove they'd all stood on her feet. This time was different.

"If I'd known you were this glorious in person, I would have come back to New York earlier," Justin murmured in her ear.

"Mr. Prendergast." She protested because she was expected to, although she was secretly thrilled.

"I apologize, Miss Greenwood, but your beauty and charm have overtaken my manners. So, tell me, have you been skating in the city?"

"Yes, every day. I love getting out in the air. I miss riding in the mountains back home on my horse, Prince."

"You could go riding in Central Park."

"It wouldn't be the same. Father offered to ship my horse up to New York, but I didn't let him do that. Prince wouldn't like the lack of open space. He loves the fresh air of the mountains."

"I get the impression you find New York somewhat lacking."

Lauren flinched. *Was it so obvious?*

"Please, don't look so nervous. I feel the same about Thornton Mews, my home on the far side of Richmond."

Just then, as they continued to circle the floor, Lauren spotted her father talking to society matrons Mrs. Vanderbilt and Mrs. Astor, and noticed that all three seemed to be looking at her and Justin. She wasn't sure that she should be spending so much time dancing with one man, but she didn't want to be with anyone else.

The music changed to a Tango and Lauren stepped back, not brave enough to try such an intimate, daring dance in front of New York society. But Justin held her hand, his expression daring her. "You look and move beautifully."

"It must be the influence of your two left feet," she teased, speaking softly for his ears only.

"I may just have to step on your toes." He leaned in closer, his eyes twinkling with amusement. "Just listen to the beat of the music and follow my lead."

He held her so close he must have felt her heart almost beating out of her chest. She forgot where they were, everything else fading away as she held his gaze, following his lead around the dance floor as people stood back and moved out their way. She was oblivious to everything except the feel of him holding her, his musky scent, his gentle breathing, his legs grazing hers.

When at last the music stopped, the sound of their audience clapping brought Lauren sharply back to her senses. Blushing scarlet, she tried to pull away from her partner, wanting to disappear, but Justin simply whispered, "Would you like a breather?" his breath tickling her ear.

"Yes, please." She couldn't say another word.

Justin took Lauren's hand and led her away from the dance floor. People smiled at them as they walked by, but she was so lost in the moment that if you had asked her who they were passing, she wouldn't have been able to tell you.

CHAPTER 5

Lauren could feel someone watching her. Casting her eyes around, she spotted a man, a stranger, staring at her with a not altogether pleasant expression on his face. Unfortunately, their path was taking them toward him. Justin must have felt her hesitation, as he looked at her questioningly before following her gaze.

His shoulders stiffened. "Don't mind Belmont. Not sure how he gained entrance. I thought they were more discerning at The Ritz."

Despite thinking it was rather a rude remark, curiosity got the better of her. "What do you mean?"

"He's a Jew and a newspaper man. Would you want one at your party?"

Lauren was horrified but before she could gather her wits and answer, the man Justin had spoken about came closer. Judging by his expression, he had heard Justin's words.

"My father's Jewish, Prendergast. If you knew anything about the religion, you would know it passes through the mother." Belmont raked his eyes from the top of Justin's head to the bottom and back. "They can't be too discerning here. They admitted you."

The tension between the two men simmered, making Lauren even more uncomfortable. "Forgive me, gentlemen, but I better find my father."

No sooner had she spoken than Justin tightened his grip slightly on her elbow.

"Nonsense! Your father knows you are in safe hands. Run along, Belmont, be a good chap."

"You haven't introduced me, Prendergast. Miss Greenwood, my name is Edward Belmont. Pleased to make your acquaintance."

"Have we met before?" she asked.

"No, but I know your father. You have been away, I believe."

"Yes. I spent the last two years at a finishing school in Switzerland followed by some time traveling in Europe with a school friend and her parents. I like to see how other people live." She smiled, but his rather sour expression remained unchanged.

"The rich live in pretty much the same way no matter where you travel, Miss Greenwood."

Lauren inhaled sharply, but before she could reply, Justin got there first.

"Ignore Belmont, Lauren. He is a communist. The Jewish blood clearly has some influence."

Lauren flushed, not at the use of her first name, but at his disparaging remark. She hoped that Mr. Belmont hadn't heard, but she saw him clench his knuckles.

"Mr. Prendergast, please could we get some water?" she asked, longing to get away. "I'm rather thirsty."

"Why don't you go for some water, Prendergast, and I will keep Miss Greenwood company?" Mr. Belmont said. That hadn't been Lauren's intention, but to refuse would look churlish. She sensed Justin was too much of a gentleman to lose face during a society party.

"I won't be long, Lauren. Please wait here."

She didn't really have much of a choice, did she? She stood watching Justin disappearing from view.

"So, been friends long, have you? I haven't seen you together before. Wouldn't have thought you were his type."

"Pardon?"

"You can save your rich-girl-indignant act. You know what I mean."

"I'm afraid I don't understand what you are talking about, Mr. Belmont. I only met Mr. Prendergast this evening. He and my father are business acquaintances."

"They are a lot more than that. In addition to both owning banks, they share common investments, including some coal mines, a few quarries and of course large land holdings. They share a lot of common interests too, such as making the highest profit at the lowest possible cost, regardless of consequences."

She wondered what he meant by "consequences", but refused to let her curiosity show. "Since you seem better informed than I am, I'm not sure I see the point of your interrogation."

He laughed, irritating her even more.

She fluttered her eyelashes as she smiled, like Mary had shown her, and asked sweetly, "May I ask what do you do, Mr. Belmont? Live off your trust fund?"

"Touché, Miss Greenwood." He bowed slightly. "If you will excuse me, it appears the cavalry are on their way."

Following his glance, Lauren saw Justin approaching with her father, whose face was a stone mask. She sensed she had earned his disapproval.

"Justin told me you weren't feeling well, Lauren. I think we should go back to our hotel."

Had she upset Justin by talking to Mr. Belmont? It wasn't as though she'd had much choice in the matter.

"I'm fine, Father. We don't have to leave, it has only gone two—"

"Now, Lauren—" Her father gave her a look he rarely used, but she knew to obey it.

"Yes, Father. Good night, Jus—, I mean, Mr. Prendergast."

Justin bowed over her hand, his lips touching her skin, sending shivers through her. "I look forward to exploring the mountain trails around Delgany. I shall be back in Virginia by New Year. Your father has invited me to stay at Rosehall over the holiday."

"I will look forward to it," Lauren replied, her nerves tingling as she tried to pull her eyes from his.

CHAPTER 6

"Have you decided on what to buy those poor girls?" Mary asked as they headed into Macy's. "I've been praying for them. Why take a child from their loving parents? It's not right."

Lauren squeezed Mary's hand, aware that her maid hated being an orphan. At least she had a father.

"Let's see what they have in children's clothing before we view the toys. After that, I want to buy Maggie a Mickey Mouse doll. Come on."

"On those?" Mary eyed the wooden escalators dubiously. "I don't think I like stairs moving under my feet."

"Just stand still. It will be fine. Children's is on the third floor."

Mary paled, her lips tight as she stepped onto the stairs, but after a few seconds she relaxed. "Look at all these people, Miss Lauren."

All around, Lauren could see customers jostling one another in their bid to buy gifts for friends and family. When they reached the third floor, she led Mary over to the girls' clothes, recalling how Maggie and Biddy had stood in front of her with barely a thread between them.

"The girls both need a coat, a hat, mittens, and a scarf. A few dresses too. The baby also needs some clothes, diapers, and some warm blankets. Oh, what do you think of these, Mary?" Lauren held up a red velvet coat and a white fur muff.

"They are nice to look at, Miss Lauren, but that velvet won't wear very well and white is not practical. They are clothes designed for rich children to wear to church. Look"—Mary held up some woolen coats—"these are more suitable. Buy the darker colors as they hide the dirt better."

Lauren listened, knowing the maid knew better than she did.

"Miss Lauren, you could buy some material. Most women can make clothes for their babies. We'd need dark colors, not baby blue or white as they pick up the dirt."

Lauren's skin crawled as she recalled the mildew-speckled tenement walls, the cobwebs, the mouse droppings, the garbage spilling in the corridors. She wanted to pick up the whole Cullen family and transplant them to Rosehall, where the air was sweet, the house clean, and Cian could wear pale blue.

Swallowing to calm her roiling stomach, and forcing herself to focus on their purchases, Lauren smiled. "Mary, you think of everything." She turned to the sales assistant, who duly produced some soft dark blue and dark gray cotton material. They picked out two pieces, adding matching thread and some needles to the pile. The shop assistant wrapped up their parcels. "Anything else, miss?"

"Yes, please. I need a toy for a baby, a Mickey Mouse doll, and a suitable gift for a pretty girl of about seven. Also, some small gifts for some boys aged between five and twelve." Lauren was thinking of Mrs. Murphy's boys, Charlie, Mikey, and Seamus, Jnr. "Have you any ideas?"

"The children have little room indoors so small toys would be best," Mary added.

The woman returned with a few boxes as well as a Mickey Mouse doll. A baseball bat, some Balsa wood kits, and a Flossie Flirt doll. For the baby, she brought a blue bunny.

"The doll is three dollars and fifty cents. We price each Balsa wood kit from eighty-three cents up to two dollars." The sales assistant placed the bunny on top of the pile. "This bunny is twenty cents."

"I'll take them all." Lauren clapped her hands, getting carried away with the Christmas spirit. Mary smiled, an indulgent expression on her face.

"Will I wrap them up for you, miss?"

"Yes, please. May I come back and collect them? We have more shopping to do." Lauren signed for the check, putting the items on her account. "Mary, we need something for Mrs. Cullen. The poor woman's nightgown was almost in rags."

The maid's hand gripped the rail on the escalator, her knuckles white. She sighed with relief when they got off at women's wear. Here again, Mary proved invaluable, steering Lauren toward harder-wearing materials and away from frivolous items.

They chose two cotton nightgowns, two dresses from the rack, and then looked for a coat.

"I think this is the one, Miss Lauren," Mary said, holding up a coat. "It's made from broadcloth, half wool and half cotton. It will be warm but will also help keep the rain off. If you buy one hundred percent wool, although it's softer, it's too difficult to dry."

"Good. I'll take all those."

"Perhaps add in two aprons so Mrs. Cullen doesn't worry about getting the dresses messed up with household chores," the maid suggested.

"Wonderful idea," Lauren agreed. "I'll get some in a larger size for Mrs. Murphy too." Once again, Lauren added the items to her account.

"Are you finished now, Miss Lauren?" Mary asked, after she had collected the clothes and toys from the children's department.

"Almost. We'll do the food shopping at the store where Mrs. Murphy shops."

Lauren enlisted the help of an assistant, who helped them to carry all their parcels to the front door of the store.

"We'll need a cab to transport all these items," Lauren said, and was very grateful that the doorman of Macy's was happy to oblige.

This time, when they got into a cab outside the store, Lauren was ready to deal with any arguments from the driver about going into Hell's Kitchen. She offered him twice the fare and a bonus if he stopped and waited outside the food store to allow her to buy food.

In the food store, Lauren had no idea where to start, so Mary did the shopping on her behalf. As Lauren watched, the girl picked out Irish potatoes, real butter, apples, carrots, cabbage, canned fruit, including peaches, an enormous bag of beans, flour, baking powder, coffee, tea, and cocoa for the girls. Mary added some cans of condensed milk before asking the storekeeper for advice on where to buy meat. He was more than happy to help them.

"Can you please double the order and send the second lot to Mrs. Murphy's? I assume you deliver?" Lauren asked.

"For you, yes, ma'am."

Lauren added some candy for the children.

"You will need some coal as well?" the storekeeper suggested.

"Can you please send around the coal direct to Mrs. Cullen? And a bag for Mrs. Murphy." Lauren paid the bill in cash, while Mary carried some of the lighter goods out to the waiting cab. The driver took directions from the storekeeper as Lauren wasn't sure which tenement was the correct one.

"Aren't we lucky, Miss Lauren?" said Mary, as the cab approached Hell's Kitchen. "We can pick apples from the trees at Rosehall, beans and peas from the garden, and peaches from the orchard. The gardeners keep bees to give us honey. All these things we take for granted. People who live in the tenements can't pick a blackberry or taste an egg straight from a chicken. I feel so sorry for them."

Mary's words brought a lump to Lauren's throat. She suppressed the urge to head straight for the train station and home to Rosehall.

*

A cab approaching Hell's Kitchen immediately caused a scene, with children dashing out onto the street to discover who was arriving. The driver stopped the cab, looking from left to right as the tenement children drew nearer.

"I don't think you should stay here, ladies, that lot'll mob you when they see all the stuff you have."

"Thank you, driver, but we will manage. The items belong to families who live here," Lauren replied.

"You bought stuff from Macy's for some of these people?"

"Yes, sir." Lauren got out of the cab, hoping she sounded more confident than she felt. How would they get everything she'd bought into the alley and up to Mrs. Cullen in safety?

"Hey, it's them ladies Maggie found!"

At the sound of the boy's voice, Lauren whirled around and recognized Charlie Murphy. "Charlie, what a godsend! Please can you help us with these packages? We have quite a few, so maybe you could call your brothers."

"Oi, you—get off! Leave the ladies alone. Go on, or I will get our Frankie after ya," Charlie screamed at some boys who'd edged too close to Lauren. They didn't leave, but at least they didn't come any closer. Charlie whistled, an ear-piercing sound. He whistled again and it seemed like children came running from all directions.

"Are they all from one family?" Mary asked, curiously.

Lauren shrugged her shoulders. "Charlie, can you ask your friends to carry everything up to Mrs. Cullen's place, please? We can sort things out up there," she said.

"They ain't me friends, they is me bruvvers. Sure thing, missus," Charlie said politely, before turning and roaring at some kids to move back, and threatening them with all sorts. He pointed to a taller boy. "That's our Frankie. Ain't nobody will mess with him."

The Cullen girls had also raced down the stairs to greet them, and were offering to help carry the parcels.

The cab driver had been watching all these things happening. Lauren paid him his fare, but to her surprise he wouldn't take the bonus she'd offered him outside Macy's.

"I don't know where you are from, lady, but I ain't seen nobody do anythin' like you did today. Keep the extra money, give it to those families you are lookin' out for. I got kids and they got kids, but none of us live like this. We ain't rich, but after seein' this, I reckon we do all right. God bless you, lady."

As the words fell out of the driver's mouth, Mary stood with tears streaming down her face.

"Mary, what is the matter?" Lauren asked, putting a hand on her arm.

"You can't even see the sky here," she said, sobbing. "There's no birds or any animals. Only dirty buildings. How can you keep children healthy in this muck?"

"They do their best. Dry your eyes before someone sees you. They have very little but their pride," Lauren whispered as she hugged Mary before picking up a parcel and heading into the darkness of the tenement where the Cullens lived.

CHAPTER 7

Lauren stopped as they crossed the step into the room. The double bed with the bumpy mattress still dominated the small space, but it had been pushed into one corner near some nails on the wall that held the few bits of clothes the family owned. The baby lay in the open top drawer of the chest sitting under the nails. A tiny, ragged-looking Christmas tree occupied the other corner. It was as bare as the floor it stood on.

Sadie Cullen faced the small fire, staring intently into the flames. For one horrifying moment, Lauren thought she had offended the woman. Before she could say anything to her, Frances Murphy ran into the room and lifted Lauren off her feet in a giant hug. As Mary held a bag in front of her, and was edging toward a small table beside the fire, Frances settled on a squeeze of Mary's arm.

Biddy and Maggie danced around in their bare feet. "You got presents in those bags, I can see the wrappin'. Are they for us?" Biddy asked excitedly.

The young girl's question earned her a slap across the backs of her legs. "Aw, Mammy, what did ya do that for?"

"Your nose is too long for your face, girl. Let the ladies come in and sit down. Look at the state of you, you'd swear you never saw visitors." Sadie stood back, gesturing at Lauren and Mary to sit on the only chairs at the table. Frances followed them, perching on a stool by the fire, a large, dirty white hanky in her hands. She mopped her eyes and sighed every few seconds.

"Not like these. Look at all those bags. Can we just have a little peek inside? It's almost Christmas? Please, Mammy, go on, will ya?"

Mrs. Cullen looked at her eldest girl and then to Lauren and back before sitting down heavily on the bed. "I don't know whether to laugh or cry. I'm so happy I could burst and so sad that a stranger had to be the one to look after us." Her face paled. "Not that I'm ungrateful. Do you know what I mean?"

"Sure you're makin' no sense at all, Sadie Cullen. Will you let the young girl have a wee peek inside the bags?" Frances almost leaped off the stool she'd been sitting on and handed a bag to Biddy. "They ain't never seen so much stuff all at once. Not likely to again either. Let them enjoy it."

"Please, Mrs. Cullen, Mary and I would love to see the girls' reactions. You would be doing us a great favor." Lauren moved her chair closer to the wall to make room for the Murphy boys crowding at the door. "There's plenty to go around."

Charlie nudged one of his many brothers and winked. Maggie reached for Lauren's hand. "Can I help ya?"

Lauren looked to Mrs. Cullen for permission. The woman inclined her head. "Why don't you sit at the table, Maggie? Mary and I know who each package is for."

Moving to kneel on the floor, Lauren caught the scent of ammonia from the cleaning solution Sadie Cullen used. There wasn't a speck of dirt to be seen other than the soot and ashes from the fire.

"Maggie, why don't you give this one to your mother?" Lauren said, handing her a parcel.

The child squeezed the parcel tight. "Feels awful soft. Must be clothes. That's boring!"

Everyone laughed, although Mrs. Cullen flushed. Mary whispered something to her and the woman gave her a weak smile.

"This next one, Maggie, is for your baby brother. Do you want to open it for him?"

"Nope! I want to open me own present. Did you buy one for myself, just for me?" Maggie's voice shrilled. Lauren couldn't help but smile at her.

"I might have, but first, you have to give Cian his present, okay?"

Biddy stepped forward. "I'll look after his."

"Thank you, Biddy. Now my turn?" Maggie stared at Lauren with a pleading look in her eyes.

"This one is yours, precious."

The girl squealed with delight as she hugged the present to her. She squeezed it, smelled the wrapping, and tried to shake it. "Do I have to wait for Christmas Day?" Maggie glanced at Lauren before sending a pleading look to her mother.

Everyone turned to look at Mrs. Cullen. Lauren held her breath. More than anything, she wanted to see the look on the little girl's face when she saw Mickey Mouse.

"Maggie, if you open this, Father Christmas may decide you have enough things and not leave you a Christmas present," replied Mrs. Cullen.

Maggie looked from her mother to the gift and back again. Biddy moved forward, less sure than her younger sister. "Miss Lauren, may I see my gift, please?"

Mary took Biddy's doll out of the sack, thankful the shop assistant had wrapped it first in a box and then in paper. The child wouldn't know what the gift contained no matter how much she tried to squeeze or shake it. But to everyone's amazement, Biddy took the gift and put it under the small tree, then sat back.

"Mr. Murphy found two trees at work and brought one home to us. We didn't have no decorations but now it looks like a Christmas tree," the little girl told them.

Lauren's eyes prickled, her chest tightening. She'd taken for granted her beautiful home, the lavishly decorated Christmas tree with countless presents waiting for her. Biddy had nothing, yet the child had more gratitude in her little finger for this one gift than Lauren had for all she had in her life. Humbled, she resolved to count her blessings more often.

Maggie stamped her foot. "Aw, Biddy. Do I have to put my present under the tree too?"

"That's your choice, Maggie, but I am putting Cian's right there for Christmas morning. When the Murphys come over, we can share our gifts with them. Is that right, Cian?" said their mother.

Cian gurgled as if to say yes. Mrs. Cullen swept her arm across her eyes. Lauren glanced at Mary but her maid's eyes were fixed on Maggie.

Lauren picked another parcel out of the sack. "Biddy, could you put this under your tree for your mother? And this is for Mrs. Murphy. These gifts here are for Charlie and his brothers."

At the sound of their names, the Murphy boys closed in around Lauren. They didn't take the parcels in their hands to shake them but stood staring at them with their mouths hanging open.

Mrs. Murphy bawled at them. "A bunch of heathens, I reared. Not one of them got the manners they were born with. What do you say to the ladies?"

"Thanks, missus. You really mean them for us?" Charlie stuttered. Gone was the confident lad who'd run for the cab. He stared at the tree as if he expected it to disappear.

"I don't see any other Murphy boys around here, do I?" Lauren teased, but even as she spoke, she wondered whether there were more. The boys were like a staircase, each one just slightly taller than the next.

Lauren gave the rest of the sack to Mary who, with Biddy's help, arranged the remaining gifts around the tree. When she'd finished, Mary handed a couple of boxes to Charlie. "You might want to put these under your tree as this one's getting a little crowded."

The boys fought over who would carry the boxes until a swift sharp slap from their mother silenced them. They fled, falling over one another as they scrambled out the door. They were soon back, empty-handed but overexcited.

"Maggie, have you decided what you want to do?" Mary asked as she started opening a box of tinsel and other decorations for the tree.

The child handed over the present, her eyes not leaving it. Then she sat on the floor and stared at the tree. "How long will it be till Christmas?" she asked, sighing loudly.

"Longer than ever if all you do is sit there watching. Why don't you help me decorate the tree? You can ask Miss Lauren will she lift you up to put the angel at the top. That all right with you, Mrs. Cullen?" said Mary.

"Thank you, Mary. I'll make a nice cup of tea. Is that an Irish accent I hear, girl?"

"I believe so, ma'am. Cook said I have Irish blood but I didn't know my parents so can't be sure."

Lauren giggled as she watched one of the Murphy boys trying to put a bauble on a branch. It kept falling off, yet he wouldn't give up. "Mary drinks tea like the Irish do—strong and wet, Cook calls it," she said.

Mrs. Cullen nodded in a knowing way and went back to work. Lauren watched as she drew water from a bucket, rinsed the pot, and threw the dirty water into another bucket. Then she drew more water, putting it in a kettle held on a hook over the open fire. How hard it must be to cook a meal in these places, Lauren thought. Where would Mrs. Cullen cook a turkey? It wouldn't fit in the Dutch oven, sitting to the side of the grate.

"The Murphys have a proper oven, they let us share it," Mrs. Cullen said, intruding on Lauren's thoughts.

Lauren flushed, realizing how easily her hostess guessed her thoughts. "Sorry, I didn't mean to seem critical. I was just thinking how much easier it would be for y'all to have running water."

"Aye, it would. The tap is down near the back entrance. We all share it," Mrs. Cullen replied as she went back to making tea.

As Mary decorated the tree and had the youngsters in hysterics with her joking around, Lauren sat back at the table.

"I can't believe you came back," whispered Mrs. Murphy, leaning toward her. "I paid the money like you said and my Seamus got the landlord to give Sadie an extension. Hard to say no to my Seamus. You'll meet him. He's coming but had to get dressed up first. Wait till he sees what you've done. Nobody ain't ever treated the Cullens this well."

"The storekeeper at the food store will deliver similar items to your place," Lauren told her. "He will also get a turkey and ham delivered from a butcher he knows. I paid him."

"For us? Why?"

"Mrs. Cullen told me you were the reason her family survived this long. I figured you should have a nice Christmas too."

The door opened and Lauren thanked God she wasn't alone as a giant of a man entered. His height, broad shoulders, and bald head gave him a menacing look. She could understand why the agent had been so lenient.

"My Charlie says you're the one who got all this stuff," he said, eyeing Lauren up. "I can support my family, missus. We don't take charity."

Lauren opened her mouth but before she could say anything the man held out his hand.

"But I wanted to say thank you for the Christmas gifts. You've blessed my wife and my lads." He jammed his hands back in his pockets, his face flushing slightly. She figured he was embarrassed, a proud man who did his best for his family.

"It was your example that led me back here," Lauren replied. "You taking care of Mrs. Cullen and her girls. Now, Mary, we should be going."

But the two women wouldn't have it. Mrs. Murphy insisted Lauren and Mary stay for tea and they all crowded around the small table in the Cullen household. For all his size and strength,

Seamus was so gentle with baby Cian that Lauren found herself squeezing back the tears in her eyes. Mrs. Murphy watered down the condensed milk and fed the child as Mrs. Cullen set out some candies on a plate. She offered to make them something more substantial but both Lauren and Mary refused.

Lauren couldn't remember a more enjoyable afternoon. The children sat comparing the merits of different pieces of candy— they were allowed two pieces each if they sat quietly. Lauren listened as they made their choices.

"This one lasts forever. If you take two pieces of hard toffee, you will still have some left tomorrow."

"But, Charlie, this makes your mouth all fizzy." Maggie opened her mouth to show him. "Like the soda pop the ladies brought us last time."

"I don't like toffee, it sticks to me teeth. I prefer these candy balls," Biddy said as she put another lemon drop into her mouth.

"Nothing beats a Snickers bar. They taste just as good as they smell. See?" Frankie held his up and Charlie took a bite, earning himself a cuff around the ear. He didn't seem to care from what Lauren could see. There was an expression of pure bliss on his chocolate- covered face.

"We best get on back to the hotel, it's getting late," Mary said eventually.

Reluctantly, Lauren stood up to leave, knowing the maid was right. It took a while to say goodbye and she promised to return to see them if she was ever back in New York. Seamus escorted them from the tenements and helped them find a cab to take them back to their hotel.

"Seamus, I've paid an attorney to secure Daniel's release from Sing Sing," Lauren said, as she bade him farewell. "He should never have been imprisoned. I've cleared his fines. Hopefully, he'll be home for New Year, if not before. I tried to locate where the boys were sent, but I drew a blank."

His eyes were misty with tears. "You did a beautiful thing today, ladies. I thank ye both sincerely. Both families will never forget this Christmas, no matter what the years ahead bring us. God bless you both."

CHAPTER 8

Lauren tried to keep her eyes open, wanting to make sure her home town of Delgany wasn't full of soup kitchens and breadlines like those in New York, but the lengthy journey beat her and sleep overcame her. She woke just as they reached the road leading to Rosehall. In the distance, she could make out the snow-covered mountains before they reached the foothills and finally, their grand home. She hugged herself as she glimpsed the pair of twin chimneys marking each end of the main house. The steep roof was covered in snow just like a painting on a box of chocolates. She leaned forward, eager to see more.

The eighteenth-century wrought-iron gates reminded her of her trip to the stately homes in England. For the first time, she had understood why her ancestors had imported the ancient gates from England. They must have missed their English roots as much as she missed Rosehall when she was away from it. She wanted Jackson, her father's butler-cum-chauffeur, to drive faster. *Will Nanny be waiting?*

"Mary, we're home," she whispered, squeezing her maid's hand. Mary didn't speak, but her eyes glistened with tears.

Someone had cleared the snow and leaves from the drive, and only a few yellowing leaves still remained near the top of the one hundred-foot high tulip poplars. Their size and strength—standing proud for hundreds of years—somehow confirmed how resilient her home was.

The world outside was changing. The stock market crash of 1929 had brought about the Great Depression, with many thousands of desperate people now out of work, some committing suicide, and many families on the breadline. Scandalous headlines graced the newspapers every day, but here at Rosehall, nothing seemed to have changed. Today, the redbrick house looked just the same as always, the windows gleaming in the winter sun.

Nanny was there, standing on the steps outside the front door with the rest of the staff. *Was she always so small? And when did her hair become so gray?* Lauren jumped from the car and ran up the steps into Nanny's outstretched arms. The old woman's eyes glistened with tears as she held Lauren tight. "You're home, you came back."

"Lauren!"

Lauren stiffened at the disapproving tone in her father's voice.

"Go, child. We'll catch up later." Nanny gave her a last squeeze before releasing Lauren to step back, almost but not quite into the line of waiting servants.

Lauren looked for her father, but it seemed that he'd already marched off into the house. She should follow him, but she was far too excited.

"Patty Kelly? Oh, my goodness, you've grown so tall and beautiful! Cook, what have you done with the child and who is this youthful woman?"

Patty, the kitchen maid, turned crimson at Lauren's teasing. Cook held out her hand to shake Lauren's, but she gave the older woman a hug instead.

"I missed your cooking. They have never heard of grits in Europe and nobody in New York can make them like you do. As for your fried chicken, please tell me that's on the menu tonight."

"Lord above but you haven't changed a bit, Miss Lauren! You still thinking with your stomach." Cook held her apron to her eyes. "You got so grown up, you is a lady now. A proper lady."

"Not quite, Cook. Just ask Mary." Lauren turned to find Mary supervising some male staff in unloading trunks. "Mary, leave that for a minute and come say hello."

Cook gave Mary a hug, the smile lighting up her whole face.

"Patty, could you please bring some tea to my room?" Lauren said. "I need to change."

"I'll do it, Miss Lauren."

"No, Mary, you take a break and catch up with Cook. Patty can fill me in on what I've been missing since I've been away."

Mary gave Lauren a questioning look, but Lauren indicated she should accompany Cook.

"Patty, come up as soon as you can. I got you a present."

"Me, Miss Lauren?"

"For your birthday in October."

"You remembered?"

"I did. How could I forget?" Lauren took off her hat and gloves and left them on the table just inside the door. The scent of lemon and beeswax competed with the tantalizing kitchen smells. Her stomach groaned, but there was no one nearby to scold her. Her heels clicked on the marble floor in the hall.

She glanced toward her father's study, but it was closed. Where had Nanny gone? She walked up the grand staircase, avoiding the creaking ninth step from habit. Opening her bedroom door, she smiled. The small fire took the chill from the room, and a bouquet of winter flowers stood on her writing desk over by the window. She glanced out at the snow-topped mountain standing proud.

She had only just sat on the bed when a knock at the door admitted Patty, carrying a tray of tea things.

"Sit down and drink some tea with me, Patty."

The girl's eyes darted from side to side.

"Please. Just for a minute. Cook won't mind. She'll want to speak to Mary in private."

"Yes, Miss Lauren." Patty handed her a cup of tea, went to bow, and almost fell over.

"Patty, stop doing that. I'm not the Queen of England."

The girl's lower lip jutted out, reminding Lauren just how young she was.

Lauren stood up, placed the china cup on a lace doily to protect the oak furniture, before reaching for her purse. She pulled out a package and handed it to the girl. "This is for you, Patty. I hope you like it."

The servant's hands shook as she opened the package, her blue eyes widening as she picked up the chain inside. "For me? This is the prettiest present I ever got."

"It's not every day you turn thirteen. Put it on. Let me close the chain for you."

While holding up her long blonde braid to allow Lauren to secure the chain, Patty stared at her reflection, fingering the necklace, before turning and throwing her arms around Lauren. "Miss Lauren, you just the best person ever! I missed you. Please don't go away for long next time."

A knock on the door startled them, and Patty jumped away as if scalded.

"Relax, Patty, it will be Mary or Nanny," Lauren whispered, trying not to let the girl see that her reaction shocked her. "Come in."

The door opened, admitting her father, a scowl deepening the lines on his face.

"Patty, what are you doing up here? Go back down to Cook."

Patty ran.

"You didn't have to be so stern, Father. I asked her to help me."

"Lauren, don't correct me. This is my house. Now you are back home, you will act as my hostess at Rosehall. Given my position, my household must run seamlessly. I will hold several dinners, large occasions, and more private affairs. I expect you to act your part as the well-brought-up young lady you are. You are not to run and greet servants as if they are family members."

"Father, Nanny is a member of the family, she's Mama's aunt. I grew up with Cook, Mary, Patty, and the rest."

But he carried on as if he hadn't heard her. "Should you continue to be too familiar, I won't hesitate in firing everyone. Maybe I should hire professionals from Richmond."

"No!"

His glare made her use a softer tone.

"Sorry, Father, I'm tired after the journey. Don't replace anyone. I apologize for my behavior. I have missed everyone and let my sentiments overcome me. My education included grooming to become a society hostess. Nanny will help me with anything I need."

Her father nodded and turned to the door, before pivoting. "I almost forgot. Justin Prendergast and his mother will be arriving here on Friday. They will spend a week at Rosehall before driving on to their home. Mrs. Prendergast was in Florida visiting friends, and Justin is driving her home."

Lauren hugged herself with glee at the thought of Justin being at Rosehall. She couldn't wait to introduce him to Nanny. What would she make of him? It was important she liked him too. He'd won Father's approval, that was obvious, but Nanny was a tougher nut to crack.

CHAPTER 9

Lauren washed and changed her dress before heading down the main staircase to Nanny's rooms. Knocking, she entered to find Nanny sitting near a small fireplace, an unfinished quilt on her knee. She seemed distracted.

"Nanny? Can I come in?"

"Lauren, when did you ever need permission? Come in, child. It's wonderful to have you home."

"I missed you, Rosehall, and our walks so much. Want to walk to the lake?"

Nanny shivered. "Not today, darling. It's rather chilly for an hour's walk."

"Cold? It was freezing in New York." Lauren drew up the soft-cushioned chair. She told Nanny all about her adventures in Europe and New York.

"Have you got the traveling bug out of your system?"

"Yes, Nanny. I'm home for good."

The elderly woman sighed, causing Lauren to study her more carefully.

"What is it? You seem exhausted and sad. Aren't you glad I'm home?"

"That's a silly question. You are the child of my heart."

"So what is it?"

"Nothing, darling. I'm just tired." Nanny leaned back in her chair. "Tell me about the Woolworth Ball. I read a little bit about it in the newspaper. The reporters weren't happy about the cost of it; they said it was about sixty thousand dollars."

Lauren nodded. "I can see how it might have cost that. It was fabulous but with all the people starving in New York, did they really have to bring in silver trees and eucalyptus trees? They even had real live roses. Father wasn't happy because I kept staring at everything."

"Did you meet anyone nice?"

Lauren flushed, causing Nanny to smile gently.

"Someone special?"

"He might be. His name is Justin Prendergast. He's from the other side of Richmond. He's tall and so good-looking and a wonderful dancer." Lauren glanced at Nanny, expecting some reaction. But the old woman was rubbing the heel of her palm against her chest.

"Nanny, talk to me, please. I know something's wrong. I'm an adult."

Nanny touched the cross at her throat, staring distantly at the fire. She spoke so softly, Lauren had to strain to hear her.

"I didn't want to ruin your homecoming, darling. Things are ghastly here. I've never seen anything like the poverty. And not just here in Delgany, but in Charlottesville and Richmond too."

"The Depression has had a horrible effect on New York as well," Lauren told her. "Mary and I visited some families in the tenements and the children weren't going to get a gift from Father Christmas. Is it that bad here? I read in the papers that the Depression isn't having as much of an impact on rural areas as on the big cities."

"I don't know about the Depression. It's the drought here that is causing the main problems, as far as I can see. The farmers can't do anything but watch their crops die in the fields, those that had seeds to plant in the first place. Tobacco values have fallen so low, it would often suit the farmers better to lay their crop back on the ground. They can't afford to pay the warehouse fees or the shipment fees."

"But people aren't starving, are they?"

"Yes, they are, Lauren, particularly those in the mountains or down in Richmond. The churches have organized soup kitchens, the Salvation Army has set up some places too, and the Red Cross has been giving people flour and other foodstuffs. There are many in need and few resources."

Nanny's chest whistled as she tried to speak. Coughing, she turned red in the face before going pale. Lauren grabbed a glass of water, pressing it against the older woman's lips. It took a few moments for her to recover.

"I caught a chill at the weekend. Silly of me," she wheezed.

"How is Father? Are you getting along together?" Lauren asked, her father's earlier stern words echoing in her head.

"Your father… He's more difficult, more challenging to please. He isn't sleeping well. At night, I hear him pacing. It was a relief when he went to New York to meet you. I wish he had brought you back in time for Christmas. You were missed."

"Don't talk to me about that. I couldn't believe Father left Mary and me alone on Christmas Day, while he went out with some business acquaintances. There was no atmosphere in the hotel where we were staying and the food was nothing like Cook's fabulous home cooking. Next Christmas will have to be twice as good to make up for it." Lauren stared at the fire. "What do you think is wrong with Father? The crash didn't affect him too badly. He said he'd protected his investments." An icy fear hit Lauren's heart, her mind going to the many suicides she had read about, including the fathers of at least two of her former classmates who had been hit hard by the stock market crash.

"The crash hit everyone, Lauren, some more than others, but he's not worried about money. It's his position. There have been rumors and articles in the newspapers that have been less than flattering."

"I don't understand why. I met a man in New York, Belmont was his name. He didn't hide his disapproval of Father's and Justin's business but didn't give me any real details." Nanny's eyes found hers at the mention of Belmont. "You know Mr. Belmont, Nanny?"

"Only by reputation. He is one of those who are writing editorials about your father."

"What does he say?"

"Not today, Lauren… Now, tell me, what else happened in New York?"

But Lauren wasn't going to be so easily distracted. "Stop it. I'm not a child, Nanny. It's better you tell me what is going on than someone in Delgany does, isn't it?"

Nanny sighed, standing up and walking into her bedroom. Returning, she handed Lauren a copy of the *Charlottesville News*. Lauren gasped at the headline:

How Greenwood lined his pockets from your misery.

"How dare he? Father should sue Belmont. Has he contacted Carlton, his attorney?"

"You can't sue if the article is true."

Lauren's mouth fell open as she stared at Nanny, before turning her attention to the paper. She read rapidly.

"I don't understand. It says here Father buys up struggling businesses. Those that overextend their investments, or that hold their cash deposits at failed banks. His expertise helps them bounce back. What am I missing?"

"The businesses may heal but the owners don't. Child, your father has plenty of cash, something that's in short supply with the banks failing. That alone causes suspicion. According to Mr. Belmont, the source of that cash may be illegal. The Greenwood name has become associated with foreclosures and evictions."

"But people take out mortgages knowing that if they miss the payments, the bank will foreclose and take the property. How can Father be responsible for that?"

"He could exercise a little understanding, Lauren. Farmers can't pay mortgages if the drought means there are no crops. If the banks won't lend them funds to buy seeds, there won't be a crop next year. If the farmers pay every cent into the mortgage payments, what will their families eat? The banks over in Farmville have been extending their credit. If a farmer has a mortgage of ten years, those banks have extended it to fifteen or twenty. They are working with the farmers and other borrowers, best they can. Can you imagine if anyone came to take Rosehall? How would you feel?"

"Devastated, Nanny, this house means everything to me. It's where Mama lived until she died. I couldn't bear it if a stranger took it."

Lauren went back to the newspaper article and read every word, her anger building. "The journalist is wrong. Father's a businessman, but he wouldn't fire people only to rehire them on lower wages. That's immoral."

"Yet it's happening."

"What's Justin Prendergast's involvement?"

"I don't know. I'd never heard of him before you mentioned him." Nanny glanced toward the fire.

Lauren's stomach hardened, fighting down the nausea. Her throat tightened. Nanny wasn't being truthful, but why was she lying to her?

"Nanny, tell me the truth, please," she pleaded.

"I would if I had facts, child, but I'll not spread rumor and gossip. Your father, although bad-tempered occasionally, has treated his servants well. He may not pay the highest wages in the county, but he has let no one go." The old woman pursed her lips into a thin line and Lauren knew nothing would make her say another word.

CHAPTER 10

Despite it being the depths of winter, Lauren hadn't closed the drapes in her bedroom, not wanting to miss her first glimpse of the wintery sun rising above the mountains. She jumped out of bed and ran to the window. It wasn't snowing and for a change the sky looked rather more blue than gray. After washing, she put on a warm woolen dress, wishing she had the nerve to wear pants. She knew Nanny would have heart failure if she did.

Her mouth watered as the aroma of Cook's strong black coffee rose up the stairs, followed by the smell of frying bacon. Her stomach rumbled in anticipation of a Southern breakfast.

Going down the stairs two at a time, she ignored Jackson's look of disapproval as she arrived on the first floor. She pushed open the door to the breakfast room, taking a second to drink in the view of the mountains. Her grandfather had installed three full-length windows to allow those eating to enjoy the beauty of their surroundings. In the background the mountains rose majestically into the sky, piercing the clouds.

Beyond the windows and closer to the house were the kitchen gardens. Despite being seasonally bare, a few winter plants were trying valiantly to push their way past the snow and frost. In a few weeks, they would be a riot of color. Rosehall's gardeners were a talented team and could grow just about any vegetable Cook needed.

"Morning, Miss Lauren, I didn't expect to see you this early."

"Cook, I couldn't wait for breakfast. I haven't eaten a decent meal since I left for school over two years ago."

"Go on with you, Miss Lauren."

Although Cook protested, Lauren knew that she was pleased. She was smiling as she instructed Patty on how to fix the various dishes on the sideboard. Lauren and her father always ate breakfast buffet-style. Father liked to take time to enjoy his food and read his paper.

With her father not being down yet, Lauren picked up the newspaper from the table and began to read an article about investors who'd lost their life savings by investing through Colombia Finance Corporation. They'd staged a demonstration in Jefferson County. The paper said men in their late fifties and some women had been seen crying in distress.

Men didn't cry in public unless they were at their wits' end. Just imagine saving all your life only to find the money had disappeared like smoke up a chimney. Lauren hoped something would happen to give those people some of their hard-earned savings back.

"Lauren, I thought you would be in bed for the morning. Aren't you tired after the journey?"

Lauren folded the newspaper and turned to greet her father, not having heard him come into the room. "No, I'm not, Father." She put the paper beside her father's place, then picked up a plate before crossing over to the buffet. She couldn't decide between buttermilk pancakes or bacon and grits, so had both. Some fried green tomatoes and a cup of strong dark coffee completed her choice.

Her father chose fried bacon, sausage, and eggs, along with two biscuits and some cornmeal gravy. As he sat down, he realized he'd forgotten his coffee. Lauren jumped up and served him, earning her a smile.

"What were you reading in the paper?" he asked.

"An article about how a lot of people are starving because of the drought, and some of the men have lost their jobs."

"There's plenty of work if they want it. Some people are just too fussy."

"I don't think that's the case, Father. The newspaper says—"

Her father banged the table with his fist. "I know what the papers say, Lauren. The Depression is bad in the big cities. Virginia has been spared, thankfully. If the mountain people weren't such ignorant *inbreds*, they would fare much better."

Lauren sipped her coffee, her appetite vanishing in the wake of her father's outburst. Should she apologize, she wondered. But why should she? She disagreed with him but she wasn't brave enough to voice that out loud.

"Justin Prendergast and his mother are our guests this weekend, Lauren," her father reminded her, as well as changing the subject. "I expect you to show them the beauty of Rosehall and the surrounding countryside. For goodness' sake, don't talk to Justin like you do to me."

"Yes, Father." Butterflies flew about in Lauren's stomach. She couldn't wait to show off her home and the land around it. It was the most beautiful place on earth.

"What does Justin do, I mean for a living, Father?"

"His family has lived in Virginia since the time of King James. Thornton Mews was the biggest tobacco plantation in the county, and Justin's grandfather invested his money in property in New York and other northern states. He made a lot of money in the war and bought a bank. Justin is now chairman."

"How did his grandfather earn money during the Civil War? I thought the Yankees destroyed most of the plantations. Nanny always said Rosehall was lucky to escape." Lauren had heard rumors of men who made fortunes through their contacts in Britain. Despite Britain being supposedly neutral during the Civil War, many British ships were used to bring contraband to the South.

Her father's eyes narrowed as he took up his knife and fork. Speaking slowly, he said, "I don't think we need dwell on the past, Lauren. What matters is the future."

He ate slowly as if savoring every mouthful, his gaze on the paper beside him. She knew better than to ask any more questions. Why couldn't her father just give her a straight answer? She ate a couple of mouthfuls but her stomach twisted.

"May I be excused, please, Father?" Lauren managed to ask. "I want to go see Prince."

"I swear you love that horse more than anyone or anything."

"I love you too, Father," she said, dropping a kiss on his head as she passed him. She didn't linger, wanting to exchange the feeling of walking on eggshells for freedom.

Lauren passed through the kitchen to the stables. "Thank you, Cook, for a wonderful breakfast. If Nanny comes looking for me, I'm going down to say hello to Prince."

She didn't wait to hear the reply but ran out the back door and headed in the direction of the stables. The path crunched under her feet as she left footprints in the frost. She shivered. She'd been stupid not to grab her coat. She should go back, she thought, but then she heard Prince calling.

Her heart beat faster at the sound. *He hasn't forgotten me.* Checking to see there was nobody watching, she picked up her skirts and ran under the gables, now covered in brown wisteria vines, and on to the stables. Her nose twitched at the combination of the smell of saddle oil and alfalfa mixed with hay.

"Morning, Miss Lauren. You still racing around like a little heathen?" said Sam, the head groom, taking in the sight of her.

"Morning, Sam. How are you? How's Prince?"

"I is just fine. Prince, on the other hand, his heart is breaking."

"Why?" She blinked rapidly as she tried to see what was wrong with the horse. He looked clean and healthy, as far as she could tell.

"He heard you was home last night and you never came to see him."

"Oh, you! I was worried there."

She moved closer to her horse, taking her time to allow him to smell her. She didn't want him to panic and injure himself. He looked snug and happy, his finely woven horse blanket keeping him warm. He sniffed and then butted his head against her as if to say hello. The soft fuzz of his nuzzling lips against her neck made her giggle. She wrapped her arms around him.

"I missed you, boy." Lauren gave him the carrot she'd grabbed from Cook's pantry on her way out. "I can't wait until it's just the two of us up there on the mountain."

After she returned from the stables, Lauren went to see Nanny.

"Father told me Justin and his mother are coming to visit for the weekend. I can't wait for you to meet him. He is just perfect. He's a real gentleman and an amazing dancer. People at the ball in New York actually applauded our Tango."

"I'm glad you met a nice man, Lauren. But what of your aspirations to write? You always said you wanted to follow your mama's dream and become a writer. I thought you were going to ask your father for permission to go to university."

"I did, but he refused. He said I'd had enough schooling and I needed to settle down, get married, and raise a family. The way he went on you would think I was an old maid."

Nanny didn't comment. Lauren let the silence linger for a few minutes before asking, "How do you know whether a man is the right one for you, Nanny?"

"See how he treats his mother and sisters. It's usually a good indication of how he will treat his wife."

CHAPTER 11

Lauren's stomach fluttered, her pulse racing as she kept going to look out the window, where the gardeners had cleared the drive into Rosehall. She hadn't been able to eat or sleep, she was so excited.

"Can I get you something, Miss Lauren?" the butler enquired.

"No, thank you, Jackson. I'm just waiting for our visitors. They should be here any minute."

The words were barely out of her mouth when she heard the gravel crunching on the drive. "They're here! Will you tell Father, please, Jackson?"

Lauren grabbed her coat and rushed outside to greet their guests. Mary's voice floated into her head, telling her not to show too much eagerness, but she ignored it. Justin had traveled to her home to see her, after all.

As he parked his shiny red Studebaker, Lauren almost wished he would run out the car and take her in his arms, but instead he moved to the passenger door and helped an older woman to get out. She guessed that this was his mother.

"Mother, this is Lauren, the woman I told you about. Lauren, this is my mother, Irene Prendergast."

"I'm very pleased to meet you, Mrs. Prendergast. Welcome to Rosehall," Lauren said, stretching out a hand in greeting.

Irene Prendergast shook the hand she was offered and smiled at Lauren. "You have a beautiful home. Such a lovely place, sitting in front of those majestic mountains. It seems so peaceful, like a piece of history that the rest of the world has passed by."

She turned from Lauren to look at the house, her eyes traveling over the whole façade. "It's original, isn't it? Built before the War Between The States It's a miracle it survived the Yankee burnings after the war. They destroyed so many of the old plantations, yet they don't appear to have touched Rosehall."

"Mama's family was lucky. Their people, I mean, the freed slaves, spoke up for the family and prevented it from being burned to the ground. Some of their descendants still live here."

Mrs. Prendergast kept talking, just as if Lauren hadn't said anything.

"Look at those Georgian features. What skilled architects they had back in those days. Did you know they mirrored many of the homes in this area on the stately homes of England? I imagine it is just glorious when all these rosebushes flower, and is that wisteria over there?"

Lauren nodded. She was a bit taken aback by Justin's mother. Most Southern women would have walked into the house with barely a comment.

"Mother loves her history and old buildings. She has green fingers too," Justin said proudly. "Wait until you see the Thornton Mews gardens."

He's assuming I'll visit his home. Lauren's knees weakened as he looked into her eyes.

"I missed you. May I hope that you missed me?" he asked with a smile.

"Justin, you can't ask a well-born young lady those questions." Mrs. Prendergast took Lauren's arm. "It is delightful to meet you, Lauren. Justin has told me lots about you and of course I know your father. Is he inside?"

Just then Lauren's father emerged through the open front door. "Irene, you look wonderful! Forgive me, I was on the telephone with a business associate. Lauren, why didn't you invite our guests inside? Not everyone is as eager as you to spend time in the chilly winter air."

"It was my fault, William. I was admiring your home, having never seen it before. It's stunning. Just a wonderful example of late Georgian…"

Lauren didn't hear what else Mrs. Prendergast was saying as her father led the lady away.

Justin moved to her side. "Alone at last. I've missed you so much. Have you missed me?"

"I barely know you." Lauren hoped he couldn't hear her heart beating as she stared into his eyes, noting, once again, how handsome he was.

"Is that a yes?" he said, looking at her with a silly grin. He licked his lips before reaching out to brush a tendril of hair off her face.

Her skin tingled. She wanted to say something witty or charming but her tongue got all twisted.

"Lauren, bring Justin inside before he freezes to death." Lauren jumped at the intrusion of her father's voice.

Justin offered her his arm. "Shall we?"

They walked into the house arm in arm and made their way into the drawing room. The grand space was both lovely and cozy, helped by flames from the warm fire.

"I see the resemblance." Justin smiled at Lauren before looking at the painting of her mother, framed over the mantelpiece. A woman with a beautiful smile and eyes full of laughter stared back at them. She wore a stunning cream tiered lace dress with a modest neckline and the smallest hint of sleeves. A cream satin bow showed off her impossibly small waist. "Your mother was beautiful too."

"Thank you." Lauren glanced at the portrait, wishing for the hundredth time that her mother was here with her. She'd been about four when Mama died and now all she could recollect was a shadowy feminine form, a presence more than a person. She thought she could remember her laugh though.

"I lost my father two years ago but I can't imagine not having him around as I grew up. You must have been so lonely," Justin said quietly.

"I would have been if it hadn't been for Nanny. She's Mama's aunt, but we call her Nanny. It's easier than 'grand-aunt'. Come over and let me introduce you." She took his hand although that wasn't necessary; the room wasn't so big that finding Nanny was difficult. "This is Nanny, I mean, Miss Kathryn Johnson."

"Any relation to the Johnsons of Giles County?" Mrs. Prendergast asked, as she stepped up beside them.

"President Andrew Johnson was my grandfather's first cousin. The family had dinner together a few times but I don't remember him too well. I was young when he died."

Justin left the room and returned with a small bag. He dipped into it and handed a wrapped gift to Lauren's father, one to Nanny, and lastly, one to Lauren herself.

"They're belated Christmas gifts. Go on, open them."

"Thank you, Justin." Lauren glanced at Nanny to see her opening a present of a dusk-colored scarf with fine calf-leather gloves to match. The elderly woman looked really pleased, which made Lauren want to kiss Justin.

"Aren't you going to open yours?" he said to her.

Lauren pulled the paper from the gift and opened the small box to reveal a musical jewelry box.

"It's beautiful, thank you so much."

"It's a rare piece from a Swiss craftsman. I saw it and immediately thought of you. Strong, yet delicate and beautiful."

Lauren flushed, not knowing where to look.

"Thank you, Justin, for your kind and thoughtful gifts. Would you like Jackson to show you to your rooms?" Nanny asked him and his mother. "Dinner will be in about one hour."

"Lovely, thank you," Mrs. Prendergast replied, but Justin declined. "I need to speak with you, William. Perhaps we could do that before dinner?"

Lauren looked between the two men. Was Justin here to see her or her father?

CHAPTER 12

When Lauren saw Mrs. Prendergast coming down to dinner on New Year's Eve, she was glad she'd chosen to wear her Parisian gown. The older woman was wearing an elegant black evening gown with long white gloves. A diamond necklace shimmered at her throat, competing with a pair of magnificent earrings.

"Lauren, you look beautiful. How wonderful to be able to wear your hair short, it really suits you."

"Do you think so? It took some persuading with Father. He was annoyed I got it cut but short hair is all the rage. Nanny doesn't like it much though, do you?"

"I don't like the idea of you growing up, darling. It makes me feel old."

"You look wonderful for your age, Miss Johnson," said Justin's mother. "I believe you were Nanny to Lauren's mother."

"Yes, she was my niece," replied Nanny. "I promised to stay by her side when my older sister died."

Just then Justin and Lauren's father arrived, both wearing evening dress. William escorted Mrs. Prendergast to the dining room, while Justin offered his arm to Nanny. Lauren walked in behind them. They had barely taken their seats when Jackson started to pour the wine and Patty and Mary, dressed in sparkling white aprons, served the table.

"I hope you like Hoppin' John soup. Cook insists on serving it every New Year. It's a Southern tradition and she says Fortune smiles on all who eat it." Father picked up his spoon as soon as

Mary had set the full bowls in front of them. Patty added the collard greens and cornbread to the table.

"I've never tasted this before. It's delicious." Mrs. Prendergast patted her lip with a napkin. "And the crackling adds so much flavor to the cornbread. I must get the recipe for my Cook."

Lauren could have been eating anything, for she didn't taste a thing. She was too conscious of Justin's leg beside hers. Jackson hadn't extended the dining-room table so they were sitting quite close together, but Justin appeared to have positioned himself even nearer to her on purpose.

The next course was roast turkey with cornbread stuffing, orange-glazed ham, and Cook's special pork chops with gravy. The vegetables included mashed Irish potatoes, green beans, black-eyed peas on a bed of watercress, squash casserole, and candied yams.

None of the ladies ate much, but both men had hearty appetites.

"You must leave room for dessert," Lauren said. "Cook is known across the county for her flaky pastry. I asked her to make her famous apple and blackberry pie as well as a peach cobbler. All the fruit and vegetables come from the Rosehall gardens," she added.

"Lauren is very proud of her home," her father added, with a look at Justin's mother.

"So she should be. The meal has been wonderful and your home is stunning, a credit to you, William. It looks like Lauren has all it takes to be a wonderful society hostess. I suppose you had a lot to do with that, Miss Johnson?"

"Lauren is a fast learner," Nanny responded, a proud look on her face.

Once everyone had finished eating, they retired to the drawing room for coffee. Mrs. Prendergast admired the silk wallpaper, commenting on how well the colors in the suite of furniture complemented the room. She took the chair closest to the large open fire and everyone else sat close by, except for William, who remained standing.

"Would anyone like a whiskey?" he asked.

"William Greenwood, haven't you heard of Prohibition? I could telephone the sheriff and have you jailed."

Despite the fact it was obvious Mrs. Prendergast was joking, neither William nor Justin looked amused. Nanny laughed, but it sounded forced to Lauren's ears. Father always had whiskey. Even Sheriff Dillon probably knew that and turned a blind eye. It wasn't like Father was producing his own moonshine.

"What do you think of those strikes over in Danville?" Mrs. Prendergast asked. "Between those workers protesting and the four horrible robberies in Richmond over Thanksgiving, I have to wonder what our country is coming to."

"I don't think the men striking should be compared to the robbers." Nanny had picked up her new scarf and was folding it together with the gloves on her lap. "Those raids in Richmond were planned by criminals. The poor workers in Danville don't know how else to get attention to their plight. Those men and their families are starving."

Lauren noticed her father glaring at Nanny, but she seemed oblivious as she kept talking. "Did you know many mining companies pay their workers in company scrips rather than dollars?"

"What are scrips, Nanny?"

"Never mind, Lauren," Father intervened. "Let's talk about something more pleasant."

"I'd like to know the answer to that question too, Lauren." Mrs. Prendergast turned to Nanny. "Please explain."

"Scrips are company currency. You can only use them at the company stores. So when the wives and children go to buy food and other items they have to pay higher prices at the store. They are a captive audience. They can't bring the scrips down to a store like Hillmans' in Delgany or the one over in Charlottesville. They can't exchange their scrips with local farmers for milk or butter for their children."

"Why would the company do that? Why don't they just pay them in dollars like other workers?" Lauren asked, receiving another angry look from her father.

"It's a way to control the workers. The store prices are higher than at independent stores." Nanny coughed as her voice quivered. "If the families can't afford to pay off their bill in full, the company store offers them credit. That way the men keep working. They are at the mercy of the company: living in their drafty, poorly built houses, being paid in scrips and having to run up credit in the store."

"That's wrong. Surely someone could do something about it?" Lauren asked.

"They have, Lauren." Her father's tone brooked no argument. "They've called in the National Guard. They'll make those that want to work get back into line. The troublemakers will be fired and thrown out. Just as it should be. We are in the middle of a Depression, they should consider themselves lucky to have jobs."

"Father!" Lauren couldn't help exclaiming. "You can't imagine what it must be like to have your family starving. The things we saw in New York would bring tears to your eyes."

Justin leaned toward Lauren, took her hand, and squeezed it. "Your father isn't heartless, Lauren, he is just looking out for the workers. I'm sorry you saw difficult things in New York. The stock market crash has caused a lot of problems for those who were too eager to be something they weren't."

She didn't know what he meant by that but he was smiling at her, his fingers were stroking her hand, and suddenly her brain turned to mush. She was disappointed when Father suggested Mrs. Prendergast might be tired from her travels and wish to retire. Lauren wanted to protest, but with Nanny and Justin's mother going to bed, she had no option.

As she stood up, Justin caught her hand again. "Will you take me out tomorrow to see Rosehall? I assume I could borrow a horse?"

"Of course. I can introduce you to Prince. Father bought him for my eighteenth birthday. He is fabulous."

"Until tomorrow then." Justin bowed slightly, giving her a wink when her father's back was turned.

Feeling breathless, Lauren left the room and floated up the stairs. She couldn't stop smiling the whole way.

CHAPTER 13

Rosehall, Virginia, January 1931

Over the next few days, Lauren and Justin spent as much time as they could together. Mrs. Prendergast was happy to sit with Nanny, discussing Rosehall's past and its gardens, sharing recipes and talking about other matters that interested women of a certain age. They enjoyed listening to Betty Crocker on the radio and discussed the items on the news. Lauren was thrilled that the two women got on so well, and not just because it left her alone with Justin. If Nanny liked his mother, she must like him as well.

Justin was almost as good a rider as Lauren and they went further afield on the rare days the snow didn't keep them confined to the grounds of Rosehall.

One morning, they decided to drive into Delgany in Justin's car. Lauren wanted Justin to see her local town and meet some of the people she'd known from birth. Patty came with them, eager to spend her day off there with her young man, Henry.

"He is a lucky man to have such a stunning beauty as his girlfriend," Justin teased as he drove. Patty was sitting in the back seat. "So when do you two get married?"

"Justin, don't be silly. She's only thirteen." Lauren frowned, shifting in her seat. Justin was too old to be flirting with a child.

"That's old enough to get married, Miss Lauren, but Henry reckons we should wait a while. We have to save for our house and also for Henry to get his training. He is going to be the best mechanic in Virginia."

"I don't think Cook will want you getting married for several years yet," Lauren said. "She needs your help in the kitchen."

"So you can cook as well as look beautiful," Justin said, complimenting her again, and Lauren saw Patty's color rise. "I hope this Henry knows how lucky he is."

"Yes, Mr. Justin. He does."

Lauren exchanged a smile with Patty, noticing she was wearing the new dress Mary had picked out for her in Macy's. The new fashion, where dresses hugged curves and accented waists, rather than falling like a sack, as they had in the twenties, suited Patty. Although young, she had a well-developed figure. The blue dress with gray undertones was just right for her coloring. Mary had convinced Cook to let her cut Patty's hair and the new, shorter style complimented her heart-shaped face.

As they arrived in town, and Justin pulled in to a space by the curb, Robert Spencer, the owner of Spencer's Garage, walked over, an oily rag in his hand. "Nice to see you, Miss Lauren. Happy New Year to you and yours. Patty, Henry had to go out to deliver a new motor but said to go on up to his mama. She's expecting you. Henry will be there in two shakes of a lamb's tail."

"Happy New Year to you too, Robert, and your family," said Lauren, climbing out of the car.

Patty stepped out behind her and Lauren turned to speak to her. "You go on, Patty. Tell Henry to bring you home this afternoon. Cook will need your help this evening."

"Thanks, Miss Lauren." Patty smiled before running across the street and around the block.

Robert was walking back to his garage when Lauren caught sight of Justin, who was standing by the car, staring after the girl. She coughed and he turned to look at her.

"Sorry, I was miles away. This is a quaint little town, isn't it? Not so little, actually. I never knew there were so many different stores here."

Lauren glanced around her. "Nanny said a few have shut down because of the Depression. We used to have the Delgany newspaper but that's gone. Seems they couldn't find enough advertisers."

Justin and Lauren set off down the road and soon Lauren spotted some migrant workers congregating around the Baptist church. They arrived every year to help plant crops from corn to tobacco, but this year it would seem that they'd appeared earlier and in larger numbers. Some of the children reminded her of Maggie and Biddy, because they were dressed in clothes more suitable for summer weather and going barefoot. Those with shoes had cut holes in the tops to let their toes out. Lauren shivered. It was too cold to be standing around in little more than rags.

"The town doesn't seem to be doing so badly to me." Justin's voice cut into her thoughts. "I've counted two grocers, your friend's garage, and is that a grain elevator I see in the distance?"

Hadn't he seen the children outside the church?

"Yes, it's over the other side of town by the railroad. The canning factory is there too. I rarely go down that way. Father wouldn't consider it suitable."

"Your father keeps a close eye on you, doesn't he?"

"I guess like all Southern fathers do."

Did her father keep her on a tighter rein than other girls? She didn't think so. After all, he'd given her a Cadillac for Christmas after finding out she had learned to drive.

"Shall we go explore over there?" Justin asked, offering her his arm.

"No, let's go back to the car and drive into Charlottesville instead. Father likes these special cigars that we can pick up for him there."

"Your wish is my command."

Lauren smiled, thrilled they got a chance to be alone. She loved Delgany but there were far too many people interested in gossiping and she wanted a chance to get to know Justin properly.

Once back in the car, though, they didn't get far, as the skies opened and it started to snow heavily, snowflakes falling around them.

"I could drive to Charlottesville and tell everyone we got snowed in," Justin said with a grin as he slowed down.

"Justin! You're incorrigible." She didn't want to admit she was tempted by the idea. "Turn the car around and let's head back before Nanny and your mother start worrying. Robert will see Patty gets home safe. We can always drive into Charlottesville another time."

They got home to Rosehall just in time, as the temperature dropped, turning the snow into dangerous ice. Justin took off his coat and wrapped it around her before he picked her up and carried her into the house. "Ladies' shoes aren't meant for walking in this weather."

Lauren couldn't reply. She was too intoxicated with the feel of being held so close to him.

CHAPTER 14

All too soon it was time for Mrs. Prendergast to return to Richmond. Justin was keen to stay, but his mother had prior engagements.

"I shall come back soon if you want me to?" Justin said, as he and Lauren went for a last drive around Rosehall before they said goodbye. He more or less whispered this, his breath fanning her cheek. He was so distracting. When he was near, the butterflies in her stomach had a party. "Won't you miss me?"

She would, but she was also desperate to get away from him. He aroused feelings in her like none she had ever experienced. She had even gone so far as to daydream about him.

"You'll be too busy to miss me. Father said you are sending lots of business contracts his way."

"I can't dance with a contract." He had parked the car close by the house and now moved nearer, wisps of his hair tickling her cheek. She couldn't move. Would he kiss her? Lauren had never been kissed before.

"I want to hold you in my arms in front of everyone. I don't want to have to steal precious moments with you like this."

He leaned in and brushed his lips against hers. It was only a fleeting touch, but enough to leave her wanting more. She edged closer, making him laugh before he pulled her to him and kissed her lightly on the mouth, his lips barely touching hers. She broke away and looked into his eyes. Their stormy expression seemed to reflect her emotions. His gaze flickered to her lips and back to her eyes once more. She leant in, giving permission, but for what she wasn't sure. Grasping her face in his hands, his mouth descended on hers, kissing her passionately.

Dimly she remembered they were parked close by the front door. If Jackson spotted them, he would report her to her father. She could hear the warnings that Nanny and other women had drummed into her head. *Nice girls don't let men take liberties... It is a woman's job to keep a man's feelings in check.* She moved away from him, although her body screamed in protest. "Justin, stop. We can't. Father wouldn't like it."

He looked at her as if about to say something, but changed his mind. "I apologize. You're so beautiful, Lauren, I got carried away. It won't happen again."

She pushed aside her disappointment. She wanted it to happen again, but she had to think of her reputation.

*

Lauren couldn't bear the loneliness after Justin had gone. She trailed around the house unable to read, unable to occupy herself, the weather preventing her from going out riding. Mary was no help either, as she was head over heels in love with Jed, a local man who lived in Delgany. They'd met while Lauren was in Europe.

"Nanny, can I please go with you the next time you go on one of your visits?" she asked.

"I would like that. I am planning on going up the mountain tomorrow, toward Rapidan Camp. Some of the male volunteers have cleared the bigger roads."

"You going to visit President and Mrs. Hoover?"

Nanny laughed, just for a few seconds sounding like the woman of Lauren's childhood. "Not likely, Lauren, although your father has been a guest a couple of times. Perhaps he will take you with him the next time he visits. It's a beautiful part of the mountain overlooking the Shenandoah Valley. I may not be a fan of all the decisions he's ever made as President, but I totally agree with President Hoover's choice of location for his second home."

Nanny warmed her hands in front of the small log fire burning in her sitting room. "I'm going to visit some of the mountain families. Times are difficult for them with the drought having killed their crops and the Depression meaning there's few odd jobs available for the men to provide for their families through the winter. Some of those families have lived on the mountains since their ancestors came over from England, Scotland or Ireland. Generations of them have lived through the Civil War, the Great War and the Spanish flu. But many say these times are the worst they have had to endure. People are starving. The land used to provide everything they needed, but now..." Nanny coughed, but Lauren knew it was to cover up her tears. The elderly woman hated to show weakness.

"So what time are we going tomorrow and do I need to get anything organized?" Lauren adopted a no-nonsense tone. Nanny would appreciate that more than the hug she wanted to give her.

"If it's not snowing too hard, we will leave around ten. I've asked Cook to bake some cookies. We can give them to the children as Christmas presents. They won't care that Christmas was two weeks ago."

"Cookies? That's it?" Lauren had imagined the car piled high with toys and all sorts.

"We have some food baskets. Mrs. Hillman at the store in Delgany has been collecting things for us. Miss Chaney at the post office too. And Henry had a collection at Spencer's Garage."

"Henry? The boy Patty is seeing?"

"You haven't met him yet? He's Robert Spencer's nephew down from Waynesboro. Robert has got him working in the garage. He's got the makings of a good mechanic. Him and Patty have been walking out for a little while. It's serious between them."

"Yes, Patty told Justin, but don't you think she is very young?"

"Lauren, you sound like you are sixty! Girls as young as Patty get married, especially up on the mountain. But don't worry, they have to save for a home so they will take their time. Henry's good for her. He's a very nice, caring lad. His father died in a fire and he and his mother came to live with Robert and Susan. His younger brothers and sisters went to stay with the father's family."

"They split up the family? How horrible."

"Nobody can afford to take in a family of six these days. At least the children didn't end up in the County home. I wouldn't wish that on anyone."

"Why, Nanny, what's wrong with it?"

"It's a home for orphans and destitute children. Those who don't have family to look after them. As a result of this Depression, the County home is overrun by children. There are too many squeezed into too small a space. If the people in charge ever cared about a child's welfare, that feeling has vanished under the burden of constant financial worries."

"Those poor children. Let me ask Father if I can donate the contents of the attic. I must have hundreds of dolls up there."

"Maybe not hundreds," Nanny said. "But, yes, there are certainly some toys that could help the children. It's hard to play, though, when your hunger keeps you awake."

"Is it really that bad?"

"It is, and it will get worse. People blame the nineteen-twenty-nine stock market crash, but there are other reasons why poverty is rising. The continuous drought, for one, plus the blight has destroyed the chestnut trees, so many of the mountain folk can't collect chestnuts to sell at market anymore."

To Lauren's horror, Nanny started to cry. Large tears fell down her cheeks, one after another. Lauren pulled the older woman into her arms, rubbing her hand along her back. "Nanny, I promise we will help these people. Please don't cry."

"I'll be all right. You run along now, child," the old woman said, insisting Lauren leave her.

Lauren decided to go and give Prince a rub-down.

"Sam, you've been working hard," she said, when she got to the stables. "It's cleaner than ever in here." She wasn't just being polite. The place had been repainted, and there wasn't even the stench of horse manure.

"Been keepin' busy, Miss Lauren. Don't want anyone thinkin' I'm not worth keeping around."

Lauren's heart raced as she looked at his face. "What do you mean by that?"

He didn't meet her gaze. "I've been readin' the papers. All those people losin' their jobs. I can't afford to lose mine. What else do I know about? I've only ever worked here at Rosehall."

"Sam, don't be worrying about things like that. Father would never get rid of you. Everyone in Albemarle County—no, in Virginia—knows you are the best judge of horses. You're the only man Father would trust with his animals. You are worth your weight in gold and then some."

Sam grinned, but his eyes didn't lose their wary expression. "I sure wish you were in charge of my wages, Miss Lauren. I'd like to see all that gold."

They laughed together, but it was a laughter tinged with sadness.

"I'm going with Nanny tomorrow to deliver food baskets. She said things are hard for people around here."

"They is worse than hard, Miss Lauren. The soapstone quarry is on the point of being closed. Those men have only ever known that work, so what will they do? They can't turn to farmin' as the land is all dried up. Unless there is plenty of rain this year, next

Christmas is going to be worse. I thank the Lord every day I have a job and home at Rosehall."

"We are all thankful you work here, Sam." She glanced at her watch. "Thank you for looking after Prince so well for me. He looks wonderful, with his shiny winter coat."

"He's a lovely horse, Miss Lauren. Such a nice temperament is rare in a thoroughbred."

Prince whickered as if in agreement, making them both laugh. Lauren kissed the horse one last time, said goodbye to Sam, and returned to the house.

With Sam worried about his job and Nanny crying about the mountain folk, this wasn't at all like the Rosehall she'd left behind two years ago. She shivered as she walked past the vegetable garden and into the house, wishing the people she cared about weren't worn down by troubles.

CHAPTER 15

Lauren decided to drive the car herself. She didn't want to ask Jackson and have him report back on their activities to her father. Nanny didn't protest, although she held onto the door handle for quite a while, perhaps needing reassurance that Lauren wasn't going to drive both of them off the road.

They headed to Delgany first.

"I was talking to Sam, Nanny. He seems worried about his job," Lauren said, as they made their way into town.

"I reckon he is. Everyone is. Times like this make people worry about everything. The newspapers are full of sadness and every day, you hear a story more heartbreaking than the one you heard the day before. Drive a little slower, darling, the roads might be icy."

"Yes, Nanny."

Lauren peered out the window as they drove down the road into Delgany's main street, looking for signs of the Depression. She hadn't been thinking of anything other than Justin on the day they drove in with Patty.

Unlike New York, there were no breadlines in Delgany and she didn't see any children begging on the street. They drove past the post office, where she spotted the postmistress, Miss Chaney, and the Burtons' cook in conversation. On the opposite side of the block, the parking spaces outside Hillmans' grocery store were occupied, suggesting people were shopping. That was a good sign. She drove past the white-framed Baptist church, which never changed from one year to the next.

"Turn at the war memorial and come back up the street." Nanny suggested. "We can park outside the sheriff's office. That will give the townsfolk something to gossip about."

Lauren did as she was bid. She said a quick prayer as she circled the war memorial, wondering, as always, how a town as small as Delgany had lost so many men in the World War. Mr. Spencer waved to her from his garage. She pondered if the young, dark-haired man holding some tools was Henry.

"The Delgany hotel seems busy if the number of vehicles parked outside is anything to go by. That's a good sign, Nanny, isn't it?"

"Yes, Lauren. But Miss Chaney said most of the guests who are staying now were here for Christmas and New Year. Next week it will be as empty as it was the week prior to Christmas."

"Who are you and what have you done with my real nanny?" Lauren exclaimed. "The nanny that I remember didn't have a care in the world or, if she did, she hid it well. You are going around like the world is going to end tomorrow."

"Here we are. Park there, just beside Sheriff's Ford." Nanny waited until Lauren parked, before saying, "I'm sorry to be such a worrywart. I'll do my best to be like your old nanny."

Lauren threw her arms around the older woman. "I love you and I hate to see you so sad. Things will get better, you'll see. I'm home for one. I will have you driven nuts in no time at all."

Nanny laughed, and Lauren was glad to see a glimpse of the woman she loved so dearly. They both got out of the car and linked arms together as they crossed the street. Hillmans' Store looked older than she remembered, the paint on the door and around the windows was peeling. There was nothing on display outside, but it was January so that would explain it. She pushed the door open, the bell ringing as she did so.

"I'll be right with you." Mrs. Hillman sounded the same as always.

The inside hadn't changed much from how she remembered it. Candies the color of the rainbow lay in clean bins near the cash register. Wooden shelves sported all sorts of goods, including canned peaches and other fruit, jelly in glass jars, honey in others. At the back of the store stood bolts of calico fabric, some as pretty as the wild flowers on a summer meadow. If everything looked a little dusty and tired, it was because she was comparing them to Macy's and other New York stores, Lauren told herself. She walked past the end displays of canned fruit and up to the counter, waiting until Mrs. Hillman looked up from her ledger.

"Why, Miss Lauren, it's wonderful to see you. You've blossomed into such a beauty. The cut of your mother, isn't she, Gene?"

"Welcome back, Miss Lauren," Gene Hillman said, with a smile. "Is this a fleeting visit or are you home for good?"

"For good, Mr. Hillman."

"Nanny will be pleased. She's been lonesome, her being an old lady." Mrs. Hillman winked at Lauren.

"Less of the old, thank you very much, Vivian Hillman," said Nanny. "How did you get on with donations for the food baskets?"

After Nanny's talk of the desperation in the mountains, Lauren hoped the locals had been full of generosity for their neighbors. She dreaded what conditions they would find when they visited the various Hollows where the mountain families lived in small communities.

The shopkeeper's smile faltered. "Not as well as I hoped, but I guess Christmas was hard this year. Thank goodness for the new owner of the *Charlottesville News*. He donated fifty cans of peaches, two large bags of flour, and some eggs. He also insisted on some candy for the children."

"That was kind of him," Lauren said, when it appeared Nanny wasn't going to comment.

Mr. Hillman nodded before adding, "The sheriff donated quite a lot of sugar."

"That was generous of him, but why? I mean, couldn't he have given you money instead of buying lots of sugar?" Lauren asked, then was mystified as they all started to laugh. "What?"

"You've been away at school too long, Miss Lauren." Gene Hillman rubbed his moustache. "Sheriff Dillon has been chasing down moonshiners. Him or those revenuers can only bust someone if they catch them with an alcohol still."

"What do you mean, catch them with it? If it's on their property, whose else would it be?" asked Lauren.

"The law doesn't work like that, Lauren. The sheriff or the men from the Revenue—the revenuers, as the mountain people call them—have to catch someone actually using their still to make alcohol. It's not rightly fair in my book. Most mountain folk look down on those who drink to excess. They are good people, in the main," Mr. Hillman said.

"True, Gene, most have a still on their property," replied Nanny. "They brew alcohol for medicinal purposes, adding some to hot water to clear a chest cold or using the alcohol to rub on a toothache. Always have done right back before the War Between The States. They aren't the ones the sheriff needs to bust."

"No, it's the ones selling it to make a profit that he wants. The tax men want their cut of the money," Gene said, nodding. "It's a difficult job, but the sheriff got lucky the other night. Busted old man Boran and put him in jail. The old coot had half a bag of sugar he hadn't added to his apples so the sheriff took that. He would have taken the apples too but he felt sorry for Boran's family. He let them have those for pig feed. That old sow doesn't know her luck, getting all those apples."

"Didn't Mrs. Boran need the sugar too?" Lauren asked. She didn't like Mr. Boran, who drank heavily and had a long history of being mean to his wife and children, but she didn't want the family suffering.

"I guess so, but the sheriff said he couldn't leave it as she might start up the still again once he'd left."

Lauren couldn't imagine Mrs. Boran touching alcohol, let alone making it. She went to church almost every day and twice on a Sunday—and besides, Mrs. Boran was a Baptist and they didn't drink at all.

"I divided the sugar and flour into smaller parcels—got some brown paper and made it into funnels like these." Mrs. Hillman returned to explaining what she had put in the food baskets and showed them her work. "Hillmans' donated some coffee, I put that into those twists there so you can tell the difference."

"Vivian, you can't afford to be that generous," said Nanny. "I know it's hard for you and Gene too."

"We get by, although more people are using eggs and chickens and canned goods to cover their bills now." Mrs. Hillman glanced away, but Lauren had seen the worry in her eyes. The woman continued, "We are now in the bartering business, not the cash business, seems like."

Mr. Hillman put his hand on his wife's shoulders. "I been livin' in these here parts since I was a glimmer in my pa's eye and I ain't never seen the likes of it afore. We've had tough times but—"

His wife cut him off. "Now, Gene, that's enough. We've got plenty. We've a roof over our heads, food in our bellies, and good friends and neighbors. Delgany is not like those big cities with all them banks that are failing and people jumping off buildings. We've had hard times before and we'll have them again but we will get through won't we, Nanny?"

"Of course we will. I have some money from the staff at Rosehall. We'll add some kerosene, lye soap, salt, and cans of condensed milk to those baskets before we go." Nanny took out the coins from her purse. Lauren watched as she counted out nickels and dimes, some pennies, and quarters. The total was four dollars and fifty-five cents. Lauren reached into her purse and pulled out a five-dollar note. At Mrs. Hillman's look, she wished she had given it to Nanny before she got to the store. She was about to explain her father had given her money for Christmas but instead stayed silent. She put the note on top of the money that Nanny had gathered, leaving Nanny and Mrs. Hillman to decide how it would be spent.

Mr. Hillman hollered for his son. "Earl, will you carry these items to Miss Lauren's truck for these ladies, please?"

Earl appeared as if from nowhere. "Yes, Pa. Morning, Nanny. Nice to see you back, Miss Lauren." He snatched the hat off his head. His eyes glowed as he leaned forward, getting closer to Lauren. "You see the Chrysler Building when you were in New York?"

Lauren smiled, knowing that Earl was as fond of buildings as she was of books. If times were different or he came from a wealthier family, he would have studied architecture at university. At sixteen, he was already known for his craftsmanship.

"I sure did. It isn't finished yet but I took some photographs of the men working on it. Next time you come to Rosehall, let me know and I'll show them to you."

"Thanks, Miss Lauren. I reckon it will be the tallest building ever when it's finished."

Lauren shook her head. "I think they plan on making the Empire State Building even taller."

"I saw that they are going to pay men three whole dollars a day to work on that. I wish I could go up and build it." Earl cast a longing glace at his ma.

"Over my dead body," Mrs. Hillman retorted. "I ain't reared you to send you off to a city like that. It's full of heathens. You saw the pictures of those workers in the papers. If God Almighty had wanted you to work up that high, He'd have given you wings."

Lauren hid her smile, knowing Mrs. Hillman would never forgive her if she thought she was laughing at her.

"Ma! You said yourself Charles Lindbergh was a hero and that lady flier too. They don't have wings."

"Don't you sass me. They had an airplane to keep them safe. Your pa said that was as good as wings. Still I reckon that Miss Earhart should settle down and raise a family like any good woman. She should leave flying to the men."

Nanny took Lauren's arm. "We best be going. Thank you, Vivian, and you too, Gene, for your generosity."

Earl picked up the parcels and Lauren held the door open as his pa said goodbye.

"Be careful up there on the mountain. I don't want to have to come and dig you out. You drive slowly, you hear, Nanny?"

"I'm not driving, Lauren is."

"We'll say a prayer," Mr. Hillman said as his son grinned at Lauren.

CHAPTER 16

The wintery sun had risen high into the sky, clearing what was left of the morning mist. Lauren drove carefully, leaving Delgany behind them, heading for the mountain.

"Where are we going first, Nanny?"

"We'll call at Meehan's Hollow first. The roads leading there are fairly decent and should be cleared of the worst of the snow. We may have to leave the baskets for the other hollows with the folks at Meehan's. I don't want you sliding off the road. Your father would kill me."

Lauren didn't argue; she was too busy admiring the countryside around her. Some trees had little or no leaves left, the bare branches swaying gently in the wind. Others looked like Christmas trees topped with a small white hat, and then the road narrowed, bringing them closer to a collection of towering trees.

"What type of trees are these, Nanny? They look like bears or some other wild animal attacked them."

"These are the chestnuts. The blight causes spores to burst open in patches. It leaves a tree dead but still standing." Nanny sniffed. "Some folks depended on those chestnut trees. They'd harvest the chestnuts and sell them to get through the difficult winter months. Now they haven't anything."

"How bad is the blight?"

"They reckon it has destroyed most of the trees, those that haven't been cut down in a bid to stop it spreading. This on top of the drought, which turned the cornfields black for lack of rain, has piled misery on the decent folks living up here. Usually they let the animals forage for food, but I've heard that a lot of farmers slaughtered their animals rather than let them starve to death."

"How awful."

"I guess it's better to slaughter a pig, rather than leave it to die and then wonder if the meat is safe to use. These people survive on a diet of cornpone, Irish potatoes, and pork, Lauren, with a little extra for the pot if the men go hunting for wild turkey, deer or rabbits. The creeks used to be full of fish, but with the high temperatures some of them have run dry for the first time in living memory. We don't know how bad it is for the families living higher up the mountain. They don't come down to town too often and nobody's got a hope of visiting up there during winter. Pull over when you can. Widow Tennant lives just over yonder."

Lauren parked and hopped out of the Ford, then walked round to the other side to open the door. Nanny went to the back of the truck and grabbed one of the bigger baskets.

"Lauren, let me handle Mrs. Tennant. If the woman could live on pride, she would be the size of this mountain."

Lauren followed Nanny up a cleared pathway. On either side there were brambles and bushes but someone had worked hard to keep the access clear. As they got nearer the building, she saw it was barely more than a shack. The roof sloped down at an angle, making it look like a heavy wind would blow it right off. It was covered in broken twigs and dead leaves with dots of white snow. There were no windows on the second floor and the two on the first floor hadn't any glass or curtains, just sheets of newspaper. There were shutters, but they had fallen into disrepair.

Nanny knocked on the door. After a while, someone pulled it open with difficulty as the bottom scraped along the floor. A thin, wrinkled woman came outside, a toddler on her hip.

"What you doin' up here? I done told those government men, I won't give my children up. They is not goin' to the County home."

"Henrietta Tennant, is that any way to greet a neighbor? I'm not here to take your children, I'm parched for a drink and a chat. What happened to 'Come in and I'll put the kettle on?'—Good morning, Donnie, how you feelin'?" The child gave Nanny a wide smile, showing a lack of teeth.

Lauren glanced at his mother, who sighed and turned away, leaving the door open. "You can come in if you like, but all I got to offer you is boiled water."

"That's good as I brought the coffee. This is Lauren Greenwood. Lauren, Mrs. Tennant has lived on this mountain since she was a girl. We used to be friends, but judging by our welcome today, looks like that may have changed."

Lauren nodded to the woman before coming to a standstill as she saw seven pairs of eyes looking at her. The red-headed children all stood around, staring. Their bellies were protruding, and for a second, she thought the eldest girl was pregnant.

"How are you, Hetty?" Nanny spoke softly. "What do you mean about the children being taken?"

The woman just stared, silent tears flowing down her cheeks. Nanny took a step toward her and pulled her into her arms, patting her back.

"We're here now, don't you be fretting. I expect you are tired. It's not easy rearing all these children on your own." Gently, she helped her to sit down in a chair.

Lauren shivered. It was colder inside this cabin than it was outdoors. The walls were covered with what looked like newspapers and pages from Sears Catalogs, utterly useless at preventing the cold from seeping in. She spotted blackened sticks and ashes in the fireplace.

"Can we build a fire?" she suggested to one of the children, a young girl of about twelve.

The girl wiped her snotty nose in her sleeve. "We ain't got nothin' to light it with."

"Matthew, John, Luke and Robert, you get dressed and go find me some small pieces of wood," Nanny ordered before turning to Lauren: "Can you unpack what we brought with us?"

Mrs. Tennant stood up, but Nanny pushed her back down in the chair. "Hetty, I want you to rest up. Lauren and I can manage if the children help us. Becky, can you show Lauren where to put things, please?"

Becky, who looked to be a few years older than Patty, moved toward the kitchen. She pointed to a plate of chicken bones and a pint of flour. Then she opened a cupboard to show a collection of about fifteen cans. "We put these up in the summer but we didn't have a lot to spare. We ain't got nothin' else."

Lauren tried not to show her horror. These children were starving. She put the basket on the rickety table, taking out the lye soap and giving it to Nanny, who sent Becky out to the well to get some clean water. Nanny pushed up her sleeves and cleaned out the ashes from the cooking stove.

"Lauren, can you bring me the kerosene from the truck, please?"

When the boys came back with the firewood, Nanny doused a couple of sticks in the kerosene and, in no time at all, a fire was burning. She heated some of the water that Becky had brought inside and washed some pots, instructing Lauren as she went.

"Lauren, will you wash those potatoes? We'll bake them in their jackets. Best nutrients are found next to the skin."

Lauren did as she was told, while Nanny sliced off some bacon and set it to fry in the pan on the fire. She made some sort of corn mush and cooked it in the bacon fat. The children crowded round, sniffing the air with glee.

"Boys, go gather more firewood. This won't be enough to keep you warm. Sarah, take Donnie and watch him over at the fire. Give your mother a break. Becky, can you show Lauren what you have left outside."

"Nothin'. Some thievin' son of a—"

"Becky Tennant, you watch your language or you'll be tasting lye soap for a week." Hetty turned to Nanny. "Chickens were stolen night before last. All three of 'em. Gone."

"By a fox?" Nanny asked.

"Not unless he was wearin' boots and a fur cap. It was them Bramley brothers, I'd swear on it," Becky said. She looked fit to spit but Hetty just rubbed her arms.

"They must be hungry to lower themselves to takin' chickens."

"We're all hungry, Ma."

"Becky, watch your tone. Just cause you be fifteen doesn't give you the right to sass me." Hetty stood up as the kettle whistled. "Can I do somethin'?"

"No, Hetty. Sit down and let me. Only room for one woman in a kitchen." Nanny smiled to take the sting from her words. She opened the coffee and added some to a pot, before pouring in the boiling water. Soon, the aroma of thick black coffee dominated the room.

Becky's eyes watered as she brushed the tears roughly away. Watching the girl, Lauren thought it best to take her out of the house for a spell. "Can you show me where to get some more water, please, Becky?"

Becky glanced at her, opened her mouth to say something, but instead huffed and grabbed the bucket, marching outside. Lauren followed in her wake.

The girl hadn't any shoes on yet she didn't hesitate to march through the muck in the back yard toward the well. They passed the remains of the chicken coop. It looked like the wire had been cut, neatly, not by a fox or other wild animal.

"You believe me, don't ya? It wasn't no foxes that stole our chickens."

"I'm sorry, Becky. I can't understand what would drive anyone to take from a family with so many mouths to feed."

Eyeing Lauren's coat, gloves, scarf, and hat, Becky said, "Yeah, I guess you wouldn't." As she pumped the water, she asked, "Do you own that big house where Nanny Kat lives?"

Nanny Kat? She'd never heard Nanny called that before. Father called her Kathryn or Nanny. Nanny Kat suited her.

"Rosehall? My father does."

"How comes you never came here with Nanny Kat afore?"

"I've been away in school and then Europe. I only arrived back home at New Year."

"I'd love to go back to school. Did you get to read lots of books? I wanted to be a teacher. You know, when Pa was alive I was good at learnin'. Good with teachin' the young'uns too. Our teacher said she relied on me. I had patience then." Becky smiled shyly.

"So what do you want to do now?" Lauren asked.

"Survive." Becky coughed.

"I'm sorry, that was stupid of me."

"You're all right. You weren't to know. I'd like to get a job but who's goin' to give one to a mountain girl? I knows how people view us down there in Charlottesville. They think we ain't got a mind of our own and we marry our brothers and sisters. I read the stupid things they say in the newspapers."

Lauren had heard similar things so she couldn't deny what the girl had said.

"What did your mother mean about people wanting to take her children away?"

Becky's lips trembled as she put the full bucket on the ground, putting her arms around her body. "They be people from the government. So they said. They told Ma that Donnie and some of the other 'uns had something called pellagra. I never 'eard of it but they said it was why their stomachs look like they was havin' a baby. The men said if they took the children to the County home, they would get rid of whatever that pellagra thing is and get better. The home would give them the right food. They said

Ma wasn't able to look after us properly and if she was a good mother, she would agree to them taking the children. I ain't ever seen Ma so mad. She acted like a bull with a spur under his skin. She took the broom and threatened to hit those men if they didn't get out of her house. She didn't want to listen to what they said. Then they told her they'd be back with the sheriff."

"When was this?"

"The week afore Christmas. Then the snows came and blocked the road so they couldn't come back. Ma hasn't been sleepin' since. She's been walkin' back and forth the whole time. She's worryin' and frettin'. One minute she says those men were right and she is a bad ma and the next, she's sayin' she'd rather throw us all down the well than give us to the County home." Becky shuddered. "Ma said there was all sorts of stories about how us girls would be treated over there. She wouldn't tell me the details but I knows it's bad. I heard some of the women whisperin' about it back in the summer when they came around to do quiltin'."

Lauren couldn't think of anything to say. Surely it would be better for the children to have regular food and proper shelter? She was relieved to hear Nanny calling them.

"You won't say nothin' to Ma about me tellin' ya? She's worried the Bramley Brothers will take revenge if we complain. She thinks they would burn the house down with us in it."

Lauren shook her head, not knowing what to say in front of such fear. Holding out her hand, she said, "Why don't I help you with the bucket?"

Together, they carried the full bucket past the chicken coop and into the house. Lauren couldn't believe the amount of food Nanny had produced. The potatoes wouldn't be ready until the evening, but for now the family had fried bacon, biscuits, and gravy and the corn mush. The children gathered along a bench beside the rickety table that threatened to collapse anytime someone moved to reach for a biscuit or second helpings. Lauren sipped her black coffee. The Tennants didn't have a cow and she hated condensed milk. The children clearly loved it though, given how fast they drank the watered-down version Nanny produced.

After the little ones had been fed, Becky took them into the living area and told them a story. Lauren helped Nanny to wash up the dishes and put them away, refusing to let Mrs. Tennant move a muscle.

"Hetty, we'll be back to you tomorrow. I can't promise a cow but I'll get you a goat. You need milk for the children and yourself. We'll find you new chickens, too, and get someone to fix that chicken coop. What you need is a dog. That will keep chicken thieves in line."

"What will I feed the dog?" Hetty asked, her voice soft. All fight seemed to have gone out of her. "Kathryn, maybe I should put the children in the County home. At least over there, they would be looked after."

"Children belong with those that love them, Hetty. For as long as there is a breath in my body, those children are going to stay with you. I'll speak to Mrs. Hillman and some of the other good folk in Delgany and see if we can come up with a plan. You just rest now, you hear?"

"Yes, Nanny Kat." But this time Mrs. Tennant smiled.

CHAPTER 17

Nanny didn't seem in the mood to chat as Lauren drove to their next stop. It was a two-story home with a wraparound porch. Smoke was swirling out the chimney. The door opened and a man came out hollerin' at his wife to put the kettle on as they had visitors.

Lauren recognized white-haired Mr. Thatcher, who had come down to see Sam about some horse issues over the years. His wife had visited with Old Sally, Sam's mother, who lived in a shack in the old part of Rosehall's grounds. Many of the mountain women came to Old Sally to learn her cures.

"Why, Miss Lauren, you all grown up," Mr. Thatcher said. "You used to look like a wind would blow you over, you were such a skinny little thing. Your pa must be proud of the way you turned out."

Truly, Lauren didn't know if her father was proud of her or not. He never said. Mr. Thatcher turned to Nanny and enveloped her in a big hug, causing Nanny to swat him on the arm. "You put me down, you great big heathen! You know better than to treat a lady like that."

"Aw, shucks, Nanny Kat, I wish you'd make an honest man of me. I'd run all the way to New York and back if you'd marry me."

Lauren burst out laughing as Nanny turned crimson. "John Thatcher, I'll tell the preacher on you! You with the best wife this mountain ever saw waiting on you in that lovely house."

"My missus don't mind sharing. She loves your cornbread gravy almost as much as I do. Ah, don't mention the preacher. He never stops badgering me to go to church and confess my sins. Doesn't he know if I start now, I'll be still kneeling there next spring?"

"Oh, you!" Nanny patted his arm.

"What'cha doin' up here anyways?" Mr. Thatcher looked at the truck before turning back to Nanny. "You ain't aiming to go much further up the mountain in that, are ya?"

"No. You can go visiting for us."

"I can?"

"So nice of you to offer." Nanny smiled at the tall, white-haired man. "We have some supplies for the families that needs them the most."

"Come inside and get warm. It's not a bad day but it's a mite chilly to be standing around. The missus would never forgive me if you went away without saying hello."

They walked up the steps into the house. Lauren kicked the snow off her shoes before stepping onto the shining wooden floor. A roaring fire lit the chimney in the main room. Her mouth watered at the smell of gingerbread baking and she followed Nanny into the kitchen. Everything shone, the stove had been blackened recently, and the floor was as clean as the counter tops. Pretty red and white curtains graced the large glass window and a butter churn stood over near the back door. Was that what Mrs. Thatcher had been doing before they arrived?

Mr. Thatcher sent his son, Ben, to empty the truck and bring the items into the house.

"Miss Lauren, you turned out right pretty," said Mrs. Thatcher. "Lovely to see you, Nanny Kat. It's been a while."

Mrs. Thatcher kissed Nanny on either cheek before doing the same to Lauren, then she turned back to Nanny. "I heard you saying to John you got food for the families on the mountain. Those that need it. That's just about every family up here. Times are tough. How do you tell which family gets what?"

Nanny exhaled noisily. "If I could, I'd help everyone, Alice, but I'll leave it to you to choose. You know who's genuinely hurting and who's been drinking too much 'shine to pay attention to their loved ones."

"You been to see Hetty?" Mrs. Thatcher asked as she set the table with cups and plates. She took the warm gingerbread out the oven and placed it on the table with a jug of heavy cream.

"Yes. She told me about her government visitors."

"I don't like it, Nanny Kat. Those government men been going backward and forward all summer." Mr. Thatcher ran a hand through his white hair. "Ain't nothing good comin' from men in suits on the mountain. Not the place for them."

"Maybe they are just trying to help." Nanny accepted a cup of coffee and a slice of gingerbread.

Lauren did the same and bit into the gingerbread. It crumbled in her mouth. "Mrs. Thatcher, this gingerbread is delicious. Your family is lucky to have such an excellent cook."

"Thank you, Lauren. See?" She thumped her husband on his arm. "Some folk appreciate the effort I make and don't insult me by offering marriage to every woman that crosses the doorstep." The twinkle in Mrs. Thatcher's eyes showed she was joking.

"What do you make of the trouble over in Arkansas?" Mr. Thatcher slurped his coffee loudly. "I couldn't believe what I was reading in the newspaper, but then it came on the radio."

"You mean the food riot?" Nanny put her cup of coffee back down on the table. "I believe Mr. Coney, the farmer who led the protest, should get a medal. President Hoover should put him in charge. I'm fed up hearing stories about how the Red Cross folks won't distribute the relief as they promised. The people are starving and they need to eat. They say Coney got food for five hundred families for two weeks. That just proves the food was there."

"I know, Nanny Kat. I think the Red Cross means well but some of those agents they employ like the power trip it gives them." Mr. Thatcher scratched his head. "Did you read how some of the papers want the stores to mount machine guns? That's just plain dumb. Coney's protest was peaceful, not a riot. Those reporters would say anything to sell a newspaper."

Mrs. Thatcher crossed herself. "I thank the Good Lord every day that I married a wonderful provider and we got lucky with our land. Even with the drought, we managed to put away a lot of food. Ben and I walked up high into the mountain and picked blackberries, gooseberries, and just about every sort of berry we could find. Same with the vegetables. I canned the lot. We collected apples from the trees and dried them on the roof, just like my parents did, back in the old days. John put word out that Reckless, our dog, likes nothing better than to chew the legs off chicken thieves. We might have to make a few cutbacks here and there, but we's doing all right."

"You are an excellent homemaker and a good manager, Alice," replied Nanny. "I told Hetty she should get herself a dog. I'm coming back tomorrow to see her. I can't bear to think of those lovely children going into that home. There has to be a way to keep the family together."

"John and our Ben will go over later with some eggs and fresh milk. The problem is Hetty is so private, she won't let us help."

"I told Lauren she has a lot of pride, but I think you'll find she's willing to accept help from good people like yourselves." Nanny stood up. "Now, we best be heading back to Rosehall or Lauren's father will send out a search party. If you need anything from the things we brought up, you help yourself. But mind you don't let those Bramley brothers near. They been helping themselves to what doesn't belong to them."

"I heard some folk sayin' that. They need teachin' a lesson. Sheriff Dillon should head up this way and do some real work rather than sittin' on his fat a—"

Nanny's steely glance cut off Mr. Thatcher's rant just in time. Lauren turned her head away to hide her smile. It amused her to see the tiny woman take on a huge mountain man and win.

Lauren drove very slowly down the mountain as it had started snowing again. It wasn't cold enough for it to turn to ice on the road just yet, but in a few hours it would be like trying to drive over glass. She shivered, despite her warm coat. How would Becky and her family survive the next few weeks when the weather would be the coldest? She glanced across at Nanny, but she appeared to be sleeping. No wonder she looked older now than she had when Lauren had headed off to school and Europe. She'd been working too hard helping others. Lauren resolved to help her as much as possible.

CHAPTER 18

Lauren slipped quietly out of bed, not wanting to wake the household. She dressed quickly before pulling out a large suitcase and opening her wardrobe. She sorted through her older clothes and filled the case with warm jumpers, some day-dresses, clean underthings, and stockings. On top, she laid two quilts, one of which she had made with Nanny's help. The stitching wasn't neat and certainly wouldn't win any awards, but she doubted the Tennant children would care. The last thing she added to the case were some books, including a copy of *Little Women* by Louisa May Alcott and *A Christmas Carol* by Charles Dickens. With the heavy case in one hand, Lauren crept as quietly as she could along the corridor and down the backstairs. She didn't want Jackson to see her.

The aroma of strong black coffee wafting toward her told her that Cook was awake. She turned the handle to open the kitchen door and entered the warm room.

Cook gasped at the sight of her. "Oh my, Miss Lauren, you almost gave me a heart attack! I heard footsteps and didn't know who it could be coming down those stairs." Cook stared at the case: "You going traveling again?"

"Sorry, Cook. I couldn't sleep and I didn't want to wake everyone else. The case is full of old clothes for charity. May I help myself to coffee?"

"I'll get some for you, miss."

"No, you have things to do. I am not completely helpless." Lauren poured the hot liquid into two cups and handed one to Cook. "Where is Patty this morning?"

Cook took the cup. "I sent her out to collect the eggs. Why?"

"Could I borrow her for a while, please? I heard Nanny coughing last night. I think she may have caught a chill. She'd planned to go visiting on the mountain today but I'm going to go instead. I'm not telling her so she can't argue and insist on coming with me. She should be taking things easier at her age."

Cook lifted one eyebrow.

"I know you try to get her to rest, Cook, but Nanny is stubborn. It's the Scottish blood in her veins. I will be gone before she gets up. I do need a second pair of hands, though. I'd ask Mary, but she has the day off to go visit Jed and his family."

"I don't know, Miss Lauren. What if your father brings back company?"

"He won't. He's gone over to Richmond. He told me last night. Something about trouble at the coal mine."

"Well, in that case, I can't say no, can I?"

Lauren leaned forward and kissed Cook on the cheek. "Thanks, Cook. You won't regret it."

"I have a feeling I will."

*

Patty was thrilled to have some hours away from the kitchen. She walked with Lauren to the back of the kitchen garden, where the Rosehall trucks were parked. Lauren stowed the case in the back of the Ford.

"Where are we going, Miss Lauren?" Patty asked.

"I have to see a man about a goat or a cow."

Patty's eyes bulged, making Lauren laugh. "Before that, I have to see Sheriff Dillon. And I thought you could introduce me to

Henry. Is he any good with making things? I need someone to fix a chicken coop."

"You are acting real funny, Miss Lauren. What do you know about goats and chickens?"

"Nothing, but I have to learn fast. How about I drop you off at the garage and you can spend some time with Henry? I'll go on to Hillmans' and then go speak to the sheriff. I will be back at the garage after about thirty minutes, when you can introduce me to Henry."

Patty turned crimson, but she nodded. "You'll like my Henry, Miss Lauren."

Lauren dropped Patty at the garage, catching sight of the welcoming smile Henry had for his girl. She drove slowly down the main street and pulled into a parking spot right outside Hillmans'.

"Miss Lauren, two days in a row? People will talk," Mr. Hillman teased her, as she went inside the store. She took a brown envelope from her pocket. "I brought these for Earl to look at. I figured it would take him forever to ask to come to Rosehall to see them."

"They the photographs of New York? I better hide them from the missus." He took the envelope and lodged it behind the cash register.

"Mr. Hillman, I need some help. Where can I buy some chickens and a cow or a goat?"

Mr. Hillman put his finger in his ear, as if to clear the wax. "Pardon me, Miss Lauren?"

"You heard right. As you know, Nanny and I went to see a couple of families yesterday and there was one woman who had nothing but some chicken bones and a small amount of flour left. No milk or eggs or anything. I don't have the first idea where to buy animals and, even if I did"—Lauren glanced at the floor—"I wouldn't know the difference between a cow and a bull."

Mr. Hillman developed a coughing fit, and she suspected he was trying hard not to laugh at her.

"I don't mind you laughing, Mr. Hillman. I'm fairly useless. Nanny had to light a stove yesterday. I wouldn't know the first thing about that. I've never boiled water. I'm about as useful as a chocolate coffeepot."

"There now, Miss Lauren, it takes all sorts to make this world of ours go around. You have other gifts. You have brains and beauty. I'll give you two of our chickens and if you take Earl with you, he can show you where Williams Farm is and you will find a cow or a goat there. Just leave it all to Earl."

"Thanks, Mr. Hillman, but please put the cost of the chickens on my… I mean my father's account. He won't mind me spending a few dollars."

"Your wish is my command, Miss Lauren." The storekeeper smiled as he said it.

"I have to see the sheriff now. Will you ask Earl to meet me at Spencer's Garage? I left Patty there."

"With her new man? He's a very nice young man, Henry Spencer. Patty has fallen on her feet there. He worships the ground she walks on. There will be wedding bells soon, I reckon."

"Patty is only thirteen."

"My Vivian was fourteen when we found ourselves a preacher. Most folk around hereabouts get married young."

"No wonder my father thinks I'm an old maid."

Lauren could still hear the sound of Mr. Hillman's laughter as she let the shop door swing shut behind her, leaving the bell ringing. Walking to the sheriff's office, she hoped his cell would be empty. She didn't relish having to speak to him with any local drunks as witnesses. What she had to say needed to remain a secret, or Mrs. Tennant and her family could pay the price. Mountain folk didn't like people snitching on them to the law.

The cold weather seemed to have kept people at home. The streets of Delgany were almost deserted as Lauren pushed open the door of the sheriff's office. Sheriff Dillon was standing with his back to the door, in front of a large fire, where he was holding out his hands to the heat. Once through the door, Lauren glanced over at the cell, and was relieved to see the bunk bed was empty, a rolled-up blanket and pillow sitting on the thin mattress. She let out her breath now it was clear she wouldn't have to deal with the morning-after stench that came with overnight prison guests.

As the door shut behind Lauren, Sheriff Dillon turned round. "Lauren Greenwood. Of all the people I thought to see in here, I would never have picked you. How are you?" He caught himself. "Are you in trouble? Something wrong out at your place?"

"No, Sheriff, not at Rosehall, but I do need your help. Nanny and I went up the mountain yesterday for a bit of a drive."

Frowning, the sheriff folded his arms across his chest, not even trying to hide his impatience. "Nanny was spreading her Christian charity again, wasn't she? Who did she upset this time? I keep telling that woman that not everybody wants her parcels or her sermons."

"Sheriff!" Lauren couldn't help jumping to Nanny's defense. "She is trying to help people and the ones we met yesterday were very grateful. There is real suffering up on the mountain. Children are starving and all sorts of mischief is going on. For one thing, when did it become normal to threaten to take a woman's children from her?"

The sheriff's foot tapped. "You talking about the County home? They are just trying to help the poor mountain folk that don't know any better. Those children never see inside a classroom. They wouldn't be able to tell you Hoover was President. Some of them probably think the Confederate flag is the real flag."

"I don't know what families you're talking about, but the ones I know are good people. Their children go to school when the weather permits. If they have decent clothes to wear."

"Lauren, did you come in here to give me a lecture? Cause I ain't in the best of moods this morning."

Kicking herself for getting his back up, Lauren spoke softly. "I'm sorry, Sheriff. Father says I get carried away at times. I am looking for your help. Please. I'm here about the Bramley brothers. They're causing trouble and someone needs to have a word with them. Otherwise there will be those on the mountain who may take matters into their own hands."

"What have the Bramley brothers done now?"

"They stole Mrs. Tennant's chickens, only you can't let the Bramleys know I told you. Mrs. Tennant is worried they'll come after her and burn the house down around her. She wanted us to believe it was foxes."

"But you know different? Spy them from Rosehall, did you?"

How dare he imply she was spreading gossip? But Lauren counted to ten before she answered. She wouldn't do anyone any good by losing her temper.

"I have a witness but she won't stand up in court so it's pointless you knowing her name." Lauren smiled at the sheriff, hoping he wouldn't see through her bluff. "I'm sure you have a long list of offenses you can arrest the Bramley brothers for. A few nights in the cells should put a stop to their gallop."

"Miss Greenwood, don't you come in here batting your eyelids while trying to tell me how to do my job. If I catch the Bramley brothers breaking the law, I'll lock them up."

Lauren decided it was time to leave. "Thank you, Sheriff."

After getting into the Ford, she drove to Spencer's Garage, where she waited for Patty to introduce her to Henry. He was older than he'd looked from a distance.

"Nice to meet you, Miss Lauren. Patricia has told me a lot about you. Do you need some gas?"

"Yes, please, Henry." She glanced at Patty. *Patricia?* She'd never heard anyone call the girl her full name before. Mr. Hillman was right. These two couldn't keep their eyes off one another.

Lauren spotted Earl walking down the street. He was dressed for the job in his older denim dungarees. "Patty, Earl is coming with us on our trip. Are you ready to leave?"

"Yes. Can Henry come too? Please, Miss Lauren. Mr. Spencer said he could have the rest of the day off."

"Sure, although you may regret it, Henry. We are stopping off to collect some animals on our way."

"Thanks for the photographs, Miss Lauren, they were wonderful," Earl said, when he reached the truck. "I left them back at the store in case they got damaged on the trip. Pa gave me these for you." He held out a box containing two chickens. "He said they are good layers." He looked up at the sky. "We should get going. Those are snow clouds on the horizon and we have to get to Williams Farm to buy a cow or a goat." He put the box of chickens in the back of the truck.

Lauren looked at the gray sky. She could see a few clouds in the distance, but they seemed far enough away not to worry about.

Earl's hands were clutched together as he held her gaze, speaking quickly. "Want me to drive, Miss Lauren, seeing as I know the short cuts to Williams Farm?"

Sensing Earl was eager to drive, she handed the keys to him and got into the truck on the passenger side. Despite the cold, Patty elected to travel in the back with Henry by her side. She was glowing with happiness and, judging by the look on Henry's face as he snuggled closer to her, the cold weather was the last thing on their minds.

"There's better places to go courting than in an open truck on a winter's day, Patty!" Lauren teased.

CHAPTER 19

A sharp noise made Lauren jump as the sound echoed through the mountains.

Earl laughed. "It's only a tree limb snappin' under the weight of the snow. Nothing serious. It's those clouds over yonder that has me worryin'. I don't want to get snowed in up here. Your father would kill us all."

She doubted her father would miss her, he was so busy with work all the time, but she didn't argue. "Look at that house up there, Earl." Lauren pointed through the windshield at a house perched on rocks high above the road. "It looks like it could slide off the mountain at any time."

"That's the old Menton place. Rumor has it, his grandpappy deserted from the Confederates and hid right up there for the rest of the war. He didn't want to fight no more. The Yankees and Feds came looking for him but they couldn't find him. He just disappeared into the hills. Didn't come out from wherever he was hiding until eighteen sixty-six, and only then because his woman convinced him the War Between The States was over."

Lauren loved hearing stories of the mountain folk. She could have listened to Earl all day long. "Do you know what happened at Rosehall during the war? Why was it left intact?"

"That's a long story, Miss Lauren, but I think it was because your mama's people turned it into a hospital. They treated all soldiers the same from what I've heard. Reckon the Yankees liked that, although local folk might have had an issue with it."

He glanced at her before continuing. "The people of Rosehall, I mean the slaves, they spoke up for your mama's family. They told how they were treated well. Your grandmama fed them the same food as the family ate during the war. Rumor has it the ladies even helped to bring in the cotton."

"She could hardly have let them starve, Earl."

"Miss Lauren, you got no idea of what happened during and after the war years. Your grandmama was different to many."

Lauren grinned. She'd studied the paintings that graced the walls at Rosehall and had always thought that her grandmother looked like a woman with a mind of her own.

As they got closer to Meehan's Hollow, Lauren couldn't see the tops of the mountains anymore, blocked as they were by dense gray clouds. They arrived at the Tennants' place just as thick snow started to fall, sticking firmly to the windshield despite the wipers being on full blast.

"I don't like this, Miss Lauren. That snow is falling thick and fast. I reckon we need to head back to town. Get you and Patty back to Rosehall."

"We won't stay long, Earl, but the family really needs these things."

On hearing the truck, Becky had run outside, followed by a couple of her younger siblings.

Lauren helped Patty carry the chickens in the box. Henry carried Lauren's case inside the house and Earl tried to persuade the goat to get out the back of the truck. One of the children grabbed some grass from the side of the house and ran over to tempt the goat. It worked.

Mrs. Tennant came out to greet them, ushering them all inside as soon as she saw the falling snow. "Goodness me, Miss Lauren. What are you and your friends doing out on a day like this?"

"It wasn't snowing when we left Delgany. Nanny asked us to bring you these." Lauren indicated the chickens and the goat. "We asked for a cow at Williams Farm, but the farmer doesn't have any to spare at the moment. He does have a heifer that might be good in a few weeks though. In the meantime, I packed some things into a case. It should help to keep you warm. Nanny wanted to come, but she caught a chill so is resting in bed."

Becky opened the case and pulled out the books, looking at them in wonder. Her eyes filled up as she glanced at Lauren. "These for me?"

"I thought you could read them to your brothers and sister."

The girl held them to her chest and smiled. "Thank you, Miss Lauren."

The children pulled out the quilts, with Sarah, Becky's younger sister, trying on the coat Lauren had worn the previous day. It was far too big on her, the material dragging along the floor.

"That's for Becky, Sarah. Take it off," Mrs. Tennant commanded.

Lauren couldn't bear the sadness on the little girl's face as she turned her green eyes to her mother. "Please, Ma, I ain't never had a coat like this. Why does Becky have to get it? She got the books."

"The books will be enjoyed by everyone. Becky is the oldest and when she goes out to find a job, she'll have to look smart. Thank you kindly, Miss Lauren."

Sarah pouted before muttering, "I wish I was fifteen like Becky. Then I'd get nice stuff too."

"Shush your mouth and watch your manners, my girl, or you'll regret it."

"Sarah, I'll bring you something new the next time, I promise," said Lauren, wanting to put a smile on the youngster's face.

Sarah's pout disappeared. "Thank you, Miss Lauren. I like pink best."

Mrs. Tennant rolled her eyes but said nothing. Becky tried on the coat, her face a picture.

"I thought it might suit you better," Lauren whispered to Becky, before turning her attention back to Mrs. Tennant.

"The boys were going to fix your chicken coop and a place for that stubborn goat, but we best be getting back to town. Earl warned me earlier about the snow, but I thought I knew best."

"You listen to Earl Hillman, his pa is a wise man. Go on, Miss Lauren. Thank you kindly. The boys will help me sort out something for these chickens."

"Goat, Ma, she's hawgry." Donnie went to his mother's side, pointing at the animal.

His ma shrieked at the goat, who was munching happily on one of the quilts. "Get out of there!"

"We best go, Miss Lauren. I don't want your daddy blaming me if you get snowed in on the mountain," said Earl.

Lauren nodded, then she sent Earl, Patty, and Henry out to the truck.

"Mrs. Tennant," she said. "I spoke to the sheriff about the trouble that's been happening on the mountain. He seemed to think the government men meant no harm. If they come again, send someone for me or Nanny or Mr. Thatcher. You are not facing this alone."

Mrs. Tennant squeezed Lauren in a hug. "Thank you, Miss Lauren. You are just like your mama."

Lauren's eyes watered, but she blinked hard so she wouldn't cry. "I will be back as soon as the weather allows." She turned to Becky. "I hope you like the books. When the weather gets warmer, maybe I can bring you some more."

"It's like Christmas every day you come, Miss Lauren. Drive home safe."

Outside, the snow was falling fast and furious, and they all piled into the truck's cabin. Patty sat on Henry's lap with Lauren squeezed in the middle and Earl driving. He had more experience than she had driving in icy conditions. The wipers were on full blast, yet you couldn't see out the window for long. Even when Earl turned the lights on it was still dark. He slowed right down.

"No point in rushing down a ravine. We'll be fine if we just take it nice and slow."

Lauren, twisting her fingers, hoped he was as confident as he sounded. After all, it was her fault they were up here. She'd been the one who had insisted they visit the Tennants. She should have put it off to another day. Squinting, she tried to see Rosehall or even Delgany through the windshield. Surely they should be able to see some lights in the distance? All she could see was thick, falling snow everywhere she looked.

CHAPTER 20

"Last time you and Patty made the trip to the mountain, Miss Lauren, you got snowed in. At least we don't need to worry about that now. Spring has come early." Mary was sitting beside Lauren in the Cadillac, looking at the view, as they drove into Delgany.

Lauren didn't need reminding about that trip during the snowstorm. Her father had confined her to the house for three days for worrying him so much and for putting both herself and Patty in danger. When they had eventually arrived back at Rosehall, Cook had decided they were going to die from frostbite and insisted on wrapping them both in hot towels and giving them steaming sassafras tea with lemon. Lauren had never liked the taste and the latest experience of it hadn't changed her mind. Initially her father had banned her from setting foot on the mountain for two months, but, as the weeks had passed, she assumed he'd forgotten. He was rarely home now, but when he did come back to Rosehall, he always brought Justin with him.

Once again, Lauren tried, but failed, to push all thoughts of Justin from her mind. She didn't know how to handle her feelings about him. They disagreed on many important matters, and he showed little interest in her views, but when he kissed her, her body responded to his kisses, falling helplessly into his arms. How could someone so opinionated and domineering be so attractive?

Determined to change her train of thought, she looked at the mountain, the signs of spring obvious as the snow melted on the lower hills. Areas of green grass and budding trees now greeted her and Prince on their rides. The people were hopeful that the worst of the drought was over and that 1931 would be a better year. So far it hadn't proved to be.

*

Mrs. Flannery at Newmarket Clothes Store sold them bundles of clothes by weight rather than quality. Lauren decided it was easier this way as Mrs. Tennant would be able to pick out what she needed and then maybe pass the rest on to other folks.

"All good-quality even if they are as old as Moses. Still, I don't think anyone on that mountain worries about what Chanel has designed, do you?" Mrs. Flannery glanced at Lauren's clothes. "Maybe you do, Miss Lauren, but them folks up there, they wouldn't be able to read the advertisements. About time they cleared out those mountain hollows. It's not right, those women having fourteen and fifteen children apiece. Not with fathers who would rather drink all day than do a day's work. Those men, they have numerous wives yet they never learn to do nothing but make 'shine. If they went, we wouldn't have a problem with illegal moonshine in Delgany, would we?"

"I wasn't aware we had one, Mrs. Flannery." Lauren tried to be nice, but it was difficult. The mean-faced, wiry-built woman never had a nice word to say about anyone. It was well known that her husband was often to be found at his still up near his old hunting cabin, producing his own moonshine. Sheriff Dillon never caught him there, though, because Mr. Flannery was as wily as a fox. "Thank you very much for the clothes."

Lauren and Mary almost ran back to the Cadillac in their hurry to get away.

"I wonder if she was always so mean," Mary whispered. "There's no need to talk about ordinary folk like she does. Very few women on the mountain have that many children. Most die in childbirth cause they can't afford doctorin' from qualified people. That's why men have three or four wives. Not at the same time, but they marry quick to have someone to look after the children."

"I wonder if Mrs. Tennant will marry again," Lauren mused, as she put the Cadillac into reverse and headed out of town toward the mountain.

"Who'd take on all those children?" Mary shook her head. "She's a nice lady, but nobody wants a ready-made family, Miss Lauren. Not these days."

*

When they arrived at Mrs. Tennant's home, they found Becky looking after the younger children.

"Becky, I'm sorry it's been two months since I got back up to see you," Lauren said. "After our last trip, Father banned me from leaving the house for weeks. He blamed me for getting Patty and the others lost in a snowstorm."

"That's because you told him you were driving so as to protect Earl Hillman from his anger." Mary turned to Becky. "I'm Mary, Miss Lauren's maid. It's lovely to meet you after everything Nanny has said about you and your family."

Becky blushed. She nodded in Mary's direction before saying, "Nanny Kat and a friend of hers, Mrs. Carson, took Ma up to Mrs. Thatcher's house. They are sortin' out things for the families up there. I wish I could help but I have to mind this lot. Can you stay for a cup of coffee?" It wasn't hard to tell Becky was bored.

Lauren answered for both of them. "Sure, we have some cookies. I also brought a couple of books for you, Becky, and something special for Sarah."

"For me? Myself?" Sarah asked, pushing her younger siblings out of her way.

"Yes, just for you." Lauren handed her a pretty parcel tied with a ribbon.

"Can I have the ribbon for my hair?" Sarah turned the parcel this way and that. "This looks too pretty to open."

"Do it carefully and then you can use the paper for something else," Mary suggested. "Let me help you."

With Mary occupied, Lauren glanced around the house in awe.

"Becky, whatever happened? It looks so different."

A new roof wasn't the only addition to the property. Someone had fixed the broken shutters and put glass into the window frames. Gone were the newspapers and in their place hung gingham curtains. The front door opened without scraping the wooden floor, which now shone under their feet. There were no signs of cobwebs, leaves or any less desirable items.

"Earl Hillman and his friend, Big Will, came up after that snowstorm." Becky explained. "They reckon it will take them a year to do everythin' they need to do as they have to fit the work around their jobs. Earl is good with his hands and his head. He told Ma he'd build her a new roof and a proper kitchen. Big Will, he can build and fix just about anythin'. He put the glass windows in and fixed the shutters. The children can sleep in the loft again and they don't have to worry about the snow pilin' in on top of them."

The old table had been replaced with a longer one, with benches on both sides, which didn't rock when Lauren sat down. There wasn't a speck of dust to be seen. Piles of wood were piled neatly beside the fire.

Becky put a pot of coffee and three cups on the table. She added a jug of cream but the bowl of sugar was almost empty.

"Things are looking up, aren't they, Becky?" said Lauren.

"Yes, miss. You, Nanny Kat, the Hillmans, and Big Will helped a lot. If things keep goin' the way they are, I might be able to leave Ma and go find a job."

"Where?"

"I don't know but I could work just for board and shelter. That would save Ma as she wouldn't be worried about how to feed me. If I could earn a dollar or two a week, I could send her the money. If the drought goes away, we can find enough to eat in the mountains, but we need cash for salt, flour, and other things."

"Like coffee?" Mary suggested as she raised her cup. "Here's to a better year for you, Becky."

"For all of us."

They stayed chatting for about an hour, and Sarah came into the kitchen wearing her new dress. Although Sarah had wanted a pink dress, Lauren had picked out one in pale green, thinking it would suit her red hair and freckles better.

"Do I look like a princess?" Sarah said, twirling around. "I ain't never had a new dress. Not ever. Look, Becky, this one still has the label on it. It's so pretty. I want to wear it to church on Sunday."

"You look lovely, Sarah."

Donnie waddled up to Lauren, his bowed legs made it hard to walk straight. "Me want dress."

Becky picked him up. "Boys don't wear dresses, Donnie."

"Me want dress. Me want dress." The child's tears ran down his face.

"What about a cookie, Donnie? Like this one?" Lauren held a shortbread circle out to him.

His grubby fingers grabbed it from her hand and stuffed it into his mouth. Mumbling through the crumbs, he kept asking for a dress.

"Sarah, take the dress off and put it upstairs till Ma comes home."

"Aw, Becky, do I have to?"

"Go on."

Sarah went, mumbling about bossy big sisters. Donnie got down from the table and went back into the main room. Becky stared at her departing siblings for a few seconds, stirring her coffee with a spoon. Feeling Lauren's eyes on her, she looked up and put the spoon down.

"Miss Lauren, I really don't know how to thank you and your friends."

"There's no need for thanks, Becky, it was our pleasure."

"I mean it, Miss Lauren, not just for the goat and the chickens and the clothes. Nanny Kat and you visitin' meant the world to Ma. She's like a new person. She's up cleanin' and cookin', she never stops. She doesn' talk about bad stuff happenin'. She's as happy as a bee in a meadow of flowers and I want to thank you for that." Becky stood and walked over to the window, her back to them, her shoulders suddenly stooped as if the weight of the world stood on them.

"What's wrong, Becky?" Lauren asked softly. "Why are you so worried if your ma is happy?"

"Cause it's all about to change. I knows it and there's nothin' I can do about it."

Lauren and Mary exchanged a look. The maid stood as if to leave them in private, but Lauren indicated she should sit back down.

Turning to face them again, Becky folded her arms around her stomach, her forehead creased with worry.

"Becky, do you want to tell us? Mary can keep a secret," Lauren reassured the girl.

"Ma said I shouldn't say nothin'. She says I'm imaginin' it."

"What?"

"Big Will and I, we went walkin' up the mountain for a bit. He wanted to find the right tree to cut down to make into this table." Becky's face flushed and she wouldn't meet their eyes.

"And?" Lauren prompted.

"I think we saw those men from the government back again. They certainly didn't look like anyone I know and Big Will didn't know them either. They didn't say hello or anythin'. Ma says they might have ten different reasons why they would be on the mountain, but it didn't sit right with me. Two of them were talkin' to the Bramley brothers. They is trouble on their own. They don't need no help from others." Becky bit her lip. She came back to sit at the table and picked up her coffee cup.

"Becky, I'm sure it's nothing. Maybe it was the revenuers talking to the Bramleys about their moonshine. I know they can't bust them unless they find them operating the still, but they could have been warning them off."

Becky sipped some coffee. "Maybe, but they all seemed kinda friendly. They moved off fairly quick when they saw us comin'."

"They could have thought you were courtin' and wanted to give you some privacy." Mary teased. Becky's cheeks flushed so hot you could have heated the coffee pot on them.

"I'm never goin' courtin' with nobody. I don't want to end up with a parcel of kids. I'm done with babies." Becky set her cup down so forcefully the liquid spilled over.

Mary giggled at the look on Becky's face. "I'm sorry, Becky, I was just teasing. Miss Lauren will be getting married before any of us."

"Mary!" Lauren exclaimed, as Becky clapped her hands.

"Tell me, Mary, what's he like?" Becky asked.

"He's handsome enough… maybe a bit too handsome."

"Becky, ignore her. Justin is a gentleman, tall, good-looking, and he's nice to his mother." The roar of laughter that came from both girls caused Lauren to add, "Nanny said that was important."

CHAPTER 21
April 1932

Lauren sat at the desk by her window, reading the paper. The rainstorm outside was welcome, as the ground had been crying out for rain. Why was it the grass looked greener and the flowers brighter during April showers? The smell of damp earth and freshly cut grass filtered through the open window.

"Hard to believe you've been home over a year, Miss Lauren. The days are flying past."

"Hmm."

"You listening to a word I saying?"

"Sorry, Mary, I was reading about the poor Lindbergh baby. There's still no sign of him, and it's over a month since he was taken. How could anyone kidnap a twenty-month-old child?"

"Money. Some people would do anything for a dollar, never mind thousands of them. Do you reckon they paid the ransom, Miss Lauren?"

"Yes, wouldn't you?"

"It isn't likely anyone would want to kidnap my child if Jed and me are lucky to have one. We don't have five dollars to spare, never mind thousands."

Lauren glanced up to catch Mary's smiling face. She and Jed would be married in October and the maid was saving every penny she earned.

"Mary, are you ready to drive into Delgany? Nanny wanted us to collect some more clothes to take up to the Tennants."

Lauren parked just opposite the now-shuttered Delgany bank. Her father had smirked when telling Lauren the story of why it had closed, saying soft-hearted men had no place in the business world. Mr. Allen's family had owned the bank for almost a hundred years. Folks had assumed it was safe as it survived the first two years after the 1929 crash. It appeared now that Mr. Allen had been too lenient with borrowers. He'd given folk with overdue accounts time to pay just because he'd known the family for years, or his children had gone to the same school as the borrower's family. A kind-hearted man, he'd used his personal fortune to keep the bank trading, but when the money ran out he couldn't admit it to the people of his home town. He'd closed the bank for the Thanksgiving holiday, left Delgany, and never came back to re-open. Many of the townsfolk lost their lifetime savings.

Local hairdresser Ginny Dobbs pushed open the door to her home as Lauren and Mary walked past. "Good morning, ladies, can I tempt you to a trim or a set?" she said, her hand on one ample hip. "I got some new magazines straight down from New York."

"We've been to New York, Ginny, back in 1930. We both saw enough of that place to last us a lifetime," Mary replied.

Ginny's smile didn't fade. "Miss Lauren, you look so sophisticated. I don't think it will be long before we hear church music. You and the handsome man driving a large red motor."

"Ginny! You hear everything," Mary said, as Lauren blushed. She knew it was nothing but small-town gossip, yet it still embarrassed her.

"Where you ladies off to?"

"We're going down to Newmarket Clothes Store. Lauren has a list from Nanny."

"You aren't going to see the likes of fashion you saw on your New York trip down in that old place. I don't think that woman ever opened a Sears Catalog."

"We need some children's clothes for Nanny. The children won't care that they aren't the latest fashions, will they, Mary? Ginny, have a nice day."

"Oh, wait." Ginny dashed inside to the front room she used as the beauty parlor. She came back out with her pocketbook, taking out seventy-five cents and handing them to Lauren.

"For those poor folk your nanny is collecting for," she said. "After what happened to Mr. Rock, there are some suffering here in Delgany too."

"Mr. Rock?" Lauren didn't know the man very well, having only met him at church on the holidays, but he'd run the motor dealership since he'd come back from France after World War I. He spoke funny, as if he was always trying to catch his breath. Locals said it was from the mustard gas the Germans had used.

"Oh, didn't you hear? He never opened in the New Year. Turns out your father's bank over in Charlottesville closed his accounts at Christmas. Rumor has it, he used every penny he had to pay the workers so they could have their Christmas. He took off back to Kansas, where Mrs. Rock comes from. They didn't take much with them. The bank officials were crawling over his place before most people had thrown out their Christmas trees."

"Mr. Rock has sold automobiles for as long as I can remember. His wife used to give me and the other children candy at Christmas. That poor family, they lost enough in the Spanish flu epidemic, losing all three children." Mary sniffed, taking a hanky out of her purse to wipe her eyes.

"Times sure are tough. First the bank and now Mr. Rock. Wonder who'll be next? I is lucky my old man bought this place with cash. I don't have to worry none about loan repayments. I get by, although I had to take in my dresses a little bit. Still, never hurt us ladies to lose a few inches off the waist, did it, girls?" Ginny's smile fell. "I wish I could do more for those people you're helping. When I read the stories about those mine workers on hunger strike over in Meadowville, I just want to cry. I'd march too if it were my children who couldn't go to school due to being buck naked or too starved with the hunger to concentrate."

Lauren and Mary didn't get a chance to comment, as Ginny carried on, "Oh, begging your pardon, Miss Lauren. I plum forgot your father owns some mines over that way, doesn't he?"

Stunned into silence, Lauren glanced at Mary. She pushed Lauren a little way down the street, saying, "Thank you, Ginny, for your donation. Have a great day."

"Mary," said Lauren, once they were out of earshot. "Did you know Father had mines over in Meadowville?" She herself had no idea.

"Only since yesterday, Miss Lauren. I heard him arguing with someone on the telephone and later with Nanny. He seemed very cross so I kept out of his way. Put it out of your mind for now."

CHAPTER 22

After seeing another headline in the *Charlottesville News*: *Disaster at Meadowville Mine, five miners dead, some missing* Lauren decided to visit the mine to see if she could learn the truth. Mr. Belmont had written the article and appeared to blame her father for causing the disaster. But didn't accidents happen? Coal mining was a dangerous business, after all.

Spring was in the air as Lauren and Nanny headed up the mountains. Lauren borrowed the Rosehall Ford rather than use her car. The flowers were budding and the smell of damp earth from the rain that fell almost daily filtered through the windows into the truck.

Nanny was holding onto her seat for dear life, even though Lauren wasn't going more than twenty-five miles per hour. "Lauren, I can't believe I let you talk me into this. Your father will be furious. Take the left turn up above."

"It's important I understand what Father does."

"Lauren Greenwood, don't you try that tactic on me. We both know you want to see whether Mr. Belmont's article is true. You haven't been yourself since you read about the disaster and the children working in the mines."

"Those children aren't supposed to be working in the mines, Nanny, they should be at school. The law says so." Lauren shifted in her seat, pretending to pay more attention to the road. Nanny was correct as usual. *Was Father lying, or was it Mr. Belmont?* "Father dismisses Mr. Belmont's newspaper articles as lies. I want to see for myself."

Nanny gave her one of her told-you-so looks, but remained silent.

Lauren slowed as the first dwelling came into view. It was little more than a shack, with a tin roof and holes in the walls for windows. She could see pieces of old rag pushed into crevices between the wooden planks, she assumed to keep the cold out. *Surely people don't live in there?* It had to be used for sheltering animals.

She kept driving until a crowd milling outside a church caught their attention.

"Looks like a funeral," Nanny said. "Better pull in over there, Lauren, and wait."

Lauren parked under some Dogwood trees and waited for the small crowd to disperse. She saw a woman, presumably the widow, clinging onto a miner's cap, her pale face staring into the grave. Five children of various ages stood behind her, the biggest holding a baby. All were barefoot and wearing ragged clothes. The younger children were crying, but the mother seemed impervious.

The funeral over, the crowd dispersed as they walked back to their homes. Nanny and Lauren stayed where they were, but they could hear muttered conversation coming through the window. Two miners, their faces lined with black marks despite them wearing their Sunday best, walked slowly down the hill toward the trees. Their voices carried.

"Nugent should be shot and thrown down a coal shaft. He knew those shafts were dangerous, yet he still sent the men down. Some mine manager he is."

"He makes a profit and that's all the boss wants. He don't care our men are dyin' or injured. You should throw Greenwood into that shaft too and follow it up with a stick of dynamite."

"That would be too fast. They should be entombed like the boys over at Coaltown. Six days and nights they were down there before someone managed to dig 'em out. They were alive for three days, judging by the markers on the wall. We could have rescued 'em, if we'd had the right equipment. When will the owners put in proper ventilation and supports? How many more have to die? Reckon those miners' union boys have a point."

"Shush your mouth, Forest, you can't let no one hear you talkin' like that. If Nugent gets to hear anythin' of this talk, he'll have us all out."

Lauren shifted in her seat as the men walked past the truck, continuing their conversation. They blamed her father for the explosion, there was no doubt about that. She looked back at the graveyard, where a soft drizzle coming down from the mountain was making the scene even more miserable. She had to wipe away a tear.

Nanny stuck her head out the window. "Hattie Benfield, how are you?"

"Heart sore and weary, Nanny Kat. I be too old to be goin' to young folks' funerals."

Lauren didn't recognize the wizened old woman, who looked older than Old Sally, back at Rosehall. She had a shawl wrapped around her thin shoulders and was wearing a hat that could have dated from the war.

"That be young Colt Dunston and his pappy, Davy, they buried today. I brought both of 'em into the world. Never thought I'd see 'em buried together. We've had our share of funerals this past week, but Lord Almighty, two men from the same family. It ain't right. Minnie, Davy's widow and Colt's ma, she don't know if she is comin' or goin'. She was so thankful when they got them out alive but hurt—they lingered for days—and thought they might have lived. But the damage was inside. Colt wasn't even fifteen years old. Reckon his pappy went back for him and a beam trapped both of them."

Hattie glanced behind her, before addressing Nanny again. "How many more will have to die before them owners see fit to change things?"

"Want a ride home, Hattie?" Nanny asked.

"Aye, that would be right kind of you. Can you take Minnie and the children too? They might as well enjoy the shelter of their house for one more night." Hattie crossed herself. "Any other company would have let them bury their men folk in peace before they gave them the eviction notice, but not ours. Nugent, the company man, gave them twenty-four hours. They'll be out by tomorrow."

"But where will they go?" asked Lauren, unable to stop herself. "The baby and the other children need shelter and their poor mother looks dazed. It's not fair to expect her to find new accommodation now."

Hattie gazed at Lauren, her eyes wide with curiosity. Nanny hadn't introduced them. "None of the children be old enough to go into the mine so the family has to leave. He's an evil son of a witch, that Nugent, and don't get me started on the owner."

Lauren swallowed hard to dislodge the bitter taste in her mouth. Her father couldn't know this family was being put out just as they buried their father and brother. "Where will they go?"

"Minnie has family back in Kentucky. She's hopin' they can take them in. She doesn't know for certain, as they haven't had time to reply to her letter. She'll just go over the mountains and see what they say. Reckon if they can't help them it's the poor farm for her and the County home for the young'uns."

Lauren couldn't stop herself from protesting. "They'll be separated. That's not right. The children need their mother. They've already lost their father and now their home."

The look Hattie gave her spoke volumes. "Not sure who you are, young lady, or how long you been livin' around these parts, but that's the way of things in Meadowville. Nobody around here can risk offerin' Minnie and her family shelter. Nugent would have them out on the street before darkness fell."

Hattie gestured at Minnie and the children, who were walking away from the graveyard, to come and pile into the truck. Lauren didn't speak, but followed Hattie's directions. They pulled up at the end of a row of houses, each one more pitiful than the last, although some of the women had tried to pretty their homes up. Minnie's one-bedroom house boasted dark red curtains and someone had planted a small garden with a few flowers out front.

Getting out of the truck, Lauren saw a tiny vegetable plot with spinach, corn, and beans at the back of the house. It looked like Mrs. Dunston had tried her best to turn the hovel into a home.

They all got out of the Ford, but it was only when the widow reached her front door that she seemed to remember to invite them inside. Lauren fell back behind Nanny, not wanting to be part of this sadness yet unable to stay away. She followed them into the house, seeing a scrubbed table covered with a few dishes.

"The neighbors sent down some food if you'd like to help yourself, Hattie. Your guests too."

"No, thanks, Minnie. Let the children eat. This here is Nanny Kat and her young friend."

Lauren stepped forward. "I'm Lauren, ma'am. I am so sorry for your loss."

Minnie didn't reply as she stared at the walls of her home. "I best get packed up. Truck will be here in the morning. Some of the men said they would take us down to the railway. We'll get a train to take us back to my parents' home. The men had a collection for us, to cover the cost of tickets."

"Ma, I don't wanna leave. I wanna stay here." A young freckled-faced boy in patched trousers wiped his nose on his sleeve.

"I told you, boy, we can't and there's no point in wantin'."

Lauren beckoned Nanny to go outside. Once out of earshot, she spoke. "We can't just stand by and do nothing, Nanny. That poor woman isn't in any fit state to talk to anyone let alone move her family away. I have to find this Nugent person."

"And do what, Lauren? Your father won't like you interfering."

"He'll be fine, he wouldn't stand by and let a widow and grieving mother be thrown out either. Do you know this Nugent man? Where would I find him?"

"Lauren, you can't do anything. What do you think would happen if people knew who you were? They could turn on you."

"That's not likely. They'll see I am trying to help." Lauren glanced around and spotted what looked like a store. "The people in there should be able to find him for me. I'll be back soon."

"Lauren, wait!"

"No, Nanny. This is wrong and I'm not going to stand by and let this happen."

Lauren marched off in the direction of the store. She pushed the door open, hearing the bell chime. The man behind the counter looked up to acknowledge her and went back to finish dealing with his customer.

"How can I help you?" The assistant said, his eyes roving over her dress, distrust on his face.

"Could you please tell me where I could find Mr. Nugent, the manager of the mine?"

"Nugent know you lookin' for him?"

"No, but he will speak to me."

The man rubbed a dirty hand across his chin. "You a friend of his?"

Lauren had had enough. "Can you please tell me where he is or do I have to ask everyone in this town?"

"Geez, you is a bit fiery, ain't ya?" The man went to the back of the store and yelled out the door, "Nugent, there's a feisty young woman looking for ya. Get in here quick before her temper burns up my store."

Lauren didn't appreciate his tone or the look on his face, but she decided now was not the time to address his lack of manners. Instead she examined the items in the store, trying not to wrinkle her nose at the smell. The shelves needed a good clean and the windows didn't let much light in through the dirty glass. But maybe that was a good thing, seeing as the floor appeared to be covered in mouse droppings.

Lauren opened the store door to try and let some clean air in. A heavily built man with wide shoulders and bulky arms stood in the passageway to the rear of the shop. He leered at Lauren, his expression making her feel like she was naked.

"Mr. Nugent?"

"Who's askin'?"

"I am. Can we talk somewhere less public, please?" Seeing the grin Nugent exchanged with the storekeeper, Lauren corrected herself quickly. "Perhaps we could take a walk outside?"

"Ain't every day a purty little thing like you asks me to take a walk. Reckon I could." He bowed in her direction and she walked out the door in front of him. His body odor turned her stomach and she could sense his large hands coming a little too close for comfort.

Once outside, Lauren turned to face him, stepping back at the same time. "Mr. Nugent, my name is Lauren Greenwood. I assume you are acquainted with my father, Mr. William Greenwood?"

His attitude changed immediately. He almost bent in two as he gave her some excuses about keeping her waiting and for his appearance. She let him babble on for a couple of seconds before interrupting him.

"Mr. Nugent, it has come to my attention that Minnie Dunston and her family are being evicted tomorrow. I am certain there is some mistake. Hence I came to see you."

"Mistake? What you be meaning?"

"Nobody would put a widow and her children out on the streets when they have nowhere to go. Especially when she has just lost her husband and firstborn son to this mining operation. I can only imagine it was an oversight and I'd like it to be addressed."

Nugent stared at her, his mouth falling open.

"Mr. Nugent?"

"These is the rules, ma'am. I don't make 'em, I just enforce 'em."

"You are blaming this decision on my father, Mr. Nugent?" she queried, piercing him to the spot with a look.

"Well, no, not exactly. You see he—Mr. Greenwood, that is—he tells me what he wants and I attend to it. He wouldn't want to dirty his hands. I am mighty surprised he sent you up here, if you don't mind me saying so. You are very young and purty. I mean a fine-looking lady to be around roughneck miners."

"Mr. Nugent, kindly deal with the matter in hand. I want your reassurance that Minnie Dunston and her family won't be thrown out of their home for the next month."

"*Month?* I can't have a no-good widow and her brats in the house for a *month*. I need it for the new miners."

"I want you to make an exception. This woman needs our help. I intend to see she gets it. Have a good day, Mr. Nugent."

Lauren turned on her heel and almost ran in her eagerness to leave the odious man behind her.

"Miss, what will your father say?" Nugent called out after her.

Lauren pivoted. "You can leave my father to me. Just do what you are told."

She almost smiled at his narrowed eyes and pinched lips. His anger radiated in waves, but for now, she was in charge and they both knew it.

She walked slowly back to the Dunston house. Minnie would have to leave before the month was out and Lauren had no doubt Nugent would make life difficult. But at least she had gained a little bit of time, maybe enough to get word from her kin.

Minnie's eldest daughter stood beside the truck, shushing the baby. She didn't acknowledge Lauren as she walked into the Dunston home. Inside the house, Nanny, Hattie, and Minnie sat around a small fire, a cup of something in their hands. The younger children had eaten, judging by the empty dishes on the table, but there was no sign of them.

"Lauren, thank goodness you're back, I got worried," said Nanny.

"I'm fine, Nanny. Mr. Nugent has agreed to you staying for a month, Mrs. Dunston. I know it's not a lot of time, but perhaps you will hear from your family in the next week."

The three women stared at her. Finally, Hattie spoke.

"Who are you? An itty bitty thing like you couldn't get Nugent to take a breath not unless—"

"I'm Lauren Greenwood. My father owns this mine. I never knew what went on up here. I'm sorry I can't do anything for the other people here. I will try, but I doubt my father will listen to me. Here is something for you to help not only this family but the others too. I know it isn't enough, but it's all I have." She held out twenty dollars to Hattie. "Nanny, we best go home now."

Nanny took Lauren's arm before speaking to the speechless women. "Hattie, Minnie, I reared this young woman and her kindness and integrity are second to none. She has my family's values running through her veins. Please don't tell anyone who she is or that she was here."

Hattie nodded, Minnie still stared.

"Lauren, it's time we were leaving. Before word spreads." Nanny escorted her from the house, but not before she spied Minnie's eldest daughter glaring at her. She must have heard Lauren admitting who she was.

"You killed my pa and my brother," the girl said. "I wish a thousand bad things for you and your family."

CHAPTER 23

Back at Rosehall, Lauren was passing her father's study when she heard the sound of him shouting, despite the door being closed.

"Kathryn, you had no right taking Lauren over to Meadowville to see the mineworkers. She could have been harmed."

"Lauren is a grown woman, William. She heard about the explosion in the coal mine and wanted to offer assistance. She is a kind-hearted young lady with a lot of questions."

"What if they had recognized her? What were you thinking of? She didn't need to see how those people live."

"I disagree. The Greenwoods are responsible for how those people live. Lauren benefits from your investments, doesn't she? It is only right she sees where your wealth comes from."

"Be careful, Kathryn. I tolerate you living here because of my late wife. I won't have anyone undermining me in my home."

"William, Lauren's a well-educated young lady. She reads the papers. She wants to find things out for herself. That new editor, Belmont, he prints enough articles in his *Charlottesville News* on your activities."

"Lauren doesn't read the *Charlottesville News*. I no longer purchase it. We only read quality newspapers in this house."

"You mean the ones you pay off or own."

Lauren gasped. She had never heard Nanny speak to Father like this before, nor did she know he owned newspapers. Was there any industry he didn't have a slice of? She moved closer to the door, her pulse racing.

"I'm warning you. Don't come between me and my daughter. You'll regret it."

"Are you threatening me? You should know by now, I'm not afraid of you."

Why would anyone be afraid of Father? Lauren knew she shouldn't be listening but she wanted to know more.

"Lauren, what are you doing standing outside your father's study? Why don't you just go in?"

She whirled at Justin's voice.

"I was about to but it sounds like they are arguing over something. I didn't want to intrude."

"I'm sure it's nothing serious."

Justin took her hand and before she knew it, they were inside the study. Her father was standing behind his large walnut desk, a glass of whiskey in his hand. Nanny was seated on the blue upholstered chair over by the fireplace. Despite the small fire her father liked to keep burning in the room, the atmosphere was chilly.

"What are you two up to?" her father asked.

"I just met Lauren outside your study so I don't know what she wanted. I hoped to have ten minutes of your time. We've had a call from Nugent, up in Meadowville. He's worried about some of the miners. Their feelings are getting out of hand. He thinks they may bring in the Union organizers. One of us should show our face."

It hadn't taken Nugent long to contact her father, but why was he calling Justin? He couldn't be involved in the mine too, could he?

"Not you, Justin, please. You only got here yesterday. I had all sorts of things planned for us…" Lauren's voice trailed off as her father glared at her.

Justin kissed her cheek. "I was looking forward to the time with you too, darling, but business has to come first. Why don't you and Nanny go to her rooms and let your father and me talk business?"

Lauren didn't argue, she'd long ago learned it was pointless. Nanny had already walked out the study and Lauren hurried to catch up with her.

"Are you all right, Nanny? I'm sorry for getting you into trouble with Father."

"You didn't, Lauren."

"But I heard you—"

"Eavesdroppers never hear good things. Excuse me, child, but I have a headache. I think I shall go back to bed."

Lauren stared after her as she walked away. She knew Nanny was making an excuse not to speak to her about the conversation she'd overheard. She would have pushed for more information, but just then the study door opened behind her and Justin came out.

"I have to go see the mine manager and then go home to Richmond, darling. Walk me out?"

"Now? Can't you even stay for lunch?" She tried to swallow her disappointment as they walked together to the front door. She hadn't seen him since February. Soon it would be Easter. She missed him.

"Not today. I know I promised to stay the week and I meant it. I didn't know there would be an issue in Meadowville. From there, I will drive to Richmond. I'll be back at the weekend and we'll do something then." He looked around before kissing her lightly on the mouth. "I like how you miss me."

"Justin, those people in Meadowville need help. The children only get one meal a day, if they are lucky. I hate to see poor people suffering. Can't you do something to help them?"

They had reached the front of the house and Justin opened one of the large double doors, ushering Lauren through before he followed her outside.

"There will always be rich and poor in society, that's the way the world works," he told her. "America gives people a chance to make their own money, and if they don't achieve financial freedom, why should we care?"

Lauren didn't want to upset him, but nor was she willing to remain silent. Not after the devastation she had seen.

"People are suffering, Justin. It isn't the Hillmans' fault that people are buying less produce in their store. Is Mr. Rock to blame because people aren't buying new cars anymore? He's worked hard all his life. I don't think it was his fault that he had to close and all the workers lost their jobs."

Justin took her hand and rubbed it as though she was a child. "Lauren, please stop talking like a communist. You are doing your best to help people. You collect money for charity, you help Nanny with the clothes collection. You've spent days up on the mountain, helping people who are beyond saving. Your father told me you even wanted to volunteer in the soup kitchen."

"He didn't agree to that."

Justin grasped both her arms now, staring into her face. "I'm glad. You don't know where some of those people have been and what diseases they may carry. Let's change the subject. Mother misses you so you must come for a visit to Thornton Mews soon. She's been trying out new seeds in the gardens. She got the idea from her friends over at Monticello. Now kiss me. It will take me three hours to drive to Richmond and I want to remember the feel of you on my lips for the journey back."

Lauren wanted to reply, to stand up for the mountainfolk that she had started to see as family, but she didn't have the chance. He swept her into his arms, kissing her goodbye, sending all her thoughts flying.

Turning back inside the house, she headed to her bedroom, where she found Mary taking an inventory of her clothes.

"I am just checking if anything needs mending," Mary told her. Then she caught sight of Lauren's face. "Why are you looking so glum, Miss Lauren?"

"Justin just left. He had to go to Meadowville and from there to Richmond."

"He'll be back soon. He's just as infatuated as you are, Miss Lauren."

"I would like to see where he works though, Mary. I need to understand what Justin and Father do. You didn't see how those families at Meadowville live. The children… some were almost naked, despite it being April. One mother had just buried her husband and son. They had been killed in a mine explosion and the mining company had already evicted her. She had six children, Mary, and nowhere to go. The man in charge"—Lauren shivered in revulsion, remembering Mr. Nugent—"he doesn't even pretend to care."

"Nanny shouldn't have let you go to Meadowville." Mary put her hand to her mouth. "Sorry, Miss Lauren, I shouldn't have spoken out of turn. I forget myself sometimes. I can't afford to lose my position here, not with saving for the wedding."

"Mary, this is your home. I hope it's more than just a job. You're my friend."

"I am, Miss Lauren, but I'm also your servant. You remember that, especially when in public. You have a role to keep up. Your father expects it, but so does the circle you belong to. Don't go making waves. It gets awful rocky when you are out there by yourself."

CHAPTER 24

By lunchtime, Nanny had still not appeared and Father did not come to the dining room, so Lauren had lunch sitting alone in the large room.

Cook fixed a tray of lunch for Nanny and Lauren insisted on carrying it to her rooms. She knocked gently on the door to the suite, which had been given to Nanny by William some years previously, and called out to her. She was relieved when a weak voice answered, inviting her to come in.

Lauren found Nanny sat on the sofa in her sitting room. "Cook has made you some buttermilk biscuits and cream of chicken soup. She says it's good for the soul," she told the older woman.

"Just leave it on the table, please, Lauren, I'm not hungry," Nanny replied.

Lauren put the tray down. "Have you a chill?" She checked her face for signs of fever, but her eyes were clear, not glassy, and her face wasn't pale or flushed. There was, though, an air of sadness and resignation about her. "Nanny, are you all right?"

"I'm fine, Lauren. Stop fussing." She fixed on Lauren's eyes. "Now what has you all flustered?"

"Justin left. I miss him already," Lauren said.

Nanny sighed. "You barely know this man, but first love can provoke strong feelings."

"I love him, Nanny. He is—"

"Not the right man for you, darling."

Frowning, Lauren waited for her to elaborate. Nanny beckoned her to come sit beside her on the sofa. Lauren loved Nanny's sofa. It seemed to cradle you when you sat in it, not like the formal suite in Father's drawing room with all its stiff chairs.

"Lauren, darling, you need a man with a kind heart," Nanny began, when Lauren had sat down. "You are strong-willed. I don't mean it as an insult. We both know you won't be happy just playing the hostess for the rest of your life. You aren't like other girls of your class. You want more from your life, more independence and freedom. That comes at a price, my darling. But with the right man by your side, you can have happiness too. Someone who loves you so much they will support you in your search for fulfillment. That man is not Justin Prendergast."

Lauren didn't want to hear all this, but she didn't say anything. Nanny didn't know Justin, not like she did. Besides, what *did* she know? She was old and had never married.

"Darling, you know I love you and want only your happiness. Don't rush into any decisions. Marriage is for life and you want to be as sure as you can be that you're marrying the right man. The feeling of being swept off your feet will wear off quickly when you have to listen to his snores every night."

"Nanny!" But Lauren giggled despite herself. She sat up and threw her arms around the woman who she saw as a grandmother. "I love you."

"Your mother would be so proud of you, Lauren. She had dreams, too. She wanted to be a writer. But her father never allowed her to do anything. He said education was wasted on a girl. Your father is different, I'll give him that. He never stinted on your education."

"Did my mother love my father?"

"Yes, child, she did."

"It must have been so awful for him when she died. For you too." Lauren saw the shadow in Nanny's eyes. "I don't remember her. Not really. But you make her come alive in my mind."

"Nobody can expect you to remember her, child. You were four years old. I swore to your mama that I wouldn't let you forget her so I'm glad my words help. The greatest tragedy in all of it was your mother missing out on raising a child who has become a beautiful young woman with a kind heart. She'd be so proud of you. Whatever happens, Lauren, always treat folk with kindness. It costs nothing."

CHAPTER 25

Richmond, Virginia, May 1932

Lauren tried to be polite as Mrs. Prendergast outlined the story of their home, Thornton Mews. Sitting on the edge of an extremely uncomfortable sofa, she plastered a smile on her face. Mrs. Prendergast had been talking for about an hour about the War Between The States and Lauren had long since lost interest. After all, it wasn't the first time she had heard all this.

Under her eyelashes she glanced around the sitting room. It had been painted in an off-cream color, which didn't help to warm up the room. Despite it being May, the room was chilly and Lauren shifted in her seat, the springs poking her in the wrong places. The place could do with a good clean, but it wasn't the dust that attracted her attention. There were black outlines on the walls, as if paintings hanging there for years had recently been removed. Maybe Mrs. Prendergast was having them cleaned…

"Of course, the Yankees burned down the original house, leaving most of it in ruins. Thornton Mews was rebuilt long after the war. They had some excuse but the reality is they were jealous of our lifestyle. They didn't live in such splendid houses. My grandmother told me about the balls they used to hold around these parts. Don't you think it would have been romantic to live in those times, Lauren?"

Hearing her name, but having no idea what she'd been asked, Lauren replied, "I suppose," and forced a smile.

Mrs. Prendergast smiled and continued chatting, until suddenly Lauren couldn't stand it anymore. "Mrs. Prendergast, Irene, would you mind very much if I went out for a walk? It's stopped raining and I would love to take a turn round your gardens."

"Of course, my dear, they are beautiful. I will call Justin to escort you."

Thank goodness she was going to get some peace for a while. Justin was much easier to be with than his mother. At least he didn't chat incessantly.

As they walked around the property, Lauren stopped to admire a blossoming rose bush, laughing when Justin picked a rose for her and tucked it behind her ear.

"Has Mother bored you to death yet?" he asked.

She turned away from his gaze, not wanting to say anything impolite.

"It's all right, relax, Lauren. I know what she is like. Father used to say empty vessels make the most noise."

"That isn't a nice way to speak about your mother, Justin. She is a little over-enthusiastic about your home, but I guess she doesn't have a job so she may be bored."

"A job? Her role is to keep this place in top condition. It takes a lot of commitment and work, not to mention money."

Lauren couldn't help thinking that the house really wasn't in top condition. The roof of the main house was sagging slightly, and inside the home smelled of damp. It was almost as if Irene was operating on a tight budget. But she pushed the thought from her mind. Justin's family was one of the richest in Virginia.

In the distance she spotted some huts. "What's over there?" she asked as they walked in their direction.

"That's the old slave quarters. The sharecroppers live there now."

"People live there? In those places?"

"Lauren, don't compare their needs to ours. They are quite happy with a roof over their heads and some food in their bellies. Not too much food, mind you, or then they wouldn't work."

"What are sharecroppers exactly?" she asked him.

"They are people who work the land in return for a share of the harvest. We provide living quarters and food at the start of the year. The workers repay our generosity when the harvest is brought in."

"What happens if there is no harvest? The drought must have affected the yields."

"It has, but don't worry, Lauren, these people know how to work. They have to or else they will be homeless. They run up debts, but there are enough family members to make sure they are paid back."

"The children don't work in the fields, do they? They should be in school."

His forehead creased in irritation. "None of this is any of your concern, Lauren. If you were to live here, as my wife, you wouldn't be in charge of the working areas. I have a manager to see to those things. Now, tell me, where would you like to go this evening? We can go to the new restaurant on main street or to a movie theater, your choice."

"I think I'd prefer not to go out. Everywhere you go, people are talking about the recent discovery of the Lindbergh baby. The poor thing didn't stand a chance. It's hard to take in that the body was buried so close to the house all this time. The parents must be devastated."

"I'm sure they are, paying all that money and not getting a living child back. Still, the mother's young, there will be other children."

Lauren stopped walking, causing Justin to stagger slightly. "What's wrong, did you catch your shoe?"

"Justin, did you hear what you said? This was a baby that died, a living human being. You can't replace a baby as you would a painting."

"Of course you can't. Sorry if I spoke a little too bluntly. I forget women are sensitive creatures."

Now he was being condescending. She'd found he did that. He either treated her like a princess, who couldn't do a thing for herself, or he dismissed every opinion she held. He could give her a look that sent her pulse racing, but most of the time he just irritated her. His opinions about those devastated by the Depression were just vile.

"Lauren, there's something I've been meaning to speak to you about. The manager at the bank in Richmond told me that you tried to clear the arrears on a mortgage so a farmer could hold onto his land. Why would you do that?"

"I felt sorry for him. I happened to be in the bank and heard his story. He owed less than fifty dollars. His family has lived on that land in the mountains since the American Revolution. His ancestors are all buried up there. If you'd been there, you would understand." She glanced at his face, hoping to see understanding but he looked incredulous. "He was crying, Justin. An old man of seventy shouldn't be worrying about his land, never mind crying in public."

His expression grew frosty. "He should have kept the payments up. He knew the consequences."

"It was his son who had taken out a loan for a hundred dollars and not made the repayments. The old man wasn't even aware of the loan. And now he will spend the rest of his life at the poor farm with strangers. I could have paid the fifty dollars and given the man his home back, but your manager refused to let me."

"He was right to refuse. I have plans for that land."

"But it was his home."

"This isn't personal, it's business. Women don't understand. They are too soft-hearted."

CHAPTER 26

After a week with Justin and his mother at Thornton Mews, Lauren was desperate to get home. She missed Nanny and her father, Cook and her home cooking. If she had to listen to another word about garden seeds or flowers, or how wonderful Justin was, she would have screamed. She now saw exactly what Nanny had been trying to tell her.

"Miss Lauren, can you slow down, please? You're making me dizzy driving so fast." Mary was holding onto her seat.

"Sorry, I just want to get home. I've missed it so much. I can't believe I lasted a week with Justin and his mother. How did I ever think he was a nice man? He never stops talking about himself, and the things he says about those poor families in Meadowville and elsewhere…"

"He just repeated what is happening across the country. The poor farms are overflowing with people who've lost everything in the Depression. In the old days, the folks that landed in those places were ones that didn't have families to look after them. Now, the young and old end up there."

"Only because banks owned by people like Justin and my father are repossessing their farms if they miss one or two loan payments. How can they justify doing that? Some of those people had lived on their land forever. What does Father need more land for? He could give those people time to find the money to pay the loans. We have a Depression, a drought, and the lowest crop prices in years—could it get any worse for farmers?"

Mary ignored her comment, probably because Lauren had ranted for most of the three-hour drive. "There it is. I can see the chimneys over there, can you?" she said, sounding relieved.

Lauren turned her head, happy to see Rosehall in the distance. They were almost home.

After parking the Cadillac on the front drive, Lauren ran inside looking for Nanny. She always missed her when she was away from Rosehall.

"Nanny, we're home," she called, as she ran up the first flight of stairs to Nanny's quarters. But Nanny wasn't there. Maybe she'd gone to do her charity work. Running back downstairs, Lauren headed for the kitchen. She could hear Jackson moving the Cadillac off to the garages.

"Cook, we're back. How's everything? We missed you. Mrs. Prendergast's cook didn't get the same train... What is it? What's wrong?"

Cook stared at her, her eyes watering. Mary looked paler than the clouds in the sky. She held a white envelope in her shaking hands, which she now handed to Lauren.

Lauren looked at the envelope and saw her name in Nanny's handwriting. "I don't want it."

"You have to read it, Miss Lauren."

Lauren clenched her teeth. Opening the envelope, she took out a single piece of paper from it.

Dear darling Lauren,

You have to forget about me, my dear child. I have another role to fill. I can't come back to Rosehall, not now, not ever. God has chosen another path for me to follow and we must respect His wishes.

I am so proud of you, Lauren. You have grown up into a lovely young woman. Remember, darling, be kind. Kindness costs us nothing.

I love you more than you will ever know. By the time you've read this letter, I will have left Delgany. Do not try to find me, for both our sakes.

Nanny x

Lauren couldn't speak, couldn't swallow. *How could Nanny leave her? What did she mean "for both their sakes"?* She looked up, but neither Cook nor Mary would meet her eyes.

"Do you know where she is?" Her voice came as a whisper.

Cook shook her head.

Lauren grabbed the older woman by the arms. "Don't lie to me, where is she?"

"I don't know, Miss Lauren. I swear. I went to call her and her bed was empty. That was on the pillow. The Master wouldn't tell me anything." Cook was shaking and tears now fell down her cheeks.

"Stop, Miss Lauren! You're hurting Cook. Why don't you ask your father?" Mary said.

Lauren released Cook, apologizing, before racing out of the kitchen to look for her father. She burst into his study and he stood up so fast that his chair toppled over behind him.

"Lauren, what's the matter?"

"Where is she? What have you done with Nanny?"

"I thought the house was on fire. Get a hold of yourself, young lady. Kathryn felt it was time to move on. She did her job and reared you to adulthood, just as she promised your mother. She's entitled to a life of her own now."

"She wouldn't just leave. Not without speaking to me first."

"Well, she did. Judging by the way you are acting, she was right to leave. You're hysterical. Go lie down before you do yourself a mischief."

"Please, Father, bring her back. Tell me where she is and I'll drive to fetch her." Lauren's voice was etched with desperation, tears stinging her eyes.

"I told you, I don't know where she is. Accept she's gone. You're a grown woman, Lauren. Ask Cook to give you something to calm your nerves. Now, I'm busy, close the door behind you."

Her father righted his chair and sat back down at the desk, picking up some papers as he did so. She wanted to beg, throw herself on his mercy, but it was useless. If he did know where Nanny was, he wasn't telling.

CHAPTER 27

The days passed by and no word came. Lauren tried not eating in the hope that her protest would make her father relent, but he threatened to take her to the hospital and have her force-fed.

She spent hours in her room, refusing to see Justin when he came to visit. Her only saving grace was Prince, who she took out on long rides through the acres around Rosehall. The leafy buds on the trees in the orchard turned into blossoms, the bees buzzing from one tree to another. Everything looked normal, yet it had all changed.

Mary tried to get her involved with Nanny's charity work, but her father forbade her to have anything to do with the mountain "*inbreds*", as he called them. He indicated that he would have the families removed by force if she went anywhere near the Hollows.

Lauren cried as she tried to sleep in the hot, humid nights. "Please, Nanny come home," she wailed into her pillow. "*Please.*"

Fed up with staying inside, Lauren dressed carefully in some older clothes. She would go up to the mountain to see Becky and the other families there. The weather was perfect and the sun shone bright in the sky. She packed a small bag with some clothes and a few more books for Becky. Singing, she almost skipped down the stairs, but restrained herself when she saw Jackson.

"Where are you going, Miss Lauren?"

"Out, Jackson."

"Your father asked me to check that you don't go up to the mountain. The government has some men working up there and your father said it was safer for you to stay here."

They must be the men in suits that Becky spoke about. She *had* to see her friend. Mrs. Tennant might have heard from Nanny.

"Father is being overprotective. Please excuse me, Jackson."

"You can't go, Miss Lauren. I have the keys to your Cadillac. Your father felt that would be best."

He was smirking at her, knowing there was nothing she could do. But she refused to let him see how upset she was. Turning on her heel, she retreated upstairs. *She* might not be able to go, but nobody could stop Mary.

*

On her return from the mountain, Mary reported that Sarah Tennant and two of her younger brothers had died from an outbreak of fever. Donnie and his mother had been taken to the Colony—a home for feeble-minded people. Nobody knew where Becky was.

"Poor Becky, she must be distraught. Someone has to have heard from her, you don't just disappear overnight," Lauren said, her voice thick with emotion.

"But Nanny did. Maybe they are together, Miss Lauren. But there ain't anyone coming back to live in that house. Someone has taken the glass from the windows and all the furniture. It looks like they tried to burn the house down."

"Why would anyone do that?" She studied Mary's face. "What aren't you telling me?"

"They are saying about town that the Tennants never owned their house. Their pa never filed a deed in the County office. They were squatters."

"That's ridiculous. I saw where Becky's grandparents and great-grandparents were buried. She showed me the graves when I called up there last. That family has lived there for over a hundred years or more."

Mary shrugged. "Not any more they don't. Miss Lauren, you can't help anyone by getting into a state over things we can't control."

CHAPTER 28

Rosehall, June 1932

Lauren paced back and forth in her bedroom, wringing her hands, trying to still the negative voice in her head. Her father was up to something, she was sure of it. He'd been too nice over the last few days, even going so far as to tell her about a donation he'd made to the soup kitchen in Delgany. He'd resorted to offering an additional donation of one hundred dollars, provided the dinner she was hosting went well.

Miss Chaney, the postmistress in Delgany, had called to visit Lauren and had drummed home the need for cash donations. She'd told her of the scores of people coming in to Delgany from all areas, walking for miles in search of jobs. Miss Chaney cried when describing the plight of these destitute families.

Cook had worked hard on the perfect menu and they'd set the dining-room table with the best silver and cut glass. Lauren chose the Old Country Roses china set, and the red and white pattern with the gold edging looked wonderful against the crisp white linen tablecloth.

The gardens were at their best, too, with freshly cut lawns. Even the flowers had worked with her. The view out of the dining-room windows was a multitude of flowering magnolia, roses, poppies, jasmine, and lilies. She'd opened the window to allow their beautiful scents to perfume the room.

What was so special about this dinner? Her father had hinted that it had something to do with his work. He'd warned her to be on her best behavior.

As she stared out at the view from her room, Lauren thought of Nanny. Every summer, Nanny would take her blackberry picking with the children on the Rosehall estate. Sam and some of the men occasionally came with them, to help clear out any copperheads or rattlers hiding in the brambles. Those days had been filled with laughter as they returned with mouths dyed purple from eating as many berries as they had picked. She could still hear Nanny's laughter…

"Miss Lauren, don't you look beautiful?" said Mary, as she entered the bedroom, carrying something in her hands. "Your father has sent this for you to wear… What's wrong? You look like you are about to cry."

"Do you remember Nanny taking us blackberry picking when we were children? Mary, where can she be?"

Mary shuddered. "I remember the red bugs. Never understood the attraction of berry picking like you did."

Lauren laughed as Mary screwed up her face.

"Why would anyone go picking berries where they know the snakes love to hang out, Miss Lauren? Just asking for trouble. We should have stuck to gooseberries and blueberries."

"You love blackberry jelly just as much as I do."

Mary grinned. "Nanny made the best but don't tell Cook." Then she adopted a serious expression. "I don't know where Nanny is now, Miss Lauren, but she'll be thinking of you. Whatever made her go away, it was to protect you." She took a deep breath. Her voice was steadier when she went on, "This is from your father."

The maid opened the scarlet-colored box to reveal a stunning sapphire necklace with matching earbobs. "Oh, Miss Lauren, look at how the stones shimmer in the light. They look like little candles, don't they?"

Lauren held her hand out but couldn't bring herself to touch the jewelry. "Mama wore these for the portrait she had painted."

"She did?" Mary draped the necklace round Lauren's neck and secured the clasp, then she clipped the earbobs in place. She stepped back to admire her handiwork. "I don't remember seeing any pictures with something this beautiful. Hurry, Miss Lauren, your father's waiting."

Just then her father called up to her room, his voice booming: "Lauren, you're running late. You know I can't abide tardy timekeeping."

Mary pushed her out the door. Lauren lifted her skirt and made her way carefully down the stairs.

Her father glanced up at her, his eyes widening. "My dear, you look stunning."

"Thank you for Mama's jewels, Father."

"*Your* jewels now, my dear. Come here and give me a kiss."

Lauren did as he bid her, leaning in to kiss his cheek. The familiar scent of tobacco and his aftershave hit her, reminding her of how much she'd loved him. Once. How could he take advantage of people's misfortunes? Banning her from visiting Becky and the families in the mountain had been the last straw.

"You look perfect, Lauren. Justin won't be able to keep his eyes off you. You two are made for each other."

She couldn't agree, but she wasn't about to argue with her father. She'd tried that but he didn't listen. He just raved about how their future depended on her making a good match.

The doorbell chimed, and she listened as Jackson opened the door, hearing Mrs. Burton's shrill tones. Lauren glided forward, on her father's arm.

"Good evening, Mrs. Burton, Mr. Burton." She greeted their neighbors with kisses on cheeks, trying not to choke on the pungent scent of Mrs. Burton's lily-based perfume. The woman always wore too much.

"Lauren, darling, don't you look so grown up. You've become almost beautiful." Delilah Burton's voice trailed off before she turned to Lauren's father. "William, how handsome you look. You get younger every year."

"Delilah, you look wonderful and you too, Harold."

Other guests arrived, giving Lauren the perfect excuse to remove herself from Mrs. Burton's company. She greeted all her father's friends and their wives or companions. She stiffened as she spotted Justin arriving. Instead of moving to his side, she sent him a watery smile and turned to greet their neighbors, the Ackermans.

Justin moved to her father's side, William treating him like the proverbial son. How could she ever have found Justin attractive? His belittling remarks toward those less fortunate seemed to amuse her father. How alike they were. Neither had an ounce of empathy. The Depression might as well be happening on Mars for all the allowances the two of them made for people.

"Hello again," came a voice. Lauren looked up into Mr. Belmont's eyes. It was the man she'd met at The Ritz party. She hadn't seen his name on the guest list, although his parents' names had been there. In her role as hostess she'd have to rearrange the table settings and set up a spare place. "Miss Greenwood, you look radiant tonight."

"Thank you, Mr. Belmont. I'm so glad you could join us."

"How could I miss the social event of the year?" he answered, kissing her hand. She caught a look in his eyes, almost as if he was mocking her.

"How are you finding the newspaper business?" Lauren asked.

"Fascinating," he replied, his tone now openly mocking her. She couldn't stop herself from glaring at him, only to find it made him laugh.

"I cannot see what is so amusing," she hissed, trying to remain smiling so the other guests wouldn't notice.

"*You* are, Miss Greenwood. Why pretend to be interested in something like a newspaper? It's clear what your role is."

"Really, sir? Would you care to enlighten me?"

"The daughter of the richest banker in the county, walking out with his up-and-coming heir, surrounded by vast wealth. Entertaining guests at what will most likely be a sumptuous feast with plenty of expensive wines, despite the country being under the restraints of Prohibition."

"I don't understand your offensive tone, Mr. Belmont. You accepted the invitation."

"Darling Lauren, what's the matter?" Justin appeared at her side, his hand taking her arm. "You look flushed. Do you want to take some air?"

She forced herself to smile and restrained the urge to shake him off.

"No, thank you. I was just making sure everyone was enjoying themselves. Tonight means a lot to Father."

"To me, too," he whispered.

CHAPTER 29

The dinner went better than Lauren could ever have expected. As she glanced around the table, everyone seemed to be enjoying themselves. Even Mr. Belmont was entertained, conversing with the people sitting to his left and right. They seemed to find him charming, if Mrs. Ackerman's smiles and her husband's occasional nods of agreement were anything to go by.

She glanced up a few times to find her father looking at her, an unreadable expression in his eyes. Was he happy with the way the evening was progressing?

Toward the end of the meal, her father stood up and clinked his glass. Everyone stopped talking at once, turning expectantly in his direction. He walked to where Lauren was sitting, bringing all eyes on her.

"I would like to thank my daughter Lauren for organizing this wonderful evening. I am pleased to see her years in finishing school have paid off. We have something to thank the Frenchies for." Lauren squirmed as the guests laughed as her father expected. She caught Mr. Belmont's sardonic gaze and immediately looked away.

"Lauren has inherited her mother's charm and beauty. Tonight is a very special occasion."

Lauren stared at him. *What was he talking about?*

"I'd like you all to raise your glasses and congratulate my daughter on her upcoming marriage to Mr. Justin Prendergast. A man I am delighted to call my son."

Marriage? Justin hadn't even asked her what she thought of getting married. She opened her mouth but closed it again. What could she say? Everyone was looking at her as they cheered her three times.

Justin came to stand beside her, pulling her to her feet. He kissed her cheek and held her hand. Her smile froze in place as she forced herself not to pull away from him. She wanted to be anywhere else but in this room. His touch burned her skin and she longed to scream at him, at her father, and their guests how she'd prefer to be an old maid than marry Justin Prendergast. But she said nothing.

"Thank you, William, for giving me permission to wed the woman of my dreams. Together, Lauren and I will make you proud."

"Give me grandsons to inherit all of this, won't you?" Hearing her father's words and the guests' laughter, Lauren wished she could simply disappear. Anything would be preferable to having everyone stare at her. She glanced at her now fiancé, but he didn't seem to share her concerns. He looked ecstatic and not at all surprised.

Justin and my father have planned this. Together. Without even asking me how I felt. How could they?

She was no longer the star-struck girl she had been the night of the Woolworth Ball eighteen months ago. Nanny's voice, warning her about young men's dazzling powers dimming with time, popped into her head. How right she had been.

Lauren took a deep breath, trying to keep the smile plastered to her face. Her father glanced at her before turning to the butler: "Bring in the champagne, Jackson."

"Sir." The butler nodded at the footman and they returned carrying trays of glasses filled with champagne. Lauren felt distanced from it all, as if it was happening to someone else and not her. She saw Justin go down on one knee and present her with a large diamond and sapphire ring. She didn't say a word, but he took that as a yes and kissed her quickly on the lips to more cheering from the guests.

Lauren blinked away the tears. She couldn't break down now, not in front of these people. Blood was pounding in her ears. The urge to take off the ring was overwhelming; her fingers itched to yank it off. She wanted to tell the world she didn't agree to this marriage, yet she kept silent. If she obeyed the rules of society, her father might listen to her later.

The torture continued as the party moved to the drawing room, where the ladies exclaimed over her ring, asking countless questions about wedding arrangements.

She grappled with her thoughts, wondering how to change the conversation. As she rose to get more water, needing an escape, Mrs. Burton made her way toward her. Lauren swerved to avoid her, almost crashing into a server with a tray of champagne. Maybe a drink would calm her nerves and help her get through this horrible night. She apologized with a smile and took a glass.

Taking a small sip for courage, she moved from guest to guest, making chit-chat, but if you had asked her what she spoke about, she wouldn't have been able to tell you. She took a seat, but to her dismay, Mr. Belmont sat down beside her. She couldn't very well stand up again as it would appear rude.

"Lovely evening, Miss Greenwood. Thank you for the invitation," he said.

"Be careful, Mr. Belmont, you almost sound as if you mean what you say."

He laughed, a nice soft sound this time. "Touché." He leaned over to clink his glass to hers. "You should smile, you look as if all the worries of the world have landed on your shoulders."

She took a sip of champagne and tried not to cough as it burned the back of her throat.

"If you don't mind me saying so, Miss Greenwood, you don't behave like someone who just got engaged to the man of her dreams. I'd hope my fiancée would look more enthused."

It took every ounce of her restraint not to poke her tongue out at him. Instead, she settled for silence.

CHAPTER 30

Justin and her father were in deep conversation, and Lauren was hoping to slip by unnoticed, but her fiancé spotted her.

"Darling, there you are. I haven't seen you all night," he said.

"My fault, Lauren," her father said. "I have been monopolizing your young man. I am so happy for the both of you."

Lauren held herself rigid as her father kissed her cheek. She saw he had noticed by the lift of his eyebrows, but she ignored his reaction.

"Would you like to take a walk in the garden, Lauren?" Justin asked her. "It's not too cold and you can wear my jacket."

"I don't think that would be app—"

"She would, wouldn't you, Lauren." Her father's faint but unmistakable command was evident. Lauren turned toward the door, knowing better than to disobey his instructions.

Once outside, Justin took her hand and led her to the garden seat beside the ornamental pond. The air smelled divine with the scent of jasmine, moonflowers, and water lilies. The gentle breeze brought in the scent of the flowering tobacco, although it was planted past the stable, near to where old Sally lived.

"Did you know water lilies flower at dusk, hence why their scent is so strong?" *What am I doing talking about flowers?* "Nanny told me the gardeners planted lemongrass, basil, and cedarwood around the pond in a bid to reduce skeeters. Burning lavender and peppermint in ornamental jars works too as the mosquitoes hate them."

"Lauren, stop talking and come sit down." Justin laid his jacket on the bench before he sat down and pulled her into his lap. She struggled but his firm grip made her worry for her clothes. The dress was delicate and it wouldn't take much to tear it. For a second she wanted to giggle, imagining the stares of the guests if she arrived back from the garden looking disheveled.

"Alone at last. Where's my kiss?" His words sounded slightly slurred. Concerned about making a scene, Lauren let him kiss her, hoping that would suffice and they could return indoors. He tried to deepen it, but she pushed him away.

"Our guests could see us," she protested.

"Let them. We just got engaged." He nuzzled the back of her ear.

"Justin, stop it. My father—"

"Your father doesn't care. He wants us to get married. Haven't you seen how happy he is?" His hands played with the back of her dress.

"Justin, please. You're messing up my hair."

He pushed her off him roughly as he stood up. "We best get back inside before you turn into a real ice goddess."

"There's no need to be nasty," she protested, but realized immediately it was the wrong thing to say because he grabbed her arm in a vice-like grip. "You're hurting me."

"Watch your tone with me, Lauren Greenwood. You may be Daddy's little girl, but he's given you to me. Signed, sealed, and soon to be delivered. I expect my wife to know her place."

"Justin, that's just it. I don't want to get married. Not yet. I want to work. My teachers, they said I have—"

"Work? Are you insane? No wife of a Prendergast has ever worked. Your father doesn't let you have a job, so why do you think I would?"

"But he sent me to school, and I thought he would, he might—"

"He might what? You're one of his assets, darling, just like any other asset. You go to the highest bidder. In this case, that's me." He yanked her to him and kissed her once more, his skin grating roughly against hers, his hands fumbling with her dress.

"Stop it," Lauren said, pulling back. "How dare you!"

Justin raised his hand as if to hit her, and Lauren shrank back. But a voice calling to her stopped him.

"Lauren, some of our guests are leaving." It was her father.

"Saved by Daddy. Go on, he won't be around to save you next time," Justin snarled.

CHAPTER 31

In the empty bedroom where Nanny used to sleep, Lauren picked up the photographs that she had left in her bedside drawer. She glanced through them, smiling at pictures of Nanny with her sister, Lauren's grandmother, and Mama holding Lauren on her knee. There was a photo of her parents looking relaxed and happy as they posed in front of a baby carriage, and there were photographs taken a year after Mama died. Nobody looked relaxed in those later pictures. Her father was scowling at the camera as though he'd been forced to pose.

"Nanny, where did you go? Why haven't you written?" Lauren said quietly. "I wish you were here to talk about Justin." She put the photographs back in the drawer and picked up Nanny's scarf, the only piece of clothing she had left behind, which still held her lingering lavender scent. "I know you never liked him and now I agree with you."

Lauren stared out the window. Nanny would have looked at this same view hundreds of times. Could she see the mountain tops from wherever she lived now?

What was she doing, standing in a room talking to herself? Wishing Nanny back wasn't going to achieve anything. If wishing worked, her life would be very different.

*

"Look, Miss Lauren, you are in the papers." Cook held up the paper and read out: "*Engagement Announced to Guests at Sumptu-*

ous Party. Mr. William Greenwood announced the engagement of his daughter, Lauren, to Mr. Justin Prendergast, only son of Irene Prendergast and the late Jerome Prendergast."

Lauren sat before her legs gave way. Mary took the paper from Cook and read more quickly: *"Breaking from tradition, in a very romantic gesture, Justin presented the blushing bride-to-be with a large sapphire and diamond engagement ring shortly after her father's announcement. Miss Greenwood is a vivacious, charming, beautiful woman known for her keen interest in horses."*

"They make me sound like an empty-headed fool." Lauren snatched the newspaper, fighting her impulse to shred it. "How could they get the information about the engagement so fast?"

Mary took the paper back.

"Your father or Mr. Justin must have sent them a notice. Isn't it so romantic?" Cook smiled before reading more of the paper over Mary's shoulder. "Lord above knows how I will cater for so many guests. Mr. Justin's family has lived here since King James was on the throne of England. He'll know everyone."

"Stop it, Cook. You're working yourself into a tizzy for no reason."

"Miss Lauren! Surely you want me to cater for the wedding? You aren't bringing in no strangers to my kitchen?"

"I'm not bringing anyone anywhere. Why won't anyone listen to me? I'm not getting married to Justin or anyone else. I want to be free to do what I want."

"Miss Lauren, you can't go around saying things like that. Your father won't like it." Cook turned to Mary. "Tell her. She might listen to you."

"Tell Father to marry Justin then," Lauren said, as she stormed out of the kitchen.

Lauren hadn't calmed down by the time luncheon was served. She walked in without acknowledging either Justin or her father.

Taking a seat at the table, she thanked Cook for serving up another array of dishes.

"Pork chops with apple sauce is just about my favorite meal, thank you, Cook." Justin fixed the older woman with a wide smile. Lauren caught the flush on Cook's cheeks before she hurried away. Justin could be so charming when he wanted. He must have felt her staring at him as he met her gaze.

"You look beautiful today, darling. The color of your dress brings out the blue in your eyes."

"They're violet," she snapped, causing her father to glare at her.

"Behave yourself, Lauren, Justin is our guest."

"He is *your* guest, Father. Nobody asked *me* if I wanted him to stay, in the same way that nobody asked *me* if I wanted to marry him. You and Justin planned it together, didn't you? My views about my own wedding don't seem to matter to anyone." She took a breath. "And you've announced the engagement in the papers already. What is the big hurry to marry me off? I didn't know you were so tired of my company, Father."

Her father's eyes bulged but his mouth was full and he was too much of a gentleman to speak.

"Lauren, darling, it wasn't like that. Please don't blame your father. I wanted to surprise you by being romantic. I guess I made a mess of it. I'm so sorry. Will you forgive me?" Justin pleaded.

Her father coughed and took a sip of water before adding, "Justin didn't do anything wrong, Lauren. Women complain that their men aren't romantic fools like those they see on the big screen, but when they try to plan a surprise, they end up being treated like cads. How can we win?"

Lauren squirmed in her seat. *Was she overreacting? Maybe Justin had planned a surprise he thought she'd love. Even so, it just went to prove how little he knew her.*

"I apologize." She spoke through gritted teeth. Justin put his knife and fork down and pushed his chair back, grating the wood against the floor. He moved to her side and leaned in near her face. "It's fine, Lauren. I'd forgive you anything. I love you."

Lauren turned her head just in time as his kiss landed on her cheek.

"So, when is the wedding going to take place? Where would you like to be married?" her father asked, but he hadn't even looked up from his plate.

"I don't think we should start planning..." Lauren took a deep breath, ready to say she didn't think that she and Justin were suited, but Justin interrupted.

"That's nerves talking, darling." Justin rubbed her arm before resuming his seat. Picking up his fork, he said, "I suggest a wedding here in Rosehall would be perfect, and September would be cooler than August."

"This September?" Lauren's stomach roiled as she pushed her plate away, any appetite for food having vanished.

"Do you want it sooner? I thought you gals like time to plan things? But any time before Christmas is fine with me."

Lauren's mouth fell open. "I don't think we know each other well enough, Justin. For instance, your surprise was—"

"Lauren, are you finished?" her father interrupted. "I have some business to discuss with Justin. Run along, dear, be a good girl."

CHAPTER 32

"There you go, all rubbed down and ready for your oats." Lauren hugged Prince, laughing as he tickled her ear with his lips. She put away his brush and only when she was sure he had enough clean water did she leave the stable and head outside, intending to go back to the house.

Mary ran toward the stable block, her face bright red, a vein pulsing at the side of her neck. "Miss Lauren, thank goodness you're back." The maid seemed to be struggling to find her breath. "Can you come in to the kitchen? We need you."

Lauren's stomach roiled. Mary didn't create a fuss and she wasn't one for drama.

Mary ushered her under the flowering wisteria arch, past the roses and the blossoming garden, and into the kitchen. Patty was sitting on a chair, rocking backward and forward, moaning to herself. Her eyes, swollen from crying, widened as she glanced around the room, but didn't appear to focus on anyone or anything. The girl's arms were wrapped about her middle as if she was in severe pain.

Lauren pulled off her gloves, placing them on the kitchen table, and rushed over to her. "Patty, what's the matter? I've never seen you so upset. Please talk to me." Lauren put her arm around the shaking girl. She glanced up at Cook, who was praying loudly and wringing her apron between her hands.

"I don't know what's wrong with her, Miss Lauren. She won't say a word. Just rocks back and forward like that."

"Patty, please tell me what's wrong."

"I'm going to have a baby." Patty's cheeks burned as she continued to mutter. "What have I done? Why is this happening to me?"

Lauren looked at Cook, now sitting with her elbows on her knees, her face covered by her hands, and then back at the girl. "Are you sure?"

"I'm poor, not stupid, Miss Lauren. I'm having a baby in September." Patty pressed the palm of her hand over her mouth.

Lauren couldn't blame the girl for snapping back at her. Looking at her closely, she could see the tiny mound under her apron. *But... September?*

"Patty, please don't cry. We'll look after you, won't we, Cook?"

But Cook remained silent. She didn't even lift her head to acknowledge the question.

Lauren squeezed Patty's hand. "Have you told Henry?" she asked.

"Henry doesn't want to know. He said he never wanted to see me again. I can't blame him."

Lauren tried to hide her shock. Henry, from the little she knew of him, seemed like a nice man.

"What does that mean, Patty? It takes two to make a baby. I'll go speak to him. He has to face up to his responsibilities."

Patty paled, shaking her head violently. "You can't do that. It has nothing to do with Henry. He's a good man, but he can't take on another man's child. It's not fair to ask him. The priest is right, I'm evil and brought this on myself."

Lauren used her hanky to wipe the servant's face.

"I don't know this priest of yours, but he's wrong. You may have made a mistake, but we'll find a way to deal with it. You'll see."

"You mean it, Miss Lauren? You won't throw me out on the street?"

"Of course not." Lauren ignored red-faced Cook shaking her head. "I won't let anything happen to you."

"Don't make promises you can't keep, Miss Lauren," Mary replied on Cook's behalf, her hand on her fellow servant's arm. "We all know that as soon as your father finds out, there will be no job for Patty. She was planning to marry Henry but now what will she do? It's a bad day, so it is."

Lauren knew she had to take control before the servants dissolved into mass panic.

"Cook, can you go make some tea with plenty of sugar and bring it to Nanny's rooms? We can talk privately there. Come on, girls, let's go upstairs and Patty can freshen up. She won't want anyone to see her in this state."

Mary kept her arm around Patty's waist as she helped the girl to climb the stairs to the suite. If they ever needed Nanny, it was now. Lauren brushed aside tears of frustration and longing.

"Sit down, Patty, please. You didn't really think I would turn my back on you, did you?" Lauren said gently, once the three of them were seated in Nanny's sitting room. "I meant what I said downstairs," she carried on. "I'll do everything I can for you."

A knock at the door interrupted them, and Cook walked in with a tray of tea and some cookies.

Lauren saw there was only two cups. "Will you not join us, Cook?"

"No, Miss Lauren. It's best you and Patty are left alone for now. Mary, come back to the kitchen. You can do Patty's chores."

Lauren glared at Cook, but it didn't change the stony expression on the older woman's face. Confusion whirled inside Lauren. Surely Cook wasn't going to turn her back on the very girl she usually treated like a daughter, was she?

CHAPTER 33

"Patty, don't let Cook upset you. She's older and traditional in her views. She won't turn against you, she just needs time, that's all." Lauren hoped she was right.

Patty sat with her hands on her lap in Nanny's reading chair, looking so tiny and alone. Lauren pushed a cup of tea into her hands. "Take small sips. It will help you feel better. At least that's what Cook always says."

"Cook says in Ireland they treat all news with tea, good and bad," Patty hiccupped.

Silence lingered between them for a couple of minutes. Lauren was hoping the servant would tell her the story, but when she remained quiet, she finally asked, "Have you spoken to the baby's father?"

Patty shook her head so violently she spilled some tea in her lap. Jumping up, she set the cup down on the dresser and used a rag from her pocket to dry her dress and the chair.

Lauren reached for her maid's hand, rubbing it as she tried to think of the right words. "Patty, please sit down. Help me understand so I can help you. Why can't you talk to him?"

"He doesn't want to know," she replied, shaking her head.

"But how do you know that if you don't speak to him? Maybe you'll be pleasantly surprised. I mean the two of you… well, you had to…" Lauren's cheeks flushed as she tried to say the words. Nothing at her finishing school had prepared her for a conversation like this. How she wished with all her heart that Nanny was here. She'd know exactly what to say.

"I didn't get into bed with him, if that's what you're trying to say, Miss Lauren. I'm a good girl. Or at least I was." The tears came again.

Lauren kneeled on the floor in front of the chair. "I'm not judging you. Far from it."

"Miss Lauren, you don't understand. I didn't, I couldn't, I wouldn't do that with anyone. I was waiting to be married."

"But—"

"I was forced. I didn't have any say. He just…" Patty stared at her lap and wrung her hands.

Horrified, Lauren moved slightly back from the girl. "You mean you were assaulted? This man… raped you?"

Patty nodded but wouldn't meet Lauren's eyes.

"And you've fallen pregnant?"

Patty's eyes blazed. "You don't believe me, do you? You've heard them say you can't get pregnant on the first time, haven't you? Well, they are wrong. You can and I did, because believe me, if he ever tried to do it again, I'd fight harder. I'd cut him. I'd scream. I'd do something other than just stay silent and still like a statue while he… he…" Patty covered her face with her hands, her shoulders shuddering as sobs racked through her body.

"Patty, don't. Please don't torture yourself." Lauren pulled the shaking servant into her arms. She rubbed her back as the girl sobbed so hard, she thought her heart was going to break. "None of this is your fault, Patty. We better call Sheriff Dillon. He can—"

But Patty pushed her back so violently that Lauren lost her balance and fell onto the carpet. "Sorry, miss. I didn't mean to hurt you, only you can't call the sheriff. He'll never believe me. I just have to go away before people find out about the baby. Before Henry becomes a laughing stock. People will know it isn't his. They know he's a good man, my Henry." Patty twisted her hands. "He's not mine no more though, is he?"

Getting up from the floor, Lauren shook her dress back into place. Who on earth could be cruel enough to hurt Patty? Not only was she so young but she was a pleasure to be around, always laughing or smiling. Everyone loved her. There hadn't been any strangers at Rosehall lately, yet someone had brutalized this innocent girl. Whoever it was had to be held responsible.

"We have to think of something. Who is this man? Maybe I can appeal to his better nature."

Patty laughed, a harsh sound emerging from her. "He hasn't got one."

"Well, I'm sure he would give you money."

"I'm not a whore, Miss Lauren."

Shocked at Patty's language, Lauren remained open-mouthed. She could hardly blame the girl, though.

"Sorry, miss, for my language, but I'm not taking a penny from that man. I have to get away from this town. I'd be obliged if you keep the news to yourself for now. Henry said his mother might help me. She may know a place for… for girls like me. Just give me a week or so to get sorted. I know I shouldn't ask, but if you tell your father he'll throw me out today, no question about it."

Hurt that Patty would think so little of her, Lauren steeled her facial expression. "Of course I won't tell him. Take whatever time you need."

"Thank you, Miss Lauren." The servant, her voice quaking, sounded as terrified as she did when she addressed Lauren's father.

CHAPTER 34

Lauren was admiring the views through all the windows she passed as she headed through the house to the dining room. The sky was blue over Rosehall, but she could spot clouds over the mountains heralding a rainstorm later in the day. The last of the strawberries were ready for picking, and the new crop of blueberries would soon be ripe. In the distance, she could see the peaches pulling down the branches of the trees with their weight. Soon the pickers would arrive to harvest them. This morning, the gardeners were already working in the sunshine, taking advantage of the less humid temperatures to deadhead the flowers, prune the bushes, and cut the grass to keep the garden looking neat.

She had dressed carefully in a light cotton dress, which she knew her father admired, letting her hair fall around her face and applying no lipstick. Now she was anxiously awaiting his arrival in the dining room, where the sun was streaming through the glass, the light dappling the floorboards, when he made his appearance.

Lauren walked over to the dresser, where breakfast was keeping warm. "Good morning, Father. I asked Cook to make all your favorites today. Bacon with maple syrup on the side, country ham with red-eye gravy and grits, smoked trout, buttermilk pancakes, and cinnamon rolls."

"Thank you, Lauren. What have you done now, I wonder." His tone may have been jolly, but his eyes held a guarded expression. He helped himself, then kissed the top of her forehead before taking his usual seat at the head of the table. He waited until

Lauren had brought her plate to the table and sat down, before asking, "May I read my paper, or do you have something to discuss with me?"

Lauren hesitated. Was this the right time? He hadn't started his breakfast, never mind his paper, but he was in a good humor.

"Lauren? What is it?"

"It can wait until you have finished your breakfast, Father."

"Something seems to be wrong, so tell me. Just spit it out, no dillydallying."

She took a deep breath. "One of our servants is in trouble. She's pregnant and I want to help her."

Her father's smile dropped instantly. "Really, Lauren, I hardly think that is something I need to deal with. Jackson can handle it."

"But it's Patty and she's so scared," Lauren told him. "She has nowhere to go. I thought she could stay here with us, I—"

"What? That's out the question. She'll be dismissed just like any other girl with loose morals."

"No, Father. This wasn't Patty's fault."

He turned bright red, but she decided to plow ahead regardless. "I don't want to embarrass either of us, but"—this was much harder than it had been when she'd rehearsed the speech using the mirror in her bedroom—"Patty is innocent, Father. She didn't do anything wrong."

"Are you trying to tell me we have another Immaculate Conception? A miracle, perhaps?"

"Father!" She regretted her sharp comment immediately. "I apologize for my tone. What I meant was someone took advantage of Patty. *They* should be held responsible, not her."

"So, you want me to force the boy to marry her? Henry, isn't it?"

How little bypassed him.

"Henry was the boy she was courting, yes, but the baby isn't his."

Her father slammed the table, catching her unawares. "Lauren, I've heard enough! There will be no taking in someone's by-blows, you're out of line." He stood up and strode to the door. Opening it, he roared for Jackson.

The man appeared in an instant.

"Find Patty and bring her and Cook to me right away."

"Yes, sir."

Lauren rose to leave. "Father, please don't take your rage out on the staff. Punish me, but please…" She didn't see his hand rising. The sharp slap was enough to send her flying onto a chair. Stunned, she held her hand to her cheek.

CHAPTER 35

Patty and Cook arrived, the older woman clinging to the younger girl's hand. Cook looked absolutely terrified, but it was Patty who Lauren was more concerned about. The servant didn't even attempt to look at her master, blushing and staring at her feet.

"What did you mean by getting my daughter involved in this, Cook?"

Lauren's father looked at Patty with such distaste, the young girl took a step back away from him.

"I'm very sorry, sir. I wasn't sure what to do, never having any experience of such matters. Nanny used to deal with personal issues like this."

At the mention of Nanny, her father's eyes protruded even further. She wished she knew what had happened to turn him against a woman he had once admired and trusted with his child.

"Patty, pack your bags and get out," he boomed, his spittle hitting the girl in the face. "You won't get a reference, but Jackson will give you your pay for the rest of the month." He turned his back on the girl, his breath coming too fast.

Lauren took a step closer, instinctively trying to soothe his temper, but she froze as he pivoted and glared at her.

Patty gave a small gasping noise, focusing his attention back to her. "I don't want to see your face in this house or on my land again, do you hear? Or anywhere in the town, for that matter."

Lauren was lost for words. Her father couldn't insist on Patty leaving Delgany, could he? He didn't own the town, did he?

"I can't leave Delgany yet, sir. I don't know anyone anywhere else. I've never been—"

Her father thumped his fist on the mantelpiece at the same time as Mary entered the dining room. "I don't care where you haven't been or who you don't know." His tone chilled the room, despite the sunshine pouring in the window. "You knew enough to get into the mess you've caused. *Get out!*"

Patty pulled her hand out of Cook's grasp. Lauren thought the girl would run, but instead she took a step toward Lauren's father.

Lauren saw an incredulous look appear on his face. This was most likely the first time a servant, and a female one at that, had had the nerve to speak to him directly.

"I told the mistress and I will tell you, sir. I didn't do nothin' wrong. I'm a good girl. I wanted to wait to get married, but—"

Mary stepped forward at that moment, her cheeks beetroot red. "Come along now, Patty. Sorry, sir, I will help her pack. She didn't mean to answer back. It's her delicate condition, makes her say all sorts of things. Excuse me, sir." The maid put her arm around Patty's shoulders and half dragged the girl out the room.

Cook remained where she was, her hands tugging at her apron, silent tears running down her face. Lauren couldn't get a handle on her thoughts. She took a step to follow Patty, but knew Mary would be of better comfort to the girl. She couldn't believe her father's reaction nor Patty's bravery in standing up for herself, but now poor Cook was in her father's sights. There was nothing in his manner to suggest it would be a pleasant experience.

"I am sorry, sir. I didn't know anything about it. I've never had any experience of anything like that," Cook said.

Lauren couldn't help but be sorry for poor Cook. She didn't know where to look and couldn't even use the word "pregnant" in front of her master.

"Father, please leave Cook be," Lauren said, finally finding her voice. "She dealt with the situation as best she could."

Her father opened his mouth but, at a moan from Cook, snapped it closed again, marching out the room and slamming the door behind him. Lauren and Cook jumped at the loud bang and silently stared at each other until they heard the front door to Rosehall crash shut and the sound of a vehicle roaring away, the gravel shrieking in protest as the wheels churned up the stones.

"I'm sorry," Lauren said, relieved to be away from her father. "This is all my fault. Please sit down." The older woman's color worried Lauren, she was so pale.

"Mother Mary and Joseph, I never saw the Master that angry before and I've seen some things that would make your hair stand on end." Cook glanced up at Lauren. "Miss Lauren, your face is all red. The Master didn't hit you, did he?"

Lauren flushed as she caught sight of her reflection in the mirror over the fireplace. Her cheek looked like it wore a fresh burn.

"Don't mind me. I have to find Patty. Are you all right, Cook? Can you get back to the kitchen or do you want me to call someone? From the garden staff? Sam, maybe?"

"Don't worry about me. You best get a steak on that cheek, Miss Lauren, or you're going to have a nasty bruise. What was the Master thinking of? You, his own precious daughter. This house isn't the same as it was. Not since Nanny left."

CHAPTER 36

Lauren paced her room, trying to figure out a solution to help Patty. She checked her money sock again but she only had ten dollars. She could go to the bank and take out some money but, glancing in the mirror, she saw the red shiny mark on her face was already turning black and purple—she couldn't be seen in public.

Going to Nanny's suite for the umpteenth time, she searched the room for some clue as to where the woman had gone. Nanny would have helped Patty. She sat on the floor beside the closet, holding Nanny's scarf in her hands. How could her father be so cruel and insensitive? If only Nanny were here, she could have made him see reason. Burying her head in the soft wool, Lauren cried until she didn't think she had a tear left.

The sun was now high in the sky, its rays beaming into the room. Crying wasn't going to help anyone, she determined, as she put Nanny's scarf away. She had to find Patty and see what plans they could make for her.

Lauren found Patty in Sam's rooms above the stables. She hesitated before entering. She could hear the girl crying, and Mary and Sam trying to soothe her. Making her way up the stairs, she knocked, waiting for permission to enter. She knew she could have just waltzed in, like her father would have done, but she tried to give the people who lived on the estate the respect she felt they deserved.

Sam opened the door, his face giving nothing away.

"May I please speak to Patty?"

Sam shrugged, but Patty's cries rose in protest.

"Patty, you behave yourself," scolded Mary. "Miss Lauren only tried to help you, much good that did her. Look at her face. Miss Lauren, you should get Sam's mother to look at that. Old Sally, she be used to dealing with injuries of all sorts."

Lauren stepped past Sam into the room, leaving the door ajar. "Don't concern yourself with me, Mary. My face looks worse than it is. Patty, I'm so sorry. I made things worse. I only meant to help you, I still can."

"What can you do for me, Miss Lauren? I ain't got a home, Henry, nothin', not even my good name."

"I can't fix your name or Henry, but I can try to find you a home. But you have to trust me. Can you trust me, Patty?"

They heard noises coming from beneath them. It was Cook, staggering into the stables, her red face glistening with sweat, her hands held out in front of her as if she needed something to hold onto. She came to a stop at the foot of the steps up to Sam's room: "Miss Lauren, your father's back." Cook took some loud, deep breaths. "Jackson called him. I heard him say something on the telephone about Patty. Come back to the house quickly."

Patty's eyes widened with terror, but Lauren squeezed her hand. "Have faith, Patty. Mary, will you please come with me?"

Lauren and Mary strode to the house, slowing as they reached the hallway. Lauren's father was waiting, but he wasn't alone. Jackson was with him.

"Father—"

"Where is the girl, Lauren?"

"Please—"

"Mary, get Patty and her things. I know she is still here. Bring her to me now or I will turn everyone who is sheltering her out." His roar echoed around the house.

"Father—"

"Enough, Lauren."

Lauren held her breath. *What was he going to do with Patty?*

Mary arrived back some minutes later, with a silent Patty in tow. She was carrying a single bag. There was no sign of Cook or Sam.

"Leave us, Mary."

"Yes, sir." The maid walked away, her shoulders hunched.

"Jackson will take you to your new home, Patty. He tells me he knows of a suitable place. I don't expect to see you again. Lauren will have no contact with you either. Is that clear?"

"Yes, sir," Patty mumbled.

Lauren couldn't speak. Her mouth was too dry, her heart beating too fast. *This is wrong. What is Father doing? And why does Jackson look so self-important, almost as if he is enjoying the young girl's agony?*

Lauren watched as the butler grabbed Patty by one arm, his fingers digging into her flesh, causing Patty to flinch and try to twist away, but to no avail. He marched her in the direction of the drive.

"Patty!" Lauren called, finding her voice at last. But before she could move, her father held her firm. "You go to your room. Now."

She didn't just go, she ran.

*

Lauren, dumbstruck, sat in the kitchen with Cook until Sam's mother, Old Sally—a wizened old lady, who seemed to be about eighty years old—strolled into the kitchen. The woman took one look at Lauren's cheek and tutted. She moved her fingers over the cheekbone, barely brushing the most tender spot.

"Not broken. Lucky. I have something to put on it. It helps with bruising."

She opened a pot of salve and Lauren's stomach heaved from the vile smell that emanated from it. She saw Cook having a similar reaction.

"Don't smell pretty, but works mighty quick. You'll see. Tomorrow, you'll look better, the next day, you won't even know you got hit."

Lauren glanced at Cook for reassurance.

"Miss Lauren," Cook said, "Sally's own mother used to nurse all the slaves when this was a working plantation. Sally learned all her tricks. You do as you are told and go to bed. I don't want anyone thinking that stench is coming from my cooking."

Lauren submitted to Sally's ministrations, trying not to gag as the woman rubbed the substance over her face.

Sally tutted as she worked. "Men always manage to catch the sorest patch of the face. Their knuckles be attracted to it."

At her words, Lauren looked into her eyes. Just how many horrible things had this woman witnessed over her lifetime? She'd have been old enough to have lived through the war and the years of reconstruction afterward. Sally turned and, in the light, Lauren caught sight of what looked like a brand mark on the side of her neck, just under her ear.

Sally caught her looking. "I got that the summer I turned fifteen. The war was going on so long and I didn't have the patience I was born with. I tried to run off. It was during the War Between The States, when I was living on the Prendergast plantation. Plenty ran away but they caught most of us. They kilt the men who they said were the leaders and branded the rest of us with an iron white-hot from the fire. Never could disguise that, no matter what I tried. I was lucky, though. They said I was too pretty to mark my face. It would reduce the price they'd get for me at market. So, they put it on my neck."

"I'm sorry, I'm so sorry." Lauren knew she wasn't responsible for something that happened fifty years before she was born, but somehow in her heart, she felt she was.

*

The following morning, Cook served up breakfast in silence. Her father didn't appear, leaving Lauren to sit in the large room alone. She had no appetite, so she carried the dishes back to the kitchen. The look she got when she entered was hardly warm, but she had to ask, "Cook, have you or Mary any idea where Jackson took Patty? Has he said anything?"

"No, Miss Lauren."

"I'm sorry, Cook. I tried to stop my father taking things out on you."

"You had no right putting the girl's hopes up. We all know servants who get into trouble leave. That's the way it has always been, in every house I worked at. Girls will always get themselves into trouble."

"Patty didn't do it on purpose. You saw her. She isn't that good an actress."

Cook sniffed.

Mary glared at the older woman before turning back to Lauren. "Miss Lauren, do you think the Master will tell you where Patty is? Jackson is behaving like he's guarding the President's biggest secret. He won't say a word."

CHAPTER 37

Lauren's father had stayed away from Rosehall for three days but he'd phoned earlier to say that he and Justin would be home for dinner.

Lauren heard the men arrive, but decided that before she had to face them, she needed to see Prince. She walked through the kitchen, grabbing a carrot for the horse. No matter how heartbroken she was, especially over Nanny going missing, Prince helped her. She craved his comfort and his unconditional love for her.

"Don't be long, Miss Lauren. Dinner isn't going to keep," Cook called after her.

"I'll be back in five minutes, Cook. I'm just sneaking this down to Prince. I've been neglecting him."

"You and that horse, Miss Lauren. You'd think he was your child, you cosset him so much."

Lauren smiled as Cook continued speaking behind her. She loved the evenings when the sun was slipping down behind the mountain, the sky a mix of blues and pinks. The air was clear, thanks to a thunderstorm earlier in the day.

The gardens had been grateful for the rain, the roses almost looking like they had flowered just to drink more water, and the smell of damp earth and cut trimmings vied for dominance. Cook's strawberry patch was almost depleted, but Lauren couldn't help bending down to steal a big red strawberry. There was nothing to beat the taste. She walked on past the four fruit trees Father had had moved from the orchard nearer to the house. He said they provided a nicer view than that of the stables and the barn.

"I told you, it was you. I never done that before."

That is Patty's voice. What is she doing back here? She sounded angry yet frightened. *Did Father change his mind?* Lauren picked up her pace, heading toward the distressed voice.

"Stop that! Stop!"

Lauren turned the corner to see Patty standing with her back pressed to the wall of the old kitchen, a man's form hovering over her. *Who was he?* Patty was wearing the same dress she'd worn the day Jackson took her away, only it was dirtier now, with the hem hanging down.

"Patty? Are you okay?" Lauren asked, approaching them.

The man whirled around, his face coming into the light.

"*Justin?* What are *you* doing here? I thought you were in the drawing room with Father."

"I was, darling. I didn't want to spoil the surprise, but I think I have found a lady friend for Prince. I went to ask Sam if he would come view her with me tomorrow. It's part of your wedding gift. I was walking back to the house for dinner when I came across this girl, crying."

"Patty, what are you doing out here?" She couldn't ask the girl what she was doing back at Rosehall, not in front of Justin.

"I thought he might—" Patty's words were cut off by Justin taking Lauren's arm.

"The girl had an argument with her beau. Let's go back to the house before your father sends a search party. You know how he hates meals to be late."

"You go ahead, Justin, I'll just check on Patty."

Justin hesitated, but Lauren walked closer to the servant, who wouldn't meet her eyes. She saw the streak of tears on the shaking girl's face, her hands clenched so tight her nails must have been digging into the flesh of her palms. As she moved closer, she almost covered her nose as the stench of sweat and fear hit her.

"Patty, please come inside. You shouldn't be in this state. It's not good for either of you." Lauren dropped her voice so Justin wouldn't hear the reference to the baby.

"I did as you said, Miss Lauren. I tried to speak to him but he just denied it. Said I had it coming." The servant's voice quaked as she spoke to Lauren under her breath.

"Henry said all those things?"

"No, miss."

"Who then?" Lauren responded in a whisper. "You can confide in me."

Patty's eyes darted from left to right as she clenched her fists by her side.

Lauren wrapped her arms around the terrified girl. "Who?" she asked gently.

"Him." Patty's outstretched finger shook as she pointed at Justin. Lauren released Patty, and folded her hands over her stomach as the girl uttered the words she didn't want to hear. "It was him, he did this."

As Lauren turned to look at her fiancé, trying to make sense of what Patty had told her, Justin paled, before recovering and moving to her side.

"The girl's hysterical, Lauren. Please come inside. I'll send Mary or Cook out to her. She's clearly out of her mind."

Lauren bit the inside of her cheek. *Justin couldn't have hurt Patty, could he? She's so much younger than him. She is practically family.*

She glanced at the girl but the servant held her gaze. Justin was looking everywhere but at his fiancée's face.

"*You*, Justin? No, you couldn't. You wouldn't—"

"Of course I didn't. The girl has no idea what she is talking about. I should call the sheriff and have her arrested for slander."

Patty groaned.

Justin gave the servant a pitying glance. "Well, these things are best kept quiet. Lauren, we have to go inside or your father will be furious. Surely there is someone who can help this poor girl?"

In that moment he genuinely sounded like he cared.

Lauren turned to Patty. "Go back to your old room for now, Patty. I will send Mary to you."

"I knew you wouldn't believe me," the servant said in a trembling voice. "Your sort always stick together. I'm telling you the truth, Miss Lauren. I swear it." She ran away before Lauren could respond.

Taking off his jacket, Justin put it around Lauren's shaking shoulders. "Lean on me, darling, that's right. We will get you inside. Just take one step after another."

Like a child, she silently obeyed him, unable to do anything but put one foot before the other. *Could Justin really have hurt Patty?* He was always so civil to the servants, a perfect gentleman. He even made Mary blush on occasion by teasing her on how well she looked. Yet now she remembered what he had said in the car that first time they visited Delgany—how attractive Patty was, what a catch she was.

She knew he didn't care much for his own workers. The conditions at Meadowville were ample proof of that. He was opinionated, old-fashioned, and lacked sympathy for those most disadvantaged by life. *But was he a monster? Could he attack a young girl?*

Back inside the house, Lauren turned to her fiancé. "Justin, go have a drink with Father, won't you? I'll just run up and wash my face. Mary should check on Patty."

"You know, your father won't want you having anything to do with that girl."

She stopped on the staircase and turned back to face him. "What do you mean?"

"He's told me about her already. Said he'd sent her away and warned her not to come near Rosehall again. Your good heart is going to be your undoing, Lauren. She's obviously trouble."

She knew she had to act fast to prevent him talking to Father about Patty being back at Rosehall. Descending quickly to stand by his side, she put her hand on his arm. She forced herself to smile and lean in toward him. "Please don't say a word to Father," she whispered.

He held her gaze, his finger tracing a line down her cheek, before he bent and kissed her briefly on the lips. It took every ounce of her restraint not to flinch at his touch.

"Of course I won't say a word, darling. Just don't take long. You know your father doesn't like to be kept waiting."

"Thank you, Justin," she said as she took the stairs two at a time, hoping to find Mary upstairs. She was in luck.

"Mary, Patty is outside. I've told her to go to her old room. I don't know where she was taken to, or how she came to be back here at Rosehall. She needs a bath and some new clothes. She and Justin had a row. Patty is in a bad way. Can you find her and make sure she is safe? I have to go down to dinner." The words spilled out of Lauren in a panic.

"Will Mr. Justin tell your father Patty's back?"

"He won't say a word. He promised. Mary, did Patty tell you that Justin was the baby's father?"

Mary wouldn't meet her eyes.

Lauren wanted to ask why Mary hadn't told her but she heard her father calling out to her. "I have to go downstairs. Make sure Patty is okay? Please?"

"Yes, Miss Lauren."

Mary ran down the backstairs, leaving Lauren to check her reflection before heading to the dining room. Her heart was thumping so loudly that she feared she'd give herself away, but Father and Justin didn't seem to notice.

The table was covered in dishes of mashed potatoes, gravy, creamed corn, green beans fresh from the garden, fried okra, and black-eyed peas. The smell of rib-eye steak turned Lauren's stomach, as did her favorite fried chicken. Cook had added smoked trout, her father's favorite, to the menu, possibly trying to soften him up. She watched as both her father and Justin heaped a mound of food onto their plates.

The men ate heartily, but Lauren merely added some creamed corn and a piece of fried chicken to her plate. She couldn't eat, so just pushed the food around on her plate from one side to the other, her mind seething with questions she couldn't answer. *Just what were the men who were sharing this table with her, the men she shared her life with, capable of? Rape, obviously, in Justin's case. But what of her father? Had he ever hurt someone so viciously? What of the stories in the papers?* Her head was spinning with it all.

"Lauren, why aren't you eating?"

Her father's voice cut into her thoughts. "Wedding nerves, Father." She said the first thing that came into her head.

"You have nothing to be nervous about, darling. Delgany will never have seen such a beautiful bride. Isn't that right, William?"

Justin reached out to touch her hand, but she avoided him by taking up her glass. She didn't dare to look at him for fear her revulsion would show.

"Of course. Stop being silly, Lauren, and eat your dinner. Think of all those who have nothing to eat."

Later that night, Mary crept into Lauren's bedroom, where Lauren had almost paced a hole in the carpet, walking around it in circles.

"Miss Lauren, you awake?" Mary whispered.

"I am. I've been waiting to hear how Patty is. Why did I ever introduce her to that monster?"

"Patty's beyond helping. She's hysterical, or at least she was until Old Sally gave her something to calm her. Now she's sleeping. She said the place Jackson took her to is horrible. It's an orphanage called the Home for Unloved Children. The matron is mean and hurts the kids who lives there. She doesn't feed them either and you know how Patty likes her food. She's terrified your father will find her here and blame Sam for hiding her."

"What have I done?" Lauren put her head in her hands, tears escaping through her fingers.

"Miss Lauren, this isn't your fault. You didn't make that man the way he is. You will find someone else to marry, you'll see."

"I'm not worried about that, Mary. I'm crying for Patty and all the other helpless girls like her. I'll not let him get away with this. I'll get justice for Patty, just you see, but first, I will have to take her back to that godforsaken place. I've tried to think of somewhere, but there's nowhere else I know that will take her."

"Miss, I love you as a mistress and as a friend and I know you don't want to hear this, but sometimes you don't use your head. Nobody is going to get justice for Patty. You should accept that."

CHAPTER 38

In the pale light of dawn, Lauren listened to the sounds of the household waking up. Her mouth watered at the aroma of strong black coffee wafting up the stairs, followed by the sweet smell of baking biscuits.

She mustn't let Jackson see her and she didn't want Cook to know. It was best if she knew nothing, then Father couldn't put blame on the old woman. Lauren went down the back stairs and sneaked out the house through the back kitchen. She ran to the kitchen garden and borrowed one of the estate trucks, then drove around to the back gate to collect Patty and Mary.

Patty had slept in Old Sally's hut overnight, but Old Sally was nowhere to be seen. Sam was standing with his arm around Patty. The young girl looked dreadful although she'd clearly had a bath and was wearing a different dress. Her hair wasn't brushed, her lips were bruised from biting them, and her face covered in tear stains.

"Miss Lauren, Cook said I wasn't to go with you," said Mary. "If we're all missing, the Master will suspect something. Patty's told me where the home is." Mary carefully repeated the directions to Lauren. "Will you be able to find the way there on your own?"

Lauren nodded. So, Cook knew Patty was back at Rosehall. Nothing escaped that woman.

Patty clung to Mary before Sam gently lifted her and set her down in the truck with a blanket for comfort. Lauren saw his eyes glistening and she had to look away and swallow hard as she heard him whisper, "It will be all right, Patty, child. It will be just fine. Miss Lauren will look after you."

If only that were true. But Lauren would do anything if it meant she could secure a happy future for Patty. She drove off slowly, engine rumbling gently, only gaining speed when they had left Rosehall behind.

"I'm so sorry about what happened to you, Patty," she said, turning back to the girl as they drove along. "If I hadn't encouraged Justin's…"

Patty shrank in the seat at the mention of his name.

"…that monster's attentions at that ball in New York, he would never have come to stay at Rosehall. I know nothing I can say will change anything, but I wish I could put the clock back. I can tell you I won't marry him. I won't let anyone force me to live with that beast."

Patty continued to stare out the window in silence. The main road ran along the creek, but following Mary's directions, Lauren continued to drive slowly as the road turned into more of a dirt track. She hoped she was going the right way as they drove through the forest, the branches of some trees hanging so low she almost ducked at times.

This place was only a twenty-minute drive from Rosehall, yet there was no sign of civilization. Patty had to have been desperate to walk all these miles back to Rosehall. There were no houses, not even a cabin. Nothing and nobody seemed to live where this track was. Just as she began to wonder if she should turn back, she saw a signpost: "Home for Unloved Children".

She couldn't help glancing behind her to check she wasn't being followed. She knew it was silly, but her father had expressly forbidden her to see Patty again. He'd promised dire consequences if she did. Goodness knows what he'd do if he knew Lauren was driving the girl to the home.

"Patty, we are almost there. Dry your eyes and smarten yourself up. You have done nothing to be ashamed of."

The girl straightened up but remained silent as they drove up the lane, ducking occasionally when the overgrown trees almost grazed their heads. A couple of times Lauren was tempted to get out and walk the rest of the way, the dirt road was so full of chuck holes. She was worried she might get a wheel stuck in one and be unable to drive home—then what would she do?

They came to a large clearing, a dilapidated old barn to their left, its door hanging at an awkward angle. Then the house came into view. It was bigger than Lauren had imagined, but more run-down than anything she had seen before. It was two stories high with what she supposed used to be a wrap-around porch, much like Mr. Thatcher's, only his was in one piece. There were several gaps in this one. The screen door was broken in places, mosquitoes the size of rats would be able to fly right into the house. Paint peeled off every surface and a couple of windows had missing glass panes. The place looked abandoned, with rusting tools lying on the ground near the barn.

Lauren parked the truck and she and Patty got out of it. Lauren looked at Patty's face, which mirrored her own feelings, but she tried to force a smile. She could see why the girl had run away from here. Even so, this place was her only hope.

Nobody came to greet them, despite the fact that anyone living there must have heard the truck. A trembling Patty slid her hand in Lauren's and together they walked to the front door. Lauren knocked and waited. Nobody came. She knocked again. The door was eventually opened by a grubby young girl. The child struggled with it as it scraped across the wooden floor.

"What do you want?"

"Good morning. My name is Lauren Greenwood. May I see the person in charge?"

"She ain't up yet. You is here too early. Came back, did ya?" This remark was thrown at Patty, who didn't reply.

Lauren checked her watch, and saw it was coming up to nine thirty. She didn't have much time, she had to be home by half past ten or her father would surely know that she'd been somewhere other than at her usual charity meeting.

"Can you please tell her I'm here? Thank you."

The child ran off, shouting someone's name. They heard shouts, followed by a short scream and then silence. Lauren resisted the urge to run back to the car and leave. Patty squeezed her hand. They heard footsteps and creaking floorboards. A disheveled woman, who smelled like a whiskey bottle, appeared at the main door. She spoke through the screen door.

"What d'ya want?"

"Good morning, ma'am. My name is Lauren Greenwood, this here is Patty Kelly."

"I knows who she is. She was here afore she ran off. We're full. Can't afford to take in no one else. Bye."

The woman turned to leave, but not before Lauren's hand shot out to the screen door, wrenching it open.

"Ma'am, you don't understand. There is nowhere else for her to go. I will pay you something to cover her costs." Lauren would find the money somewhere even if she had to ask her father to increase her allowance.

"You? How much?" The woman seemed sharper as her eyes grazed Lauren from her head to her toes and back.

"Enough. Perhaps we could come inside to talk? It's rather warm and Patty could do with something to drink."

"Same as myself."

"Water would be lovely," Lauren replied hastily. The last thing any of them needed was liquor. Where was the woman even buying alcohol in the middle of nowhere? She'd heard the revenuers had closed most of the stills with the exception of those way up high in the mountains.

Lauren stepped gingerly over the half-rotten step and through the warped door frame into the hall. The wooden floor was covered in dead leaves and small twigs. Cobwebs glistened in the poor amount of sunlight filtering through dirty windows. A battered kerosene lantern hung on a rusty hook under some wooden shelves, which looked as though they had been put up by a small child totally ignorant in the ways of woodwork.

Lauren jumped as a mouse shot across the floor right in front of her feet. At least, she hoped it was a mouse. She pulled Patty in through the door behind her and followed the woman, who was making for a room on their left. Lauren gazed around what she could see of the house, imagining how it once was, with its high ceilings and fabulous space. But instead of being airy and open, the house felt claustrophobic. A chill settled on the back of her neck, making her shiver as they entered the woman's office. The nameplate read: *Veronica Werth, Matron.*

Inside the room was a desk and chair, with a few low cupboards set against the walls. Papers covered almost every surface, dotted here and there with liquor bottles, most of them empty. A few other chairs, piled high with papers, were scattered around. Since she had entered the house, the stench of unwashed bodies, sweat, and a sweet fragrance that Lauren didn't recognize made her feel nauseous. She glanced over at the unopened window, the murky glass almost hiding the view of the forest outside. The windowsill was covered in dead flies and bees caught in cobwebs.

"Push those papers onto the floor and take a seat. Smoke?"

The woman offered them a cigarette, but both of them refused.

"Could we please have some water, Miss Werth?" Lauren asked when it became obvious they weren't going to be offered refreshments.

The woman rang a bell and soon a girl, almost as skinny and dirty as the one who had answered the front door, came into the room.

"Carly, get these guests some water."

The child didn't answer, but the look she gave them was inquisitive. Lauren smiled, but the girl didn't react. She left, returning relatively quickly with some water-filled glasses. The liquid was tepid, the glasses marked.

Lauren's anger rose. This was supposed to be an orphanage, where children were to be looked after, but the woman in charge looked incapable of looking after herself.

"Patty, perhaps you can tell Miss Werth why you ran away, while Carly shows me the facilities," Lauren said pointedly.

Carly looked at her blankly, causing the matron to bawl, "She needs to pee, show her the outhouse."

Lauren flushed. Standing, she fought to remain pleasant.

"Would you mind, Carly?"

The girl shook her head and walked out the door, leaving it open for Lauren to follow. She kept her pace slow in the hope of seeing more of the orphanage. As she entered the kitchen, there were more children in various states of dress. Not one of them made a sound or held her gaze. With their hands stiffly by their sides, they didn't behave like children but like statues. Some of the children wore dresses made from flour sacks—she recognized the 'XXXX' label from Cook's kitchen at Rosehall.

Lauren followed the girl into the yard behind the house, where the forest had almost taken over. In the distance the mountains were beautiful but the immediate view was nothing but ugly. Everything was in a state of disrepair. From this angle she could see the barn had a hole in its roof. She didn't hear the sound of any livestock, there were no chickens pecking at the ground. Carly pointed to a wooden structure slanting to the left. It looked as if it would fall right over if a child laid a hand on it.

Inside, it was worse than she'd expected. There was a plank of wood hung crossways from side to side, a rough hole cut into the middle of it. Some pieces of newspaper hung on a nail to one side. There wasn't a bucket of water to rinse anything and the stench put a strain on her already compromised stomach.

Leaving the facilities, she saw there was plenty of land around the orphanage. It looked like someone had once tried to sow a vegetable garden but like the house it had been abandoned some time previously. There was an orchard, too, although now only recognizable by the apples ready to be harvested. Each tree seemed to grow on top of the next. She bet nothing had been pruned for at least five years. Further away, beyond the orchard, she could just make out what seemed to be a lake.

Carly had run off before Lauren had opened the outhouse, so she made her own way back into the orphanage. The ground squished under her feet with rotten fruit, no doubt the source of the numerous flies. She kept her eyes peeled for snakes. They loved to hide in tall grass, especially when there seemed to be a large supply of rodents to keep them happy.

How could she leave Patty here? This wasn't a home for unmarried mothers but one for orphans. Matron would use Patty's labor but after the baby was born, where would Patty and her baby go? They couldn't live here. She racked her brains, but there was nowhere else she could take the girl. She climbed the rickety back steps, hoping they wouldn't collapse under her as she walked back into the kitchen.

CHAPTER 39

Everywhere Lauren looked was covered in grease and grime apart from the kitchen's cooking area. The table, while old and worn, had been scrubbed clean, as had the sink, and the stove had recently been blackened.

She heard footsteps coming down the stairs, and she glanced up, shocked to see who it was: "Becky? What are you doing here?"

The girl turned away, walking toward the stove, but not before Lauren had spotted the disdain in her eyes.

"Becky? I can't believe it's you. When you disappeared, I never thought we'd see you again."

Becky stoked the fire in silence.

"Why won't you talk to me, Becky?"

"Why should I? You let us believe you'd help us and then you let them take everything. Ma, my brothers, my family." Hatred burned in Becky's face.

Lauren took a step back. "It wasn't like that."

"Really? That's how it felt. What are you doing here now?" Becky asked, her eyes looking to Lauren's stomach. Lauren blushed, understanding that Becky thought she was pregnant and in need of help, but she held her ground.

"I brought Patty back. She didn't tell me you were here."

"Why would she? I haven't seen her. I've been up in the mountain for days, trying to find food. Even wild turkeys are slim pickings these days. Why's Patty come here?"

"Patty's baby is due in September. There is nowhere else for her to go."

Becky paled. "She's so young. What happened to her man? He seemed nice when you brought him up to the mountain. But then you seemed kind too. How stupid was I to believe that?"

"I did try to find you, I did." Lauren had tried to check on Mrs. Tennant and Donnie at the Colony, but was told in no uncertain terms to mind her own business. A guard had escorted her off the premises with a warning not to return. "Stuff happened at Rosehall. Nanny left and things changed."

"Did you lose your whole family? See your ma cave in to strangers and agree to go to the Colony? A place for the feeble-minded? She could die there. Donnie too. Sarah's dead, and two of my brothers, too. The others ran away. Nobody's seen them since. Your sort are all the same."

Lauren's temper rose. Putting her hands on her hips, she asked, "And what, may I ask, is my sort?"

"Rich woman looking to ease her conscience by helping poor white folks. I've seen plenty of women just like you coming up the mountain, turning their noses up at our ways, finding blame where there was none, making judgments just cause we was poor."

Lauren stared at the girl as she carried on.

"We do our best with what we have so don't you stand there in judgment, you with your pretty clothes and nice things. You got money while these kids got nothin'. Poor food, little fuel for baths in hot water, and a roof that leaks when it rains. Do yourself and your friend a favor and find somewhere else."

"For someone who tells me not to judge, you don't seem to take your own advice. I never meant to hurt you. I can't do anything for Patty, I only have a little money of my own. Appearances can be deceptive." Lauren took a second. "Patty is having a baby she doesn't want and the world isn't interested in. She's barely more than a child herself—she's fourteen. She has nowhere else to go.

Please help me to convince her to stay here. The matron doesn't seem to care." Lauren hated the begging tone in her voice.

"Leave her here then, but you get going. You have a home."

The implication was clear. If she really cared about Patty, she wouldn't be trying to get rid of her.

"Miss Lauren, maybe your heart is in the right place but you need to leave. Do your friend a favor and go now. She'll be all right. Now go on."

"Not before saying goodbye." Lauren didn't wait to hear Becky's reply, going in search of Patty. She found her outside the front of the house, standing by the truck.

"Miss Lauren, please don't leave me here."

Lauren hugged her, her tears mingling with Patty's. "I wish I could take you home, Patty, but we both know that isn't going to work. If I had enough money of my own, I would run away and take you with me." She pushed the girl away, putting her finger under Patty's chin, forcing her to look her in the face. "I'll come back soon. I've been searching for Nanny, but I'll try harder. You are part of our family. Just try to make the best of things here. You remember the family we visited during that snow storm?"

Patty didn't reply.

"Becky, the eldest daughter works here now. She'll help you. I will see you soon."

Blinded by tears, she kissed Patty on the cheek once more before getting in the car and driving off. She glanced in the rearview mirror just in time to see Becky come out and put her arms around Patty. At least she had one friend in that godforsaken place.

CHAPTER 40

Tears blurred Lauren's vision as she drove home. Patty couldn't stay in that hovel. And what of the children who lived there? They were too silent. A home full of children should be filled with happiness and laughter. She had to speak to her father. He wouldn't leave an animal in that place, would he? She tried not to think of the conditions the Meadowville mine people lived in. This was Patty, someone her father had known for years. He would see it differently.

Back at Rosehall, she washed and dressed and had lunch with her father. But she couldn't taste any of the food. Her father ate an enormous helping of fresh river trout with mixed greens and wild rice, followed by a large slice of pecan pie, while she pushed the same food around on her plate. How could she eat when the children and Becky had so little?

"Father, may I talk to you, please?" she asked, once he had finished his meal.

"We are talking." She caught the wariness in his expression.

"I mean, I need to speak to you, Father. Please would you come into the drawing room? It's more comfortable than sitting at the table."

"You are being very mysterious, Lauren." But he smiled at her as he opened the door, holding it open for her to pass through in front of him. She walked, wondering how her feet moved so steadily when inside she was quaking.

"So, what is this all about?" he asked, standing in front of the fireplace, as she perched on the edge of the sofa.

She took a deep breath. "I don't want to marry Justin."

"Lauren, don't tell me you two had an argument."

"No, but—"

"Darling, it's normal to get nervous when the wedding is looming, but everything will work out wonderfully. Justin is a good match for you, and he comes from an excellent family. As a Prendergast, you will want for nothing."

"I don't need anything, Father. You give me everything I want and more."

"A woman needs a husband and in time, a family." His lips pursed, signaling that the conversation was over.

Lauren hesitated before continuing. "I don't believe Justin is the man you think him to be."

"Oh?" Her father stared at her, and she couldn't read the expression on his face.

She fiddled with her hands on her lap before saying, "I... that is, a couple of nights ago, I—"

"Lauren, your conversational skills are appalling. You can't string a simple sentence together. Perhaps we should speak tomorrow when you are more composed."

"No, Father, I need to talk to you today. The thing is... I have found out that Justin took advantage of a young girl and left her in... in the family way." She couldn't mention Patty by name, not when he'd expressly forbidden her to mention the girl again.

"All men sow their wild oats, my darling. It's something your mama, God rest her soul, would have explained to you. Perhaps I should have found someone to have a talk with you. I have been rather remiss about things like this. A woman would explain certain marital issues to you."

"But this is not marriage. Sometime last December, Justin forced the young girl and now she is pregnant with his child and he won't do anything to help her."

"Should he?" he replied, nonplussed.

Her head jerked up, her eyes locking with his.

"Don't look at me like that. You're an innocent, well-brought-up young lady. The girl… she probably doesn't know who the father of her brat is. Why should Justin be the one to pay? Young ladies do best not to think about their husband's dalliances, Lauren, in particular those that occur before marriage. Boys will be boys, you should know that. She will have been one of many and you will probably be thankful for this when it comes to your wedding night."

Scarlet with embarrassment, her face, neck, and ears feeling hot, Lauren didn't know what to say. She swallowed, pulling at the neckline of her dress. Feeling choked, she could barely believe that these words were coming from her father's mouth.

"You shouldn't have any involvement with this girl. How did you even find out about her?"

"I walked in on an argument between them." Lauren paused, then decided that it was best to tell the whole truth. "Father, it was Patty." Maybe he would think differently if he knew it had happened at Rosehall and to a girl she considered to be family. When he didn't react, she carried on, "Our serving girl was extremely distressed."

"She probably expected more money than he was prepared to give her," he said simply, seemingly unaffected by the news.

Was he deaf? Or just completely heartless? Patty was a servant, yes, but also a young girl under their protection. Lauren needed to let her father know just how badly Justin had treated her and that she was now languishing in a disgusting hovel.

"Patty is only fourteen years old, Father, an innocent who was forced. Justin r… treated her very harshly. How can I marry someone like that?" she snapped.

Her father turned around, resting his hand on the mantelpiece, his back to her. "Justin is the perfect husband for you, Lauren.

Don't you think I would know? You'll marry Justin Prendergast September 29, as planned," he said, turning back to face her.

"And if I don't want to?" Lauren asked, stunned, a tremble in her voice. This conversation was not going in the direction she had intended.

"Don't be childish. You're promised to Justin. We have announced your engagement in all the papers. To call it off now would put us in a bad light. It could compromise our family name and that would be bad for business."

"But, Father, what about me? I don't love him." Her voice shook despite her best efforts. She clenched her fists, willing him to listen to her.

His eyes bored into her. "What has love got to do with marriage?"

If he hadn't looked so bewildered, she would have thought he was trying to be humorous. Her heart raced and she clasped her clammy hands together, restraining the urge to wipe them on her dress. She forced herself to speak softly, her voice barely above a whisper. "Please don't make me do this," she begged.

"Lauren, this is all my fault."

Her hopes soared.

"I've indulged you from the moment you were born. I was warned I would spoil you, but until this moment I have never had cause to worry. You have always done what you were told and while your charity fundraisers can, on occasion, be rather irritating, overall I have nothing to complain about."

Lauren went to open her mouth, but he hadn't finished.

"This marriage between the two families is very important to me for several reasons, not least because Justin reminds me of myself. You, Lauren, need a firm hand to keep you from becoming too soft-hearted. I don't want to hear another word about breaking off the engagement, do you hear me?" His lip curled with disdain. "I shall put today's talk down to female hysteria owing to wedding nerves."

Tears pricked at her eyes. She could not fathom what he was saying. "I love you, Father, I do. But you are wrong about this. I won't marry Justin. I can't. Not now. Not after this. I wouldn't marry him, not even if he was the last man on earth."

"You will marry him," her father replied, his voice booming as he stepped toward her. "Don't think for one moment you will defy me. You will become Mrs. Justin Prendergast, or I will have you committed to an asylum."

Lauren reeled. *Who was this man before her?* "You can't do that. This isn't the eighteen fifties."

"I think we both know that I can do as I wish." Her father's cold expression chilled her to the bone. Then, with a shake of his hand, his demeanor changed. "Now, let's talk about something more pleasant. Have you two decided where you shall honeymoon? Your mother loved Paris."

CHAPTER 41

After a sleepless night, with her father's words ringing in her ears, Lauren didn't go down to breakfast. Cook, obviously worried about her, sent up a tray heaving with food. She'd cooked scrambled eggs with fresh asparagus from the garden, and sweet potato pancakes on the side. Unable to stomach the food, Lauren put the tray, untouched, on the bed.

All night long, she had tried and failed to understand her father's logic. If he loved her, as he said he did, why was he insisting she marry an animal like Justin? Once more, her thoughts turned to Nanny. If only she was here, she would talk to her father and convince him he was wrong. Nanny would find a way to make Father listen. She hadn't spoken to him about Patty and the horrible orphanage. She'd failed. Around and around her thoughts swirled, but nothing made sense.

Pushing away her confusion, she decided she would drive out to see how Patty had settled at the orphanage. She could hear Mary singing off-key as she went about the housework, and there were already some tantalizing smells coming from the kitchen, which suggested Cook was baking up a feast. Getting dressed quickly, Lauren opened her bedroom door to find herself face to face with Jackson. She tried to walk past him, but the butler moved.

"Please let me pass, Jackson. I'm just going to take the car out for a while."

"Sorry, Miss Lauren, but your father requested you stay home today."

"Excuse me?"

"He said I was not to give you the key to the car."

"Don't be silly, Jackson. You must be mistaken. I have plans to go into Delgany."

"I'm not mistaken, Miss Lauren. Your father was very clear. He said to tell you Mr. Prendergast will call here this morning. You will have lunch and then he will take you to Thornton Mews for the weekend. I believe Mrs. Prendergast wishes to discuss some last-minute wedding details."

So that was why Cook was baking. She was preparing lunch for Justin. Maybe she could persuade her to add arsenic to his portion.

Lauren ran her tongue over her dry lips as she wondered what she should do. She wasn't prepared to let the butler keep her prisoner.

"Your father told me to call him if you should leave, Miss Lauren."

Reeling, Lauren didn't wait to hear another word. *Her home. Her prison.* For that is what it was and when she married Justin, she would only swap one prison for another.

Just then, Mary came to tell her that Justin had arrived. Lauren walked downstairs, trying to calm her nerves and her temper. She was furious with her father and with Jackson, and filled with disgust for her fiancé. How was she supposed to treat him as normal, knowing what he'd done to Patty? It was all his fault that the girl was now living in that horrible place.

Justin was already seated in the drawing room, waiting for her. Her skin crawled and she fought the instinct to take a step back as he stood up to greet her. "There you are, darling. I thought you had found someone more interesting. You look beautiful, that dress really suits you."

She didn't even smile in his direction. Instead, she walked to the drinks cabinet and poured a whiskey for Dutch courage. The woody scent made her nose itch and she hoped it would taste nicer than it smelled.

"Darling, it's too early for me but thank—" His words cut out abruptly as she downed the drink herself, then slammed the empty tumbler onto a nearby table. She savored the sting as the harsh alcohol burned her throat.

"Lauren, what on earth are you doing? Nice girls don't drink straight whiskey at lunchtime."

"Don't they? So, is that what I am? *A nice girl?* What was Patty?"

Justin's cheeks reddened, and his eyes darted to the door. Walking over, he closed it before marching to her side. He took her by the elbow, forcing her to sit on the sofa as he filled a glass of water for her. "Drink that. Now."

She refused, but he held her head, pushing the glass to her mouth. When she continued to refuse, he held her nose until she opened her mouth and then he poured the water into it, making her gag.

"Drink it down. What would your father say if he saw you like this?" he hissed, the effort of keeping his voice low making his face flush a deeper red.

"He doesn't care. He told me he would lock me up if I don't marry you."

Justin's arm fell away as he recoiled in shock. "What?"

"You heard me, he said he'd lock me up."

"Why wouldn't you marry me?"

She tried to stand up, but he pushed her down by the shoulders.

"I told him I wouldn't marry you if you were the last man on the planet."

"Why?" He was so still she hardly saw his lips move. "Why would you tell your father such a thing?"

"Patty. You raped her." She spat the words out.

He grabbed her arm, twisting it as he pulled her up to her feet, her face inches from his.

"You're hurting me."

Her words only made him tighten his grip at the top of her arm.

"Stop saying things like that. I didn't force that girl. She came to me willingly and she enjoyed it. Just as you will."

"I won't marry you," she said furiously.

"Let's see about that." Before she knew what he was doing, he strode over to the door and turned the key in the lock, then in a flash was back beside her. She tried to move away, but he fixed her in place, pressing his fingers into her arms.

He pulled her to him as his mouth came down on hers, forcing her to kiss him and pushing her back onto the sofa. The shock wore off as she realized his intentions. She tried to shove him away, but he was too strong for her. She tried to kick with her legs, but he pinned her down. She opened her mouth to scream, but he smothered her face with his large hands as she panted for breath, panic soaring through her. She heard her dress rip and her mind went to another place, away from this darkness, away from his attack, as if this was happening to someone else entirely.

From far away, Lauren heard the handle on the door rattling, but when the door didn't open, the person outside started to knock. Taking advantage of Justin's distraction, she pushed him away from her.

"Miss Lauren, I apologize for interrupting and talking through the door," a loud voice called out. "It's important. I forgot to remind you to telephone Mrs. Cullen before she leaves for the afternoon. She wants to talk to you about your next visit."

Mary. Dear Mary.

Lauren scrambled to her feet, ran over to the fireplace, and grabbed the poker. "Get out of here now, or I will scream for help."

His scathing grin was almost her undoing. He turned his back, adjusting his clothing, and then he poured two drinks. One he drank greedily, the other he threw over her. "Now you smell like you drank the bottle." His last act was to slap her hard across the face. "From now on, you remember you are mine to do with as I please. Your father, the cold old varmint, sold you to me just as he would a piece of his company or a used car. I need a wealthy wife with a good name to be the mother of my sons. I'm not marrying you for the pleasure of your body, I have other women for that. But if you ever, for one second, think you can defy me, remember this." He struck her again before leaning closer to squeeze the arm holding the poker and it dropped out of her hand to the floor. Now he pinned both her arms, whispering in her ear, with his sour, whiskey-tainted breath, "Your maid, Mary, she's more my type. I wouldn't mind having her."

At his words, she spat at him; it was the only thing she could do, given he now had her hands pinned behind her back. He released her to wipe the spittle from his face, and then he smiled. It sent a river of fear through her.

"I have to admit you have more spirit than I expected," Justin said. "Our wedding night should be fun." He went over to the door and unlocked it. Then, to her surprise, he hurried back to her side and picked her up in his arms. She tried to claw him, to stop him.

"I *will* hurt Mary," he said, determination in his voice.

At that, she gave in, realizing how powerless she was. She lay in his arms, limp and defeated, as he carried her toward the door of the room, calling for help. "Jackson, can you help me, please? Seems my bride-to-be got carried away with celebrating. She will have a sore head in the morning as she has no tolerance for whiskey. Poor dear girl fell over her own feet so will have some nasty bruises on her face. Perhaps you can escort us to her room. I can't very well carry her up there alone. That would destroy her reputation even if we are to be married in September."

Lauren closed her eyes in shame, not wanting to see the butler's expression. She counted back from ten, trying not to scream as her mind relived the harrowing attack. When they got upstairs, the butler showed Justin her room. He opened the door, standing back to allow her to be carried inside.

"Thanks, Jackson, that will be all."

"But, Master Justin—"

"I can take it from here, thank you. I will be downstairs in just a second. Perhaps you could pour me a drink."

The butler wavered for only a second before he left them alone. Justin didn't close the door.

"Can't ruin your reputation, can we, my dear?" He laughed as he positioned her on the bed before turning down the covers. "Would you like me to help you undress?"

She shrank back from him. "Get out before I scream."

He leaned in closer. "I think we both know you won't do that," he said, his lips brushing light as a feather against hers. It took every ounce of her willpower not to cry out. "I can't wait until we're wed."

Horrified, she felt the onset of tears. She turned away from him, but it was too late, he had already noticed. His smile widened.

After the door had closed behind him, she heard him loudly telling Mary that he'd been too generous in giving her a drink of whiskey and the alcohol had gone to her head.

"I'll help her get into bed, then, sir."

"No, Mary, leave her be, please. She said she didn't want you to see, she's embarrassed. Why don't you come downstairs and we will discuss your position after the wedding? I think my wife-to-be deserves a lady's maid and you seem ideally suited for the position. Come and talk to me."

Lauren wanted to scream, but she didn't dare to say a word. He would only punish Mary. The tears fell faster, until she heard the maid decline the invitation.

"Thank you, sir, but I'll have to telephone Mrs. Cullen on Miss Lauren's behalf. I also have errands to run for the Master. He is due home shortly and will be angry enough at the state of Miss Lauren. I can't afford to upset him as he'll dock my wages. My ma relies on them, she does."

Lauren clasped her hands to her chest, waiting to hear Justin insist. But he believed Mary's story, despite her mother being dead for years. Her maid was safe—for now. Relief flooded her.

CHAPTER 42

Lauren ripped off what was left of her clothes and threw them in a pile in the corner of the room. She wrapped a towel around her bruised body. She could smell the whiskey on her skin and in her hair and longed for a bath, but what if he was still outside? What if he came back to hurt her again? She shivered, rocking backward and forward, waiting to hear the sound of the motor car on the gravel outside. What was taking him so long? Why didn't he leave?

She buried her head in her hands. Her body hurt, her head most of all. She lay on the floor unable to stand, until the blackness took over.

*

The scent of roses and wild honeysuckle filled her room as the curtains danced in the soft wind. The sunlight streamed through the crystal-clean glass windows warming Lauren's body. As she roused, she heard someone rattling at the door.

"Miss Lauren, it's me, Mary. Let me in, please. Your father's home and he's angry. Jackson told him what happened. Please, Miss Lauren, he wants to see you downstairs immediately."

Lauren pulled herself to a standing position, grimacing with pain. She ambled over to the door and slowly turned the key. When Mary saw the state of her, she gasped.

"I knew he was up to something. That's why I made up the telephone call from Mrs. Cullen. I knew you would know those

New York tenements have no telephone. Oh, Miss Lauren, I swear if I had guessed he'd hit you I would have got something to hit him harder. Oh, goodness!" She pushed Lauren's hair back from her face, her breath making a hissing sound as she noted the bruises. "What did he do that for? And why did you drink so much? Miss Lauren, you smell worse than the inside of an old whiskey bottle."

"I had a small drink for Dutch courage. I had to tell him we were finished, I would never marry him. He threw a whole glass of whiskey over me."

"Why would you think of doing something like that on your own? You don't stand a chance against him, Miss Lauren. What will I say to the Master? I can't bring you downstairs looking like this. And look at your new dress. The state of…" Mary froze as she stared at the dress discarded on the floor. Gasping, she held it up to the light. The ripped material told its own story.

"Miss Lauren, what else happened in that room?"

Lauren held her hands to her chest, trying to stop them trembling. She opened her mouth to speak, but it was too dry.

"Did he? He did, didn't he, the rogue!" Mary threw the dress at the door before wrapping her arms around Lauren.

"No, he didn't… Mary, you saved me. Your knock at the door…"

Lauren closed her eyes, trying not to see Justin's expression just prior to Mary's interruption. He hadn't cared that he'd hurt her and he'd been ready to hurt her more. She wasn't a person to him, just something for him to use. Sobbing, she let Mary hold her just as Nanny would have done. The maid rubbed her shoulders until Lauren got a hold of her emotions.

"I can't ever thank you enough, Mary."

"I had a bad feeling. I never trusted that man even before he hurt Patty. Miss Lauren, I'll go ready a bath for you. Soaking in hot water will help ease your aches and pains. I'll tell the Master the whiskey made you very ill. He'll be angry, but at least he won't see you in this state. After today, he's away for the week. When he returns, myself and Cook will have you looking at least half decent."

Lauren almost cried again at the maid's kindness, but she wouldn't hide what had happened. "I will dress and go downstairs. Father needs to see me like this."

"I don't think that's a good idea, Miss Lauren."

"Mary, I know my father. He loves me. Whatever else he does, he loves me."

CHAPTER 43

As Mary went downstairs to tell Lauren's father that his daughter would be down shortly, Lauren wrapped her towel more tightly around her before tiptoeing to the bedroom door. What if Justin was hiding, waiting for her? She'd forgotten to ask Mary if he had left. She opened the door, looking both ways, before shuffling to the bathroom and locking the door behind her.

After running a hot bath, she scrubbed herself until her skin was red raw but still didn't feel clean. She tried to remove the feel of his hands, and the smell of his skin, but she couldn't erase the sound of his taunting voice from her head.

She froze when she heard knocking at the bathroom door, her veins turning to ice.

"Miss Lauren, let me in."

Taking a deep breath, Lauren forced herself to get out of the bath and let the maid in. Mary washed her hair as gently as possible, but Lauren couldn't help flinching from the pain.

After she had helped Lauren to dress, Mary carefully dried and arranged her hair to hide as much as she could of the purpling bruises on her face. When all was done, Lauren tried to stand up, but her trembling legs wouldn't let her.

"Miss Lauren, please let me tell your father you are unwell."

"No. He has to know."

Lauren braced herself, her shaking legs slowly carrying her to the door. Her head throbbed, her stomach threatened to revolt, and her body cried out in pain. Taking one gentle step at a time, she made it downstairs and headed for the drawing room. As she neared the door, her heart hammered against her chest. Forcing herself to be brave, she opened it, relieved to find her father alone and sitting on the sofa. She didn't walk over to kiss him as she would usually, but took a seat. She pushed back her hair and looked him straight in the eye, wanting to see his reaction. His eyes widened as his expression turned to distaste.

"Good Lord, Lauren, when Justin came to see me to tell me—"

"He told you?"

"Yes, he said he was so ashamed."

Relief crept over her, as she let out her breath. *He believed her. Justin would soon be history.*

"I told him he had nothing to be ashamed of."

Lauren blinked, thinking she must have misunderstood him.

"What were you thinking, Lauren? I don't know what has come over you. First, it was our conversation yesterday, and now this. The sooner this marriage takes place the better."

She reeled with shock. What was he saying? "Father, no. You can't make me marry him, Justin did this." She pointed at her face with a quivering finger.

Her father barely glanced at her. "Justin explained that he hurt you when he tried to stop you falling over. You wouldn't have hit your face if you hadn't been drunk. The fact that it has taken you more than an hour to get ready to come down to see me proves you were inebriated. I trust that this is a one-time occurrence, young lady. Nobody likes a drunk, much less a female one."

Lauren stood, swaying with the effort of doing so. "You can believe what you want, Father, but I didn't get drunk. Yes, I had a glass of whiskey to spite you and Justin. I wanted some Dutch courage to tell him the wedding was off. But that's all I had. Justin did this and this"—she pointed to the bruises on her arms and on her face—"and he tried... *he tried*... to do worse." She said the last sentence in a whisper.

Her father reddened as her meaning became clear. He stood up, clearing his throat. "Well, yes, Justin did mention that things got a little heated and you both got carried away. I can't say I'm impressed, but these things happen."

Lauren's blood boiled. "I did not get carried away. He battered me, and could have done worse, if it were not for Mary's timely intervention. Is that the type of man you want me to marry?"

"You're becoming hysterical again." Her father looked at his watch. "I am already late for my social engagement."

"I'm sure whoever you are meeting will wait."

His expression darkened. "Be careful, Lauren, this is my home and you will treat me with respect."

"Respect should be earned. What about me, Father? My fiancé beat me this afternoon. Can't you see? If he's prepared to do this to me while we are not married, what will he do when we are? He knows divorce is not an option." Her father's expression grew stonier. Desperate, she threw herself at his feet, letting the tears flow, as she pleaded with him, "I'll do anything, but don't make me marry him. I'm begging you."

His eyes, hard as flint, blinked rapidly, his lip curled with distaste. He hissed, "Get up and behave like the lady I raised you to be. I hold you responsible for today's events. You behaved badly, drinking, and Justin disciplined you. You have only yourself to blame for that. You will marry him, Lauren. Too much depends on this union for you to throw it away in a tantrum. The entire country is having to make sacrifices to survive and thrive."

She tried to get to her feet but her bruised body refused to respond. She got as far as her knees. Her father made no effort to help her, but took a step backward, his tone as cold as the look in his eyes. "Retire to your room. I will see you get all meals served up there until those bruises disappear. You won't leave Rosehall until that happens. Should anyone call for you, we will tell them you have a severe cold." She watched the heels of his shoes as he strode out the room.

After the front door banged shut, Mary came into the drawing room. The maid ran over to help Lauren to her feet. "Miss Lauren, you need to go to bed. Do you want me to call Doctor Danby?"

Lauren shook her head. Her bruises would heal but the doctor wouldn't be able to cure a broken heart.

CHAPTER 44

The next morning, after another sleepless night, Lauren went over every bit of the conversation she had had with her father. Disbelief mingled with despair. Her father had always loved her, or so she had believed. At least, she had interpreted his gifts, his sending her to the best schools, and allowing her to travel, as love. She realized now that her clothes, education, and the life he had provided her with had been solely to cement his role in society.

Knowing she had to see to her bruises, Lauren managed to sneak away to the former slave quarters of Rosehall in search of Old Sally. She rarely ventured down to this part of the estate. She knew it was fanciful, but she could feel the years of hurt, anger, frustration, and misery the slaves had endured.

She found Old Sally sitting outside her small shack, a pipe in her mouth. The woman seemed to be expecting her, not showing any surprise at Lauren's visit or at the state of her face.

"Sally, could you please help me again? I made a promise to Patty to visit her soon and I can't go out looking like this."

The woman disappeared into her shack without a word. Lauren moved from one foot to another, wondering if she should leave or wait. She got her answer when Sally reappeared with the same jar she had treated her with last time.

"Sit down, Miss Lauren. I can't reach your face from here."

Lauren sat, cringing, as the stench hit her nose.

Sally was as gentle as before, tutting over the bruises. "You be lucky, child. If he'd hit you a little lower, you could have lost your eye. He's got a mean spirit, that man. You should stay away from him."

"It wasn't my father this time, Sally."

"I know, child. I know."

The old woman put her hand on Lauren's shoulder, her gentle touch reminding Lauren of Nanny. She tried to hold back the tears, but to no avail.

"Your man will get worse, child. There's an evil in his soul, same as in his grandfather's. If you knew the things they did to their people over at the Thornton Mews plantation, it would turn your hair white. That's why it was destroyed after the war. The people made sure nobody would work in conditions like that again. Or at least they tried to."

"How do you deal with your memories?" Lauren whispered. "How can you be so kind to me?"

"You did nothing to my people, child. You try to do good by folk. Sometimes the end result isn't what we would have chosen, but at least you try. Your grandmother offered my people sanctuary at Rosehall. They gave us a house, a small garden to grow some food, and a wage to work. It wasn't much, but it was all they could afford and we was starvin'. Other plantation owners threw their people off the land. Folks like the Prendergasts"—Sally spat on the ground as if to cleanse her palate—"they be evil, it's in their blood. You can't stay with him. Your children would carry his blood and bring more evil into the world."

Lauren slumped, thinking of Patty. The baby would be treasured and loved, she'd make sure of it. She would support the young girl however she could.

"You need to rest now, child. Go sleep and let the body work its own magic."

"Thank you, Sally." Lauren stood up, her legs a little shaky. "Please come up to the house later and Cook will have something for you."

"I have enough, child. Old folk like me don't need much. A roof over my head and food in my belly."

Lauren's face felt hot from embarrassment. She hadn't realized the old quarters were in such disrepair. The roof of Old Sally's shack didn't look that solid to her. How little she knew about how other people survived.

"Go on now, child, before someone comes looking for you. I don't like to bring attention to Old Sally. She's outgrown her usefulness. Someone may get a notion to send her away."

"No, Sally. You belong here at Rosehall."

But even as she said the words, Lauren knew they were hollow. She didn't have any more control over Old Sally's future than the old woman did.

CHAPTER 45

By Monday, the bruising had faded to brown and yellow patches, enough to be covered with some light make-up, so Lauren took the opportunity to visit Patty. She tried to hide her plan from Mary, as it was better for her not to know where Lauren was going, in case she was asked, but her maid wasn't so easily fooled.

"I know your heart is in the right place, Miss Lauren, and don't worry, I'll take care of Jackson. You go on now, but don't be gone too long. We don't want anyone asking any questions. Give Patty my love."

Lauren packed a small case with some items that she and Mary had liberated from the attic a few days before. Rather than gather dust at Rosehall, they would benefit the orphanage. She'd also asked Cook to prepare a basket of food, insinuating that she was heading to a charity meeting.

Cook fussed around her like a mother hen. "Are you certain you should be driving, Miss Lauren? I am sure that Jackson would be pleased to drive you to your meeting and collect you later."

The last thing I need is my father's spy watching my every move. "Thank you, Cook, but I'll be fine. What could possibly happen at a charity meeting?" She took the small case and the basket and hurried out to her car. Thankfully, Mary had sent Jackson away on a made-up errand for the Master.

*

Lauren sighed with relief as she left the streets of Delgany behind her. Now it was just miles of country road before her, evergreen trees on either side, in parts forming a canopy overhead. She drove carefully to the orphanage, taking the turn off the road that she now knew was Orchards' Pass.

If possible, the potholes seemed almost bigger than before. On nearing the tumbledown house, she thought it looked even more depressing than before. Perhaps it was because the sun was shining brightly, highlighting all the decay and cracked paint. She parked the car, picked up the food basket, but decided to leave the suitcase of attic things in the car. She got out and walked across the yard to the house. She knocked on the door and the same tatty-looking child eventually opened it. This time she didn't ask who Lauren was but left the door open and ran away.

Lauren made her way inside, hearing some noises coming from the kitchen area. She knocked on the matron's office but there was no answer, so she hesitated for a few seconds before making her way to the kitchen. A quick knock and she pushed the door open in time to see Becky bathing a badly beaten child in a tin bath. She was so engrossed in her task, she hadn't noticed Lauren come in. The other children in the room remained silent, their eyes growing wider.

"Becky, sorry for butting in—"

Becky jumped as if she'd been caught doing something wrong. "Why are you back? Didn't we make it clear before, we don't need do-gooders like you here?"

"I beg to differ." She kneeled down beside the tin bath. "Don't fret, little one, I won't hurt you. I bet they are very painful." She pointed at the lines on his back; in places the skin had been broken. The boy didn't say a word, his eyes never leaving Becky's face. "Who did this to him?" Lauren asked.

"This has got nothin' to do with you. Why are you back?" Becky repeated. She helped the child to climb out of the bath, covering him in a threadbare towel. Lauren got to her feet. The boy couldn't be more than six or seven, given his lack of height.

"I got in trouble. I stole an apple and Matron gave me a whippin'," the child whispered. His eyes were filled with fear as he looked at Lauren.

She bent down again, so her face was on a level with his. She spoke softly: "You must have done something worse than take an apple, child."

"No, ma'am. I took one apple. Lottie, she's my sister, she's hungry. She was cryin' and I couldn't bear it no more. I is sorry. I told Matron I is sorry but it didn't make no difference."

Lauren bit her lip hard to stop the tears falling. "What's your name?"

"Fred."

"Fred, I'll pay Matron for the apple you took so you can forget all about it now."

"You will?"

"I will. Now why don't you take the towel and go get dressed? I need to speak to Becky."

The young boy glanced at Becky, who gave him permission to leave with a nod of her head.

"Where's Patty? Why isn't she helping you?" Lauren asked.

"She don't do nothin' but lie in bed. She barely eats. Says she has nothin' to live for."

"But the baby?"

"You and me both know she don't want that baby."

"Of course I know that, but I'm afraid it's coming. Where is she?"

Becky started to empty the bath water in the sink, ignoring Lauren's question.

"Becky, I asked you a question."

"Nothin' wrong with my hearin'. Don't see why I got to tell you. You left her here."

"For goodness' sake, I explained that." When Becky stayed standing, she glared at her. "Will you show me where she is or do I have to go looking myself?"

Becky gestured upstairs. "That's where the children live. Help yourself. I will be up in a minute, after I see to Fred."

Lauren walked up the stairs, listening to them creak and groan beneath her feet. She held onto the worn, aged banisters, thankful she hadn't taken off her gloves. She could feel the roughness of the wood through the cloth.

Upstairs, the carpet was threadbare and dangerous—a child could easily trip and fall headfirst down the stairs. She wondered why Matron hadn't just removed it. Bare wood would surely be safer. The walls had originally been covered in wallpaper, which was now peeling and flaking. Someone had made an attempt to whitewash one wall, but appeared to have run out of paint halfway through. She knocked on a closed door before opening it—she thought the room might be empty as it was so quiet.

She held a hand to her nose as the stench inside the room made her eyes water. The conditions the children were kept in weren't suitable for pigs, never mind human beings. How could anyone let innocent children live like this?

Glancing out the window, to the far side of the barn, she spotted a tree under which she saw some little crosses protruding from the soil. They were barely visible, given the brambles and long grass growing around them.

Graves. How many children have died here?

Lauren left the room and quickly checked the rest. In each one she found children of different ages, yet all of them in a similar state of undress. The rags they wore barely covered them. More than one child had open sores on their legs, some had them on their faces. Their sunken eyes and protruding cheekbones spoke of prolonged hunger. The stench was overpowering everywhere, but whether that was the children or the rooms, Lauren wasn't sure. Some of them shrank from her in fear. Others just stared. None of them spoke.

"Patty, there you are. I've been looking in all the rooms, trying to find you," she said, entering yet another room. Patty lay on a scruffy bed. Her face and hands were as dirty as the dress she was wearing and her eyes looked lifeless, as if all the joy in life had been sucked out of her.

"You ain't my mistress no more."

"No, I'm not, but I thought I could be your friend. Please get up. You need a wash and we need your help."

The girl just stared at the wall, unmoving.

Lauren went to the grimy window, fiddling with the catch until it finally gave way and the window opened, sending some much-needed fresh air into the room. She pushed the drapes, such as they were, back from the window edges. The room looked even worse in the daylight. The floor was filthy, while a layer of heavy dust covered every surface. In the corner, she spotted what looked like mouse droppings. A shiver ran down her spine. Spiderwebs covered the light fitting and the dusty corners. Her stomach turning, she stared at the girl in the bed. The sheets were gray with dirt, the blankets showed signs of a moth invasion.

Lauren took a step closer to the bed. "Patty, I'm so sorry for what happened to you and if I could turn back the clock, I would. If I could punish Justin somehow, I would. I know you don't feel good about the future," she said, "but you can't let him win. You must fight back. You have to do something to help yourself and I will do everything I can to support you. You will be an amazing mother, your heart is so full of love and kindness. Lying here dwelling on things isn't going to do you any good."

The girl simply turned over on her side, her back to Lauren, who kicked herself, knowing she was making a mess of this. Nanny would know exactly what to do.

"Please get out of bed," Lauren implored. "You can't just lie here. This won't do you any good, none at all." Maybe Patty wouldn't help herself, but she'd always helped others. Perhaps the secret to getting her out of bed was to pull on her heartstrings. "Patty, there are children here who need you. Becky needs help. Will you come down? Please?"

Still, she didn't move. Lauren took a deep breath.

"Can you imagine what Nanny would say to you when there are poor children around you who are even worse off and in need of help?"

CHAPTER 46

Matron Werth nearly fell off her seat as Lauren slammed the door to her office shut behind her. The room was in just as much disarray as before. Lauren was seething with anger. The matron wasn't the right person to look after a pack of wolves, never mind a child. These children, Patty and Becky, deserved to have someone in charge who cared for them. Someone who loved them. As Nanny had often said, kindness didn't cost anything.

"How can you sit there while the children upstairs live in such filth? It's disgusting." Lauren clenched her teeth to give the woman a chance to answer.

"I do my best," Matron replied, taking a large drink from a bottle. "The County don't pay me nothing to look after the brats. I can't be expected to work miracles."

"It doesn't cost a lot for hot water and clean clothes. Those children are sick from neglect."

Matron tried to stand, but she couldn't, flopping back into her chair. Filled with disgust, Lauren tried to keep her voice calm, although her nostrils flared, and a vein in her neck pulsed hard as her face flushed.

"Why did you beat Fred so badly?" she spoke slowly in an attempt to curtail her anger.

"He stole, that's a sin." Matron glanced at her quickly before looking away. Her hands shook until she clasped them together, her breathing coming fast. Lauren could smell the woman's fear.

"And battering a child until they bleed isn't?" Lauren hissed, losing control. She moved closer, now towering over the woman. "What sort of woman are you? Get out of here now! You have no right to run this place and these poor children into the ground. No right at all!"

"You're all the same, you people. You can't do anything to me, you don't have authority."

"You have a choice, get out now or face charges of abuse and neglect."

"Who will run this place?" The matron pushed her face in Lauren's and sneered. "You? You wouldn't want to get those pretty rich white hands dirty, would you?"

"It's no longer your business who runs this place. Go on, get out! Now, before I change my mind and call Sheriff Dillon out here. You have the day to get packed. When I come back tomorrow, I expect you gone."

"Two can play that game, Miss Greenwood. What would Daddy say if I told him you brought your fiancé's lover back here after she ran off? Mr. Jackson seemed quite certain your father prohibited you to have any contact with Patty."

Lauren's blood was pounding in her ears. She stood even closer to the woman, trying to ignore the stench coming from her body. "Don't ever try to get the better of a Greenwood!" She turned on her heel and marched out the office and through to the kitchen, calling for Becky.

CHAPTER 47

The girl didn't come running to Lauren, but kept her waiting while she saw to a number of children who seemed to be working outdoors. Lauren walked outside, almost falling through the rotting step into the yard. It was yet another thing that needed fixing in this horrible place.

"What are the children doing?" Lauren asked, trying to avoid piles of dirt and long grass as she walked over to Becky. She was terrified of snakes and knew they loved to hide in the grass.

"Matron insists on every child pullin' their weight so they have to grow crops. We sell what we can."

"But they are so little and they don't even have hats. They will get burned."

"Matron don't care nothin' about that."

"Don't the older children go to school?" Lauren asked, wondering what they were supposed to be growing. The whole area looked like it had been attacked by brambles and weeds.

"Sure they do, and they get three meals a day and are wearin' rags cause they like 'em."

"Becky, stop it. I'm not the enemy, I've told Matron to leave."

"You have?" Becky swung around and held Lauren's gaze. "Who's going to run this place?"

Lauren gulped. She'd been too busy thinking about getting rid of Matron to face the consequences of her leaving. "I was hoping you would," she said on impulse.

Becky cocked her head, one eyebrow raised.

"Please, Becky, hear me out. I'd help you as much as I could. You wouldn't be alone. I can get some money to fix things up. My father has accounts in most stores in Delgany. I can buy supplies, food, and clothes for the children."

"No."

"But you love these kids. Don't try to deny it. I've seen how you treat them, how you try to do your best. I can't wait to see how you get on once we get you some real help. We're going to clean this place up. The children are all going to be bathed and dressed properly. No more rags and no more beatings. They will have proper beds and food and…" Lauren realized that Becky was laughing. "What have I said that's so funny?"

"Beggin' your pardon, Miss Moneybags, but where is this money tree growin'? I sure don't see no dollar bills hangin' around."

"I told you, my father has accounts everywhere."

"Your father? The same man who made Patty come live here? You thinkin' he's goin' to care about strangers?"

Lauren kicked at some dirt, knowing Becky was right. As soon as her father found out what she used his accounts for, the source of funds would be cut off. Why did everything come down to money? She had no idea how much it would cost to keep a place like this going, but she wasn't going to let Becky know that.

"I'll find the money, if you just say you'll do the job. I'll pay you extra," she pleaded.

"You have money to pay my wages?"

For a fraction of a second, Lauren was tempted to lie but something told her honesty was her best policy. "I don't know."

Becky whistled.

"Where did Matron get her funds from, because she had to get something from somewhere? Unless you have a still up here, I haven't seen where she could brew all the apple shine she drank."

"The still's over yonder, down by the apple trees," Becky teased.

Despite herself, Lauren glanced in the direction Becky indicated, making the other girl laugh.

"I don't know where Matron gets the money from, but nearly all of it goes on that apple shine. A couple of mountain men deliver to her on a regular basis. She must have been cheatin' these children out of the money that was meant to feed and clothe them ever since she came here." Becky took a breath. "See, you don't know what you're doin' and neither do I. You can't employ me to run this place."

"Why not? You have the experience, you care about the children. You'd be much better than Matron Werth."

"I'm backward—a hillbilly, they call me. I ran away from them people who wanted to put me in the Colony with Ma. I ain't goin' to stay nowhere that brings attention to me." Becky looked up, tears glistening in her eyes. "I love these children, yes, but if you put my name on any papers, the County folk will know wheres to find me. What if they want to lock me up? I can't go live in a place where the doors are locked. They only let you into a yard for exercise once a day and they throw you into a locked room by yourself if you ask questions. I can't live like a bird in a cage."

Lauren held her hand up. "What do you mean, you ran away from the people who wanted to put you in the Colony? I don't understand. I thought your mother took Donnie to the Colony herself. That's what I was told. After Sarah and your brothers died."

"Ma went willingly, if you can call it that. She didn't have no choice. They were goin' to take Donnie from her. She couldn't give him up so she went too. The other boys ran off. I hid and waited every day for two weeks for them to come back for me, but they didn't. Then one day, those Bramley boys came sniffin' around so I took off as soon as darkness fell. I stayed with some friends higher up in the mountains, but they got their own troubles. I came here about six weeks ago. I had no choice, nowhere else to go."

"So, no one knows you're here?"

"Big Will does. I had to tell someone in case Ma came back. Or my brothers. But he hasn't heard nothin'. He went to the Colony once, to ask after Ma, but they sent him way. My family, they all just disappeared."

Lauren recoiled in horror, her breath catching in her throat. She shook with shame. She hated asking Becky to risk her freedom, but she couldn't take on the orphanage without her. She didn't know the first thing about looking after a house, cleaning or cooking. She'd never entertained a child for more than a few hours, never mind taken responsibility for one.

"I promise you, Becky, that you are safe. Those men aren't interested in you now. They wanted to clear the land for the Park. You can trust me, believe me. Please, Becky, I need you and the children need you."

"Miss Lauren, they'll find me. I can't go into that Colony place. I'd rather die free on the mountain."

Lauren grasped Becky's arms. "You aren't going there, Becky. And I don't want to hear any more talk of dying either. You can stay here and help me. We can do this together."

Becky wrenched herself out of Lauren's grasp, putting a small distance between them. She shook her head and although her voice faltered, she sounded like she'd made up her mind: "No, Miss Lauren. It just won't work. You'll have to find someone else to help you."

"I don't know how to do it and my father—"

"Well, then, why don't you just run along back to your life? You're just the same as all the rest of those God-lovin' rich women who came to visit: all mouth and no action. We don't need your sort here. Go on with you!"

Lauren stamped her foot in the dirt, sending up a cloud of dust. "I don't think I ever met such a stubborn girl in all my life. I do care, thank you very much, and I'm not going anywhere. I just need to be able to make things workable. The truth is my father wants me to get married. I am trying to find a way to change his mind, but if I were to work here it wouldn't help matters, it would just annoy him."

At Becky's knowing expression, Lauren wanted to explode.

"What about if I put my name on the papers for the orphanage and write to the people who are supposed to be in charge to tell them that I am taking over? In reality, it would be you who would run the place. That way, no one at the County office will know you're here."

Lauren waited for a response, but Becky just stared at her.

Lauren hated begging but she couldn't simply walk away from what she had seen. "I can't move in here, Becky. It's just not possible. But I can visit. I'll come most days and help you out." Lauren crossed her fingers, knowing that her father and Justin might find a way to stop her. "Patty will help too," she carried on. "We can employ some other people."

"And pay them with what? Your head is still in the clouds."

"But what options do you have? You would have stayed on the mountain if you could have made it work, yet you ended up here. You could have run away, but you stayed. You love those children. I know it and so do you. Please, Becky, can we just try it? For three months? If it doesn't work, you can leave, but you will have a reference and will be able to get a paying job in Charlottesville or Richmond, or even leave Virginia."

Becky's face broke into a smile. "You're about as ornery as the mule my daddy used to have. I guess we will give your way a try for a time."

Lauren wanted to hug the girl, but knew that wouldn't be appropriate. She settled on a smile.

"I think you goin' to give me some sleepless nights, Miss Lauren. You soundin' just like Nanny Kat."

"Thank you," Lauren said, relief washing over her.

"Don't thank me yet, you have no idea what you've taken on."

CHAPTER 48

Back in the house, Matron hadn't moved from her desk.

"You want me to help you pack?" Lauren asked.

"I've been thinking," the woman said, slyly. "You can't just throw me out, you got to pay me off. I have wages due."

"I know how much money you've spent on moonshine. Cash that should have been spent on the children." Matron's face paled. "After what I've seen, I've decided you're not spending another night here. Get packed and I'll give you a ride to the nearest bus station." Lauren started to leave the room, then turned back. "How do you keep the orphans so quiet? I would have expected them to be crying or screaming, or maybe even laughing, although that's hard to imagine, given how they live. What have you done to them?"

The woman's eyes shifted to the whiskey bottle. Lauren put out a hand to the wall, the realization hitting her. "You feed whiskey to the children?"

"Keeps 'em quiet, don't it?"

"Get up and pack your things now." Lauren's voice filled the shabby room.

"What if I refuse?"

"I will drive you to the local sheriff's office and have you charged with murder of a child."

"I ain't murdered anyone."

"Haven't you? You may not have killed a child with your own hands but you are culpable. How many children have died during your tenure at this orphanage?"

"They come in with all sorts of diseases. I'm no doctor."

"You don't need a medical qualification to know children need clean clothes, clean surroundings, and good food. Now what's it to be?"

The matron seemed to crumple before her eyes. Lauren steeled herself, trying not to let pity into her heart for the woman as she put her head in her hands and sobbed. She forced herself to think of Justin Prendergast to keep her anger alive. Otherwise she might find herself hugging the woman.

Matron swallowed noisily. "I was like you once. I can see myself in your eyes. You won't believe me, but I didn't run a children's home for the money. I always loved children. Fifteen years ago, I had my life all planned out. My family was never rich, but my parents were comfortable. I was engaged to be married to the nicest man you ever met. Steve Murray was his name. We were going to run a store and have a large family. But then he went to France, to fight in the war."

"I'm sorry," Lauren replied, feeling her resolve starting to crumble.

"No, he weren't killed in the war. If he had of been, I might have understood more. Steve came home but he brought that nasty flu with him. His whole family died over the space of two weeks. They didn't stand a chance."

Lauren listened, letting the matron carry on.

"I couldn't look at another man so I decided to work with children. I was good at it too. I had an empty heart and they had lots of love to give. Whooping cough hit us in nineteen twenty-seven. At one point we had fourteen children in quarantine. I nursed them day and night, but only five of them survived." Matron's temper flared. "I nursed them properly, just the way I'd been taught, but we didn't have the right facilities or the medicines. The County wouldn't help us once the money ran out."

"Oh my..."

"Yes, ma'am." She took a deep breath. "After ten years of spending my own money, scrimping and saving, and trying to get donations from friends to run this place, I just couldn't do it anymore. We managed until the stock market crash, just about. We didn't get to do any painting or repairs, but the children didn't go hungry. They didn't have new clothes but they had plenty of cast-offs. We made do and we were all happy. But then the money dried up and the food donations, the clothes, everything that had been holding us together fell apart."

Matron looked up, catching Lauren's stare. She held her gaze.

"At first, I had a little drink in the evenings to help me sleep. Then it was a drink in the morning to get me going. Soon, I was drinking a bottle of apple shine a fortnight, then it was a week. If there's one thing we got around here, it's plenty of apples." Matron held her shaking hands up for Lauren to see. "I can't function without it now. I know what I've done and what I've let happen to the children living here. I'm sorry for it, I am, but I can't change the past." She pulled herself into a standing position, straightened her dress, and stood up straighter.

Despite all the woman's faults, Lauren found herself softening toward the matron. "I'm sorry your life turned out like it did," she said. "Do you have somewhere to go? Family to take you in?"

Tears gathered in the matron's eyes. "Yes, I've kin living in Washington. My widowed sister, she'll take me in." The woman swallowed hard. "I hope you succeed, young lady, but I can tell you now your chances are next to impossible. Don't nobody care about children like this lot in the good times. In these bad times, they ain't on anyone's list of priorities."

"But they are on mine."

CHAPTER 49

Lauren, Mary, and Patty stood looking at the orphanage, two days after Matron had gone. Becky was busy in the kitchen. Lauren saw that Patty was holding onto Mary's hand as though her very life depended on it. Justin had so much to answer for, she thought. Even as his name popped into her head, she pushed it out again. She had more important things to consider than that man. He was worse than the dirt beneath her feet. Worse than one of those snakes that she was sure were hiding in the grass on one side of the house.

Thinking of those snakes, Lauren said, "That grass has to be cut back. There could be all sorts hiding in it and this area will make a nice play area for the children." She imagined the grass cut down, the brambles cut right back, and the children playing on a rope swing or having a game of baseball.

Mary shrugged. "I don't think a play area is the first thing you should have on your list." She pointed to the house. "Look at the roof. The shingles are loose and some are missing. It doesn't look like it's straight to me. See, if you pick out that mountain peak over there and keep that in view as well as the roof, isn't it listing to one side?"

"We'll get someone to look at it. We need to make the house bigger."

"Miss Lauren, you need to fix it up first."

"I know that, but we need more space. The kitchen area is too cramped for everyone. It'd make more sense to rebuild the kitchen and at the same time put in a bathroom."

"You can't get used to that outhouse, can you?" Mary teased. Lauren had told her of the horror of the place.

Lauren shivered. Just thinking about the outhouse brought the stench right back into her nostrils.

"Miss Lauren, how are you going to pay for everything?" Mary asked.

"I have accounts at the stores."

"You mean your father does. He isn't going to like you funding this."

"He's away at the moment so he won't notice. We should take advantage. Anyway, part of his money was Mama's and from what Nanny told me about her, I know she'd want me to do something like this. Oh, Mary, I've just had the best idea! You and Jed could work in the orphanage when you get married."

Mary's face fell, but before she answered Lauren, she turned to Patty. "Patty, you should go back in the house, it's rather hot and you need to think of your baby. Have some water to drink. I will be in just after I finish talking to Miss Lauren."

They watched as the girl disappeared into the house.

"Miss Lauren, you can't afford to employ me and Jed and even if you could, I… I can't stay here. Jed is going West and I love him, Miss Lauren. He's my future. We'll get married right after his latest job finishes in October, and then head out to California."

"Don't mind me, I was just being selfish." Lauren tried to cover her hurt. "Now, where was I?"

The maid surprised her then by wrapping her in a hug. "Miss Lauren, you know I love you. I always will, no matter where I live. Don't you forget that."

"I'm thrilled for you, Mary, I really am, but I can't help hating the thought of losing you. I know it's selfish, but with you and Nanny gone, who will I have as friends?"

"The post works in California, too, Miss Lauren. I'll write to you. We've been together almost our whole lives, apart from when you went away to school or to Europe. We've got shared history and nobody and nothing can take that away."

Lauren dabbed at her eyes. "Right, come on, we have a lot of work to do."

"Miss Lauren, are you really going to clean the orphanage?"

"Of course I am. It's too disgusting for words."

"But you've never cleaned a pot, never mind a house."

Lauren shrugged. "How hard can it be?"

*

Lauren soon regretted those words. How did Mary and Patty deal with these chores every day? It was never-ending. The following day, Mary had got everything they needed from Hillmans' Store and together, she and Lauren had driven over to the orphanage. At the last minute, Sam had jumped on board, wanting to see how Patty was doing. With William Greenwood still in Richmond on business, Sam could take a few hours off.

When they had arrived at the orphanage, Patty had run out to meet them and Sam had swung the girl around like she was a small child. The transformation in Patty was miraculous. Becky had been pleased to see Mary again, and Sam soon put Becky at her ease. Now he was busy fixing shelves and doors for her downstairs.

Lauren and Mary agreed to tackle the upstairs while Patty would help Becky look after the children. Today, Lauren had given Becky the suitcase of clothes and other things that she and Mary had found in the attics at Rosehall: "Don't let the children try on any of the clothes until they've had a bath, Patty."

"I won't, Miss Lauren."

Lauren climbed the stairs, determined she would do her share of the work. She started by sweeping the floor of the room the younger children used.

"What are you doing, Miss Lauren?" Mary asked when she came to check on her.

"Sweeping. What does it look like?" Lauren answered, blowing dust out of her mouth.

"Miss Lauren, you have to clear out the room before you can clean it. You need to tackle those cobwebs and all these cots need to be stripped down, the bedding washed or incinerated. The floor is the last thing you should do." Mary bent down and pulled up a patch of carpet. "I reckon you should get rid of the carpet. There is no vacuum cleaner and no amount of tea leaves will get the dust off this thing. The moths have already been feasting on it. Goodness knows what else it's infested with."

Lauren's skin crawled at the maid's words.

Mary glanced at Lauren and started laughing.

"What's so funny?"

"Miss Lauren, you should see yourself. You have more dust in your hair than there is on the dresser downstairs! You should have wrapped a towel around your head."

Lauren had never felt so useless.

"Miss Lauren, why don't you do some work in Matron's office? There is so much paperwork to be sorted out in there. You might be able to find out how Matron Werth funded this place. Go on now, leave the cleaning to us."

Defeated, Lauren handed the broom to Mary and walked downstairs to the office. Someone had already removed the whiskey bottles, dirty glasses, plates, and cutlery. The window had been cleaned too. All the papers had been placed on the desk so the chairs were bare now. They looked worn and threadbare in places, but at least they were clean. She guessed Mary had already worked her magic in this room. Her suspicions were confirmed when Patty arrived in with a cup of tea.

"Becky said to give you this and ask you to figure how to pay the bills. She doesn't want anyone calling here for payment."

"Thank you, Patty."

"Miss Lauren, thank you for bringing Sam today. I missed him. When my parents died, Sam and his ma, Ole Sally, they looked after me."

"He's a good man."

"Yes, Miss Lauren, he is."

"Patty, could you introduce me to the children? I have to learn their names."

She smiled. "They're nice. Well, most of them. Shelley needs patience. She's very angry but I think she's just hurt at being dumped by her parents."

Curious, Lauren waited for Patty to explain.

"Shelley says her ma had two children, her and a boy. She heard the parents talking one night about not being able to feed four mouths. They decided to leave Shelley here so they could go to California."

"Shelley heard all that? No wonder she's angry."

"Yes, but all the others have sad stories too, Miss Lauren. Shelley isn't the only one. You just wait till you get to know them." Patty walked with her out to the yard, where some of the children were standing around. "This is Terry, he's the eldest. Fred is the red-haired boy next to Lottie, his sister."

"Fred is the boy Matron beat. I don't think I'll ever forget his name." Lauren shuddered, pushing that image out of her mind. "What about the girl with the red birthmark?"

"That's Ellie-Mae."

"And her brother?"

"Dalton, but he isn't her brother, at least they aren't related by birth. They came here together and Dalton won't let anyone near Ellie-Mae unless he is present."

"How am I going to remember all these names?" Lauren addressed the children, smiling at them as she spoke.

Terry answered. "Just call us boy or girl. That's what Matron did."

Lauren stared at him, not wanting to believe him, but she could see that he wasn't making it up.

"Nice to meet you, Terry. I may forget some names until I learn them all, but I will never address you as boy. That, I promise you."

Terry just blinked, he didn't smile or scowl. His face was almost expressionless. He turned and limped away. She wondered what happened to his leg.

"Miss Lauren, you best get to the office. Becky said to keep—"

"Keep?"

"Keep you out of trouble," Patty whispered, her eyes on the ground.

Lauren leaned in and hugged the girl. Then she grinned. "Best do what Becky says then."

CHAPTER 50

Lauren sat at the desk, working her way through the mound of papers. She might not be able to clean, but she would get on top of this paperwork or her name wasn't Lauren Greenwood.

The hours flew by and the problems she had taken on grew in magnitude. It looked as though Matron hadn't bothered to make any payments in a long time. There were notices from the electricity company and demands for payment from most of the stores in Delgany. The orphanage owed Hillmans' Store, Miss Chaney the postmistress, and there were unpaid bills outstanding at the sawmill and the garage. She hadn't seen any trucks on the property, so what had Matron used to ferry the children or supplies around in?

A knock on the door broke into her thoughts. "Miss Lauren, you and I need to head back to Rosehall now. It's getting late."

"Is it?" Lauren glanced out the window. The evening dusk was slipping down from the mountain, through the trees in the orchard. The wind carried the sweet scent of apples, making Lauren realize how hungry she was.

"Isn't that a gorgeous view?" she said as she watched the dying sun disappear, turning the sky delicious shades of red and pink. "*Red sky at night, shepherd's delight.*" Was that how the old rhyme went?

"How did you get on in here?"

Lauren screwed up her face.

"That bad?"

"Mary, it's worse. The orphanage owes money all over town. I can't think of a store that isn't due payment."

"You knew it would be a mess once you met the woman in charge."

"I did, but I guess I underestimated just how bad it was." Lauren looked up in time to see Mary trying to hold back a yawn. "I've worn you out, haven't I?"

"I'll live. Come and see the changes we've made."

Leaving the office, Lauren found they had stripped the stairs bare of the carpet. "Sam pulled it up and threw it out," Mary told her. "It was a hazard, particularly if Patty was to fall. Her being pregnant and everything."

"Good for Sam." Lauren followed Mary up the stairs to the second floor.

"We weren't able to get all the rooms done, so we prioritized two. We've made one for girls and one for the boys."

Lauren walked into the first room. Barely recognizable, it reeked of petroleum fighting with lemon polish. She wrinkled her nose, and when the smell became overpowering, she put her hand over it.

"Sorry about the smell, but what we've used will kill everything that shouldn't live in here," Mary explained.

There were fewer cots in the room and those that had survived all had clean bedding. Every surface shone. The window sparkled and the light streaming in no longer highlighted dust motes floating in the air. The ceiling and light hanging were free of cobwebs and the floor, although stripped bare, looked spotless too.

"Mary, you've performed a miracle! This doesn't look like the same room at all."

"It still needs work. A new rug for the floor would be nice, to keep out drafts in the winter. We had to throw out some cots, but Sam reckons there are some he can repair. These have been stripped and treated with the flint gun, that's what causes the smell. It should be gone tomorrow."

Lauren hoped she was right.

The next room had the same strong scent and they had cleaned it from top to bottom. A couple of the beds were bare and the room was practically sparkling.

"We had to throw out most of the mattresses, owing to them being infested. Nothing would have saved them. The children will have to sleep on the floor until we can buy or make new ones."

"I will speak to Mrs. Hillman." She could see by the maid's expression she wanted to argue. "Mary, I have to get Mrs. Hillman on side as we will need things regularly. We can trust her, we have no choice. You can't go shopping for me when you live in California." She knew Mary disagreed, but the maid was too tired to argue. "We'll also need sheets and blankets. How are the children faring? Did Becky and Patty get them all washed and treated?"

"Yes. Some boys got their heads shaved. It's easier to get rid of the nits that way. But the girls, it would be too cruel to do that. Becky used a ton of larkspur. There were lots of tears, but Patty doled out the candy you brought so that helped."

Despite herself, Lauren scratched her head. She caught what she was doing and exchanged a grin with Mary. "Can't help it. Every time I think of those things crawling on the children, I get itchy."

"Maybe we should dose your hair with larkspur too?"

Lauren burst into laughter.

"Come on, Miss Lauren. You, me, and Sam have got to get back to Rosehall before Cook sends a search party. Tomorrow is another day."

CHAPTER 51

Lauren groaned when she spotted Jackson at the front door. She'd dropped Sam and Mary off at the servants' entrance first. She'd also changed into a fresh set of clothes before leaving the orphanage. The blouse and skirt were old but clean.

"Evening, Jackson, were you waiting for someone or just admiring the mountain view?" she said sweetly as he walked over to hold the door for her.

"Your father came home early, Miss Lauren. He requests your presence in the study."

Her heart beat faster, but she contained herself. She refused to let this spy see the impact of his words.

"Thank you, Jackson. I will just go up and change."

"He said as soon as you got in, Miss Lauren."

"I'm sure Father would expect me to make myself presentable." She knew it was childish, but she had to have the last word.

She walked into the house and as soon as she knew Jackson couldn't see her, she ran up the stairs, undoing the buttons on her blouse as she did so. She threw her clothes on the bed and changed into a new dress. Combining it with heels and a spray of perfume, she was back downstairs to greet her father in the study within moments.

"Father, you're home early. I wasn't expecting you this evening." She forced herself to walk over to him and kiss him on the cheek, ignoring his glare of disapproval. Then, over his shoulder, she spotted Justin rising from a chair. Her heart plummeted. She could hardly stand the sight of him. She tried to hide her trembling hands behind her back, not wanting either man to see her fear.

"Justin, you should have sent word you were calling over. I would have—"

"Where were you, Lauren?" her father asked, sitting in a chair by the fire. "We called the house, but Jackson didn't know where you were or when you would be home. He couldn't find Mary either. One might almost deduce you had run away."

"Run away? Why would I have done that? I have a wedding to plan." Lauren sank into a chair opposite her father, relieved that her shaking legs no longer had to support her body. "I was out shopping. I have seen the most gorgeous new designs that I must have for our honeymoon, Justin." She smiled at him briefly, telling herself not to overdo it and hoping that her white knuckles on the arms of her chair didn't give her away.

"Darling, I will buy you as many dresses as you like," Justin said. "Mother was wondering when you would come over to discuss the wedding. She had expected to see you before now, as I think you know."

Lauren ignored the rebuke, laughing as if he amused her. "That's my fault—getting married ties up so much time. I shall telephone her and call over."

"Tomorrow, Lauren."

She nodded in response to his curt remark.

Dinner and the rest of the evening dragged by. Lauren wanted to run and hide but forced her feet to stay still. The combination of little sleep and hard work at the orphanage meant she was exhausted, but she couldn't risk Father's or Justin's disapproval by requesting an early night. She made herself appear docile and compliant, even if she did have to bite her lip more than once. Especially when they discussed the *Charlottesville News*.

Justin was particularly incensed. "Belmont should be taken out and strung up with a copy of his paper shoved down his throat. The gall of the man!"

"Just ignore him, Justin. If my sources are correct, his distribution is reducing, and he's finding it difficult to source advertising," her father told him. "Without the money from the advertising, the paper will fold. It is only a matter of waiting."

"In the meantime, I just let him print his scurrilous lies, do I?"

"Could you not sue him for character defamation?" Lauren couldn't resist asking the question. She knew the answer. Justin could only pursue that route if he was innocent and, knowing her fiancé, that was unlikely.

"He could," her father jumped in, "but Justin has more important things on his mind, like your wedding and upcoming honeymoon. He has to make sure all his various businesses are best placed to thrive in his absence. Your husband-to-be is such a hard-working, actively involved man that he will be difficult to replace, if only for a few months."

"Months?" Lauren repeated.

"Justin has told me of your plans to visit London and Europe and the Far East. I never knew you wanted to travel to the Pacific Islands, darling. Wouldn't fancy it myself. Can't tell a Chinaman from a Jap."

Lauren couldn't bear her father's racist remarks, but it was useless trying to correct his views. *Why does Justin want to visit Japan?* She would love to see the country, but not with him. *What is he up to?* She shivered.

"Lauren, darling, I'm tired. I think I'll call it a night and leave you two lovebirds to it."

"Actually, Father, you beat me to it. I was just going to ask to be excused. It's been a long day." Lauren yawned loudly, earning a look of rebuke for her unladylike manners. But she didn't care about that. She just had to get out the room before her father.

Her legs shook as she stood up, staggering slightly as she clumsily knocked over her cup. She was terrified of being alone with Justin, and she willed her father to understand, but she might just as well have wished for Nanny to appear.

"Please excuse my clumsiness, I'm having trouble sleeping." She couldn't bear to touch Justin, never mind kiss him good night. She strode to the door, only turning when the handle was in her grip. "Good night, Father. Justin, sleep well."

She was gone before her father or her fiancé could call her back.

Lauren feigned a chill for the rest of the weekend. Only when Justin had left for Richmond, did she come out of her room.

"You will have to find a better way to deal with that man. You can't fake illness every time he visits." Mary was tending to Lauren's hair at the mirror.

"I have to get away, Mary. I know that. But when I leave Rosehall, Father will cut off all my access to his accounts. I must buy everything we need before I burn my bridges."

"Don't leave it too long or you may end up being burned, Miss Lauren."

CHAPTER 52

Lauren parked outside the orphanage and watched as several of the children ran outside, but stopped short of coming near her Cadillac. They looked cleaner than they had on her first visit, she thought, but they were still too quiet.

As she looked around at them all, she found she could remember most of their names. Some children were easier to identify than others. Ellie-Mae always had her hair down, covering her large red birthmark, her eyes glued to the ground. Dalton was never far away from her side. Brother and sister, Fred and Lottie, clung to each other's hands. Shelley, whose temper Lauren had witnessed a few times, often stood with her hands on her hips as if she was about to launch into battle.

These kids still expect something horrible to happen to them, Lauren thought to herself. *The days of being punished are all too real in their minds. What could she do to encourage them to run around and play in the grass, jump in the muddy puddles, and go fishing for frog spawn?* She pushed her worries from her mind, put a smile on her face, and forced cheer into her voice: "Good morning, everyone."

Most of the children didn't answer, simply staring at her. She smiled at them all, but they didn't react. Then the door flew open and Patty came running out.

"Morning, Miss Lauren." Patty's face fell. "Are you on your own today?"

"Yes, Patty. The others had to work at Rosehall. How are you feeling?"

The girl didn't reply. She turned around and walked back into the house, her shoulders slumped.

Tempted to call her back to help her, Lauren enlisted the children's help instead: "I have some things to bring in for Becky. Can you help me, please?"

"What you got?" asked Terry, who had joined the other children in the yard.

"Food and…" She didn't have time to finish as the children crowded round the trunk, waiting for her to hand out the packages.

"Take the basket to the kitchen, please. The other bags you can leave in Matron's office. Be careful, don't carry anything that's too heavy. Don't let the basket drop, it has cookies in it."

The children cheered as they carried the items inside, and Becky came out to see what all the noise was about.

"Morning, Miss Lauren, be you limping?"

"Becky, I have pains and aches where I never had them before. They've lasted all weekend. How do you manage every day?"

"Practice, miss. You'll learn."

She wished she shared the girl's optimism. She handed Becky two books she'd brought her. Becky's eyes glowed as she read out the titles. "I love Charles Dickens. Thank you, Miss Lauren."

"We need to do something about the track up here. Hitting the holes in it makes my bones shake every time."

"I reckon we got other things to be worried about first, Miss Lauren. Like the new bed mattresses, ticking for covers, clothes…"

Lauren threw her hands in the air, cutting Becky off mid-sentence. "Coffee first, please, Becky. I can't think until I'm awake."

"You don't usually get up this early? That figures."

As she sipped her coffee, Lauren surveyed the reformed kitchen. It looked better now that Sam had whitewashed the walls, fixed some cupboards, and put up some shelving units. The table wasn't big enough for all the children to sit around at the same time, though, and they needed a properly plumbed sink. The sink in the kitchen was old and in disrepair. Hauling water from the well, out by the barn, was exhausting and would be a filthy job once the weather turned worse.

"Sam worked hard in here, didn't he?" Lauren said, admiring his handiwork.

"Yes, he did. He's a fine man. Promised me some new presses too. If he can get the time to make them."

"I'll make sure he gets the time and the lumber. Why don't you make a list of the things you would like in the kitchen and we can see about getting them?"

"Miss Lauren, you ever managed household budgets? Is that your job at your house?"

Lauren shook her head. "Father looks after the money. I think Cook has some input, but I never get involved. Why?"

"Cause you seem to spend money like it was water. All the materials you bought in Hillmans', the glass for the windows, and the things Sam fixed. I worry you'll run out."

"Don't think of money, Becky. My father has endless credit at the stores and he owes me a lot more than a few hundred dollars. I am going to buy some more things over the next few days, so please make that list."

The girl's eyes bulged. "I never stop thinkin' of money. I gotten a lot of mouths to feed here."

"Becky, for now I aim to take advantage of my father's wealth. The time will come, maybe soon, when he will notice and close my credit facilities. Until then, we will buy what we need."

"That be stealin'." Becky's face paled. "The sheriff will close us down and send the children to the Nuns or Brothers or them other places."

"Becky, stop it! You aren't doing anything wrong and I am certainly not stealing. My father inherited Rosehall when Mama died but it will come to me eventually, so my fiancé reminded me!" Lauren swallowed the bitter taste in her mouth. "Time is running out, so do me a favor and just make a list of everything you need. Don't think about the cost. We can prioritize things later. For now, just write and don't think."

Becky gave her an incredulous look, but she didn't argue. Lauren handed her a jotter and pencil.

"How was Patty after we left? I know our going away again upset her, but is she getting used to living here, at least for now?"

"No, Miss Lauren. I think bringing those folks from your house made it worse. Showed her what she's missing. I knows you had to bring them here and I'm grateful. We got more done with Mary and Sam's help than I could have ever done on my own. But it's hard on the girl. She's young, she's got to grow up fast."

"She's lucky to have someone like you here to care for her. I'll try to speak to Henry again. He wouldn't see me the last time I called at Spencer's Garage. His uncle said he was too upset. Why won't people believe Patty was innocent and the baby is not at fault?"

"No point in askin' me about why people think the way they do."

Lauren nodded, understanding her meaning. "Would you like me to try to find out what happened to your family? I can try again."

"No, thank you, Miss Lauren." Becky's eyes shone with unshed tears. "I don't want to attract any attention to me right now. I got people lookin' out for them. Mountain folk like the Thatchers. They'll be lettin' me know if they hear anythin'. But would you mind giving me a lift into Delgany? I need some cornstarch, some bluin', and some kerosene."

Lauren smiled. "Sure, we can go right now. What's bluin'?"

Becky roared with laughter. "Easy to see you never had to do laundry, Miss Lauren. What's bluin' indeed? That's a good one."

*

When they got back to the orphanage, the children barged past Lauren and came running to greet Becky, smiling and hugging her as if she had been gone for months and not hours. Lauren walked into the house almost unnoticed until Ellie-Mae came up to her. Chocolate covered the child's lips.

"Miss Lauren, why do you look so sad?"

"I was just thinking, Ellie-Mae. What are you doing today?"

"Carly was showing me and the other girls how to cook. She let us lick the bowl."

"I can see that."

"Want to come and see the cake?" Ellie-Mae held her hand out, but her eyes were anxious. What type of world taught a young girl to be wary of affection?

"I'd love to see, thank you." Lauren held the child's sticky hand and listened to her chatter as they walked to the house and into the kitchen. A rather lopsided cake sat on the table.

"Ellie-Mae, I think that's about the nicest cake I ever saw."

"Miss Lauren, now you're smiling. Chocolate cake always makes me smile too," Ellie-Mae said.

On impulse, Lauren bent down and picked up the little girl, giving her a kiss on the cheek and swinging her around in the air. Ellie-Mae giggled before demanding Lauren do it again. Then she saw Lottie eyeing them. She held out her arms to the solemn-eyed three-year-old: "You want to do the same?"

Lottie nodded, so Lauren picked her up, kissed her, and twirled her around too. The child put her arms around Lauren's neck, her little head snuggling into her shoulder. Tears glistened in Lauren's eyes as Lottie held tighter. She hugged the girl back and swore these children would never want for love or food again. Not while she was still breathing.

CHAPTER 53

Lauren patted Prince as she rubbed him down. They'd gone riding up the mountain that morning and the horse had enjoyed it just as much as she had.

"I've been neglecting you lately, boy, haven't I? But you should just see the children, Prince. They have so little."

The horse butted her side, looking for apples. "You are just like a man, aren't you? I'm telling you all my sorrows and you're thinking of your stomach." She gave him an apple and kissed his nose. "You deserve it."

"You all right, Miss Lauren? You been talkin' a long time to that horse."

Lauren twirled at Sam's voice. "Sorry, Sam, you made me jump. I wasn't paying attention."

"That be obvious. You and that horse." He came closer, patting Prince. "How's Patty doin'?"

Lauren wanted to say something good to put a smile on the man's face but she couldn't lie.

"She's not doing too well, Sam. She misses Rosehall, you and old Sally, Mary, even Cook, although that woman was less than charitable to her. Becky and I have tried all sorts of things, but nothing clears the sadness in her eyes."

Sam rubbed Prince in silence.

"Have you any ideas, Sam?"

"None fittin' for your ears, Miss Lauren. I'll pray for her."

"Can you include me and the children in your prayers too, Sam. We need them."

"Always do, Miss Lauren. Nanny too. Someday we will all be together again."

Sam turned away and blew his nose noisily before straightening up. "Old Sally has some jars of her remedies for you. Wanted me to pack 'em up and put 'em in the car for your next trip. She says it's only fittin' for you to be ready for anythin'. Children and accidents tend to run hand in hand."

Lauren put her hand on his arm. "Thank you, Sam, and please thank Old Sally for me. Your kindness is more than I deserve."

*

Lauren found Becky in the back yard, muttering to herself.

"What time do you call this? I need to know what time you will be here, Miss Lauren. There's a man been sittin' waitin' for you this past hour," Becky greeted her.

"A man?" The hairs on the back of her neck stood up as she looked around her. Was it Justin? Her father? Her stomach clenched as she jammed her hands under her armpits to hide their shaking. She whispered, "What does he want? What does he look like?"

Becky was looking at her like she had two heads.

"What do you mean, 'What does he look like?' He's about the same as every other scruffy man we know, only he's wearin' someone else's suit. He wants us to take his children."

Lauren looked at the dilapidated house and back at Becky.

"What are you lookin' at me for? Why don't you go speak to him?"

"What do I say?" Lauren asked nervously.

"How do I know? I never met with the parents, Matron did that. So off you go."

Lauren straightened her back. *You can handle this*, she told herself.

When she got inside the house, she found the man sitting on the stairs. She hid a smile as she saw what Becky meant by him wearing someone else's suit. The trousers seemed to hang around his hips rather than his waist and the jacket was at least two sizes too big. His brown hair was speckled with gray, too long to be fashionable, and judging by the smell emanating from him, he needed a bath as much as he needed a shave. His cheekbones protruded too sharply and he looked half-starved. He hopped up as soon as he saw her.

"Sorry, ma'am, I was just restin' my legs. Name's Bart Leroy."

"Come into the office, please," Lauren said, trying to sound as professional as she could, and feeling like a fraud the whole time.

She pushed the office door open—at least the space was clean, she reasoned. Her guest hovered in front of the desk as if afraid to take a seat. He looked lost, standing there in his oversized suit, staring at the chair. *Had he borrowed the outfit from someone larger-sized?*

"Good morning, Mr. Leroy. Why don't you take a seat?"

Lauren tried to put the man at ease by taking a seat in the chair nearest the one she indicated for him. Maybe he would be more comfortable speaking to her if the desk wasn't between them.

"Ma'am, thank you for seein' me. I'm here about my two girls. Me and the wife, we've tried our best, but we just can't do it anymore. My girls are cryin' goin' to bed, too hungry to sleep. I haven't had a job in over two years, not since the Depression really hit hard. I've tried, ma'am, worn out the shoe leather walkin' for miles to find work. I found a day or two during the summer months, here and there. That kept the wolf from the door, but now we got no door."

Lauren let him speak, sensing he needed to get a burden off his chest.

"The bank, they foreclosed a while ago, but nobody came so we just stayed on livin' there. I was born in that house. It's only a small, one-bedroom place. I didn't think anyone would be interested in it, but those bank people brought the sheriff. He threatened to arrest me if we didn't vacate by Friday."

"Tomorrow?"

"Yes, ma'am. Myself and the wife can survive on the open roads, but my girls can't. They are too young for a start, but they've also been sick." The man looked stricken at this admission. "They ain't sick no more. They better, but they're skin and bones and I worry if we take them on the road and have no shelter and no food then they might…" He couldn't keep talking, tears now running down his cheeks.

Lauren pushed a clean hanky toward him, wanting to say the right thing but not able to find the words. What was this country coming to when a decent, caring human being had to give up his own children?

"Mr. Leroy, when was the last time you had something to eat?"

"Been a while, ma'am."

"Why don't you rest there a minute and I'll get you something. Then you can tell me about your girls."

"Thank you, ma'am. They say about town you be an angel sent from God to help us in these times."

Lauren's breakfast turned to a rock in her stomach. *About town*… *What exactly were they saying?* "Those people must be thinking of Becky, Mr. Leroy. I'm no angel, I just try to help a little. Now let me get the food." She hurried out the door, more to compose herself than in any rush to find food for him. She found women's tears hard to bear, but when a grown man cried, her heart bled for him.

Once in the kitchen, Lauren spotted Becky out by the washing line, playing a game with the little ones. She smiled at the sound of the children's laughter. She poured out a bowl of oatmeal, sliced a couple of thin pieces of bread, and poured water into a cup. She sensed Mr. Leroy's stomach wouldn't be able to manage more and the last thing she wanted was to make him ill.

After carrying the tray back into the office, she saw, to her relief, that Mr. Leroy was more composed. He jumped up when he saw the tray, taking it from her.

"Lay it on the desk, please, Mr. Leroy. Eat slowly. Don't try to keep the bread for your family, you need to eat too. I will pack you a small basket to take home to your wife and children." Lauren went to the opposite side of her desk and moved some papers around, trying to give him some privacy to eat.

How can I take on two more young girls, she wondered. *We are filled to the rafters already. We have too many children and not enough beds. And what will happen to this man if he no longer has the thought of hungry children driving him on? He looks so thin already, he won't survive the trek on the road.*

When Mr. Leroy had eaten, he sat back. "Thank you, ma'am," he said gratefully.

"Becky cooked. You wouldn't be able to eat my offerings, I'm still learning." She joked, trying to put him at ease, but he sat there staring at his hands.

"About my girls…"

"What ages are they?"

"Clarissa, she be comin' up for five and Bean, I mean Sophie, will be three next month. We call her Bean."

"Lovely names." Lauren smiled. "Mr. Leroy, did you farm your land?"

"Yes, ma'am. Did real well, especially the years of the war. I went off to fight and left my pa workin' fields of wheat. He got good money for it too. But then the prices fell and Pa fell sick. Between the money for the doctor's bills and the fall in prices, we got behind with the house payments. I didn't know Pa had mortgaged the place to buy more land for more wheat. When I came back, I switched to growin' cotton, but I wasn't good at that. I planted fields of cabbages, cucumbers, string beans, corn, tomatoes, sweet potatoes, Irish potatoes—you name it—and watermelons.

The girls like the watermelons." He smiled briefly, then continued, "I also grew apples and peaches. I can grow just about anythin' bar cotton. My wife, Norma, she helped me until the girls grew sick. We'd had to sell the animals to make the payments to the bank and I guess the girls were missing the fresh milk. My wife, she be the best ma you could find. She looked after our two girls and never gave up. Not even when the doctor said they didn't stand a chance. But they did. My Norma wouldn't let them die."

Lauren had listened avidly. "Mrs. Leroy knows of your plan to go on the road?"

"She don't like it, ma'am, but she knows it's the only thing we can do. We ain't got any livin' folk who can help us. My Norma, she ran away to marry me. Her family didn't take kindly to my pa's politics." He took a drink of water.

Lauren took a deep breath, holding his gaze. She felt he deserved the truth. "I think you should know, I am new to this position. If I am honest, I don't know the first thing about running an orphanage. I don't know how to clean, cook or sew. I am about as useful as that hideous ornament on the mantelpiece."

They both stared at what looked like a mangled piece of iron.

"Do you care for the children? Are they fed well? Will you give the girls back to us when we find proper jobs and can give them a home, or will you give them away to someone else?" The questions burst out of him.

Lauren's mouth fell open. What sort of place would keep children away from their loving parents? "I don't have your permission to allow them to be adopted. They would stay here, of course they would. I wouldn't simply give them away."

"The thing is, other homes don't always worry about paperwork. Especially if rich folk take a shine to a certain child. My girls be as pretty as their ma, with green eyes and white-blonde hair. They be right up rich folks' street."

"Mr. Leroy, no child will be adopted from this orphanage unless they are an orphan or their parents give written permission. You can trust me on that front. But I have a proposition for you…"

An idea had been brewing.

"A what?"

"I'd like to offer you a job."

He rubbed his ear, his eyes widening. "A job?"

"Yes, but I have to warn you, the pay will be next to nothing. Instead, I'll give you a share of the crop you grow. We have plenty of land but no knowledge on what could be grown here, and no idea what to do with the plot. We need to produce food for the children but also to sell it to help pay the bills. The land has been neglected for years."

Mr. Leroy didn't speak, seeming to have forgotten how.

"Your wife, she could help Becky with the children and the cooking and cleaning. We have some rooms on the second floor and they are a mess, but maybe with some hard work, one of them could be used as your bedroom. Clarissa and Bean"—Mr. Leroy smiled at that—"could share the girls' dormitory, or they could sleep with you. Whatever you wish."

"You mean all this?"

"Yes, but I don't know how much I can pay you." She flushed. "I have inherited quite a number of bills and I'm not sure how much money I have to spare."

"I don't need payment. I'll work hard for you, miss, and my Norma will too. We'll do just about anythin' if it means we get to keep our girls, have a place to live, and somethin' to eat. When can we come here?"

CHAPTER 54

Bart headed home with a basket packed with some supplies for his family, promising to return the next day with his wife, Norma, and their two girls.

After he left, Becky was quieter than usual. Lauren wondered if she was missing her family.

"Are you okay, Becky? Are you thinking of your ma and Donnie?"

"I do that at night when I've time to think," Becky snapped. They were in the kitchen and Becky was busy preparing food for the children.

Lauren stayed silent, despite the urge to fill the uncomfortable silence.

"Miss Lauren, you can't go offerin' jobs to every tramp who knocks on the door. The place be fillin' up in no time."

"Mr. Leroy's not a tramp, he's a farmer. He will help us grow food and make this place some money."

"Hmph! He don't look like no farmer. What type of farmer wears a suit too big for him?"

"Becky, don't be mean. He hasn't eaten properly in a long time. I reckon that was his best suit at one time. I like him and I'm glad he's going to live here."

"But where, Miss Lauren? You going to fix him up in a hotel in town?"

"No, I told him he has to make one of the upper rooms habitable."

Becky stood, her hands going to her hips. "So, he's fixing the roof too?"

"Becky, please don't be like this. I had to help him. You didn't hear his story."

"I've heard plenty of stories in my life, Miss Lauren. You need to grow a thicker skin or we might as well call this place Hooverville, where anyone can set up home, expect to be fed, and be done with it. If you have your way, we will have tents with all sorts livin' all over the place. *This is an orphanage.*"

Lauren glanced out the window, biting her bottom lip. *Was I silly to offer a man a job without knowing anything about him?*

"Becky, all we can do is try," she replied, trying to save face. "If it doesn't work out, we'll ask him to move on."

"Raise his hopes and then pull the rug from under him. That's a good idea." Becky sighed loudly.

"I really am sorry, Becky. I should have discussed the Leroy family with you before I offered Bart a job. I didn't think about or consider your feelings."

"You don't need to. I just work here." The girl picked up a rag and started cleaning down the kitchen table.

"No, this is your home and I have invited strangers to live here. I would promise not to do it again, but as you have gathered, I am very good at making mistakes."

The girl pursed her lips.

"Do you want me to go tell him I've changed my mind?"

"You can't do that."

"I can. You are the backbone of this home. I can give him a few dollars and send him to Charlottesville. The charity workers there will help him."

"You'd do that?" Becky cocked her head, lifting one eyebrow.

"Yes. I told you from the start, you should be in charge. As you can see, I make a mess of things."

"You don't, Miss Lauren, but you have a soft heart. Not everyone you meet will tell you the truth. You just need to be careful, is all."

"You forgive me?"

"I'm thinkin' about it," Becky said, but her eyes were smiling.

CHAPTER 55
Delgany, September 1932

Mary stood in the middle of Mrs. Hillman's living room, holding her hands out by her sides as Mrs. Hillman and Miss Chaney argued over the correct fit for her wedding dress. She exchanged a smile with Lauren, who was sitting beside Jed's mother, Maureen. Lauren had taken Ellie-Mae and Dalton into Delgany to do some shopping and to see how Mary's dress fitting went.

"I'm glad you're here, Lauren. I thought I was the only one behind the door when God gave out good sewing skills." Maureen laughed self-consciously.

"No, I was definitely behind the door, too. Although I can embroider a hanky, if that's useful."

Everyone laughed at Lauren's joke, aware of her lack of housekeeping skills. Still, she was learning—she hadn't burned eggs all week.

"Ellie-Mae, would you bring me over those pins on the table, please?" Mrs. Hillman asked. The young girl jumped to help, carrying the pins like they were gold dollar pieces. She lit up when Mrs. Hillman praised her.

"I wish Patty would have come into town today," Mary said, her face a mask of concentration as both women told her to be still. "I don't move my arms when I speak," she protested to a round of "shush". Mary rolled her eyes, but Lauren could see the excitement in her face.

"Patty was scared people might make unkind comments. You know how some can be," said Lauren.

Lauren stared at Mrs. Hillman's carpeted floor for fear Mary would read the sorrow in her eyes. Patty wasn't doing well. As the weeks flew past, she seemed to be sliding further into despair. She hated her baby bump and took her temper out on the younger children. Lauren missed the happy young girl who used to sing all the time, who seemed to be lost to them, but she didn't know how to help her.

"That Flannery woman from the Newmarket Clothes Store for a start. Who died and made her head of this town? I wish her husband would put manners on her." Miss Chaney pulled a piece of material into place and sighed with satisfaction.

"Miss Chaney! You're not suggesting he should hit her?" Maureen held a hand to her mouth.

The old postmistress shook her head. "Of course not, Maureen. Just make her sit home until she has something nice to say to someone."

"Ha! She'd have to be buried in the house." Mrs. Hillman turned scarlet. "Sorry, ladies, that wasn't kind and young ears are present."

Ellie-Mae glanced up from the buttons she was playing with. "I think you are kind all the time, Mrs. Hillman."

"Jed wrote this morning that he doesn't like the new job much but the money is good. He needs to build up his savings before he and Mary go to California after the wedding in October." Maureen brushed at her eyes but not before Lauren saw the tears. She squeezed the woman's hand. Lauren would miss Mary, but this lady was going to lose her son.

"I'm lucky my mother-in-law-to-be likes me enough to put up with me." Mary smiled, but Miss Chaney glared at her. She shrugged.

"Put up with you? You're a joy to have around, Mary. I wish you could both stay in Delgany, but I know there is more for young people out in California," Maureen said. "I just hope I can visit one day."

"I hope to go too, Maureen, so maybe we can travel together… to check up on Mary and her brood of twelve children," said Lauren, and she saw Mary poke her tongue out when Miss Chaney wasn't looking.

"Miss Mary is going to have twelve children. Is she opening an orphanage too?" asked Ellie-Mae.

Lauren grabbed the child and tickled her until she shrieked with laughter. "Off you go find Dalton, darling. Some of this conversation isn't fit for little ears."

"Mrs. Hillman, would Earl be able to take the children back to the orphanage?" Lauren asked. "I have to go to Richmond for a few days."

"Of course, I'm sure he'd love to. They can have their supper here first." Mrs. Hillman tucked some more pins into the wedding dress.

"Great. Please tell Becky I will be back in a few days' time. Mary is coming with me so I can buy her a wedding present. I thought I might buy her a nice silk nightdress with a lovely lace bodice."

As the ladies laughed, Mary's face glowed. "Miss Lauren!"

On their way back to the car, Lauren spotted Henry alone at Spencer's Garage. She handed the key to Mary. "You get in, Mary, I will be back in a moment." She didn't wait for the maid to try to dissuade her, but strode down to the garage. "Henry, could I have a word, please?"

"I'm busy, Miss Lauren," Henry said, his reply just about polite.

"So I can see." Lauren responded, sarcastically. She immediately regretted it when she saw his eyebrows shoot up.

What was it Nanny said? *You catch more flies with honey than with vinegar.*

Lauren started again. "Henry, please. I wanted to ask you to come visit Patty. She needs a friend and I know you loved her so. She still loves you."

"Go away, Miss Lauren."

"But, Henry…."

"Patricia and me are not together no more. That's the way it is and nothin' will change it. Nothin' and nobody."

He walked into the office, leaving her standing on the garage forecourt. With a last look in his direction, she turned on her heel and walked back to the car.

"What was all that about, Miss Lauren?" Mary asked as Lauren got into the car and turned the key in the ignition.

"Just me making a fool of myself. Again."

CHAPTER 56

The trees were changing color. All around Lauren the leaves were different shades of purple, orange, yellow, and red. When she was a child, she'd wondered why the trees at the top of the mountain changed color first. Nanny had explained that it was due to the cooler temperatures at the summit. Lauren missed her more than ever now. She had even placed a personal ad, but to no avail.

Lauren had been away in Richmond for four days, setting up a bank account and arranging a mortgage to buy the orphanage and surrounding lands. She'd told her father she had wedding dress fittings and needed to stay in the city. Closing her eyes, she thought of the conversation with her father.

"I'm so happy you've come to your senses about marrying Justin, Lauren. This is for you." He handed her a check for seven hundred dollars. "I know you have been spending money on my accounts but just in case you need some extra dresses or accessories."

She'd taken the check despite feeling guilty that he believed the money she'd been spending at various stores was in preparation for her wedding. It just showed how little attention he paid to the bills.

His gift allowed her to purchase the orphanage as the bank had been happy to finance the additional five hundred dollars by way of a mortgage. She guessed the Greenwood name had helped her application.

As she drove along the bumpy dirt track that led to the orphanage, tufts of yellow witch hazel dotted the ground. Becky used the plant for everything from treating sore throats to soothing away bumps and bruises. She arrived at the house and was surprised when nobody came out to greet her. Usually, at least some of the children would come running out at the sound of her car.

Lauren walked into the kitchen, where she found Becky at the stove. Her friend didn't even turn around, although she must have heard her.

"Good morning, Becky."

"You came back? I thought you'd got fed up of playin' matron and stayed home in your mansion."

Tears pricked Lauren's eyes. What did she have to do to prove herself to this woman?

"Why are you being like this, Becky? Where are the children? How is Patty?"

Becky glanced round and Lauren saw the look in her eyes.

Her heart stopped and she swallowed to get rid of a sudden sour taste in her mouth. "What's wrong? Where's Patty?"

"I sent a message to you. To Rosehall."

"I didn't get a message. I haven't been at Rosehall, I came straight here from Richmond. I went there to set up a bank account and get this property transferred." The hairs on the back of her neck rose as she moved closer to Becky. "Where is Patty? What have you done with her?"

"I ain't done nothin' with her. She made her own decision when she… when she…"

Lauren grabbed the girl's arms with both hands. "Where's Patty? What do you mean?" She had an awful sinking feeling in her stomach, and her head was spinning.

She saw the children come racing in and then shrink into the background, before disappearing from the room. Only then did she come to her senses.

"I am so sorry," she said, letting go of Becky. "I shouldn't have done that. I didn't mean to hurt you. Please tell me I didn't?"

"I'll live."

"Please tell me what is going on."

"Patty's baby arrived the day after you left. He came early and he died."

Lauren's heart broke on the spot. How much more could Patty bear? Hadn't she been through enough? "The poor girl, she must be distraught. Where is she? Can I go see her?"

"She killed herself," Becky said in a whisper. "Bart found her hanged on a tree outside."

Lauren fell into a chair at the table. She knew enough about the Catholic religion Patty had followed to know that, in her faith, the girl had committed the biggest sin. The pain in her heart was nothing compared to the pain of hearing her father tell her she must marry Justin. It was a thousand times worse.

Her anger rose. Justin Prendergast was rich, yet his son and the mother of his child had died in a run-down orphanage out in the middle of nowhere. Putting her head in her hands, she sobbed her heart out.

"Miss Lauren, I'm sorry. I didn't mean to tell you like that. I'm just so angry. Not at you, but at the world. I thought you had deserted us. That you got scared and ran back to your real life. I didn't blame you for that, but I hated you for not telling me."

Lauren raised her head. "I swear never to run out on you and these children, Becky. If I ever disappear again, you will know my father or Justin is behind my disappearance. I can't understand why you didn't get my message. I asked Mrs. Hillman to tell you when she dropped Ellie-Mae and Dalton back after Mary's dress fitting."

"If word gets out and the sheriff comes out here, Miss Lauren, there will be trouble. I shouldn't have said those things to you. I let Patty down and I've hurt you too."

"You let no one down. I won't hear of it. None of this is your fault, Becky. But how did the children react? Stupid question, I suppose."

"Bart and Norma were wonderful. Bart got Patty down before the children saw her. Norma explained to them she had died because of the baby. Most of them know women die having children."

That gave Lauren an idea. "That's it…"

"What's it?"

"I'll tell the sheriff Patty died because of childbirth complications."

"You can't do that, Miss Lauren."

"I can and I will. It's true. She'd never have killed herself if she wasn't pregnant and had just lost her baby. Justin is to blame and we can't let the children pay the price by risking this place closing down. Suicide is a crime."

"So is covering it up," Becky whispered.

"I will speak to Mr. Leroy and see if he will keep quiet. None of you need to come with me to the sheriff. He won't come out here. He'll take my word for what happened."

Becky didn't look convinced. "I'll do whatever you think best, Miss Lauren, but I don't think you're livin' in the real world."

"Maybe not. But I have to try. We have to give Patty and her baby a proper burial. It's the decent thing to do."

"How you goin' to do that? The priest won't do it, on account of what she did."

"Don't worry—I don't want that priest here. Patty went to him for help when she first fell pregnant and he told her she was evil. We'll have our own service. We can all say our goodbyes and tell her we loved her." Lauren clenched her fists, willing herself not to cry. She had to stay strong for Patty—what good would her tears do?

CHAPTER 57

Lauren walked through the tulip trees that lined one side of the property. Her mind was whirling. It seemed like a normal day, the birds were singing, and the clouds looked like fluffy blankets in the sky. Even the sun was shining for the first time after a week of rain. It did its best to add some warmth to the air. Yet she was frozen inside.

She found Mr. Leroy and his wife standing at the barn.

"Morning, Miss Lauren."

"Mr. Leroy, Bart, I need to ask you something."

He took off his hat, twisting it in his hands, his gaze staring toward his wife before back at Lauren.

"Your answer won't affect your job, don't worry about that," she added, when she saw how anxious he appeared. "I heard about Patty." Lauren's voice hitched on the poor girl's name. "I want to go to the sheriff and report her death. I have to. But I intend on telling him she died in childbirth."

They stared at her in silence, Bart fiddling with his hat. Norma put a hand on her husband's arm.

"I hope that Patty wouldn't mind me telling you this—I hope she'd understand, given the circumstances. Patty was the victim of a violent attack. She never wanted the baby."

Norma exhaled sharply, but it was Bart who answered, his gravelly voice betraying his emotion. "I didn't know that, Miss Lauren."

"We didn't talk about the attack. The man behind it is powerful and rich."

"Why don't you tell the sheriff the truth, if you don't mind me asking?" Norma picked at her skirt.

"If I tell the sheriff it was a suicide the County may use it as an excuse to close the orphanage. I believe they will use Patty's misfortune to their advantage, because the sheriff and others believe the children here belong in the County home. The children will suffer if they close this place down. But I need your agreement. I won't ask you to see the sheriff, I won't involve you."

She watched the couple, Bart staring at the ground, Norma using her apron to wipe the tears from her eyes. Lauren let the silence linger.

"Miss Lauren, you helped us more than any other person I know. You gave us everything when we had nothing." Bart looked to his wife, who nodded.

Lauren's heart beat faster.

"I understand the reasons for what you are doing. I can't say I agree as I believe the truth is always the best option." He held her gaze. "But this might be an exception. I won't say a word and neither will my Norma."

Norma moved to take Lauren's hand. "This can't be easy for you, Miss Lauren. We know you to be an honorable person and we saw how much Patty meant to you." She hesitated, glancing at her husband before turning her gaze back to Lauren. "I think you made the right decision."

Lauren exhaled, feeling her shoulders loosen. "Thank you both. Bart, I believe in the truth too, but the man who caused all this is too powerful to defeat. You should know he is my fiancé."

Bart's eyes betrayed his shock and confusion. Norma stiffened beside her and she held her hand tighter.

"I won't bore you with the details, but I know this man, I know just how vile he can be. So, I must see the sheriff and tell him Patty died in childbirth."

"I trust you, Miss Lauren. You don't owe me any explanation. Just be careful, we need you here." Norma hesitated again, then said softly, "Becky is wonderful, but she's young and needs you to lean on. She'd never admit it, though."

"I hoped you'd make a coffin, Bart."

"I already made it, Miss Lauren. I figured it was best to do it soon as we don't need the children seein' Patty."

Lauren tried to smile her thanks, but her lips wouldn't move.

"Come, let me show you."

Lauren held back. "I can't… I don't wish to look at her."

"No, ma'am. I closed the coffin. Ain't a sight for nobody to see."

Norma put her arm around Lauren's waist, supporting her. "Come look at what Bart did." They walked to the smaller barn, where the old tractor was housed. Lauren was surprised to see that the doors were locked with a new shiny padlock.

Bart saw her surprise. "Didn't want any of the kids gettin' too curious."

"You are a marvelous man, Bart."

"Thank you, ma'am." He opened the padlock. "Are you ready?"

No, I am not, her mind screamed, but she moved forward regardless. Bart closed the door behind them and Norma took her hand once more and guided her over to a clean stall. Lauren exhaled sharply.

The coffin lay on the ground, a beautiful carving of a tiny house and some trees on the lid.

Lauren kneeled by the simple wooden box, running her fingers over the surface. "You have carved a home and a garden, Bart. Oh, Patty would have loved this." She shuddered.

"Norma asked me to do it."

Lauren glanced up, finding Norma's eyes shimmering with unshed tears.

"When she was feeling good, she told me about her dreams. She kept talking about the house and garden she and Henry planned to have. She wanted a white picket fence and to grow a garden like the one in Rosehall. A smaller version, I mean. She really looked up to you, Miss Lauren."

Lauren shuddered as she tried to keep her tears in check. "I let her down. I should have done more."

"Nothing you could have done, Miss Lauren. Patty's hurt went too deep. Now she is home, she is happy. Her and her baby." Bart crossed himself.

"You believe that?" Lauren asked.

"Yes, ma'am."

Lauren wished she shared his faith. Maybe it would be a comfort.

"When do you want the burial, Miss Lauren? Best not to wait too long. I can dig out the site. Maybe over by the other side of the orchard near the lake would be a good place? Patty used to go sit there for a spell or two when it was warm."

"Sounds right to me." Lauren gently rubbed the coffin and stood. "Tomorrow afternoon? We should move Patty into a room in the house. I want to give Sam, Mary, and the others a chance to pay their respects."

"I'll bring the coffin up to the orphanage in a bit. Will we leave you alone with her for a moment?"

"Thank you, Bart, you too, Norma. I really don't know what we would do without you both."

The couple withdrew, leaving her alone.

Lauren took a deep breath before speaking: "Patty, I hope you can hear me. I'm so sorry for not being here for you. Not protecting you." Lauren put her head in her hands and cried. Forcing all the awful pictures from her mind, she tried to concentrate on the wonderful ones. She could see Patty playing with some dogs from the estate at Rosehall, throwing sticks for them to fetch. She saw images of the girl working in the kitchen, running to carry out Cook's demands, and her face when Lauren had presented her with the necklace on her thirteenth birthday. She could still hear Patty's laughter.

Tears spent, she kissed the lid of the coffin, whispering "Goodbye, Patty", before she left the barn and walked through the grounds.

Lauren thought the walk would calm her, but her temper flared. Patty, so innocent, so much in love with Henry, had everything to live for. But for Justin, she would have been happy. The leaves rustled with the wind as if whispering their condemnation of her not protecting Patty. Her feet slushed through the weeds and leaves carpeting the ground. She shivered slightly. As she headed past the fruitless trees, she wondered which one had been the one—she didn't want to know.

CHAPTER 58

In the end, Sheriff Dillon had barely asked any questions. Patty mattered no more dead than she had done when she was alive.

With grief like a stone in her stomach, Lauren left Delgany and drove back to Rosehall. When she arrived, she drove through the rear entrance, slowing as she passed the old slave quarters. She parked and took a few seconds to compose herself before she went to face Sam. He'd treated Patty like the daughter he never had. Lauren knew she was about to break his heart wide open.

Glancing around, she couldn't see anyone. Maybe Sam was in the stable. She tried to walk briskly but her legs felt like they were trudging through mud and not along well-tended gravel pathways.

"Miss Lauren, you gave us a fright. What are you doin' out here in the stables?"

"Sam, I have to speak to you," she said, steeling herself for what lay ahead.

"Has the baby come? Is Patty doing okay? I wanted to go see her, but with the Master back an' all…" Sam stopped speaking, realizing that Lauren was staring at him. Then he backed away from her, "Miss Lauren, I got work to do. I ain't got time to be talkin', no offense. I got to go…"

"Sam, please, let me—"

"I don't want to hear it. Don't say it, Miss Lauren. I knows by your eyes. She's gone, isn't she? She was too young to be carryin' a baby. God in heaven!" Sam whirled around and thumped the stable door with his fist. Lauren jumped but he seemed to barely notice. She took a step closer.

"Sam, I…"

"I knows, Miss Lauren. You tried your best. It's God's way."

"But—"

"I best go tell Ole Sally. She loved Patty. She'd known her from a babe in arms. She delivered her from her mama. Did you know that? Patty's mama, she worked at another place but was turned out when they found she had fallen for Patty. Sally, she held Patty's mama's hand until that little bundle arrived. She was so itty-bitty and her mama was sick. They didn't know whether the babe'd live or not. Ole Sally knew what to do. She fed Patty with milk from a goat until Patty's mama recovered from her sickness. Patty's mama loved that child somethin' fierce. When she died with the flu, Ole Sally insisted on keeping the child. Wouldn't let her go to any orphanage. The Master didn't care so long as he didn't have to do nothin'. When Patty was about ten, Cook took her into the kitchen to teach her a trade. She could have had a good life and now…"

"Oh, Sam, I'm so sorry. You and Old Sally already lost so much."

"Miss Lauren, I ain't being rude but I can't talk to you right now." Sam rubbed his eyes with his sleeve before making his way slowly toward his mother.

As Lauren watched him go, Prince whinnied for her and she ran to his stall, throwing her arms around the horse, burying her face in his neck. He butted her a couple of times as if to say he was listening, as she sobbed into him. Why did bad things happen to good folk when people like Justin seemed to get away scot-free?

*

Lauren walked into the kitchen, interrupting Cook and Mary arguing over what food to serve. What did it matter whether

Father had his favorite turtle soup or not? Patty was dead and everything else paled into insignificance.

"Miss Lauren, you look white as a sheet. What's the matter? Come, sit down. Cook, can you give her a drop of your brandy," said Mary, her eyes fixed on Lauren.

"I don't need a drink. It's... I've got something horrible to tell you both. Patty... she died, her and the baby."

Lauren looked from one shocked face to the other. Mary burst into tears and buried her head in her hands, before collapsing into a chair. Cook turned back to the soup she was preparing, adding some seasoning before taking a taste and adding some more.

"Cook? Did you hear me?"

"I did."

"But—"

"What do you want me to say, Miss Lauren? I am sorry for young Patty, of course I am, but maybe it was for the best."

Lauren felt for the wall behind her. "The best?" she croaked as Mary's head swung up, disbelief written all over her face.

"God works in mysterious ways, Miss Lauren. He knows Patty and that child of hers had no chance of a good life. He—"

"Cook, don't you dare say this was God's will. We all know who caused this and he isn't living in Heaven unless Richmond got a new name. Patty was innocent of everything. She was a child, for goodness' sake. How could you think something so horrible?" Lauren took a step before faltering, pressing her hands into her sides. She wanted to grab the woman by the shoulders and shake her.

"Miss Lauren, you don't understand, not really," Cook said calmly. "You've been protected all your life."

"Miss Lauren might have been, but I haven't." Mary almost spat at Cook. "Patty was like a little sister to me. She grew up on this estate. You knew her all her life. She used to sing every day and when she met Henry and they made plans, she was about ready to burst with happiness. How could you be so cruel? Sorry, Miss Lauren, but I can't bear to be in the same room as that woman right now." Turning on her heel, Mary ran sobbing out the kitchen.

Cook sent the contents of the bowl flying across the table with a sweep of her hand. "Why is everyone treating me like the baddie in all this? I didn't do anything to the girl. She made her bed, she should have stayed out of that man's way."

Lauren had heard enough, turning her back on Cook and heading through the door to the hall. She couldn't believe the woman's reaction. Poor Mary, not only had she lost her friend, Patty, but after today, it was doubtful that she and Cook would ever be as close as they had once been.

Outside, the gravel screeched in protest as her father drove up the main driveway. Lauren broke into a cold sweat, wiping her clammy hands on her dress, as her heart beat faster. She wanted to hide behind the bushes boxing off the kitchen garden but that was cowardly. She still had to give Mary the details of the funeral tomorrow and arrange with her father to allow the staff to attend.

Brushing the hair back from her face and checking nobody was near, Lauren wiped her nose before walking sedately out the side gate to meet her father.

"There you are, Lauren! What have you been up to? You look like you were dragged through the bushes." He held her gaze for a second before saying, "Justin wants you to go to Thornton Mews tomorrow."

She was about to protest, but he cut her off. "I don't want to hear it. I've lost patience with all your excuses, as has Justin. His mother expects you tomorrow morning. You will stay for lunch and you will finalize the wedding plans. Is that clear?"

"I am sorry, Father, I have plans. Justin and his mother will have to wait." She turned to leave, but then twisted back to face him. "Not that you will care, but Patty died in childbirth. The funeral is tomorrow afternoon. I expect you to allow the staff to pay their respects. Your presence won't be required. I hold you and Justin equally responsible for her death. Him for the attack and you for casting her out when she most needed our help."

*

Lauren pulled up outside Spencer's Garage, where Henry was polishing the hood of a Ford. When he saw her, he flushed, but he had no option other than to come over. Spencer's couldn't afford to turn away paying customers. Not these days.

"Miss Lauren, what can I do for you?"

Lauren fought the desire to drive away, to be anywhere else but here. "I haven't come shopping. I came to talk to you." She crossed her arms and just as quickly uncrossed them. She rubbed the back of her neck.

Henry blinked rapidly, shaking his head. "I've no time for talkin'. I'm workin'." He turned on his heels and walked toward the garage.

Lauren got out the Cadillac and followed him into the garage, where he started restacking a bundle of tires.

"Henry, please. It's about Patty." She hated how her voice wobbled.

"I told you the last time. Patricia and me broke up a long time ago." His voice sounded flat but she could see by the dark circles under his eyes, his nails bitten to the quick, that he was upset.

She took a deep breath, lowered her voice, and put out her hand, laying it gently on his arm. "Patty's dead, Henry. I'm so sorry to break the news to you like this. I should have gone for your uncle or your mother to make sure you weren't alone."

He shook her arm off, but didn't make a sound.

She faltered. "I thought you might like to come to the funeral. It's tomorrow afternoon. I wrote out the directions for you."

She held them out, but he made no attempt to take them. Instead she put them on the counter, using a tin as a paperweight.

"Patty loved you so much, Henry. None of this was her fault."

As she walked away from him, she heard his cough and turned back.

"Miss Lauren, what did she have?"

"A boy. They'll be buried together."

She waited for him to say something else but he turned his back on her. Wiping away her tears, she headed back to her car. As she drove back to Rosehall, she looked in her rear-view mirror: Henry remained frozen to the spot.

CHAPTER 59

Mid September, 1932

The sky was too blue, the sun shining as if in mockery of their broken hearts. Mr. and Mrs. Hillman brought baskets of food, Bart had fashioned a cross out of Oak and Norma and Becky stood on one side with the children. Bart, Sam, Big Will, and Jed carried the coffin from the house to the burial site beside the lake. They'd picked a secluded place under a collection of willow trees. Bart and Big Will had put up a picket fence around the site, to preserve it and protect it from roaming wildlife.

In the absence of a priest, it was left to Lauren to say the words, but when she tried to speak, she found she couldn't. The words in the Bible just danced on the page. She blinked rapidly, steeling herself. "*Even though I… walk—*" her voice cracked with emotion.

Bart stepped forward, taking the Bible from her, but a voice stopped him.

"May I say the verse for her, please?"

Lauren looked up and came face to face with Henry. Taking the Bible from Bart, he walked to the head of the grave.

"*Even though I walk through the valley of the shadow of death, I will fear no evil…*"

Henry's voice never wavered despite the shine of tears in his eyes. Lauren couldn't stop crying and judging by the sobs around her, she wasn't the only one. The children cried, Bart carrying Bean, Clarissa holding Norma's hand. Becky rubbed her eyes several times. Jed had his arm around Mary, supporting her. Cook didn't turn up, which only broke Lauren's heart further, and there was no sign of Lauren's father.

Finally, Henry closed the Bible and stared into the grave: "Patricia, I loved you and I wronged you. I should have stayed with you. I should have ignored Mother and my family. We could have gone away and got wed. That's what a man would have done. But I behaved like a boy and for that, I'm sorry. I will never forget you."

As Henry threw a handful of dirt on top of the coffin, Lauren cringed at the sound of the earth hitting the wood. Her chest tightened, it was hard to breathe. She closed her eyes, hearing Patty's voice singing around the house as she went about her chores. Patty, who had been so full of life and love. Lauren threw some dirt into the grave, whispering, "Be happy, Patty. I'm sorry." Slowly, she walked away, letting the others mark their grief.

Walking over to where Henry now stood some distance from the grave, staring at the mountains, she coughed so that he could compose himself.

"I let her down, Miss Lauren," he said finally, turning to look at her. "I loved her and yet I deserted her when she needed me most. Why didn't I take her away?"

"We all wish we could go back and change things, Henry."

"Who was it?" he demanded, as he held her gaze.

"Didn't she tell you?"

"No, she refused. She didn't want me goin' after him in case I got into trouble. I know it was someone important. Was it your father?"

Lauren shook her head. At one time she'd have protested that her father wasn't capable of something so horrible, but now she wasn't so certain. He hadn't condemned Justin, after all.

"I wish I knew. I'd kill him with my bare hands," Henry said, his voice trembling.

"That's why Patty didn't tell you. She loved you too much to see you hang."

He glanced over at the burial spot where Sam and Bart were now filling up the grave. "Thank you for tryin' to help her," he said, his eyes laced with tears.

"I didn't do enough." Lauren wiped tears from her face. "Are you coming inside for something to eat?"

"No, thank you. I have a train to catch."

"You're leaving?"

"There's nothing left for me in Delgany. I'm goin' to join up, see a bit of the world. Work out why I was so stupid to give up on my Patricia. Goodbye, Miss Lauren."

CHAPTER 60

After everyone had gone, Lauren headed into the office. She had realized that she must find a way to protect the children and Becky from her father and Justin. She paced back and forth until inspiration hit. She sat at her desk and proceeded to write two letters, one to Sheriff Dillon and the second to Edward Belmont at the *Charlottesville News*. She licked the envelopes, pasting them closed, hoping they would be a good insurance policy.

Now I am ready to face my father and Justin, she thought. *And I will show them that I am a strong, confident woman, not a quivering, sweating wreck. I should have left Rosehall when Patty did. If I had, she might still be alive.*

"Lauren, where you goin'? You look like you want to murder someone," said Becky as Lauren marched through the kitchen on her way to the car.

"I'm going to collect my things. I'll never spend another night in Rosehall while my father lives there. Don't worry, Becky. I'll be back soon. If I'm not, send the sheriff out to look for my body." Lauren was only half-joking. She didn't know what her father or Justin might do once they'd heard what she had to say.

Becky stared at her, opening and closing her mouth a couple of times before she finally said, "Miss Lauren, are you sure? You're giving up a home and a promising future."

"I won't marry that animal, not now, not ever. I have a home here." Lauren faltered, suddenly unsure. "I do, don't I?"

"Yes, of course, but none of us will have a home if we can't find some money. Up till now, you've bought everything on your father's credit. The new beds upstairs, the food in the cupboards, the animals in the barn… that was all paid for by your father. What will we do next week, next month, and the months after that? Thanksgiving and Christmas are coming."

"We'll manage somehow. Bart has already got some of the land under cultivation and you and Norma are canning and bottling fruit. We can sell some of those items to pay for the things we can't provide for ourselves. We'll be fine."

Becky went back to folding laundry on the kitchen table. "I can't understand why the County won't give you the money they used to give to Matron."

Lauren sighed. She hadn't told Becky the full story, because she hadn't wanted to worry her. But she'd been wrong to keep quiet. Becky was nobody's fool. It was better they all knew where they stood. There would be difficult times ahead despite her confident words.

"The County haven't paid Matron for years. She used her own funds in the end. She rented this house and used donations from her friends to pay for things. The County don't agree with private orphanages, they want public ones like the County home or religious ones like the Catholic and Baptist homes."

Becky's mouth fell open. "You mean, they could have shut us down and shipped the kids off to those other places? Is that why you had to get the mortgage?"

"Exactly—I had to buy this land. Matron was in arrears to the woman who owned it. When she died, her sons wanted to sell. Buying it was the only way we could keep the house."

Becky shuddered. "I don't like owin' banks money. They don't have hearts, those men. Look how many people they've put out on the streets. Good folk like Bart and Norma."

"Stop borrowing trouble, Becky, as Nanny would say. Now, wish me luck with my father. If I don't come back, I've left some letters in my desk. Post them for me, please."

*

When she pulled up outside the grand house, Lauren saw Justin's Studebaker parked beside her father's Red Arrow. Pushing her shoulders back, she marched inside.

"Miss Lauren, your father and Mr. Justin asked not to be disturbed," said the butler, trying to stop her.

"Get out of my way, Jackson."

"But, Miss—"

"Do as I say, Jackson. You are not the Master of this house despite what you may have told yourself. Now move!"

Lauren pushed open the door to the study, her heel almost catching in the plush blue carpet. There was a roaring fire and the two men sat drinking whiskey while Patty lay cold in her grave. A red mist descended in front of her eyes.

"Lauren, what is the meaning of this?" said her father.

"I'm glad I've caught you both together. It will save me having to repeat my message." The sight of him sickened her.

"I won't marry you, Justin," she said. "Not now, not ever."

His eyes flamed. "Behave yourself, Lauren. Your conduct is unbecoming to a lady."

She laughed, but it wasn't a pretty sound. "You talk of behavior and conduct? That's rich, coming from you!"

Leaping out of his seat, he grabbed her arm.

"Ouch, you're hurting me!"

"That's just a taste of what's coming to you. I'm telling you, no woman will ever disrespect me."

"Father, are you going to sit there and let him treat me this way?" She tried to pull away from Justin. "My father won't tolerate you treating me like this."

"Let's all calm down. Justin, restrain yourself, please," her father said.

Justin released her. Lauren shot him a glare of triumph as she rubbed her arm, but he was laughing now. It was a harsh, bitter laugh.

"You are a naive little cow, aren't you? Your father doesn't care." He mimicked her voice. "Your father wouldn't care if I had all the women in the country. All he cares about is covering his tracks. His dirty little secrets, of which there are quite a few. Isn't that right, William?"

Lauren glanced at her father, but he didn't say a word.

"I don't believe a word of it," she said, her chest heaving.

"You wouldn't. You don't believe what's written in front of your face. How do you think your father got so wealthy? You aren't stupid, Lauren. You must have asked yourself, where the money came from? Your father got into bed with some dubious individuals and I have all their details. I can ruin him in an instant and he knows it."

Her father's face had turned the color of fresh linen, and he rubbed the back of his neck, his eyes never leaving Justin's face. She expected him to say something, to protest, and was shocked when he remained silent.

"You're bluffing." Yet deep down, she knew it was the truth.

"Am I?" Justin sneered, an unkind smile spreading slowly over his face. He was clearly enjoying this.

"You just like hurting people, you're a bully." That was true, at least.

He didn't deny it. "I am also your fiancé and I demand you say no more about canceling our wedding. It's in two weeks, the invitations have gone out."

"No, they haven't. I didn't send them."

His face flushed at her remark.

"Why?" she asked, tears stinging her eyes. "Why do you want to marry me? You could marry any girl in the county, in the whole country, if you wanted to."

"Yes, but haven't you realized by now that I want what I can't have? It makes,"—he moved toward her, yanking a piece of her hair forward, twirling it around his fingers—"for a much more exciting life."

She pulled away from him, trying not to wince at the pain in her scalp.

"But don't flatter yourself, Lauren. You aren't the only attraction. Rosehall is a lovely plantation, with some fine land, which our children will inherit. Your father has a wealth of contacts and he has a knack of knowing how to make money. I have to give him that. My father made some bad investments and the '29 crash has affected our funds. The bargain I made with your father is mutually satisfying in more ways than one."

Her father paled, yet he still lied to her face: "I don't know what Justin is talking about."

"Yes, you do," Lauren said, anger coursing through her, "and it's best if we are all open with one another. You threatened to have me committed to an asylum after I refused to marry Justin. After this man raped a fourteen-year-old girl, who became pregnant and has now died because of his actions. He also attacked me, your daughter."

Her father slammed his fist onto the table, "I won't listen to this."

Lauren didn't even blink. "Yes, you will, Father. I'm telling you again that I won't marry Justin Prendergast and I don't care what the consequences are. You can disinherit me, if you wish, but I will not have anything further to do with this monster." She bent to pick up her purse where it had fallen, when Justin grabbed for her wrist. She moved out of his way just in time.

"Furthermore, if either of you try to follow through on your threats, you should know that I have written to Mr. Belmont and Sheriff Dillon. Those letters are to be opened in the event of my disappearance or early demise."

Her father got to his feet angrily. "I did not threaten to kill you, Lauren."

"No, but I wouldn't put it past Justin trying to kill me, would you? Either way, the letters I have written outline in detail what happened to me from the moment you forced me into an engagement, your reactions to my objections, and my desire to live my life on my own terms. Edward Belmont will be thrilled to give much publicity to the contents of the letter I have written to him."

At her father's sharp inhalation, Lauren smiled grimly. "I'm a Greenwood, Father, you taught me well. Justin was most indiscreet. He delighted in telling me how you had sold me to him. You valued me so poorly, Father."

Now she turned her attention to her fiancé. "You have left a trail of suffering in your wake, Justin. I'd sleep with one eye open, if I were you."

The muscle tic in his cheek betrayed his anger, "Why, you b—" He clenched his hand into a fist.

"*Don't touch me, Justin.* Edward Belmont is just waiting to take you down. He knows I'm here. If I don't contact him within the hour, he has my permission to open the letter. I also enclosed a copy of a letter from Patty."

Lauren crossed her fingers behind her back. *He doesn't need to know that the letters I've written haven't yet been posted*, she thought. She knew her plan was risky, but she also knew that both these men valued money above everything else. They wouldn't take the gamble of being ruined.

Lauren turned her back on them and, drawing herself up to her full height, walked toward the door. Even now, above all else she desperately wanted her father to beg her forgiveness, to tell her he loved her.

"Lauren…." Her father spoke softly.

She pivoted, hope soaring.

"Get out of my house and never come back. As of this moment, I no longer have a daughter. You can take Mary with you. Leave now." He leaned over his desk toward her, his face purple with rage. *"Leave!"*

"With pleasure," she retorted, and slammed the door behind her. Jackson was still hovering outside.

"You heard the man, he wants me gone."

CHAPTER 61

When Lauren went to find Mary, to tell her that she would be leaving Rosehall forever, and to ask her if she would come with her to the orphanage, she found that the news had already reached the staff and Mary had packed her belongings. Lauren went to her room and the two of them put the few things that she wanted to take with her into a large suitcase.

An hour after her father had ordered Lauren to leave, she went to the stables to see Sam to ask if he would sell Prince for her. She was concerned that he would be taking a risk in helping her, but Sam reassured her that he wanted to help so she also asked him to contact Jed. She wanted him to sell her Cadillac and buy a truck in its place. With the money left over, Jed could look for a cow. Finally, with tears in her eyes, she asked Sam to drive her and her maid to the orphanage.

Not a word passed between the three of them until the truck pulled into the yard and Sam parked by the porch. Mary and Lauren got out and Sam pulled their baggage from the back and took it to the front door. He hugged both women, his eyes full of tears as they said goodbye, then he climbed into the truck and set off back to Rosehall.

*

"I spoke to my father and Justin and my father has thrown me out of Rosehall and cut me off, just as you predicted he would, Becky. So, I guess I am another orphan." Lauren tried to hide the hurt, but her voice quivered. "Mary and I have brought our things and we will move in today."

"Will your father or Mr. Justin come after you here?" Becky asked, her face white with fear.

"No, they know it would be a bad decision to follow me. I made sure of that."

"What can you do that's so powerful, it would stop a man as rich as your father?" Becky asked.

"I've written two letters. One is addressed to Sheriff Dillon and the other to Mr. Belmont at the newspaper. They are both here, in my desk drawer."

Becky and Mary exchanged a glance before looking back at Lauren.

"What do those letters say?" Becky said.

"The truth. I know that my father and Justin can't risk what I have written becoming common knowledge. If anything should happen to me, you are to post the letters, Becky, as I have already requested."

"Miss Lauren, are you sure you know what you are doing? Nobody has ever defied your father before and come out the victor," said Mary.

"I might not like my father, but I am his daughter. He has taught me well. I will win. This time, at least."

Lauren's first night at the orphanage proved to her that she'd done the right thing. As Becky and Mary helped her to get her room ready, she brushed a tear from her eye when she saw Nanny's quilt lying on her new bed.

Two weeks later, when Lauren's father was absent from Rosehall, Sam collected Mary and Lauren from the orphanage and drove them back to meet Jed at the stables. He had sold her Cadillac and bought a more practical truck instead. There was enough cash left over to buy a cow. Sam had sold her beloved Prince, just as Lauren had asked. The money from the horse would pay for the new bathroom upstairs and proper plumbing in the kitchen.

As she set off with Mary on the road to the orphanage, this time driving her new truck, Lauren did her best to hold back tears. She stopped at Hillmans' Store in Delgany and they loaded up the truck with supplies. Big Will helped with the loading—"I was hopin' you'd be drivin' to the orphanage and could take me there to see Bart about the roof. He and I could work on it together to keep the costs down." The man looked at the ground. "Thought I might check up on Miss Becky while I was there."

Lauren grinned. "Okay, hop aboard, if there's room."

Big Will climbed in, grinning, careful to hold on tight to the chickens in the box he was carrying. "Mrs. Hillman said one of these chickens would do for the pot and one is a good layer, but now I can't remember which one is which," he chuckled. "They both look the same to me."

Lauren laughed when Mary replied, saying, "No good asking Miss Lauren to choose, she couldn't tell a rooster from a chicken."

Big Will found that funny, given how much he laughed.

"It's true. I am still learning how to be a farmer," Lauren said.

Mary turned to Lauren. "Mrs. Hillman is a nice lady, isn't she, Miss Lauren?"

"Yes, she is. And it's Lauren, Mary. You don't work for me anymore, remember?"

"I do until next week, Miss Lauren."

Lauren sighed, guessing it would be a while before Mary would ever be able to see her as an equal.

CHAPTER 62

There were some children playing outside in the yard when Lauren and Mary arrived with Big Will. All the orphans were barefoot but dressed in clothes, at least, rather than flour sacks. Terry, at fourteen, and the eldest boy in the home, stood watching. Lauren saw that he was always on guard, as if expecting something bad to happen. His limp had come about after a broken leg had been set badly, following an incident at the home some years previously. After all the tales he'd told her, she wondered just how much of an accident it had been.

Lauren climbed down from the truck, laughing as the children ran screaming for Becky to come look what Lauren had brought with her.

"Afternoon, Miss Becky, how are you today?" Big Will said, climbing out the truck as she came toward it, her hands on her hips.

Lauren bit her lip as Becky replied coldly, "What are you doing here?"

But Big Will just smiled widely. "I wish it was because I missed your pumpkin pie, but Bart has asked me to have a look at the roof. Says it needs fixin'."

Amused, Lauren watched Becky respond to his flirting: "We ain't got the money to fix no roof."

"Seems like you might be mistaken on that front, Miss Becky." Big Will picked up the box with the two chickens and held the squawking birds out to her. "Mind that first one, her bite is worse than her manners."

Becky's eyes widened as they took in all the supplies being unloaded from the truck. Mary had drafted in some older children to help.

"Miss Lauren, what you doin' now?" Becky asked her.

"I bought you some supplies, Becky, and Jed has found me a cow. It will be here on Friday. Bart or Big Will will have to put up some fencing to keep it from roaming off."

"A cow! What am I supposed to do with a cow?"

"Milk her for the children."

Becky looked thunderstruck.

"I can show you how, Miss Becky, if you want some help." Big Will grinned.

"I don't need help from the likes of you! I thought you were here to check on the roof?"

"I am, but I have a list of things to do and a man gets mighty thirsty. Do you think I could have a glass of cider?"

"Water is all I got. You'll find some in the kitchen."

When he walked off, laughing, Lauren moved to Becky's side.

"Why are you being so mean to Big Will? He's here to help us."

"Miss Lauren, we ain't got no money to pay him. Ain't right to bring folk here, thinkin' they will earn money to feed their families."

Money. It all came back to money.

"Becky, I sold some things I owned. Some of that money will go toward the roof. I sold my horse to pay for a new bathroom and properly plumbed kitchen. I will find more money, somehow."

Becky glared at her and turned on her heel, Lauren running a few steps to catch up with her. "Please, Becky, I'm here to help, not hinder. What have I done? Why are you crying?"

"I can't believe it. You livin' here and now comin' with a truck, all this stuff and help, and... well, it's just too much for a body to take in. I have to go think."

"Do you think you could make some coffee while you do that?" Lauren asked, a grin on her face. Then she hugged the girl. "Go on, smile and charm Big Will into a lower price for the roof. It's obvious he holds a candle for you."

"I told you before, I'm not gettin' married and havin' babies. That's one trap I'm avoidin'!" Becky replied, but she was smiling as she walked into the house.

Mary went over to where Lauren was standing. Linking arms, the two women walked into the orphanage and came to a standstill at the sight of some children covered head to foot in flour. Two girls, one blonde and the other auburn, looked half scared to death.

"Sorry, miss, but we didn't know what it was."

"We thought you could eat it."

"Don't tell Becky," Lauren whispered.

"Don't tell me what?" said Becky, entering the kitchen. "What on earth happened to my flour? You bunch of heathens, get out of here! Every single last one of you. Go on, get!"

The children ran, a trail of flour in their wake. Lauren and Mary exchanged glances, biting back their giggles, not wanting a fuming Becky to turn on them.

"Go on, laugh. I spent two hours scrubbing this kitchen and look at the state of it! Those men will think I sit on my backside all day long."

"So, you *are* worried about what Big Will thinks then?" Lauren teased, while Mary laughed, picking up a little of the flour and throwing it at Becky.

"Now you look like you were playing with the children."

"Miss Lauren, you will be the death of me!"

"Can you die after you make the coffee, Becky? I would offer, but I still don't know how to use a stove."

Mary took the kettle and filled it, making coffee for everyone while Lauren and Becky worked together to clear up the flour. They heard shouts and laughter coming from the yard and, looking out the windows, they spotted Big Will chasing the flour-covered kids with pails of water. Soon, he was just as soaked as the children.

"Men! They never grows up," Becky exclaimed, but there was a smile in her eyes as she said it.

*

Jed arrived to see Mary and stayed for dinner, but Big Will had to get back to town. Orphanage food was basic fare compared to Cook's adventurous table at Rosehall, but it tasted delicious. The company was even better. The children were getting used to the new way of doing things and that evening, they had even laughed as they sat around the table.

Once the children were fed and had gone to bed, Lauren asked the adults to sit around the table with her.

"We still have forty-five dollars left over from the sale of the car and one hundred and fifty dollars from the sale of Prince. I'd like your input on how we should spend the money. Personally, I'd like the roof to be fixed before the worst of the rains or the snow comes. I'd also like to make the kitchen bigger so we can have a seating area that fits everyone in. I want proper plumbing in the kitchen. There are too many people living here to be carrying water from the well. What do you think, Bart? Could you and Big Will manage those tasks by Thanksgiving?"

"Sure can try, Miss Lauren."

"Don't forget you want a bathroom too, Miss Lauren," Mary teased her.

Lauren looked at Bart, who was scratching his head. "May need some help on that one, Miss Lauren. John Thatcher will give me a hand, I reckon."

"Good. I thought we should also invest in some animals."

"Invest?" Becky queried.

"Mr. Hillman suggested we will run out of money fast if we buy all our provisions from the store every month. He said to buy some piglets and feed them up. We can then slaughter them and salt our own pork. Same with the milk, butter, and cheese." Lauren saw they were all smiling. "What did I say?"

"You ever slaughtered a pig, Miss Lauren?" Bart said, and they all burst out laughing.

CHAPTER 63

Delgany, October 1932

It was such a beautiful Indian summer's day that you wouldn't think it was October already. The sun was high in the stunning blue sky and only a few clouds hung over the mountains. It was the perfect day for a wedding.

"Mary, you look so beautiful." Lauren kissed her friend's cheek, careful not to smudge it with lipstick. The white wedding dress was stunning, wide at the shoulders and nipped in at the waist, flattering Mary's figure. The children had made a garland for her hair from wild flowers they'd collected in the meadow. Ginny Dobbs, the local hairdresser, had trimmed her red hair into a flattering style, with bangs highlighting Mary's green eyes.

It was a lovely, private ceremony, with barely a dry eye in the church. Jed's mother put on a small wedding party afterward and Miss Chaney had organized a pot-luck-style dinner to help reduce the burden on Jed's family. Every guest brought their special dish and the men had set up planks on wooden trestles, which were covered with tablecloths. In the center, stood Jed's favorite, a large stack cake.

"Why is it called a stack cake, Miss Lauren?" Ellie-Mae asked, unconsciously licking her lips as she stared at the centerpiece.

"Mary explained to me that it's a tradition in Jed's family. Every lady who comes to the wedding brings a layer to add to the cake. The higher the cake, the more popular or important the couple."

"People must like Jed and Mary a lot. It's the biggest cake I ever saw! What's in the middle?"

Mrs. Hillman, fixing things on the table, replied, "A mixture of apples and molasses, I believe. I heard chocolate cake was your favorite, Ellie-Mae."

"I've changed my mind," said the little girl. "Can I skip dinner and just have cake?"

"You'll get mighty hungry waiting. Mary and Jed have to cut the cake and they only do that when everyone is finished eating." Mrs. Hillman smiled fondly at the little girl. "Why don't you come over and try my fried chicken and my Indian bean bread? I have a special recipe my ma learned from an Indian lady."

Never far from Ellie-Mae's side, Dalton spoke out: "You're lyin'. There ain't Indians around these parts."

"Dalton, apologize at once to Mrs. Hillman. You don't speak to your elders like that." Lauren saw the mutinous expression on his face and knew an apology would not be delivered, but she didn't want to make a fuss at Mary's wedding. "Mrs. Hillman, I apologize for Dalton's rudeness. If it were not for the occasion, I would take him straight back to the orphanage."

Mrs. Hillman looked at Dalton for a couple of seconds before she spoke. "I don't appreciate anyone calling me a liar, son, and Mr. Hillman wouldn't like it either. Long before you were born, the Indians lived on these mountains. There are a lot of folk around these parts that have Indian kin. In the last century, there weren't many white women and the men needed company and families. I figure that's hard for you to understand. But just because you don't see proof, doesn't mean someone isn't telling the truth." Mrs. Hillman took Ellie-Mae's hand. "Would you like to come and try my bean bread? It's not to everyone's taste, but Mr. Hillman, he insists I make it."

"May I go with Mrs. Hillman, please?" Ellie-Mae asked Lauren.

Lauren nodded, waiting to see what Dalton would do. He never let Ellie-Mae out of his sight.

"What's it made of, this bread of yours?" Dalton's tone was brusque, but Mrs. Hillman didn't take any notice.

"You cook some dried beans and mix them into a cornmeal dough. You make it just the same as cornbread. Want to come with us and try it?"

"Dalton, please come," said Ellie-Mae. "I'm hungry."

"I'll come, but I hate beans," he replied.

Lauren wanted the ground to open up and swallow her. She expected to see anger when she looked at Mrs. Hillman, but instead spotted a pitying look in her eyes. Lauren watched as the woman spoke softly to the boy.

"Son, nobody said you had to eat beans so what are you fussin' over?"

Dalton opened his mouth, but for once he seemed to be stuck for words. He stared at the woman like he was seeing her for the first time. "Nothin', ma'am. I'm sorry for being rude to you earlier."

Mrs. Hillman ruffled Dalton's hair. Lauren clenched her hands together, waiting for him to retaliate. He hated anyone but Ellie-Mae touching him. To her surprise, Dalton reached for Ellie-Mae's other hand. "I'm hungry too."

Becky approached just as Mrs. Hillman and the two children walked toward the food table.

"What happened to Dalton? He's smiling."

"I think he just met his match in Mrs. Hillman. He was very rude and she almost killed him with kindness. Then she ruffled his hair."

"That made him smile? We should ask her what her secret is. Last time I tried that, I got a bruised shin for my trouble."

"You and me both."

*

The wedding was a roaring success. John Thatcher had slaughtered a pig and had given half to the orphanage. Becky and Norma had spent two days cooking different types of meat. Sausages in gravy, roast ham, and pork chops with apple sauce were just a few of their dishes on offer. Lauren had taken the children up to the meadows and there, they had searched for the last of the berries. They'd turned them into apple and blackberry pie, apple-sauce cake, and preserves.

Sheriff Dillon's presence made the men more careful about drinking moonshine, but as the day progressed, some of the guests got noticeably louder.

Mrs. Flannery's voice carried across the general chatter of the guests. "Good job Miss Chaney told us to bring roast ham and told the Hillmans to bring fried chicken otherwise everyone would be eating cornbread, biscuits, and gravy."

The stuck-up woman deliberately ignored the orphans and now she had criticized the orphanage's contributions to the meal, even though they had done their very best. Lauren put a hand on Becky's arm, afraid the girl would let her "mountain wild side" as she called it, come out. Mrs. Flannery would never survive once Becky got going—the girl had red hair for a reason.

Lauren handed her a Coke. "Drink that and ignore the ignorant old witch."

Ginny Dobbs chipped in then: "I'll put turmeric in her color next time she comes in to get her hair done. That'll put a stop to her gallop. These lovely kids are lucky to have you, Becky. I brought candy. Not much of a cook at the best of times. I wasn't about to show myself up at a wedding. These women will be talkin' about who made the best cornbread gravy for years to come."

Lauren smiled, knowing there was some truth in her words.

Mr. and Mrs. Hillman shared their rug with Dalton and Ellie-Mae. Both children seemed drawn to the Hillmans. Earl treated Dalton like a kid brother and Ellie-Mae like his own special princess.

Someone started singing and a man took out his banjo. Ellie-Mae danced with Mr. Hillman, while Dalton led Mrs. Hillman around in a circle. After taking turns with each of the children, John Thatcher showed Lauren how to do a jig: "It's the Irish in me. Six generations back and me legs still jiggle when I hear an old tune."

There was much fun and laughter and it was a relief to spend one day not worrying about anything other than would the rain fall. As the evening dusk slipped down from the mountain the children ran after the lightning bugs. The wind carried the sweet scent of cedar and fir trees, tickling Lauren's nose, and she watched as the sun slipped away out of sight, shivering in the coolness of the fading day.

It was like the end of an era. Mary had been such a big part of her life. First, Nanny left, then Patty died, now Mary was going away. How she wished Nanny had been here today, joining in the celebration. She could picture her and John Thatcher arguing over who had a better jig—the Scottish or the Irish? Nanny was very proud of her Scottish roots.

When the time came for Mary and Jed to leave, Lauren hugged her friend tightly, not wanting to let her go. "Thank you for everything, especially over the last few weeks. Please write to me."

"I will, Miss—, I mean, Lauren." Mary turned to Becky. "Look after her, won't you, Becky, and don't let her cook unless you want the children poisoned."

Lauren knew Mary was teasing, but the kitchen had barely survived her first attempt to cook ham and eggs for breakfast. She'd almost set the orphanage on fire.

"Miss Lauren will get better." Becky gave Mary a hug—the two had become firm friends.

"Thank you for your faith," replied Lauren, beaming.

"It's not faith, Miss Lauren. We all knows you can't get any worse!"

CHAPTER 64

Later that evening, at the orphanage, Lauren sat on the porch looking at the view. It wasn't as pretty as the view of the Blue Ridge Mountains back at Rosehall, because one area of the mountain here had been plundered by a lumber company. In the dusk light, the mountain looked like it had been given a bad haircut, with the barber shaving it bald in places.

Children's voices carried in the evening's quiet.

"Miss Mary looked so pretty today. I can't wait until I grow up and get married."

Lauren smiled at Ellie-Mae's comment. Not yet six years old, but such a romantic at heart.

"Won't nobody ever want to marry you. Not with that ugly face," came the reply. Lauren recognized Shelley's voice. She knew you shouldn't dislike any child, but when it came to the misbehaving and mean Shelley, she struggled to find any redeeming qualities.

The door slammed and Ellie-Mae ran toward the trees. Without hesitation, Lauren ran after her.

"Ellie-Mae, come back," she called after the child. "It's not safe down there by the water. Becky warned us all about the snakes."

But Ellie-Mae paid no attention, just kept running. Lauren ignored the pain of small rocks and sharp leaves as her feet moved quickly through the grass. The children often went barefoot, but her tender feet had always been encased in shoes.

She pushed past the cramp in her side to reach the child. *How can someone so small run so fast?* "Ellie-Mae! Stop! Please! I can't run anymore."

Lauren bent over to catch her breath. She panted fast and loud as she saw the young girl turn around to check on her. She stayed where she was, banking on the child's good nature to come back.

"Miss Lauren, you don't look good. You too old to run like that." Ellie-Mae came running over toward her.

Lauren fell to her knees and grabbed the child, hugging her. "You scared me, darling," she said, still gasping for breath. "You know we don't let you run down here in the long grass after sundown. It's too dangerous."

Ellie-Mae looked up, the pale moon highlighting the tear stains on her face. "I'm sorry. Am I in big trouble?"

"No, darling. I heard what happened, and I'm sorry that Shelley said such a thing, but I wish you had come to me or Becky rather than run off. I'll deal with her when I get back."

"Ain't no point. Shelley only spoke the truth. Nobody will want me, the adoption people said so."

Lauren picked the child up, who was very slight for her age, and made her way back to the house, praying she wouldn't step on anything. When she reached the porch, she sat back down in her chair. "Sit here with me for a bit, Ellie-Mae. Let me recover my breath."

As Ellie-Mae snuggled down on her lap, Lauren searched for the right words to comfort the child. "Ellie-Mae, people have their own ideas of what makes someone beautiful. For example, you have glorious blonde hair. I'd love hair like yours."

"Why?"

"It shimmers in the sunlight. You look like someone painted your hair with strips of gold."

Ellie-Mae picked up a strand of her hair, her face screwed up in concentration. "I do?"

"Yes, sweetheart, you do."

"You got nice hair too, Miss Lauren."

"Thank you. It has a mind of its own. Most days, I want to cut it all off."

Ellie-Mae shook her head. "No, don't do that. You'd look like a boy."

"So what else do you think is beautiful about you?"

"Not my face."

"Why?"

"Miss Lauren, you ain't blind. You can see it right here." Ellie-Mae pointed to the strawberry-colored mark covering most of one cheek. "Mama tried all sorts, but nothin' worked. Some stuff stung, but I wouldn't have minded if it made it go away. It gets bigger every day."

Lauren didn't want to think of what cures the poor child had been subjected to.

"Darling, you have beautiful blue eyes, the color of the sea. Have you ever seen the sea?"

"No, ma'am."

"I'll show you pictures in a book tomorrow. Remind me to do that. Everyone has eyes, but some people have such amazing eyes that others can't help but stare at them. Maybe when you think people are staring at your cheek, they are thinking what gorgeous eyes you have. I'd love my eyes to be like yours."

Ellie-Mae sighed loudly. "I know you are trying to be nice, but I know what they are looking at. It's a witch's mark. It means I was a witch long ago and they burned me. Tied me to a"—the little girl scratched her head—"I can't remember the name, it's a wooden pole in the ground."

"Ellie-Mae, who told you that? It's a load of nonsense. You are no more a witch than I am."

A tear fell down the girl's cheek as she turned her big blue eyes on Lauren. "Miss Lauren, I tried to be good. They said if I was good, it would go away, but it didn't. No matter what I did."

"Sweetheart, I wish I knew who told you all these things."

"The woman at the last house we lived in. She said I would never get a mommy or daddy because one look at me told people I was a witch with a black heart." Ellie-Mae hiccupped. "She said a circus might come and take me as part of their freak show. I didn't know what that meant. One of the older kids showed me pictures of a woman with a beard all over her face. She said I should get one to cover the mark."

Lauren simmered with rage but tried not to show the little girl. She rocked her back and forth as Ellie-Mae gave way to tears. After some time, the child's breathing slowed as she fell into a deep sleep. Lauren's arms started to ache but she didn't move. She wouldn't move an inch until the little girl was better.

CHAPTER 65

Lauren was half asleep as she sat listening to the sounds of the night. An owl screeched in the distance and the roar of a puma came from the mountain top. As the stars above twinkled in the inky black sky, and Lauren searched for a wishing star, the kitchen door swung open.

"Miss Lauren, why are you sittin' outside? You will get bit all over."

"Shush, Becky! Ellie-Mae was upset and fell asleep. I didn't want to move in case I woke her."

"Poor baby. She upset again? Who was it this time? Shelley?" Becky whispered.

"Yes, Shelley started it, but the real problem is all the lies the child has been told over the years. If I ever see the woman in charge of the home Ellie-Mae lived in, I might just kill her."

"She's a nun. Those two children were in a convent home over the other side of Charlottesville. Dalton has the marks of a whip all over his back. He tried to stop the nuns sayin' horrible things to Ellie-Mae and they nearly killed him for it."

Lauren flinched at her words, her insides freezing. "How dare they hurt a child, especially one who was trying to be kind?" Her voice quivered with rage. She swallowed the sour taste in her mouth. *How many other children had those nuns hurt?* "How did they get away? And what about the other children living there? Does nobody check on the orphans?"

"The way Dalton talks, it seems a priest helped them escape, but I don't know for sure. He's so young too. Both of them were on the point of starvin' to death when they got here."

It got worse and worse. Her heart broke for the poor kids. "Who brought them here?"

"Some man picked them up in his truck on the road. He said he felt sorry for them, but he had children of his own to feed."

"Did Ellie-Mae tell you what she was told about being a witch?"

Becky crossed herself.

"You don't believe those stories, do you, Becky?"

"Not sure what I believe, Miss Lauren. We got told many things where I grew up. Some believe witches are real, some kind, some cruel, just like other folk. I knows that little girl has the heart of an angel. She is kindness itself."

Becky lifted the child from Lauren, allowing Lauren to stand up, before giving Ellie-Mae back to her. Lauren carried the sleeping child upstairs to the room the girls shared.

"I have to find those children a home," Lauren said when she returned downstairs. "Ellie-Mae needs a mom's love. Dalton needs a father's strict but caring hand. I won't stop until I find them both parents who will worship them."

CHAPTER 66

The next morning, Lauren spoke sternly to Shelley, making her apologize to Ellie-Mae in front of the other children. Lauren's voice quivered as she repeated Nanny's message to her when she'd spoken about kindness.

"Children, whatever happens, always treat folk with kindness. It costs nothing." She blinked rapidly, her mind caught up with thoughts of Nanny. *Where has she gone and will she ever come back to Delgany?*

She looked up and caught Bart Leroy giving her a thumbs up. She smiled, remembering how she had worried about giving him the job. The orphanage couldn't run without him now. He could grow just about anything, it seemed, and his wife Norma could turn what he grew into all sorts of dishes. Nothing got wasted. Norma's jams sold well at Hillmans' Store, bringing in an extra income. Lauren insisted that the Leroys took fifty percent of the profits, so that they could buy their farm back at some point.

"I'm going into town, Ellie-Mae," Lauren said to the little girl, "and I'd like you to come with me. You can choose someone to come with us."

Ellie-Mae tugged on Dalton's arm. "Dalton will come with us, won't you?"

The boy shrugged his shoulders.

Becky gave Lauren a shopping list, while Bart placed boxes of eggs and jars of pickles and fruit jelly in the back of the truck.

*

In town, Mrs. Hillman greeted them with a bright smile. "How is my favorite little girl this morning?" she asked Ellie-Mae.

"Fine," Ellie-Mae said, but her usual smile was missing. Mrs. Hillman met Lauren's eyes over the child's head.

"Ellie-Mae, will you take Dalton to the sawmill and ask Big Will to come see me, please?" Lauren asked her. "Wait outside for him, don't go into the mill. It's dangerous."

"Yes, Miss Lauren. Come on, Dalton."

When the children had left, Lauren filled Mrs. Hillman in on what had happened the night before.

"The poor child, imagine filling her head with all that nonsense. She is a pretty little girl. God must have his reasons for marking her that way."

"Shelley won't stop teasing her, and the other children often follow her example. Dalton gets into so much trouble, fighting the other orphans who upset Ellie-Mae. I need to find them a home."

"You mean, find someone to adopt them?"

Lauren nodded, biting the side of her cheeks.

"How do you go about doing that? I guess they'd have to be rich, young folk."

"Rich? No, that's not an issue, assuming they have enough money to keep the children in food and clothes. Someone with plenty of love and experience with children, I think, would suit them best. Dalton is challenging, but Ellie-Mae won't go anywhere without him."

Mrs. Hillman looked out the window at the back of the store to where her son, Earl, was now playing with Ellie-Mae and Dalton in the yard.

"My Earl is great with children. I think it's because he is still so much of a child himself."

Lauren nodded. "He's a lovely young man. The woman who marries him will be lucky. He's kind, honest, and trustworthy."

Big Will had now appeared beside her. "You were looking for me, Miss Lauren?"

"Yes, I was wondering if you had time to do a few jobs for me, Big Will. Bart needs some help with the fencing in the meadow."

"I can do that for you, Miss Lauren, but not today. It would have to be Saturday."

"Thank you. I will tell Bart to expect you. Now we best be getting back. Will you send the children inside, please?"

"Yes, Miss Lauren, see you Saturday. Will you ask Miss Becky to bake a pie?"

"She'll bake two."

The man's laugh followed him out the door. Lauren glanced at Mrs. Hillman, but her friend was staring at the two children coming through it.

"Ellie-Mae, this came in today and I thought of you." Mrs. Hillman produced a small cloth doll from behind the counter. "See her lovely gold hair? Reminded me of you."

"It did? She's pretty. What's her name?"

"I haven't named her yet, what do you think?"

Ellie-Mae tilted her head to one side as she stared at the doll. "Betty, I think that suits her."

Despite wanting the little girl to have something, Lauren knew she couldn't take the toy back to the orphanage. The other children simply wouldn't understand. "Ellie-Mae, you can play with Betty when we visit the store. Mrs. Hillman will look after her for you in the meantime. Won't you, Mrs. Hillman?"

"Of course I will. And I'll make her a new dress, if Ellie-Mae picks out some material. What color do you think?" Mrs. Hillman asked Ellie-Mae.

"I think she'd like a red dress for Christmas. Then she'd be purty, wouldn't she?"

"She sure would. I'll get working on it for the next time you call in to see us. Now, why don't take your pick of some candy before you go?"

"Yes, Mrs. Hillman. Thank you for the doll and the candy." Ellie-Mae gave her a hug, making the older woman blush, but Lauren noticed that she held onto the little girl for a few seconds. Ellie-Mae turned to Dalton. "What are you going to pick?"

Mrs. Hillman put the doll away, sending Lauren an apologetic look. Once the children were happy with their choice, Lauren settled the bill.

"Lauren, the way things are going, I'll have to pay *you* money again this week. Tell Norma to bottle more fruit. Her jars just fly off the shelves."

"I will tell her. Thank you, Mrs. Hillman. See you soon."

"'Bye, kids."

The children waved, Ellie-Mae running around the counter and hugging Mrs. Hillman once again.

CHAPTER 67

Thanksgiving, November 24, 1932

The extension Bart and Big Will had been building onto the orphanage was finished just in time for Thanksgiving at the end of November. Mr. Thatcher helped the men to install a bathroom upstairs and proper plumbing in the kitchen. They now had hot and cold water over the sink. Earl had come to help, when his pa hadn't needed him at the store, and the Hillmans had given them credit at the sawmill; credit that Lauren hoped to pay off with next year's crops. She and Becky had great plans for the land around the orphanage.

A large Monarch cooking stove had been installed in the kitchen, to Norma's and Becky's delight. Lauren's cooking skills remained non-existent. They'd tried to show her how to adjust the temperature of the oven by adding water to the reservoir, or allowing it to steam off, but she remained clueless. She couldn't even make flapjacks, something most of the children had mastered, including the boys.

A basket of wood sat by the fire, and there was more stored in the root cellar so nobody had to get wet or snowed on when the weather turned bad. Still more wood lay out in the barn. Bart had taught the older boys how to use the sharp axe and their efforts meant they wouldn't run out of firewood for about a year, maybe two.

The kitchen was now large enough to hold a long table with benches on either side. Bart usually sat at the head of the table, with Becky and Norma at the other end near the cooker. Lauren sat among the younger children.

Norma and Becky had been baking all week in preparation for today's Thanksgiving dinner. Big Will and Bart had gone up the mountain and brought back not one but two wild turkeys. The memory of butchering them made Lauren cringe. Still, their feathers would be useful; they were collecting feathers for a new mattress.

Now the turkeys were in the oven, keeping warm until their guests arrived. The heat of the ovens, and the scent of roasted meat and baked yams were filling the air, making the kitchen feel even cozier than normal.

The table was covered in plates, and there wasn't a square inch of bare wood to be seen. There were fried tomatoes, butter beans, black-eyed peas, English peas, creamed Irish potatoes, and, of course, a bowl of collard greens. Mashed squash, baked yams, and grits for Bart also sat there. *That man would eat grits ten times a day if he had his way,* Lauren thought, with a smile. Plates of biscuits and bowls of freshly churned butter dotted the table.

Lauren gazed at everything. "Becky, Norma, you've outdone yourselves. This is a real feast."

"Thank you for saying so, Miss Lauren, but I'm sure it's not what you are used to," Becky said.

"No, it isn't."

Becky's face fell before Lauren went and hugged her, her voice shaking with emotion, "It's a thousand times better."

Becky's eyes shone as she smiled wildly, and Norma placed another dish, this time Lauren's favorite, fried okra, on the table.

"Norma, the table will collapse with all this food. You planning on feeding all of Delgany?"

"I bet there isn't a scrap left for tomorrow, Miss Lauren."

Lauren had given up trying to get the others to call her by her name. Miss Lauren made her still feel like an outsider. But then that's what she was, she supposed. Norma, Becky, and the children shared similar backgrounds after all. They all grew up knowing what it was to go to bed hungry and to worry about money. It was still new to Lauren.

"When are the Hillmans going to show up? I'm hungry," Bart complained. Norma shooed her husband away from the food, when he tried to grab a biscuit. "You're always hungry. Make sure you leave room for afters, Becky's made a pie just for you."

"I love you, Miss Becky. Come here and give me a kiss."

"Don't you come near me, Bart Leroy, or I will hit you over the head with my rollin' pin."

"Becky is waitin' for Big Will to kiss her," Shelley said. She had just run into the kitchen from outside.

Lauren had to turn away to hide her amusement as Becky nearly died of embarrassment.

It was left to Norma to admonish the child. "Shelley, you keep those sort of remarks to yourself and show respect to your elders, you hear?"

"Yes, Mrs. Leroy."

"What do you say to Becky?"

"Sorreeee."

Lauren exchanged a glance with Becky. They were both worried about Shelley. Her attitude toward the staff and the other children was getting worse by the day. Becky shook her head in warning to Lauren. They would tackle the little girl, but not today.

"Thanks for your apology, Shelley, and mind you don't say anythin' like that again. Now go join the other children outside. We will call you when it is time to eat," Becky said.

The girl opened her mouth, but before she could say anything, Lauren intervened: "Now, please."

The Hillmans' arrival diffused the atmosphere. Lauren had invited them when she heard that Earl was spending the vacation with his sister, Annie, meaning the couple would be left alone over the holidays.

"I brought you some cornbread dressing," said Mrs. Hillman. "My Gene says it's the best in the County but he is probably biased. I also got some sweet potato casserole and some buttermilk rolls. I wasn't sure what else to bring."

"Your company was all we asked for, Vivian, but thank you kindly. The children can decide whether you or Becky make the best cornbread dressing. I don't think my attempt would win any prizes."

"Did you cook?"

"Mrs. Hillman, Miss Lauren ain't allowed in my kitchen, at least not by herself. She's too dangerous," replied Becky.

Lauren laughed along with everyone else. She could clean a room now, without ending up with more dirt in her hair, paint a fence, plant seeds, weed, and even pick cotton, but she still couldn't master more than making a coffee in the kitchen. And only then if someone had lit the stove already.

"We should fetch the children in to wash their hands. They are starvin', they tell me." Bart winked at his wife.

"May we speak to you first, please?" Mrs. Hillman looked to her husband, who walked over to her side to hold her hand.

Lauren's heart started to thump. *Please don't let it be bad news*, she prayed. "Of course," she said out loud. "What can we do for you, Mrs. Hillman?"

"Myself and Gene, we got to talking and we wondered if we could give a home to two of the children."

Lauren couldn't stop herself. "You want to take in two children?"

"We do. We understand you might think we are too old, us being in our forties, but we're comfortable and we have space. In our home and in our hearts."

Tears spiked Lauren's eyes at the look of love that passed between the couple. Before she could respond, Mr. Hillman spoke. "Myself and Viv wanted us more children after Annie and Earl came along, but that wasn't God's plan. Then Ellie-Mae and Dalton waltzed into our lives and they just stole a piece of our hearts. We discussed it with Earl and he'd love to have them as his siblings. But we shouldn't have put you on the spot like this. We should have had us a Thanksgiving celebration and approached this another day."

"It was my fault," Mrs. Hillman said. "I'm too impatient. I'd love to have the children in time for Christmas. It would mean a lot to us."

Lauren nodded. "Becky, why don't you give the Hillmans an answer?"

"I can't do that, Miss Lauren. You are Matron."

"I may be on paper, but we all know you is the boss," Lauren teased her friend.

"Well, in that case, yes. A thousand times yes! I don't think the children could wish for better parents than you two. You already know Dalton is a handful."

"He is, that's for sure, but he just needs some love to straighten him out. His heart is hurting. My Viv can cure that," Gene Hillman told her.

Mrs. Hillman squeezed her husband's hand but stayed silent, her eyes full of tears.

"What of Ellie-Mae?" Lauren whispered, just in case any child was listening. "I took her to see Doctor Danby and he thinks her birthmark may keep growing. He says she may need treatment in the future. It could prove expensive."

"If she does, we will take care of that just as we would if it had been Annie or Earl that needed help. These little ones will get the same treatment as our blood children got. That's a promise."

Lauren had heard enough. She walked over and hugged Mrs. Hillman and gave Mr. Hillman a kiss on the cheek. "I can't think of anything better to be thankful for but a loving family."

"Me neither," replied Becky. "But can you keep it a secret until after dinner? I don't want to make the other children sad on a day like today."

The Hillmans both nodded their agreement, and Norma sniffed loudly. "Please excuse me. I have to get something from the barn."

Bart followed his wife, leaving Becky, Lauren, and the Hillmans in the kitchen.

"You feelin' good, Miss Lauren?" Becky asked.

Lauren had been staring at the table, lost in memories of previous Thanksgivings. Nanny insisted the staff have a Thanksgiving dinner that she cooked herself. If Father was around, they would hold it the day after the holiday, as he wouldn't eat with the servants, not even on special days. Jackson had always gone somewhere for Thanksgiving, but his absence was a blessing, not a loss.

She could picture Patty and Mary fighting over the wishbone in the turkey, Cook pretending to be cross instead of amused. She could see Patty singing. She'd had such a lovely voice and her smile had been big enough to light up the whole house, never mind the room…

Now Mary was happy with Jed in California. Unlike a lot of people who went West, Jed had managed to find a job and his wife was busy making a home for them. She wrote regularly. Nobody knew where Nanny was. She seemed to have disappeared into thin air, and Lauren's heart ached every time she thought of her.

"I'm fine, just missing Mary, Cook, and Nanny," Lauren replied, dragging herself away from her memories. "I hope they are all enjoying Thanksgiving, wherever they are." Her father, too, but she couldn't admit to missing him. Her feelings were too raw and complicated. She could barely understand them herself, let alone explain them to her friends.

"So how d'you feel about president elect, Mr. Roosevelt, Lauren? Do you think he will do good things for the poor?" asked Mr. Hillman.

"Well, he has promised aid for the farmers, and unlike President Hoover, he seems to be amenable to giving to charities, and he thinks he can create jobs for workers, so I hope so," Lauren replied. "I also admire Mrs. Roosevelt. I've read some articles she recommended on children's diets. She seems to have a caring heart."

"I read about her introducing a plain menu in the White House," Mrs. Hillman added. "She plans on serving the Senators some plain, nutritious, and cheap food. I'd love to be a fly on the wall to see their reaction to bean stew rather than the usual fare they are used to."

Becky raised her glass. "Let's hope she and her husband will be able to bring some good news for more people in nineteen thirty-three."

Lauren picked up a glass of water from the table. "I'll drink to that."

CHAPTER 68

April 1933

"Are you goin' beggin' again?" Becky teased Lauren as she walked down the stairs into the kitchen area.

Shadow ran over to Lauren, but before the dog could mark her dress with his mucky paws, Becky scooped him up. Jed had given them Shadow when he and Mary left for California. He was supposed to be an outside dog and ought to protect the chickens from foxes, but the children couldn't help treating him like a pet. He wouldn't win any beauty contests but they adored him.

"I know the kids love this rascal, but he should be livin' outside. Look at the state of him," Becky said gruffly, but she patted Shadow on the head and gave him a cuddle. He was a big black ball of fluff, his origins impossible to make out.

Lauren glanced down at her cream chiffon dress, which she had brought with her from Rosehall. It was nothing like she usually wore these days. Far too fancy to be wearing while cleaning the house or hoeing in the back yard. "Too much?"

"No, you look like a lady."

"Maybe I should wear my working clothes, might make the store owners more generous with their money."

"Miss Lauren, you go in and act and look like the lady you were reared to be. If you appear to be penniless, they will see through you. Nobody takes notice of poor folk."

"I *am* penniless, I don't have to pretend to be! If this doesn't work, I'm not sure what will." Lauren sat at the table, for a second letting Becky see how the worries of the orphanage were wearing her down. It had been a difficult spring, and not just because of the cold weather and the loss of chickens to a fox. The last straw had been the school teacher sending Carly and a couple of the other girls home for wearing indecent clothes. Lauren fumed as she remembered the embarrassment on the little girl's face as she explained that the teacher said her dress highlighted her figure too much. As if Carly was wearing a too-small dress on purpose! Lauren wanted to strangle the teacher.

Becky put a cup of chicory in front of her. Their coffee supplies had run out days before. "I don't fancy your chances of gettin' money from Delgany folk. They still think you should have closed the orphanage and put the children in the religious homes or the County home. But anything you get will help, even if it's prayers. The weather needs improvin', then we may have a chance to grow somethin' to put up for the winter."

"Things will improve, Becky. You heard our new president's address on the radio. President Roosevelt will make changes. The Depression will be over in no time."

Becky rolled her eyes but didn't argue.

*

"Listen, lady, I can't afford to be givin' money to any no-good orphans. If I gave money to everyone who asks for it these days, I'd be in the poor farm in no time." The man wore a decent suit and had a gold watch hanging from his waistcoat pocket. He moved closer to her, taking one step for each word, his bony finger now wagging in her face. The smell of embalming fluid made her want to cover her nose. A woman stared from behind the counter, unable to meet Lauren's eyes.

"Thank you, sir." Lauren grasped the door handle of the undertakers' and got out just before he reached her. Shaken, she pushed her hair out of her face as she hurried down the main street. Becky was right, nobody was interested in donating for the orphans. She'd heard just about every excuse, ranging from those echoing the words of the man in that last shop to others who wanted to help, but couldn't afford it.

She couldn't go home to Becky with empty hands. They needed money for taxes and bills, but even more pressing was the need to feed and dress the children. It seemed they grew out of their clothes just as soon as they got them. It wasn't so much an issue for the boys, who could get away with wearing trousers a little too short, but the girls' dresses had to be an adequate length for decency.

Lauren pushed her shoulders back as she glanced at her reflection in the glass window of the barber's shop. She was about to push open the door when she heard a commotion.

"Stop, thief! Stop!"

A baker in his flour-streaked apron stood with his hands on his knees, struggling to breathe. Lauren saw a child darting between two vehicles, both drivers blaring their horns. Her heart in her mouth, she stepped forward, relieved to see the boy hadn't been injured. But he'd been caught by Mr. Flannery of all people. The moonshine that he consumed would make the whole town drunk, and he had a nasty temper. She screamed out in protest as Flannery gave the young boy a vicious backhander.

"Leave that child be! Pick on someone your own size." Lauren made a grab for the boy, but Flannery held him in a tight grip.

"This ain't none of your business. This 'ere boy needs lockin' up. He's a menace."

"He's a child, half-starved by the look of him." Lauren moved slightly closer, staring into the boy's eyes. "What's your name, child?"

"Cal," he muttered, staring at his feet.

"And, Cal, did you take the bread? Were you hungry?"

"Course he's hungry. So's the rest of the country, but they don't resort to stealin'. He's just like his ma. *Ow!*" Flannery rubbed his ankle where the boy had just kicked it.

"Don't you say nothin' about Ma."

"You little brat…" Flannery held up his arm again, but Lauren grabbed it.

"Don't you dare lay another hand on him."

The baker arrived, his belly heaving, his face as rosy red as his breath came in gasps. "You'll be the death of me, lad. Sheriff Dillon will have you locked up now."

Lauren saw the child pale, his eyes wide with fright.

"I can't get locked up. I ain't goin' back to that place. Never!" Taking them all by surprise, the boy bit Flannery's hand, who released him with a roar of pain, and took off at a run. His freedom lasted all of five seconds before yet another man grabbed him. He walked back toward the baker carrying Cal by his shirt collar, the boy's feet dancing just off the ground.

"Put the boy down this instant," Lauren demanded. "I will pay for what he stole and take responsibility for the child. Can't you see he is starving? Look at him, he is skin and bones."

Cal kicked out at the man now holding him, and the man cuffed him across the top of the head with his spare hand, saying, "Listen, lady, I don't know who you are or why you're interfering."

"My name is Lauren Greenwood."

"Greenwood?" the man stammered, his eyes wide, pupils darting from side to side.

She could smell his fear, but she didn't have any sympathy for him. "Yes, William Greenwood is my father. Perhaps you know him?" Lauren gave all the men standing around her a big smile, then she opened her purse and took out a dollar. Giving it to the baker, she said, "I assume this will cover your costs?"

"Yes, but—"

"I will take the boy home to his family." She bent down to speak to him. "Cal, please take my hand after the good gentleman releases you."

Cal gave her a tentative smile, but his face fell as he looked over her shoulder.

"Miss Lauren, not so fast! Cal is coming to my office. We're old friends, aren't we, Cal?"

Lauren stilled at the sound of the sheriff's voice. She hadn't seen him arrive. Keeping the smile plastered in place, she stood. "Surely you don't need to waste your time with a child, Sheriff? I've paid for the bread."

"Miss Lauren, you should go on home now. Cal ran away from a home for children like him. He'll go back there first thing in the morning."

"Please don't send me back," Cal begged. "I swear I won't steal nothin'. I just got so hungry and the smell of the bread made my mouth water. I forgot myself. If you have to send me somewhere, send me to jail. Don't send me back there, they beat me so bad."

"Stop taking nonsense, boy. The good nuns run the home. They are doing God's work."

"They threw me in the water and told me to swim. I never been in the water before. I don't know how I got to the shore. But the kid with me, he didn't come back. He's still out in that water."

The sheriff held the child by the arm, but Cal directed his plea at Lauren: "Please, miss, don't let them send me back there. I'll do anything."

Lauren couldn't stop herself: "Sheriff, why don't I take care of Cal for a while?"

"Miss Lauren, go home."

"No. Cal, where are your parents?"

"Ma is at work."

"And your pa?"

"He don't know who that is! Knowing Myra, it could be just about any man in this town or the next one," Flannery said with a smirk.

Lauren flushed at the ribald comments. She wanted to slap the smirk from Flannery's face. It was well known that he visited the wrong side of town regularly. How could he talk like that in front of the boy?

"Sheriff, why don't we discuss this in your office? It's far too hot out here."

The sheriff shrugged his shoulders. "Nothing to discuss. Move along, folks, the fun is over."

CHAPTER 69

Sheriff Dillon dragged the boy along the street. Lauren, heart sinking, watched the two of them for a second, before ducking into a store she had intended visiting to ask for a donation. She glanced around her, seeing clean but sparsely stocked shelves. An old refrigeration unit helped keep some soda bottles cool and she picked up two and walked back to the counter. An older woman came down the stairs from what Lauren assumed were her living quarters, a basket of freshly made cookies in her hand.

"What can I do for you, miss?"

Lauren didn't recognize the storekeeper. "I'd like these two bottles of soda and four of those cookies, please."

"You going to bribe the sheriff?"

Surprised, Lauren stared at the woman.

"I watched what you did out my window. Been a long time since anyone stood up for that poor child."

"Do you know him?"

"Cal? Yes, he was born here in town. His ma, well, as you heard, she isn't what some consider decent. Easy for those men to judge. She was hardly more than a child herself when she got in the family way and… well, you can guess the rest. She's taken to drinking now. She says it makes it easier to deal with the different men pawing at her."

Lauren winced.

"Sorry, miss, I forget myself sometimes. Is that all you were wanting?" The bag of cookies and the two bottles of soda were lined up on the counter.

"Yes, thank you, and please don't apologize," Lauren said. "I'm not offended, I'm horrified. Can nobody help her? Does she have family or friends?"

"None that I know of. There was an old lady who lived with them for a bit, but she's dead now. The priest came and took Cal away to some home for boys. Said he needed saving. From what the child tells me, it's the ones who are running that home that need saving. You're wondering why I don't help the child myself, aren't you? I tried but they wouldn't let me have him. I don't have a man, not anymore. He died some years back. I have this store but"—the woman waved her arms around—"as you can see, it's not doing so well. I do what I can to keep the roof over my head and help others when I have a little extra. But lately, there's more men out of work than in and my takings are way down."

"I'm sorry, I didn't mean to pry." Lauren apologized even though the woman had told her everything voluntarily.

"I heard you telling the sheriff you could take him. Would that be back to your father's house?"

"No, ma'am. My name is Lauren Greenwood. My father and I…we aren't on good terms. I live at an orphanage outside of town on the road to Charlottesville. We look after lots of children."

"You have room for Cal there?"

Lauren knew they didn't, but still she said, "We'll find it."

"You got a battle on your hands. That home Cal was taken to wasn't fit to look after dogs, never mind young'uns, but they don't give up their own lightly. He's a good boy, Cal. He doesn't tell lies. I believe his stories, although they give me nightmares. You treat the children right at your home?"

"Yes, ma'am. At least we try to. They could do with some extra food. That's why I was in town today, trying to get some donations."

"You go look after Cal. I'll try to find some way to help you with the cost of another child."

"I wasn't haggling, Mrs…?"

"Stone. Mrs. Stone. Off you go now. Tell Cal I'll look in on his ma."

Lauren insisted on paying for her goods, despite Mrs. Stone's protests. They were now packed in a brown paper sack, which she scooped up.

"Be ready to do battle, Miss Greenwood."

"I am. I've become better at arguing my case. I had to. Thank you, Mrs. Stone."

Lauren walked out the store and turned right, heading to the sheriff's office. She walked past the white picket fence of the Baptist church, waving to the baker as she saw him watching her from his store on the far side of the street. Turning left, she crossed the road in front of the war memorial and, taking a deep breath, walked into the sheriff's office. Her temper flared when she saw Cal sitting on the tattered, thin mattress in the main cell.

"Is that necessary?" she asked, looking from the child to the sheriff.

"Miss Lauren, don't tell me how to do my job. It would have been easier to keep Houdini himself locked up than this lad. Never stays where he's supposed to. Way he's going, he will end up in the penitentiary."

Lauren put the cookies and soda on the sheriff's desk. The scent of freshly baked cookies rose above the lingering smells of sweat, liquor, and other things she didn't want to identify.

"For me?"

"One soda for you and the other one for Cal, and two cookies each."

The sheriff rolled his eyes, but didn't stop her from opening the soda and handing the bottle and two cookies to the small boy. His fingers touched hers through the bars of the cell. She smiled, trying to remove the fear from his eyes.

"Thank you, ma'am," he said as he went back to sit on the mattress.

"Sheriff, I want you to release Cal into my custody. I will take responsibility for him."

"Can't do that, Miss Lauren."

"Why not? You're the law in town."

"Yes, but he was committed to the care of St. Joseph's, over past Charlottesville. He must return there."

"Why? He'll only run away again and it's at least ten miles away. He must be desperate if he keeps running away."

"And you think he won't run away from you?"

"Becky will look after him."

His eyebrows raised but he didn't respond, his mouth full of cookie.

"She's brilliant with children. I have total confidence in her."

"What do you want me to tell the priest?"

"He should pray for those who are tormenting children." At the hard look he gave her, she whispered, "Come on, Sheriff, you and I know that the child may be exaggerating, but something must be wrong if he keeps running away. Someone who knows him and his mother told me that the stories Cal has told her gave her nightmares. If only a little of what he says is true, he's better off with Becky."

Sheriff Dillon stared at the boy for a few moments before standing up and opening the cell. "Cal, you want to go with Miss Lauren or you want to wait for the priest?"

"I want to go home to Ma."

"That's not an option. Your ma isn't capable of looking after you."

The child stared at his feet. Lauren walked past the sheriff into the cell, trying to breathe through her mouth rather than her nose.

"Cal, why don't you come with me and if you don't like my home for children, I will drive you over to the other one, I promise."

Cal stared at her for some seconds, and she could almost see his mind working out his options.

"Why don't you give it a try?" Lauren said gently.

"Get going if you are going, Cal. I don't have all day to stand around here doing nothing," Sheriff Dillon grumbled as he walked back to his desk. "Father Fennelly will be here any minute. He knows you always run back here."

Cal put his hand into Lauren's. "Can we go now?" he whispered.

Lauren squeezed his hand. "You got anything you need to collect from home?"

"No, ma'am."

She glanced at the sheriff. "Thank you, Sheriff."

"Don't be thanking me. He'll have run off again within the week."

CHAPTER 70

Cal remained quiet on the drive out to the orphanage. Lauren tried to engage him in conversation but failed, the child staring silently out the window the entire time.

"Is your home up on the mountain?" Cal finally broke the silence as he looked around at the trees lining their route, the mountain coming closer.

"Not exactly. We live at the foothills. Do you like the mountain?"

"I guess. If I lived at the top, nobody would find me until I wanted them to."

"There's wild animals like bears and bobcats up there. They get protective over their territory so you might find they don't make good companions."

"I can handle a big old bear. I ain't scared of nothin'."

Lauren smiled as she turned onto the dirt track to the orphanage. "Mind your teeth, Cal. The chuckholes on this road will make the truck rattle."

Despite her warning, he bounced up and down but found it hilarious. His giggles filled the truck—and, for the first time, he seemed like the little boy he was instead of the child who had been forced to grow up far too fast—but he fell silent when he saw the house and the orphans who ran out to greet the truck. Lottie and Carly battled to be the first one to hug Lauren. She embraced them quickly before opening Cal's door to let him out. He seemed to be glued to the seat.

"You got a new boy? What's his name?" asked Carly.

"Cal."

"Hi, Cal. I'm Carly and she's Lottie. We have boys here too. Want to come inside and meet them?"

"I don't think I'm stayin'."

"We'd like you to stay, but if you want to leave, will you let Miss Lauren have somethin' to eat first?" Becky walked across the yard toward the truck. "I can hear her stomach from here. Believe me, she gets real grumpy if we don't feed her."

"Like Ma?" Cal asked, eyeing Fred, who had followed Becky out the house.

"I don't know your ma, son, but maybe." Becky smiled. "Are you hungry? I made bacon and grits."

"And gravy?" Cal's eyes bulged.

"Of course. You can't eat grits without gravy."

"Fred, will you take Cal inside and show him where to wash up, please?" said Lauren.

"Yes, miss." Fred glanced at Cal. "Comin'?"

"Sure." Cal sounded confident, but he glanced at Lauren before he moved. Only when she smiled did he follow Fred.

"You got a bag for Cal?" asked Becky.

"No, he came like he is. He ran away from a church orphanage. He got arrested for stealing some bread and his mother is a lady of the night. That's about all I know about him."

"That's enough to know that the boy needs us."

*

Lauren sat on the porch, watching the sun go down beyond the orchard, where soft hues of pink, orange, and gold painted the sky as beautifully as if van Gogh himself had picked up his paintbrush. For once the children had all settled early.

Bart had fixed screens around the porch to keep mosquitoes and other bugs out. Becky sat shelling peas.

"Do you ever stop working?" Lauren asked her friend.

"I ain't workin', I'm sittin' with you when I should be scrubbin' the kitchen floor. Did you see the state of it?"

"Becky, you could eat your dinner off that floor. You need to take care of yourself. We rely on—"

A girl's scream rent the air, making both women jump. Becky said, "That's Lottie. What's the matter with her?"

Lauren ran into the house with Becky following close behind. Lottie came flying down the stairs. "A ghost, I saw a ghost!"

"Child, it was a bad dream is all. There's no such things as ghosts," said Becky, trying to calm the little girl.

"There is. It was all white and it was movin'. I saw it, I did."

"You let Miss Lauren go check and we'll follow her."

Lauren climbed the stairs, leaving Becky to carry the girl. All the other girls were still asleep despite Lottie's scream. She looked in on the boys' room and they seemed to be fine too, apart from Cal, whose sheet was covering his head. She pushed it down to find a pillow where the boy should be. She checked under the bed, but there was no sign.

Lauren's heart raced. *What if he's run off, trying to get back to his mother? He's so small, he won't stand a chance if he comes across a black bear or a puma.* She checked each room, but to no avail.

"What is it?" asked Becky, when she returned to say that Lottie was sound asleep again.

"It's Cal. He's not in bed. I can't find him."

"Oh, Lord of Mercy! Where is that boy?"

They searched the whole orphanage, but there was no sign of Cal. Becky ran to the outhouse, but it was empty.

Lauren met her outside the kitchen door. "I should drive around."

"You won't find him on no road. He is going to stay out of..." Becky whirled around. "Cal, that you? I heard somethin'. You come out, child, you ain't in trouble. We just worried about you."

Nothing happened.

"Miss Lauren," Becky carried on, "did you tell Cal about the cottonmouth snakes that come around here? They like to settle down in the crawl space under the house."

Cal scrambled out from under the house, his eyes out on stalks. "I don't like snakes."

Lauren gathered him to her. "Cal, thank goodness you are safe. Why did you run off?" The child didn't smell as sweet as he had after his bath earlier. Lauren cuddled him closer. *Has the poor boy wet himself?*

Cal stared at the ground, his whole body trembling as if he was freezing.

Becky put her hand on his shoulder. "Please tell us. Lottie thought you was a scary old ghost."

"Yeah, sorry about that. I didn't mean to scare her."

"But why would she think you were a ghost?" Becky probed.

"Um… I…"

Lauren spotted something white in the crawl space. Hoping she wouldn't disturb a copperhead or worse, she bent down to the ground to look under the house. Cal had left a crumpled bed sheet in his hiding place.

"Sweetheart, did you have an accident?" Becky asked, as Lauren pulled the material free.

Cal shrank back from them, raising his arms as if to ward off a belt.

Becky used a softer tone: "Ain't nothin' to run off about. Happens to us all at one time or another. Reckon you had a bit too much to drink before you went to bed, is all. Or maybe you forgot to go to the toilet before you went to sleep?"

Cal stared, his mouth open as Becky wrapped up the sheet. "I'll put this in to soak, Miss Lauren, and get a new bed sheet for Cal's bed. You can change his clothes."

"Come on, darling, back inside the house. Would you like a glass of warm milk? Seems you had an eventful evening."

"You ain't goin' to hit me?"

"No."

"Am I in trouble?"

"Cal, you had an accident, that's all. There's nothing to fear."

"But at the other home we had to wear the sheet all the next day if they found out we wet the bed. The other kids used to pick on me. They got angry, because I kept doin' it. It upset the nuns, see, and then they got mean with the other boys too, and they said I was evil. That my mother had made me that way. They hung me upside down outta window. When I didn't fall, they said the Devil had saved me."

Lauren and Becky exchanged horrified glances. When Lauren sucked in her breath, Cal shrank back from her again.

"Cal, sweetheart, I'm angry but not at you. Never at you. I want to shout at those people who were so mean to you. I promise you will never be punished for wetting the bed here. Just don't run off if it happens. Find me or Becky and we will help you get a new bed sheet. You had us so scared, we thought we'd lost you."

"Would you care if you did? The sign outside says 'Unloved Children'."

Lauren bit her lip, forcing the tears back. "Yes, darling, very much. Every child here is precious, even the ones who have just arrived. We need to update the shingle to show the name Becky has picked out: 'Hope House'. You are part of our family now, Cal, whether you stay here forever or you find a new home."

CHAPTER 71

Lauren watched as Fred and Lottie ran through the meadow on their way back from town. The long grass was the color of wheat, not a lush green like it should be. The blue cloudless sky was beautiful, but more than once Lauren wished for gray clouds bringing rain. Some thunder and rain might lift the humidity. They all desperately needed it, not just for the crops but to replenish the creeks. Thank goodness for the meltwater coming down from the mountain.

Becky had come up with a reward system, whereby the best-behaved children of the week were taken into Delgany and allowed to choose a piece of candy from Hillmans' Store. Usually Lauren drove, but today the truck wasn't working properly, so they were on foot. She thought she might have hit a hole in the dirt track a little too heavily. She'd asked Mr. Hillman to send someone good with engines to the orphanage to have a look at it. That would be another bill to pay. Where were they going to get the funds to replace the cow she had bought for the orphanage? The cow had gone dry and nobody seemed to know why.

They all missed the milk the cow had produced, the butter and cream too. But that wasn't all. Bart was finding it harder to locate wild turkey, quail or even squirrels. He said it was because every farmer needed to supplement his family's food by taking what the mountains had to offer. The Depression was cutting even deeper than last year.

As they walked through the fields, Fred munched on his Snickers bar, savoring every bite. Lottie didn't like peanuts so she'd opted for Candy Buttons.

"Miss Lauren, why do they color the lime ones blue when the yellow ones are lemon? I thought limes were like lemons, only green," said Fred, looking at Lottie's colorful candies.

"They are, Fred. I guess the man who invented Candy Buttons had a good imagination."

"I prefer the pink ones," Lottie said, popping another small ball from the strip of paper into her mouth.

"They should be red," replied Fred. "Who ever saw pink cherries on a tree?"

"The blossoms are pink. You showed us that in the book, Miss Lauren."

"Yes, Lottie, I did."

"Why do you tell us not to pick tomatoes until they are red, but Miss Norma uses green ones?" Lottie was full of questions that morning.

"If the frost comes too early, we have to use the green ones. In my old house, the cook used to use vinegar and fry them," Lauren told her. "They are nice. You're making me hungry now, Lottie."

Lottie giggled.

Lauren gestured to the children to join her under the shade offered by the trees lining the almost-dry creek. Twigs snapped under their feet, another reminder of the need for rain. "Watch where you're walking, the snakes enjoy the sun too."

"What do the cottonmouths do when the water gets so low?" Fred asked, looking at the creek bed.

Lauren shivered despite herself. "I don't know, Fred, and I don't aim to find out."

"They ain't dangerous unless you bug them, Miss Lauren. Animals aren't like humans, they don't attack for no good reason."

Fred was passionate about all sorts of animals, and figured he was the authority on snakes.

Lottie shook her head. "I don't care why they bite, I don't like them. They're mean and they kill people. You be careful, Fred, they might not know you are a good brother."

The sun filtered through the leaves and the fruit growing on the trees. Soon it would be time to go apple picking. The slight breeze twirled Lottie's skirt around her legs. She was growing again and would soon need new clothes. But where would the money come from to buy them? Lauren shook those thoughts out of her mind, looking up at the majestic mountains, the tallest seeming to reach right up into the azure sky.

"Isn't Ellie-Mae and Dalton lucky to live in a store that sells candy? I bet they can eat as much as they want every day," Fred said.

"I don't think Mrs. Hillman would allow that, Fred. Too much sugar is bad for your teeth."

"Dalton is nicer now, isn't he, Miss Lauren? He looks happier too."

"He sure does, Lottie."

"They are a real family, aren't they? Do you think we will find a family one day, Miss Lauren?"

"I hope so, Lottie, but I would miss your smile if you left. I'd miss your brother too."

"Come look, Miss Lauren, this is what Ma used to cook for us," Fred said, pointing at something in the ground. "She fried it in the pan with some fat and other stuff. Tasted good, too."

Lauren looked at a plant that resembled the weeds the gardeners used to pull out of the lawn at Rosehall. She couldn't believe they were edible, but the little boy looked convinced.

"We must ask Miss Norma. Maybe she can cook some for you."

Fred nodded enthusiastically. "I know what I said about the candy store but I didn't mean it. I never want to leave you. Never."

Lottie smiled in agreement with her brother. They weren't sure what age she was, but at least she looked healthier than the first day when Lauren had met them. Fred had got over his beating, and treated Becky as his savior. He was like her shadow these days.

The little boy ran ahead as Lauren matched her pace to Lottie's. The child loved to pick wildflowers, bringing them home to Becky and Norma. "Look, ain't they pretty?"

"They are, sweetheart, but they don't smell good, see?"

"Phooeee, they smell like the outhouse!"

Lauren laughed. "Yes, they do. It shows you that not everything that looks beautiful is nice inside, doesn't it?" Lauren spotted a bird. "Look at that little one, it's pretty, isn't it? His feathers look blue like the mountains and his stomach is yellow like your flowers."

"Is he building a nest? For his babies?"

"Miss Lauren, come quick!" called Fred, who was now far ahead. "There's a girl here under a tree. Come on!"

Lauren picked Lottie up and ran toward the sound of Fred's voice. Soon she saw the little boy standing beside a tree and waving his arms. "Hurry, Miss Lauren!" he called again. "I think she's sick. She seems real bad to me."

"Fred, don't touch her," Lauren called. "Leave that to me." What if the stranger had measles or some other contagious disease? Fred, Lottie, and the other orphans could fall ill. Now she was closer, she could see Fred bending over a small girl, his arm outstretched but not touching her.

"She has a fever, Miss Lauren," he told her when, with Lottie still in her arms, she finally came to a stop beside him. "I can feel the heat off her body. Doesn't she look awful pale? Like she's dead."

Lottie screamed, burying her head in Lauren's shoulder. The girl on the ground moaned.

"Lottie, you stay here, darling." Lauren put the child down. "I have to help the little girl."

Lottie sat on the ground.

"Fred, come sit beside Lottie."

He moved reluctantly to Lottie's side, as Lauren inched closer to the child, not wanting to scare her. *What was she doing all alone out here?*

"Can you hear me?" Lauren asked as she touched the girl's forehead. She was burning up. Lauren wished she had some water, but the creek was almost dry and stank from putrid fish. She'd have to wait until they got home.

"I'm going to pick you up and take you back to our house. Then we'll get you better." The girl didn't respond. She was such a pretty little thing with blonde curls.

Lauren picked her up. She weighed about as much as a child of two should weigh, yet Lauren judged her to be about four.

"Come on, kids, let's get the little one home."

"Do you know her name?" asked Lottie.

"Not yet, but we will."

"She looks like the picture of the angel on Becky's book, doesn't she? Or what was the name of the girl whose granny died at Christmas?"

"The little match girl."

"Yes, she looks very much like her."

Lauren could feel the child's heart beating too quickly. Was it fear or fever?

"We're going to get you better, little one. You're safe with us," she whispered as she cradled the child. "Fred, please will you run ahead and let Becky know we are coming? Ask her to get her medical herbs out. Oh, and tell the children to go outside and play just in case this one has something contagious."

"Yes, ma'am."

Fred ran off, leaving Lottie to walk with Lauren. This time the child adjusted her pace to Lauren's slower one. Finally, they reached the turn for Orchards' Pass and they were in sight of home.

Lottie ran ahead, but Lauren didn't call her back. Shadow came bounding out to greet Lottie, barking and running around the small girl. Lauren heard Lottie giggling, but the child in Lauren's arms flinched at the noise.

"Shush, you're all right. That's Shadow, he looks after all of us."

The girl grew more limp and Lauren quickened her pace, meeting Bart halfway down the track. He took the child from her.

"Where did you find her? It feels as though the poor little thing has a fever somethin' bad."

"Down by the creek. She was alone. What was she doing so far from anywhere?"

"No idea, but it looks like she's been walkin' for some time. Her legs are all bruised and look at the state of her feet."

The soles of the child's feet were shredded, blood mixed in with dirt and small stones.

Bart carried her into the kitchen and set her down on a bed sheet that someone had laid on the table. Norma had boiled some water and Becky had her herbs ready. They stripped the child's clothes off, noticing welts and marks on her body.

"There's no rash so it ain't measles or the pox. Seems to me like she's got an infection of some sort. Oh goodness, look at her leg!" Becky tutted under her breath as she examined the child. "That's nasty, whether it's a boil or something else, look at that line of red. That's not a good sign. Lauren, will you hold her down? Norma, can you hold her leg?"

"Sorry, Becky, I'll go mind the children outside." Bart was gone before they could say anything.

"That big husband of mine fought for his country, but ask him to stand and watch a child being doctored and he'd pass right out in front of you," Norma told them.

Becky washed the wound with hot water, took a sharp knife and pierced the lump. The child bucked under Lauren's hands, crying out before losing consciousness. Lauren couldn't stop the tears spilling over.

Continuing to clean the wound, Becky smeared some concoction onto it before finally wrapping what looked like an onion in green leaves over it and securing it with a cloth. She ran out to the barn, returning with some walnuts. Rubbing the child's leg gently, she marked where the red line was.

"Reckon someone should go for Doctor Danby," Becky said as she eyed up the damage. "He might have to take the leg off. I can't do that."

"No, we can't let that happen," Lauren exclaimed, her voice squeaking past the lump in her throat. She threw her body in front of the child as if to shied her from an assault.

"Believe me, I don't want to, Lauren, but that red line is poison. We all knows that. I don't know how high it can get before it's too late. We need the doctor sooner than later."

Norma went to the cupboard to the right of the stove, where they kept the jar with the money. She counted it out. "How we going to pay him? We don't have three dollars between us."

"We got about half of his fee. If he's a good man, he'll wait for the rest. This little one doesn't have that luxury," replied Becky.

Norma agreed and went to find Bart, while Lauren helped Becky tenderly bathe the child's feet.

"Where do you think she came from?" Becky asked.

"I've no idea. I've never seen her before, have you?"

"You mean, is she from the mountain? I don't reckon so, but I don't know everyone that lives up there. Some people never come down this far."

CHAPTER 72

They moved the child to Lauren's bed, where one of them always remained by her side. Her temperature soared, despite a cold compress on her head. Lauren wanted Becky to take off the bandage and look at the wound, but she refused: "You got to give it time to work, to pull the poison out."

Lauren had to believe Becky knew what she was doing, but she wished Nanny or Old Sally were here.

As the sun dropped behind the mountain, still Doctor Danby didn't come. Norma fed the children, who were quieter than usual, their chatter a dull murmur traveling up the stairs. All the while Lauren held the child's hand, not wanting her to wake up and think she was alone in a strange place.

Lauren had dozed off when she heard the wheels on the gravel. Finally, the doctor had arrived. She turned up the kerosene lamp to give him more light as he came in.

"What happened to her?" he asked, gazing at the child.

"We don't know, we found her down by the creek. She's got bruises on her legs so she may have fallen. Becky is very concerned about the infection."

"It's not a cottonmouth or rattlesnake bite. There's no puncture wound that I could see." Becky unwrapped the cloth, the smell of the contents turning Lauren's stomach. She forced the bile back down her throat.

"You did well," Doctor Danby said. "Whatever that poultice was, it's worked some." He pointed out where the walnut mark was and the red line had receded, then examined the wound. "Looks like someone gave her a thrashing that opened the skin. I suspect they used something dirty like a rusty belt. She's lucky."

Lucky? How can a child who's been beaten and is near-death be lucky?

Lauren opened her mouth to protest but the doctor continued, "She's not out of danger yet, the next few hours are critical. What was in that dressing?"

"Green onion, wild garlic, and some bread to form a bind," replied Becky.

"Can you mix up a fresh batch and apply it? Change the bandage every four to six hours. Watch the redness to make sure it continues to fade. Any change, call me."

"We don't have a telephone, but I can send my husband, Bart," said Norma, who had slipped into the room.

Doctor Danby looked hesitant. "Becky," he said, turning to her, "although young, you have a good head on your shoulders. You will know if this turns worse. If I can't get back here in time, you must operate. Otherwise the child will die."

Lauren's stomach churned. The doctor was talking about cutting off a child's leg as if it was something you did every day. She couldn't believe they were being so stoic, she wanted to scream and shout about the unfairness of a young girl being so ill and abandoned in her hour of need. She watched Becky's face, her friend's eyes holding the gaze of the doctor. She didn't even flinch.

"Yes, Doctor."

"I'm going to explain to you what you will need to do, if that time comes."

Lauren pushed past the group, then ran downstairs and out to the yard. She couldn't listen to the conversation any more.

Eventually, after Doctor Danby had left—without accepting any payment, Becky told Lauren later—Norma came to find her. "Lauren, have faith. Becky did the right thing when she applied the poultice and it's working. We just have to believe it will continue to work."

The next forty-eight hours were the longest hours of Lauren's life. She was only able to sleep for a snatched hour or two, as she fretted over the little girl. The rest of the time, she stayed sitting by the child's side.

*

"Lauren, wake up." Becky shook her gently. "The fever's broken, she's going to be fine."

Lauren rubbed the sleep from her eyes before looking at the child now sleeping peacefully on the bed beside her. Becky had left the bandage off and the angry red cut was now turning pink. The walnut mark was inches away.

"Becky, you did it. You saved her," Lauren whispered, her heart soaring as she looked at the child.

"I'm going to wrap it up again, to be sure, but I think she will be fine. When she opens her eyes, she is bound to be scared. We're all strangers. Bart drove down to the sheriff but nobody has reported a little girl missing."

Lauren pushed the blonde hair back from the child's face. "Maybe she'll be able to tell us who she is and where she's come from soon."

*

"Am I in Heaven?"

Lauren jumped at the sound of a small voice. She'd been asleep.

"No, darling, you're alive and well. My name is Lauren. What's yours?"

"Ruthie. Where am I?" She pushed the blonde hair out of her large cornflower-blue eyes. She tried to sit up, but winced in pain. Lifting the covers to look at her leg, her mouth hung open as she gazed at the bandage.

"You are at an orphanage near Delgany, Ruthie. We fixed up your leg so you will be all better soon. Do you know where your mama is?"

Ruthie picked at the bed cover. "She's in Heaven with my baby sister. The angels took them away. Why didn't they take me too? I want to be with Mama." Her blue eyes shone with tears.

"Oh, precious, you don't want to die! Your mama wouldn't want that. You have to live. What about your Pa?"

Ruthie's eyes closed as her body shook. Lauren tried to pull her into a hug, but the child was rigid. "Ruthie, it's okay. You don't have to tell me anything."

Ruthie whispered, "Pa died before Mama did. I got a new pa, but I don't like him. He's mean, he kicked my rabbit. Now she's dead, like Mama."

"Oh, Ruthie, I'm sorry. Maybe your new pa is worried about you?"

"He doesn't like me. He shouts a lot. I make mistakes and he gets real mad. He told me to get out."

Lauren did her best not to show her horror. She forced a smile and kept her voice calm. "Well, don't you worry. Nobody is going to send you away from here. You can stay as long as you like. Are you hungry?"

"Yes, ma'am."

"I'll go down and get you something to eat and bring it back up here. Do you need the bathroom?"

"The what?"

"The outhouse?"

Ruthie squeezed her eyes shut, two small tears escaping to run down her cheeks.

"What's the matter, precious?"

"Will you be mad?"

"No, I promise."

"I couldn't hold on. I's wet already."

"You've been sleeping so long, that's not your fault. Let me help you."

Lauren held Ruthie as she helped her change into a clean nightgown. As she placed the child in the chair, she started to strip the bed. At that moment, the door opened and Becky entered the room.

The little girl shrank back in the chair, pushing her fingers into her mouth.

"This is Becky, Ruthie. She's the one who worked magic on your leg to make you feel better. She's my friend and she wants to be your friend too."

"Hello, sweetheart, you hungry? I can make you some flapjacks if you'd like them?"

"Yes, please," the girl whispered.

"Do you want me to carry you downstairs so you can meet the other children, or do you want to have them up here?"

"Can you carry me?" Ruthie asked hopefully.

"Sure, sweetheart. Just let me get this cleared up."

Becky took the dirty laundry. "I'll take this while you two wash up. Don't stand on your leg, sweetheart, not until it gets better."

Lauren carried Ruthie to the new bathroom, where the child's mouth fell open at the indoor toilet, the bath, and the sink.

"You must be really rich. I never saw an outhouse in a house before."

Although Lauren fought hard not to have favorites, her heart had been claimed by Ruthie. The child remained just as sweet as she had been in those early days at the orphanage. She was a favorite of children and adults alike, and, as the weeks passed and nobody came to claim her, Sheriff Dillon was happy for her to remain at Hope House. Ruthie never mentioned her stepfather again and nobody else brought up the subject, happy to welcome the little girl into the fold. The only child who seemed to dislike her was Shelley, but then again Shelley hated the whole world.

"Seems to me, little Ruthie'd be dead if young Fred hadn't stumbled across her, Lauren, and if Becky hadn't made good use of the talents God gave her," Sheriff Dillon said, when he called in to check on the little girl. He was eating a slice of Norma's apple pie, having declared it to be the best he'd ever tasted.

"Would you like more coffee and more pie, Sheriff?" offered Norma.

"I sure wouldn't say no. Your husband is a lucky man, ma'am."

"I believe I'm the lucky one. The stories you hear nowadays with men walking out on their families, ridin' the rails, heading to live in those horrible camps. What do you call 'em?"

"Hoovervilles, ma'am. It isn't the runaway husbands that bother me, it's the children who are left behind. Every day the poor farm is complaining they have too many children and not enough space. Every orphanage is full to the rafters and yet the kids keep coming. The asylums are full too."

"With people goin' mad from their worries?" asked Becky.

"No, with children. Healthy kids."

"You can't put a healthy child in one of them places. That ain't human."

"Can't say I don't disagree, Becky, but what's the answer? Despite Lauren's knack for picking up youngsters off the streets, even she can't house all these kids."

"Well, don't tell her about 'em all, or knowing our Lauren, she'll try."

CHAPTER 73

The children raced into the orphanage shouting that Ellie-Mae and Dalton had come to visit. Lauren took off her apron, grateful to get away from peeling potatoes. With so many children to feed these days, it seemed to take hours to prepare the food. As she couldn't cook, she'd volunteered to prepare vegetables.

Moving outside, she greeted Earl Hillman and the two youngsters.

"I missed you, Miss Lauren." Ellie-Mae gave her a hug.

Lauren clasped the child to her. Seeing her beaming face lifted her spirits straight away. Dalton smiled at her before chasing after Cal and Fred, with Shadow barking and bounding after them.

"Earl, you and your parents have done wonders for those children. They are so happy. The change in Dalton is amazing."

"He's still a bit big for his britches but we'll sort it out. All they needed was some love and attention." Earl turned crimson. "Lauren, I didn't mean to—"

"You didn't, Earl! You're right, they needed a real home. Would you like to come in for a cup of coffee? I think Norma might have some cookies too."

"I would, but first, where would you like me to put this present?" Earl went to the back of the truck. He climbed up and came back holding a goat in his hands. "Grouchy thing she is an' all, but Ma said the milk would be good for any babies you got. It's easier on the stomach than cow's milk."

"We don't have any cows at the moment."

"You do, they'll arrive tomorrow."

"Earl, your parents are too generous to us," Lauren replied, touched.

Earl was trying to get the goat to go toward the barn. He pulled and pushed, but the goat refused to move away from a tuft of grass she was eating: "They got the goat, someone else donated the cows. Don't know who, but Ma will know."

Lauren clapped her hands. Becky chose that moment to come around the corner, coming to a standstill as she looked at the goat: "What's that doing here?"

"Present for Lauren. Ma said she's grouchy."

"That she is, particularly when she's hungry," Becky joked, winking at Lauren.

"No, I didn't mean— Oh, heck, why do I open my mouth and put my foot in it?" Earl's ears were as red as his cheeks.

Lauren felt very sorry for him. "Come inside, Earl, we're just having fun. Sit down and tell us all the happenings in Delgany. Terry will look after the goat, won't you, Terry?"

"Yes, Miss Lauren." The boy had come silently into the yard soon after Earl and the children had arrived.

"Terry has a gift with all animals, Earl. He wants to be an animal doctor when he finishes school."

Terry turned crimson just as the girls came running up to see the goat. They crowded around, Ruthie getting a little close.

"Watch out, Ruthie, your hat—"

Terry's shout of warning was too late. The goat swiped the little girl's bright red hat and ran off with it in her mouth.

Lauren braced herself for tears, but instead the youngsters laughed and went chasing after the goat.

"She won't hurt them, will she?" Lauren asked.

Becky shook her head. "She's safe with Terry around. He'd walk in front of a runaway train to protect those children."

Later that evening, when the goat and the children returned, it was hard to know who was more tired.

"Miss Lauren, we're calling her Grouchy. She's got a mean temper and she ruined my hat," Ruthie said.

"I'll knit you another one, don't worry." Becky ruffled the young girl's hair as they stared at the goat, bits of red wool hanging from its hide.

"Girls, there are two surprises in the barn. Want to see?" Lauren asked.

The girls clapped with excitement. They followed Lauren and Becky into the barn to find a new cow and her calf in the stalls.

"Aw, they're real sweet, aren't they?" Becky said.

Ruthie went closer to the cow. "They are beautiful. I think we should call them Petal and baby Pumpkin."

"They're dumb names for animals," Shelley snarled.

"Shelley, be nice," Becky reprimanded.

"Who heard of a cow called Petal? Or a calf called Pumpkin?" Shelley rolled her eyes, her hands on her hips, daring the younger ones to argue with her.

But Carly stepped forward. "Ruthie, I think your names are beautiful. Petal and Pumpkin they are. Terry will carve their names on the posts. Won't you, Terry?"

"Yes, ma'am." Terry saluted the younger girl, making everyone laugh. Lauren exchanged a glance with Becky. Terry adored all the kids, but Carly held a really special place in his heart.

"Who's first to do the milking? Miss Lauren?" Terry offered her the bucket. Lauren took hold of it, not wanting to admit she'd never done milking before. The children were all looking at her expectantly, and Becky's eyes were dancing with laughter.

Norma took pity on her, taking the bucket from her hand. "I think the cook should have the first cream, don't you?" she said.

Becky came to stand behind Lauren. "Don't worry, we'll teach you later," she said with a wink.

CHAPTER 74

November 1933

"Which bank did you put your money into, Lauren?" asked Becky. She was holding a newspaper in her hand.

"The Richmond First National in Richmond. Why?"

Becky's face paled, her freckles more obvious than normal.

"Why, Becky?" Lauren repeated.

"That's gone. They shut the doors in a man's face. He had gone to get some money out to buy a present for his wife's birthday, but the banker shut the door just before he entered. They never re-opened the bank. The newspaper said everyone who had money in there has lost everything, as the bank had been using people's savings to try to stay open."

Lauren grabbed the paper from Becky's hands. *All gone? It couldn't be.* She read through the article, realizing with growing horror that Becky was right. She had put all their money into the Richmond bank. All the money they'd scrimped and saved from the sales of berries, pies, and canned items. They'd saved every dollar to put toward the mortgage payment due in January. They'd even collected enough to pay for Christmas for the children. *Now it was all gone.*

"Did you keep any of the money in your father's bank?" Becky asked Lauren.

"He would have stopped me having access to it." Lauren threw the paper on the table. *What will we do now? Why, oh why, didn't I put the money in a sock or a shoebox?*

"How much money have we got left?" Becky said, chewing her lip. "Tell me the truth, Lauren."

Lauren walked over to the cupboard and took out the tin. She poured the contents onto the table. "Two dollars, fifty-five cents."

Becky frowned, making a noise in her throat. Lauren couldn't look at her. She'd failed them all. Months of hard work and now they were somehow worse off than when they'd started.

The back door opened, admitting Norma. "It's chilly out there. I was just—" She came to a stop when she saw their pale, stricken faces. "What's wrong?"

Lauren could feel both sets of eyes on her, but she couldn't find the words.

"The bank where Lauren put the money we made… it's closed," Becky said at last, wringing her hands. "The money's all gone."

"All of it?" Norma asked, her voice incredulous.

"We've two dollars, fifty-five cents to our name," Lauren said. "I'm utterly useless. Why did I open the account with that bank?"

"Look here, Lauren, we've been through hard times before. This is just a setback, is all. You couldn't have known this would happen. Most of the banks that closed did so in the early days of the Depression. We thought that was over."

"Norma's right, Lauren," added Becky. "The children will be fine. We can kill one of the chickens for Thanksgiving. We'll make do."

Norma poured a cup of coffee, added some cream and a spoon of sugar. "Drink that, Miss Lauren, it'll help with the shock. Then you pick yourself back up and get on with it. We don't have time to mourn the loss of that money, we have to find a way to replace it."

"Find fifty dollars for the mortgage? How? The bank won't wait on the payment."

"Nothing will happen with that attitude, Lauren. All the orphans depend on you. You can't show weakness, at least not in front of them."

"And what about you, Norma? Some of that money belonged to you and Bart."

"We can't miss what we never had," Norma poured water into the kettle from the clean bucket. "We are strong and healthy. We'll get through this. Together."

*

Lauren dressed in one of her best Rosehall dresses, as Becky called them, and sneaked out the orphanage early the next morning. The grass was wet with dew and there was little heat in the sun, but the birds were singing. She felt crazy but she was desperate. She'd taken on these children and the people who worked here. She couldn't let her pride stop her from asking for help: they needed money and there was one person who had plenty.

She drove the truck slowly down the dirt track and out onto the main road, going over and over what she was going to say. Last night, she'd drawn up a list of what they needed, and the approximate cost. In addition to the mortgage repayments, food, and utility bills, Terry needed new trousers, he was too old to be wearing britches and the boys at school teased him enough over his limp. Carly and Shelley both needed new dresses. The young children needed shoes, the cardboard-stuffed soles let the water in. All the children required thick coats, as the few they had were in rags and wouldn't keep the winter chill out when it came.

She drove past the Delgany turn and took the back roads. It didn't take long for her to see the large chimney of Rosehall on the horizon. Stopping the car for a second, she took in the view of her home. She brushed the tears from her eyes. Her father despised weakness of any sort.

"Put your shoulders back and chest out, Lauren." Nanny's voice shone through, loud and clear. Lauren did just that as she drove the last few yards. The tree-lined avenue was more overgrown than she remembered, the paths covered in leaves and rotting fruit. She drove on until she reached the gates, then found that she could go no further.

A large padlock held the gates in place. There was no smoke coming from the chimneys, no sign of life—human life, that was. All the trees and bushes that she could see were overgrown, as if Nature was reclaiming what had once been hers. Lauren got out the car and called out, but nobody answered. Where were Sam, Old Sally, and the others? Where was her father?

If Rosehall was deserted, then with it went her hopes of fixing her money problems. She got back in the truck and sobbed her heart out. So much for keeping her shoulders back. She was crumbling under the weight of her worries. In the back of her mind she'd always relied on the very last option of going to her father to beg for his help, but now even that option was gone. What was she going to do?

CHAPTER 75

Lauren sat on the porch, a blanket wrapped around her shoulders to ward off the chill, staring at the stars in the midnight black sky. She hadn't told Becky and Norma where she'd been earlier in the day, simply saying that she needed some time to think. How would she find the money for the mortgage and the property taxes, never mind the day-to-day needs of the children? Why had she been stupid enough to put their savings in just one bank? Nanny always kept cash near to hand for an emergency. She wondered, for what felt like the millionth time, where the old woman was: *Is Nanny looking at these same stars?*

The sound of Shadow barking broke into her thoughts, together with a noise coming from inside the house. Fred must have smuggled the dog up to the boys' dormitory again. He'd wake up the whole house with his barking.

She turned to go inside when she smelled it.

Smoke! Fire!

Her heart stopped as she looked around for the source, but she couldn't see it. The weather had been unseasonably warm, leaving the grass and wood perfect fuel.

I have to get the children out the house!

"*Fire! Fire!*" she screamed at the top of her lungs. "*Get out now! Boys, wake up! Becky, are you up?*" Lauren ran up the stairs and pounded on the door of the older boys' dormitory. Shadow bounded out the room, jumping on Lauren before going back into the room, barking his head off.

Terry came out, rubbing the sleep from his eyes, but when he heard *"Fire!"* he turned back to wake up all the younger boys. They traipsed out the room with Terry leading them downstairs. Fred came out last and wouldn't leave without Lottie.

"Lauren, what on earth…?" said Bart, emerging from his quarters.

"I smelled smoke outside, Bart. I can't see where the fire is, but we have to get the children outside."

Bart pulled his suspenders up as he shouted for his wife: "Norma! Help Lauren! Bean and Clarissa, get out the house now! I'm goin' to the barn. Fred, tell the older boys to come help in the barn. And get that dog out of here."

"Yes, sir." Fred grabbed Lottie's hand and raced down the stairs with Shadow in hot pursuit, despite Lauren telling them to walk—she didn't want anyone tripping.

Norma and Becky escorted the children out, while Lauren checked every room to make sure there was nobody left anywhere inside. The smoke was thicker now, making her gag and cough. She stumbled down the stairs, seeing a fiery glow through the window.

The barn!

Outside, Norma had arranged the older children in a line to pass buckets of water from the well to the front, where Bart was valiantly trying to save the barn and their livestock.

"Petal is in there with her baby Pumpkin. Grouchy is in there too. Are they going to die?" Ruthie tore her gaze from the barn to pull on Lauren's skirt.

Lauren bent down and put her arm round the little girl. She could feel her trembling. "Ruthie, go with Carly and all the other little ones down to the lake, and take Shadow with you. Don't come back until I come and get you, you hear?"

"Yes, Miss Lauren."

"Carly, don't let the little ones out of your sight. They don't understand how dangerous it is."

Carly, white-faced in the glow from the fire, nodded. Taking Ruthie by the hand, she led her and the others down the path toward the lake. Cal went with them, carrying Shadow.

The women and older children passed the buckets as fast as they could, but it was like trying to put out a fire with a thimble full of water.

Bart pushed the line back. "Wet the house. The barn's gone."

They turned their efforts to the house, throwing buckets of water on the wood, where the paint had already started to blister and crack. Despite the heat, smoke, and exhaustion nobody gave in. A truck arrived with Big Will, Earl, and some of the men from Delgany, including Sheriff Dillon.

"Saw the glow in Delgany. You men, take this side. Keep that water coming." The sheriff turned to Big Will: "Can you handle the roof?"

"Yes, sir." Big Will and Earl climbed onto the roof of the house and stamped out any sign of sparks or cinders. Lauren prayed harder than she'd ever done. They couldn't lose the house. Where would the children live?

Then, mercifully, a drop of rain hit her face, followed by another as the clouds opened. The downpour hadn't come a moment too soon. The men cheered, but Lauren couldn't say a word. Norma hugged her silently.

The sheriff sent Becky and Norma to the lake to check on the little ones, but Lauren refused to leave the house, continuing to work to ensure the fire was completely out. Despite the rain, the danger of sparks carrying on the wind was too high to abandon the effort. The dark sky turned brighter as dawn broke and the rain moved off, leaving some clouds floating above the mountain peak.

Lauren watched as Norma tended to Bart, who had been burned by the flames, putting some of the vile-smelling salve that Old Sally had given Lauren on his hands and around his ears. Thank God Sam had given it to her when Patty had first come to live here.

Bart screwed his nose up at the stench. "I think I'll settle for the pain."

"Don't be a baby. You've smelled worse." Norma fussed around him like a mother hen.

The barn was gone, that much was evident. Big Will and the sheriff insisted on checking the house thoroughly before they let anyone inside it. Only then could the Delgany women start preparing coffee and food.

Mrs. Hillman, Miss Chaney, and Ginny Dobbs, who had turned up to help out, passed out cups of coffee to the men. Lauren's cupboards were bare, but thankfully, they'd brought their own supplies. The women cooked up bacon, eggs, sausage, biscuits, beans, and grits to feed everyone, refusing to let Becky, Norma or Lauren help.

"You women need to rest just as much as the men. You worked as hard as they did." Mrs. Hillman shook her head as she looked in the direction of the barn, before walking back up the steps into the kitchen.

Becky brought the children back to the house once it was safe. Shadow barked when he saw Lauren, but whimpered as he passed the barn. He lay down and refused to move, his eyes trained on the smoking ruins. The children trailed past in silence, tear marks causing white lines on their sooty faces. Ruthie ran straight into Lauren's arms.

"Did you save them? Pumpkin? Grouchy? Where are they?"

Lauren shook her head and held the child as she sobbed, her heart breaking.

After the children were washed and fed, Becky and Big Will took them off to the lake to do some fishing. They hadn't wanted to go but Lauren hugged them all and asked them to try to catch as many fish as possible to help her.

The sheriff and Bart inspected the remains of the barn, while Earl and the other men cleared out the debris, including the remains of their animals. Lauren couldn't bear to look. How had the fire started? They were always so careful. The children knew not to light lamps in there unless an adult was with them. Still, maybe they'd got curious.

Lauren approached the men: "Any idea how it started?"

The sheriff's grim expression caused Lauren's stomach to clench. Shadow barked at her and she bent down to pick him up, feeling his heart beating fast, just like hers.

"You got insurance, Lauren?"

"No, Sheriff. We couldn't afford the premiums. Do you know what happened?" She didn't want to ask, but his expression prompted the question.

"Arson."

"*What?*" She shook her head slowly, holding Shadow so tightly that he yelped. She kissed him and put him on the ground. He immediately ran back toward the house. Lauren was finding it hard to breathe. Nobody hated her or the children enough to endanger their lives, surely? The cows and the goat were more valuable alive than dead to most folks. "It couldn't be—"

"We found four cans of kerosene just inside the door. I know you people couldn't afford that many at once. You see anyone hanging around?"

Lauren wrapped her arms around herself. Someone had done this on purpose. What if they had targeted the house with the children inside? It didn't bear thinking about.

Her body shook, making her voice quiver. "I do recall Becky saying she saw the Bramley brothers," Lauren said. "Apparently they drove out this way last week. Said they were inspecting land for the Blueridge Park or something. You know Becky's opinion of them."

"Those brothers been causing trouble for years, but this ain't their style. Thieving, bootlegging for sure, but killing animals that could fetch a good price elsewhere…" The sheriff scratched his chin, brushing the soot off his face with his sleeve. "I just can't see it."

"Who do you think it was then, Sheriff Dillon?" Bart asked, holding his burned hands gingerly.

"Don't rightly know, but someone really wants to shut this place down. You might reconsider sending those kids away to State-recognized orphanages like St. Joseph's over beyond Charlottesville or the County home in Richmond."

Lauren folded her arms across her chest as she held the sheriff's gaze. "I told you before and I'll tell you again. I won't send a dog to those places, never mind these children. This is their home and nobody's going to run them out of it."

"That's fightin' talk, Miss Lauren, but who's going to protect them?"

"We will. Father insisted I learn to shoot. I'm a better shot than most as I had to learn not to hit the animals we hunted. Bart has a shotgun. We'll get one for Becky and Norma too."

The sheriff's eyes narrowed. "I don't want a militia out here, Miss Lauren."

"We won't go looking for trouble, but if someone sets foot on this property again with the intent of hurting any living person on it, I'm sorry to say that you will be collecting them in a box."

*

Little Ruthie insisted on holding a funeral service for the animals from the barn. Bart, Earl, and Big Will had already buried the remains, but the child wanted a marker made.

"God loves everyone, says so in the Bible. He even loved Grouchy and that took some doin'," Ruthie insisted, when they tried to dissuade her.

So, they gathered the children together and put the wreath, which Ruthie had made from grass, on top of the mound that covered the remains.

"We'll bring you flowers in the spring," Ruthie whispered.

Lauren cried, not just at the loss of the animals but for fear of what the future might hold. Thanksgiving and Christmas were coming. The money was gone and now the animals too. She'd told the sheriff that she wasn't going to abandon the children but, in reality, how on earth would she keep them?

CHAPTER 76

The days following the fire were brutal on everyone. The children, scared and upset at the loss of the animals, acted up at every opportunity. Lauren couldn't sleep, wondering who would threaten a group of innocent orphans. Becky looked just as bad as she did; she knew the girl was worrying. Not so much about Christmas—Becky had reminded Lauren that many mountain families never celebrated Christmas—more about practical matters like money for taxes, the mortgage, and food on the table.

"What we got in the cupboard, Norma?" Becky asked.

"A half-box of salt, a spoonful or more of sugar, about the same amount of baking soda. There's half a pint of lard and some milk left from what the Thatchers dropped off yesterday."

Becky picked up a basket and walked out the back door, down the steps, and toward the orchard.

Lauren followed her. "Where are you going?"

"To get us some things for Thanksgiving."

She watched as Becky gathered what Lauren thought were weeds, calling out to the boys to collect a basket of acorns for her. The girls followed them.

"What are you making with the greens? Soup?" Lauren glanced over at the children giggling as they collected the fruit of the oak tree. "And why acorns?"

"No. We are having greens for lunch, much like we will do every day until we find a way to get some money." Becky shook some dirt off a clump of greenery. "We can boil some acorns, dry them, and then use them to make flour for pancakes. The Indians used to use them."

"You'll make the children eat weeds?"

Becky gave her a look. "What do you suggest? We let them starve? When we had no money, Ma used to do this. She'd take what she could get from the ground. This here is sorrel, it can be eaten raw but it has a nasty taste so I'll cook it with some garlic and clover." Becky moved some pieces of lumber on the grass.

"What are you looking for now? Worms?"

"Mushrooms. They like to grow in the dark spaces and they come to life just after it rains. The children enjoy them."

Weeds and mushrooms. Even the pilgrims ate better than that.

Lauren turned on her heel and went back into the house. Upstairs, she took her gun from its place at the top of the closet, where she kept it hidden from the children. She hated hunting, but if it was the only way to put meat on the table, she'd have to do it. Bart couldn't operate a gun, not with his hands damaged from the fire.

As she walked down the stairs, her heart sore, Fred and Cal were on their way up.

"You goin' to kill somethin', Miss Lauren?" Fred asked. His face had lit up with excitement at the sight of the gun.

"I'm going to try to get us a wild turkey."

"Can we come with you, Miss Lauren? *Please?*"

"Not this time, boys. Next year in the spring, I'm sure Bart will take you hunting. For now, could you try to catch some fish? Becky is gathering things for Thanksgiving."

"Yuck! She's gathering greens, ain't she?" Cal grimaced. "Ma used to do that sometimes if she couldn't find work. Miss Norma can cook better than Ma, but I sure hate eating greens."

"It's either that or starve." Lauren repeated Becky's words, despite sharing Cal's feelings. She ruffled his hair. "Go on now, boys, and don't fall in that lake."

"Maybe we can catch a turtle. I like turtle soup." Fred rubbed his stomach.

Lauren briefly closed her eyes. Her father had loved turtle soup. Despite everything, she missed him, or rather her image of him. "Be careful, don't let him catch *you*."

But the boys didn't even look up, too caught up in the excitement of their upcoming adventure.

Lauren decided to go back to her room to change into her pants. It would be safer than going through the woods in a dress. She was wondering how far up the mountain she'd have to go when Becky called up to her: "Lauren, there's someone coming."

Her heart hammering at the sound of the gravel crunching outside, Lauren picked up the gun. But when she looked out the window and saw that it was Big Will driving Miss Chaney's old Ford, with the postmistress sitting beside him, she placed the gun back in its hiding place in the closet and ran downstairs to open the door.

"Afternoon, Lauren, how are you this fine day?" Miss Chaney asked brightly, before her eyes had taken in Lauren's attire. "Oh my, what *are* you wearing?"

Lauren glanced down at her pants. "Sorry, Miss Chaney, we weren't expecting visitors. I was going hunting."

"Miss Lauren, you don't have to do that," Big Will said quickly. "I can do that for you. But first, I have to unload the trunk." He walked round the car to let Miss Chaney out, then went to the trunk.

"I've brought you up some supplies," Miss Chaney told Lauren. "I figured if you hosted Thanksgiving here tomorrow, you could thank the people for their help with the barn fire."

"I would, Miss Chaney, but… well, I don't have anything to give them."

"You will if you get your skates on and help Big Will take the provisions into the house. Where are Norma and Becky?"

"Right here, Miss Chaney. We've been gatherin' lunch," said Becky, walking over. "Want to stay and eat?"

"I'd love to. Thank you. Big Will, are you in a hurry to get back to town?"

"Not when food is on the table, no, ma'am."

Lauren caught the look on Becky's face. *Would they have enough food?* Still they couldn't be inhospitable.

"You brought us some flour and beans," said Norma. "Thank you kindly, Miss Chaney. I'll rustle up lunch." Norma put her apron over the bowl in her hands. Was that to keep insects out or stop their guests knowing how bad off they were? "You keep Miss Lauren company. She's so down, her lip is sliding along the ground."

Big Will laughed heartily as he took two bags of food into the house.

Miss Chaney offered her arm to Lauren. "Walk me to the porch, my dear. My hip is bothering me. I fancy sitting on that swing seat and looking up at the view for a spell."

Lauren guided the old woman up the steps and onto the porch, where Miss Chaney sat down. "Lauren, you can't let the fire get you down. You got to be thankful nobody was hurt. I don't like to see animals dying, but it wasn't the children. It could have been much worse."

"I know," Lauren replied with a heavy heart, "but I can't help feeling I let everyone down. I put all our money in a bank that failed, now the goat and the cows are gone, and once again, we have no milk for the children. They are starving, Miss Chaney. The older kids haven't any shoes and the younger ones, well, their clothes are almost indecent. Some of the dresses the girls have are more patches than original."

"Nobody said it would be easy taking on this place. You're having a hard time but it will pass."

"You've been saying that for months now, Miss Chaney."

"Well, one of these days, it will be the truth."

"Ladies, lunch is served!" Norma called from the kitchen.

Lauren led Miss Chaney into the kitchen, where the younger children had washed and were seated at the table. The adults sat down too and Norma served up the greens as if it was prize beef. She'd made some corn mush to go with it. The children hated it, but it would fill their stomachs, at least.

"Can't we have milk? I hate drinking water," Shelley complained.

"Water is good for you, Shelley," replied Lauren. "We'll have milk again when we get a new cow."

"I sure miss Petal and Pumpkin. Grouchy too, even though she ate my red hat," Ruthie said sadly.

Lauren grinned as she pictured the goat munching on Ruthie's hat. That goat had gotten into more mischief than all the children put together, yet they still missed her.

"Tomorrow is Thanksgiving, isn't it, Miss Chaney?"

"It sure is, Shelley."

"We don't have much to be thankful for, do we?" Shelley swung her legs on her chair.

"That's enough of that talk, young lady. You have a roof over your head, food in your belly, and people who love you. That's more than some," Miss Chaney said crisply.

After lunch, when Miss Chaney was about to be driven back to the post office by Big Will, she pressed a dollar into Lauren's hand and whispered, "Things will get better." Lauren prayed that the old woman was right, as she kissed her goodbye and then watched the Ford until it disappeared from view.

Only then did she return to the house, where Norma and Becky were planning the menu for the next day. Big Will hadn't had time to go out with her gun, and it was too late for her to go hunting now.

"I can make an apple pie. I have my dried apples and now we have flour and lard." Norma looked in the box of provisions Miss Chaney had brought. "There's a slab of bacon too and some coffee."

"Thank goodness for coffee! I hate that chicory stuff."

"With coffee at thirty cents a pound, you best get to like chicory, Miss Lauren," Becky retorted.

Just then the boys came running in, shouting at them.

"What now?" Becky asked as the three of them ran to the door and down the steps.

"We got a snapper! A big one! Look!" Cal was dancing from one foot to another in excitement. He and Fred were carrying the turtle between them. It was bigger than any turtle Lauren had ever seen.

"That will make a fine turtle soup," said Norma. "Thank you, boys. Go wash up in the bath and then you'll find something to eat on the stove."

"Be careful, she's mighty cross," Cal warned as she took hold of the turtle. "Nearly took my finger off, she did."

"Don't worry, Cal. I grew up with snapper turtles, I know all their tricks. My fingers will be just fine."

"Come on, boys, bath time," Becky told the boys.

"Aw, Becky, that's not fair, we had our baths on Saturday. It's only Wednesday."

"Cal, you get up those stairs and into that bath or I will chuck the turtle into it with you." Norma pretended to chase the youngster.

The adults laughed as the boys pushed each other out of their way in their haste to get to the bathroom. Terry was the only one remaining in the kitchen.

"What are you waiting for, Terry?" Norma moved closer.

"Get away from me with that thing! I is older now. I was thinkin' I could have my bath in private, like."

Lauren hid her smile with her hand as she saw Becky trying to swallow her mirth. Terry was only two years younger than Becky, but they all forgot that.

"Of course, Terry," Lauren said. "We should have thought of that. Could you look after the younger ones first, though?"

"Yes, Norma." Terry took off upstairs.

"That boy be growin' up so fast, he'll be thinkin' of leavin' us soon." Becky picked up her spoon, sniffing the pot to check her sauce.

"Don't be thinking of anyone leaving just yet, Becky. He's not that old and nobody is going to push him to go anywhere. This is his home."

CHAPTER 77

Thanksgiving, November 30, 1933

Thanksgiving dawned with a brighter sky than they had enjoyed over the previous days.

The children put on a play for Thanksgiving, telling the story of the pilgrims. Despite the unusual food, turtle soup, and cornbread not being the usual Thanksgiving fare, they enjoyed their day. Norma had made shortbread and served it with some of her blackberry jelly. If anyone missed cream, they didn't say.

Later that evening, they were all listening to the radio when they heard someone honking a horn. The children ran to the windows: "It's Big Will and another truck behind him!"

Becky glanced out. "It's John Thatcher and his wife, Alice. What are they doin' here? Maybe they have news of Mu." She opened the door and rushed out to the truck.

Lauren watched from the window, hoping the Thatchers had been able to find out more about Becky's family. She watched as the hopeful look slid off Becky's face. Alice wrapped her in a hug. Becky trailed after the couple as they came in the door.

Becky whispered to Lauren, "They didn't find out anythin'."

John Thatcher's voice boomed, "Evening, folks. I'm sorry we are calling so late. Had a family gathering at our place and we set out a little later than planned."

"You're welcome, Mr. Thatcher, Mrs. Thatcher. Come in, please." Lauren held the door open to allow their guests to file in. She squeezed Becky's hand as she passed, but sensed she didn't want to make a fuss in front of the children.

Mrs. Thatcher was carrying a basket and the smell of cookies was making everyone's mouth water. "I brought you some cookies and my apple-sauce cake with some heavy cream. But John has some things for you that need to be put away first," Alice told them.

Mr. Thatcher beckoned them outside, where Big Will was leading a goat with a rope. Walking over to the back of his truck and with the help of his son, Ben, he took down a box with a chicken and a rooster in it.

"We heard you'd had trouble and we had a bit of a collection for you around the mountain folk. We all miss you, Becky. You and your ma and the kids." Mr. Thatcher's voice cracked as Becky's eyes filled up. "Folk don't have a lot to spare. Times are tough, but we figured you'd be needin' milk for the little ones and some eggs. You won't get many from one hen, but at least it's a start."

Becky flung her arms around the white-haired man and hugged him.

Ruthie moved closer to Lauren, pulling at her sleeve. "Do we get to keep the goat?"

Lauren's nose prickled, her throat tightened, her voice cracking with emotion, "Yes, sweetheart."

"Can I name her?"

"I think we should ask everyone to help us choose a name, don't you?"

Ruthie agreed and ran back inside, full of excitement, to tell the other children.

"Mr. Thatcher, I can't begin to tell you how much your kindness means to all of us."

"I wish Nanny Kat was here to see what you've done, Miss Lauren. I think she'd be very proud."

"I wish she was here too." Lauren fought the impulse to burst out crying. Becky had been brave so she had to be too.

The children deserved better. She swallowed the lump in her throat, digging her nails into her palms. "I've tried to find her. I've written to as many people as I could think of, but it's like she doesn't want to be found. I wanted the sheriff to put up a missing person's photo, but he laughed at me." Lauren pushed aside her feelings of embarrassment at the memory. "I thought she might reappear when Father closed Rosehall and moved permanently to Richmond." Since visiting Rosehall and finding it closed up, she had discovered where her father was now living.

Mr. Thatcher put his hand on her shoulder. "Nanny Kat will have a good reason for staying away. She'll come back when the time is right."

"I hope so, Mr. Thatcher."

The Thatchers didn't linger long. It would take them an hour to drive back to their home. "We don't like traveling too late at night in November," Alice said. "Never know when the weather will turn nasty."

Big Will stayed a little longer, helping to find a place for the goat, the hen, and the rooster in the shed where they had kept Patty's body. It had escaped the fire and would have to be where they'd live until the barn was rebuilt.

The next morning, Cal and Fred surprised everyone by starting to build a chicken coop.

"We're like a real family, aren't we?" Cal said. "All lookin' out for one another."

CHAPTER 78

"Look, Miss Lauren, the lights are up. Does that mean it's Christmas?" Ruthie's eyes filled with wonder as she stared at the colored lights decorating the town. They hung across the trees down the center boulevard and most stores had decorations in their windows.

"Can we get lights for our Christmas tree?" Ruthie asked. "I never had a tree. Mama said we would, but my new pa, he stopped us. I think they look beautiful." The little girl stared at the decorated tree outside Hillmans' Store.

"We'll have a tree, darling. We just won't have lights. It's too dangerous with so many children in the house." *How can I tell the children we can't afford lights? The tree will be free, because we'll get one from the mountain. But there's no money for decorations or presents.*

Weighed down with her thoughts, Lauren parked the car outside the post office. Miss Chaney had cut out paper dolls and put them in the window around a picture of Santa Claus. Inside, she'd hung up some paper decorations.

"I know it's early, but after all the bad news this year I thought being festive might cheer us up," Miss Chaney said to Lauren as she entered the post office with Ruthie.

Lauren forced a smile. She used to love Christmas at Rosehall, but now it was a season she wished she could sleep through. She didn't want to disappoint the children.

"Lauren, there's some post for you. Right here." Miss Chaney pulled out some envelopes. Lauren's heart sank, recognizing the mortgage demand, the notification of taxes due, and the electricity bill. Yet another reason there wouldn't be lights on the tree: their electricity would be cut off if she didn't come up with the payment.

"Lauren, chin up. The Good Lord loves us and He will provide. I'll say a prayer."

"Thank you, Miss Chaney. Ruthie, we better be going."

"Ruthie, wait, have a candy before you go. What about this one?" Miss Chaney held out a red and white candy cane.

"For me? Thank you, Miss Chaney. Will you say a prayer for me too?"

"Sure I will, Ruthie. What would you like?"

"For us all to be happy. I don't ever want to leave Miss Lauren and the rest of my family at the orphanage."

Miss Chaney swallowed hard as she nodded, but Lauren glanced away, not wanting the child or the postmistress to see the tears of hopelessness in her eyes.

She walked out the post office carrying the letters. *How am I going to find the money to pay these bills?* It had been bad enough worrying about how to pay for a nice Christmas for the children, but now these bills had to take priority. *Keeping a roof over our heads is the most important thing I have to do.*

Ruthie sucked on her candy cane, oblivious to Lauren's turmoil. "Who's that?" She licked her candy, pointing to someone.

"Who?" Lauren wasn't paying attention as she took the little girl's hand and urged her to hurry up.

"Lauren?"

Lauren's blood turned to ice and the hairs on her arms stood upright as she heard his voice.

Lauren grabbed Ruthie's hand and walked faster, ignoring him. Tempted to run, she knew she couldn't. The ground was slippery where the heavy frost hadn't yet melted and Ruthie could fall.

The little girl turned around, pulling on Lauren's arm. "Miss Lauren, that man is talkin' to you. Didn't you hear him?"

"Listen to the young girl. Turn around and talk to me."

Lauren gave the child's hand a squeeze before turning to face Justin, her heart thumping in her chest. His eyes raked her from head to foot but she used all her willpower to keep her face straight.

"Good afternoon, Justin, please excuse us as we are in a hurry."

"Well, who'd have thought we'd meet here and with you looking like..."

Lauren refused to be intimidated, although she wished she could take a bath. In bleach. She held the letters and bills tighter against her chest, her other hand clasping Ruthie's. The little girl had picked up on the atmosphere and was now hiding her face in Lauren's skirt.

"I've just returned from my honeymoon," he continued. "England was simply wonderful. My bride's family is well placed in England. Her cousin threw us a party. Everyone who is anyone was there, including David and Wallis Simpson, as she is now. Do you know her? She lived in North Virginia for a while. David and I got on so well together. My wife and I have a standing invitation to visit them whenever we wish."

Lauren noted the use of David rather than Prince Edward, the heir to the British throne. How could Justin believe she cared? Under her eyelashes she tried to see if anyone else was around, someone friendly, but there was no one nearby. She couldn't let him see her fear of him, he'd feed on it.

"Congratulations on your marriage, Justin. I hope you will be very happy. Please excuse me. I have a headache and we need to get home."

Ruthie spoke up. "I want to go home."

"Aren't you a little beauty?" Justin said, his voice sending a shiver down Lauren's spine. "You remind me of someone Lauren and I knew. Doesn't she look like Patty?"

Lauren gasped. How could he stand there and speak about Patty? How dare he utter her name? "Come on, Ruthie, we must go. Please excuse us."

"Don't go. I want to invite you to a Christmas party. You'll need to hide those hands with gloves and you can blame your tan on the French sun or something."

"Oh, I love parties! Can we come too?" Ruthie asked.

"No, thank you, Justin. Ruthie, we will have our own Christmas party."

Justin's eyes widened, his lips thinned. Instinctively, Lauren pushed the little girl behind her.

"What gives you the right to stand there and talk to me like that? If you'd married me, you wouldn't look like a hillbilly. Look at the state of you, it's a wonder you wear shoes. Most of them go barefoot, don't they?"

Lauren tried to walk on, but Justin grabbed her arm.

"You made a laughing stock of me, Lauren Greenwood. You just wait. By the time I've finished with you, you'll lose everything. Keep an eye on your girls. This pretty little thing is pleasing to the eye," he hissed.

Lauren fought back the nausea his words caused as she tried to shake off his grip, but he only tightened his hold.

He's threatened the children.

Heart beating faster, she tried to think of how to warn him off. Her hands were trembling as she saw Edward Belmont striding toward them, his eyebrows raised, his gaze focused on Justin's hand clutching her arm.

"Good afternoon, Miss Greenwood. Fine day, isn't it?" came a loud voice, causing Justin to drop her arm and turn. Lauren inhaled sharply and her fingers tingled as the blood flow returned to her hand. She wanted to thank Mr. Belmont, but she had to get Ruthie away from here; as far away from Justin as possible.

"Belmont. What are you doing in Delgany? I'd have thought you'd be stuck in your office, writing more lies," Justin snarled.

"If you men will please excuse me, I best get back to the children," Lauren said, almost running away.

"Lauren, I'll see you *soon*." Justin's parting remark made her stop for a second, but then she hurried on.

What is Justin going to do? He's threatened Ruthie. Could he also have burned the barn? She couldn't picture him carrying cans of kerosene in his suit, across the fields, though, and they would have heard a car, wouldn't they?

"Miss Lauren, are you going to cry?" Ruthie's voice broke into her thoughts. "You shouldn't let that horrible man upset you."

Lauren smiled through her tears. "Let's go home, Ruthie darling."

The child held her hand more firmly. "Did you mean it about us having a Christmas party?"

Lauren looked down at the girl. Ten minutes ago she was worrying about how to pay for the basics, why had she ever mentioned a party?

Ruthie jumped up and down. "Could we? I ain't never had a party before. Do you get to eat cake?"

Lauren couldn't bear to take away the joy in Ruthie's eyes. "Yes, cake and cookies and lots of lovely things."

"Hurry up, Miss Lauren." Ruthie dragged her toward the truck. "We have to ask Becky as she's the boss in the kitchen. Do you think she will let us?"

"She might, if you ask her nicely."

"I will. I'll say please and thank you at the same time. That will make her say yes. A party, Miss Lauren. We are going to have a party!"

CHAPTER 79

Lauren couldn't meet Becky's eyes when Ruthie ran straight into the kitchen, with a hopeful expression, asking if they could have a party. Becky tried to tell the little girl that she would do her best, but she couldn't make any promises. Yet the child wasn't in the mood to listen. When she sensed Becky wasn't going to say yes, she threw a tantrum, throwing a glass of water onto the floor before she ran upstairs.

"Why did you go tellin' that child we is going to have a party? We don't even have the money for normal food unless you met Father Christmas in town."

"No, definitely not him." Lauren pushed the pile of dishes to the side of the table and put the collection of bill envelopes in its place. She sat at the table with a sigh.

"What happened? What prompted all this?" Becky had her arms on her hips. There was no way she was going to let this go.

"I met Justin. Justin Prendergast."

Becky exhaled before sitting down and pulling Lauren onto the other chair. "What happened? What did he say?"

"He's married and just back from his honeymoon. He partied with the Prince of England."

Becky rolled her eyes. "The Prince is welcome to him from what you told me. Pity he didn't throw him in the Tower of London or chop off his head."

"Becky, they don't do that anymore." Lauren tried to smile but failed dismally.

"What are you hidin'?" Becky demanded.

"He told me he was going to make me pay. For making a fool of him. He said he'd take everything I had."

"Does he know how little you own?" Becky's attempt at humor fell flat. "Lauren, I know somethin' bad happened between you and him, but you can't let him frighten you."

"He said Ruthie looked like Patty and I was to watch myself. What if it was Justin who torched the barn?" Lauren picked at a spot of congealed mush a child must have left on the table with her nail.

Taking Lauren's hand in hers, Becky placed the other one under Lauren's chin, forcing her to look up at her. "Justin Prendergast? The man who owns half of Virginia County? Now your imagination is gettin' the better of you. A rich, well-known man like him don't have time to be goin' round the country burnin' down barns. He knows he'd stick out like a fox in a henhouse. He can't afford to get caught. It was more likely them Bramley brothers." She continued, "Why don't you go up and rest for a while? I've heard you pacin', wearin' a hole in the floor for worryin' about this place. Don't bother denying it, I can tell from the circles under your eyes. We're all worried about Christmas and how we're goin' to find the money to pay off them bills. But you will make yourself sick and now you're fussin' over this. Off you go! Take your mind off that man, he's all trousers and no action."

CHAPTER 80

December 19, 1933

Lauren relished the emptiness of her office, where she'd retreated with a cup of chicory and the newspaper. She loved to be surrounded by the children but she couldn't stop worrying about Christmas—and not just their presents. How would she feed them through the winter?

The orphanage looked so dark and depressing compared with the houses and stores in Delgany. The town was lit up like one big Christmas tree, whereas they had yet to fetch a tree from the mountain. There wasn't even a piece of holly on the front door, never mind a wreath. Inside the house, the walls were bare. Becky wasn't in the Christmas mood, being focused on finding the money to pay the mortgage. Norma was a little more optimistic, but every day she kept postponing any decorating or talk of Christmas. Lauren wondered if they were all waiting for a robin to deliver a cash bonus.

Outside the wind howled down from the mountain, bringing the occasional flurry of snow. The snow wasn't sticking to the ground yet but that could change any minute. The low-lying clouds were as gray as dirty sheets and Lauren shivered, even though the office was warm, thanks to the small fire Terry had lit earlier. Staring into the fireplace, she wondered how on earth they would get out of the mess they were in.

Lauren turned the pages of the newspaper, scanning them. She shouldn't have spent three cents, but she'd felt sorry for the paper boy standing on the cold pavement in Delgany with holes in his shoes, his red toes visible through the worn leather. She'd slipped him ten cents and not taken the change—so many folk needed money just as badly as she did.

It felt like a lifetime ago when she'd thought nothing of spending three hundred dollars on a dress and bought a different one for every ball she attended. Now she worried about paying three cents to read the news. She turned the pages, wishing for an answer to her prayers. What was she looking for? *An advert that promised full Christmas dinner and trimmings for all twenty of them for a dollar?* she thought wryly. *Or for fifty cents, the children could have any toy of their pleasing?* She laughed at herself. There was desperation and there was foolishness and she was definitely acting foolish.

A headline caught her eye, dragging her away from her musings:

RICHMOND LOCAL GIVES GIFT OF CHRISTMAS TO HIS NEIGHBORS

The article printed a copy of an advertisement that had appeared in the newspaper. Lauren sucked her pen as she read the text:

A Richmond man, who elects to remain anonymous, ran the advertisement shown below in the County newspaper to help his local folk in their time of need. When it was brought to my attention I decided to reprint it here. If you wish to write to Mr. B. Virdot, please send your letters to me, Edward Belmont, and I will pass them on. It's a pity some of our wealthier residents, such as Mr. Justin Prendergast or Mr. William Greenwood, couldn't provide a similar service to the town of Delgany.

Lauren's breath caught, seeing her father's name in print. She focused back on the article, pushing away the pain that surfaced every time she thought of him.

The advert that appeared in the Richmond paper read as follows:

IN CONSIDERATION OF
THE WHITE COLLAR MAN!

Given the harsh circumstances we are all experiencing, some more than others, I wish to follow the example set out by Charles Dickens in his book, *A Christmas Carol*. No, I won't invite myself to your home for supper. I would like to give $5 to 75 families so they will be able to spend a merry and joyful Christmas.

If you are concerned about how to find the money for your family at Christmas, please write to me, Mr. B. Virdot, care of this newspaper. I promise I will never reveal your identify and you shall never know mine.

In writing, please familiarize me with your true circumstances and financial aid will be promptly sent.

Lauren read and re-read the advertisement, wondering if it was genuine. Mr. Belmont obviously thought so or he wouldn't have reprinted it. There were so many con artists and grifters playing on people's good natures, she knew, but what could they expect to gain from this?

"You'll get lines on your face, Miss Lauren, if you sit lookin' like that for long. What's got your goat this time?" Becky said, entering the room.

"I may have found the answer to our Christmas woes. Read this, Becky. What do you make of it?"

Becky read through the article. "You believe it? That some man is givin' his money to strangers? It's a scam."

"How would that work? He's not gaining anything but letters from folk telling him how hard life is."

"Why would he want to know? If he has money to throw around, why get depressed listenin' to strangers' problems? Maybe he belongs in the asylum."

"What would you do, Becky, if you had enough money to do whatever you'd like? I'm sorry, though. You came in here to ask me something, didn't you? Is there something you need?"

"I don't know what I need more than money, Miss Lauren. I came to ask if you had any spare. We have credit at the store and the Hillmans, they be nice people, but they got to eat too. The girls here could do with some new shoes. I've tried repairin' their shoes with cardboard, but now there is more cardboard than leather. And the boys—"

"I know, Becky, believe me, I know. But I don't have any money at the moment aside from two dollars. I've been keeping that for times when it was really needed."

"Guess this is the time, Miss Lauren." Becky was almost out the door when Lauren called her back.

"What would you wish for, Becky, if you could have five dollars?"

"No point in wishin'."

"Humor me. You can't ask for anything for the children. It has to be something for yourself. A new dress, shoes, a hat. What would it be?"

Becky snorted. "You got spare dollars to give me?"

"You know I don't. I'm just curious. If Father Christmas came down that chimney, what would you ask for?"

"To go see a movie in a theater and have dinner in one of those fancy restaurant places. Ain't never been to either." Becky brushed her face on her sleeve. "If this Father Christmas of yours is flyin' nearby, that's what I'll wish for. I reckon I might as well wish for Clark Gable to come along and sweep me off my feet. It's got a better chance of comin' true. Can I go now, Miss Lauren? I got work to be gettin' on with."

"Clark Gable? I wouldn't have thought he was your type. I reckoned you would be more of an Errol Flynn type."

Becky's laugher followed her out the office. Once she was alone, Lauren re-read the advert before carefully cutting it out and placing it in her top drawer.

Later on that day, Lauren couldn't stop herself from pulling the article from the drawer. *What if it was genuine? What if the man did grant them some money? What if this was the way to give the orphans a real Christmas?*

While Becky was at the store, Lauren picked up her pen and wrote the letter to the paper before she lost her nerve.

Dear Mr. Virdot,

I know you will be inundated with letters because of your kind gesture. I don't know how you will choose who benefits from your kindness, but I would like to ask for help for my friend Becky.

Becky has dedicated herself to helping cast-off children. The children nobody else wants. She works day and night and refuses to take anything but a minimum payment.

Becky would love to go to Richmond to the theater. She's never been.

Our orphanage is low on funds and we use every penny we earn to pay down the mortgage and keep on top of our bills. We were doing just about fine, considering the times we live in, but our barn recently burned down, killing our cows and goat. Things are far more difficult now.

You may know me from rumor and gossip. I swear on my heart I don't have any access to funds. My father disinherited me some time ago. If I could, I would gladly go back in time and instead of buying endless dresses at exorbitant price tags, would have contributed the monies to places such as the orphanage. But I was selfish, self-centered and vain back then. I didn't know how to boil water, never mind fend for myself. I feel grateful that has changed. I can now cook a meal—well, "cook" might stretch things slightly—I can make a decent salad though.

I may have lost all the things that women of my age from my background take for granted—the nice house, endless shopping sprees and trips to Europe—but I believe I am richer for it. I have made many true friends in the wonderful Delgany community.

Please help my friend, Becky. She will never write and ask for anything for herself.

Thank you for reading my letter. I wish you and yours a very Merry Christmas and a Happy New Year.

Yours sincerely
Lauren Greenwood

Lauren put the pen down, looking at the letter in her hand, wondering if she could add anything more to make this Mr. Virdot see just how deserving Becky was. After everything she'd been through, Becky could still find love in her heart for any child who needed her. One thing was for sure—the world needed more people like Becky.

CHAPTER 81

December 20, 1933

With a heavy heart, Lauren parked the truck in the yard, wondering how she would tell Becky and Norma that she hadn't managed to raise any money. She'd been to see the leaders of each church in Delgany. Although they were all very pleasant, they couldn't afford to help the orphans. They had too many hungry people of their own.

The scent of cinnamon and gingerbread wafted from the house on the breeze. She strode into the kitchen, her stomach growling, and stopped at the scene before her. Norma was stirring what looked like cookie dough. Becky was showing the younger girls how to put a paper chain together with some flour paste. The boys, under Terry's leadership, were twisting green garlands with holly to make Christmas wreaths. Only Fred and Bart were missing.

"What's going on?" Lauren asked. "Where did you get the supplies?"

"John Thatcher came by earlier. He said it was an early Christmas present. He gave us flour, sugar, and freshly churned butter. He also gifted us a small ham."

Lauren hugged Becky, lost for words.

Then Cal called for her attention. "We're making presents for those who have helped us. The Hillmans and Miss Chaney and Mrs. Dobbs. The sheriff too." The little boy showed her a half-made holly wreath.

"If they hang them up on their doors, maybe some other people will see them and will want to buy some for themselves. There's plenty of holly around on the mountains. We could make some money to help you at Christmas." Terry's face turned crimson.

Lauren kissed his cheek. "Thank you, Terry. They are beautiful wreaths. I think we should take a few to Hillmans' Store. I am sure they would be able to sell some. You are all working so hard. What can I do? Want me to help you, Norma?"

"No, thanks, Miss Lauren, I can't afford to lose any cookies." Norma smiled to show she was teasing.

Ruthie pulled at her skirt. "You can help me and Lottie, Miss Lauren. We keep getting the paste on our fingers and making everything sticky. Shelley gets angry when we do that."

Shelley didn't look up, focused on working.

Lauren took off her coat and scarf and hung them on the rack by the back door.

"Show me what I have to do, please, Ruthie? You too, Lottie?" She sat at the table between the two girls, her mood lifting despite her money worries. These children were an inspiration, she thought, her spirits soaring.

Outside, the snow fell a little more heavily. If it continued at this pace, they could be cut off. The mountains were covered in a gray mist, and you couldn't tell where the mountains stopped and the sky began.

"Can we go play in the snow for a while?" Cal asked, fed up of working on the holly. He had his thumb in his mouth and was mumbling about getting another thorn in it.

"Go on, all of you. Get rid of some of your energy. You are like a bunch of overexcited puppies," said Becky.

Shadow barked as if to confirm her remark. The children, laughing and giggling, ran to get their coats and hats and all trooped out to play.

"Don't go near the lake, children. It may look like the ice is frozen but it's cracking in places," warned Lauren. She didn't want anyone trying to skate on it and fall through. She'd had enough of disasters and sickness to last her a lifetime.

"We won't, Miss Lauren," the children chorused.

As Lauren helped Becky clean up the table, Terry piled the completed wreaths to one side.

"Want me to drive you into Delgany to deliver them, Terry?"

"Yes, please, Miss Lauren. The sooner the Hillmans have them, the better."

*

Lauren and Terry returned to the orphanage with good news. "Becky, we sold all the ones we took to Hillmans' Store," Terry told her excitedly. "We have to make some more."

"Well done, Terry." Becky clapped him on the back. She and Norma were on their way upstairs to the attic.

"I think the children should come in, Terry. Could you call them? It's cold out there," Lauren said, glancing out the window. The snow was coming down fast now and footsteps were disappearing after a couple of seconds.

Terry whistled from the back door to alert the children to come in, and eventually they came trooping into the house, discarding wet woolens in a heap on the table.

Lauren counted the orphans as they came in, something she always did. One was missing, who was it? Lottie was in, as were Fred, Cal, Terry, Shelley, Bean, Clarissa, and Carly. Carly put a scarf on the table, making Lauren's blood run cold.

"Carly, where did you get this?" Lauren gestured to the scarf.

"It was out back, near the old outhouse. I thought it was pretty and was going to ask you to wash it and give it to Bart for Christmas. Why?" The girl searched Lauren's face. "Did I do something wrong?"

"No, darling, not you." Lauren's head swirled. *I once gave a scarf identical to that to Justin for his birthday.* She quickly scanned the children. "Where's Ruthie, Carly?"

"She ran ahead, said she needed the bathroom. Why?"

"She hasn't come back into the house, least I didn't see her." Lauren's heart raced, despite her best attempt not to panic. She ran upstairs but the bathroom was empty, as was Ruthie's bedroom. Becky and Norma were in the attic, working on surprise Christmas gifts for the children. They didn't have much but they wanted every child to be given a little something.

"Becky, Norma, is Ruthie with you?" Even as she asked, Lauren knew the answer. The women wouldn't allow any children to go up there to see what they were working on. Becky stuck her head out. "What's wrong, Miss Lauren?"

"I can't find Ruthie." Lauren raced down the stairs again, checking the boys' bedrooms, but they were empty too. She arrived down to find the rest of the children waiting in the kitchen. They stared at her.

"Carly, go upstairs and look for Ruthie. Terry, keep all the other children in here. Don't let anyone outside. You understand?"

"Yes, ma'am."

Lottie grabbed Fred's hand, a terrified expression on her face, but Lauren couldn't stop to reassure her. She pushed past the children and ran outside into the yard, shouting Ruthie's name at the top of her voice. Her voice was harsh with fear, bringing Bart running from the small barn. Norma and Becky heard her too and came galloping down the stairs.

"What's wrong?" asked Bart, who reached Lauren first.

"I can't find Ruthie. She isn't in the house and Carly said Ruthie left her to run to the outhouse. Some time later, Carly found a man's scarf on the ground near the outhouse. He has taken her, hasn't he?"

"Who has taken her?" Norma asked as she came running up, leaving Becky with the terrified children. "What's going on?"

"Ruthie's gone. Carly said she had to go to the outhouse. She's not there. I'm sure the scarf is Justin's. He met Ruthie in town, commented on how like Patty she looked." Lauren covered her face with her hands.

"Lauren, you're jumping to all sorts of conclusions. Let's search properly. Ruthie might think it's a game we're playing," replied Norma.

"I know he's taken her. He's done it out of spite. He said he would make me pay for humiliating him." Lauren was gasping for breath, her heart pounding.

Norma pulled her arm. "Lauren, slow down. Who is this Justin?"

"Justin is the man I was supposed to marry. The man who abused Patty." Somehow Lauren managed to get the words out. "I met him in town the other morning when I took Ruthie to Miss Chaney to collect the post. He commented how much she looked like Patty."

Lauren ran for the truck.

"Where are you going, Lauren? You can't go after this man alone," Norma called out.

"I have to. It's me he wants to hurt."

"Bart, go with her. Go tell the sheriff. He'll help, he has to. Send word to Mr. Belmont. "We'll search for her here again, just in case." Norma kissed her husband's cheek. "Be careful."

"Here, take these. Ruthie will be frozen, the poor little mite." Becky came over and bundled some quilts into their hands. She turned away to pick up Lottie. The poor child was hysterical. Norma had her arms around Carly and her own girls. Fred, Cal, and the other boys stood to one side, staring.

"Everything will be fine, children. You go back inside and stay warm. Keep working on the Christmas decorations, Ruthie will love Christmas." As Lauren tried to smile for their sake, Cal broke away from the group and ran up to hug her: "You'll find her, Miss Lauren. You will."

She hugged him back for a second before climbing into the truck, where Bart was already sitting in the passenger seat. He couldn't drive because the burns on his hands were still too painful. Lauren grabbed the steering wheel and started the engine.

CHAPTER 82

The weather slowed them down as Lauren drove, thick, dense snow coming down in buckets and obscuring their view. Someone would have to dig out the dirt track that led to the orphanage, or it would become impassible.

"He can't have got too far in this, Miss Lauren," said Bart.

"He could be anywhere. Oh, why did I have to take Ruthie into town and bump into him?"

"Just pray now. There's no point in going over what's happened."

There was no sign of Justin or any other motor vehicles on the road into Delgany. Once they'd reached the main road, Lauren had managed to speed up. Even so, before they arrived at the sheriff's office, at least an hour had passed since she'd discovered Ruthie was missing. Anything could happen to a defenseless child in an hour, she thought, her stomach churning.

"Miss Lauren, what on earth are you doing out in this weather?" The sheriff was shocked to see her bursting into his office, accompanied by Bart. "Didn't you hear the weather warnings on the radio?"

"Sheriff, Ruthie's gone. Justin has taken her. We have to find her before he hurts her." The words burst out of her in a torrent.

"*What?* Slow down, Miss Lauren."

"Miss Lauren met this man in town the other day," said Bart, more composed than Lauren. "He threatened her. Now Ruthie, one of our five-year-old girls, is missing. We have to find her. She'll be terrified, poor little mite."

"I know Justin Prendergast," replied the sheriff. "I really cannot believe that he would take a child. Lauren, don't you think this feud with him and your father has gone too far?"

"Sheriff Dillon, Justin is the man who assaulted Patty and fathered her child. He's cruel and capable of just about anything. I simply can't stand here while I'm sure he's got Ruthie. He could hurt her." She turned and ran out.

Bart sprinted after her. "Where are we going?" he asked, as Lauren opened the door to the truck.

"To Rosehall. That's where this all started."

"Your father's house? Justin's not likely to bring a child there. The place is empty. Your father—"

"Cares about nothing but himself." Lauren climbed into the driver's seat. "Bart, go round up some men and get them out to Rosehall."

"Where are you going, Miss Lauren?"

"To my home."

She turned the key in the ignition and rammed the gears into reverse, ignoring the way the wheels slid, and turned in the direction of Rosehall. *Please let Ruthie be okay. Please*, she begged silently.

Lauren drove as fast as she dared; she'd be no use to Ruthie if she ended up in a ditch. Heading in through the back entrance, she passed the old quarters, which looked like they'd fallen down. She parked and ran, slipping several times on the icy ground, the snow still falling steadily around her, blanketing Rosehall in white. Heart thudding, she kept going, through the orchard, past the stables to the back door. When she turned the handle, she found the door was unlocked. She pushed it open and entered the kitchens.

"Ruthie, where are you? Ruthie?" she screamed at the top of her lungs. The kitchens were deserted, everything covered in dust. Her voice echoed back at her, taunting her.

Is this place empty? Am I wrong to look for Ruthie here?

Lauren ran into the hall, the wide staircase empty of anyone. Then she heard voices and immediately recognized her father's. Following the sound, she ran to the study and opened the door. Justin stood in front of the unlit fireplace, her father stood by his desk, looking older but otherwise unchanged. His face wore a familiar, stony expression.

"Lauren! What are you doing here?" His eyes traveled from the top of her head to her feet and back up to her face. His forehead creased as he grimaced, shaking his head at her appearance. "You look like one of those mountain women you are so fond of."

"She's looking for me, William. That's right, isn't it, my dear?" said Justin.

Lauren charged at him, hoping to take him off guard, but he grabbed her easily, savagely twisting her arm behind her back.

"Where's Ruthie? What have you done with her?" Lauren said, ignoring the pain in her arm.

"Ruthie? Who is she? Have you finally lost your mind, Lauren?" Her father, now red-faced, turned to Justin. "What do you mean by dragging me out here on a day like this, Justin? I have a dinner to attend this evening."

"Sit down, William," replied Justin. "You too, Lauren. No, don't kick me. I do have the girl and you won't find her unless you do exactly as I say."

Lauren saw the manic gleam in his eyes. He was beyond dangerous. *How long is it going to take Bart and the others to get here?* Glancing out the window told her the weather was worsening, the snow building up on the windowsills.

Justin pushed her into an upholstered armchair. It felt damp. Her mind flitted from one thing to another in a whirlwind of panic. In this weather, Ruthie wouldn't last long out in the open. *Has she got her coat? Her hat?*

"William, you cheated me," Justin spat. "You promised me the money to save Thornton Mews and the bank. You told me to trust you. I should have known a man like you wasn't to be trusted."

"Justin, we both suffered when those deals went bad. It wasn't just you. Things will be better in the New Year. We have a new president, we—"

"Be quiet. I'm finished with listening to you. I should have made Lauren honor our engagement." He glanced at her. "I should have burned down your orphanage not just the barn."

His admission of guilt made her realize just how disturbed he was. "Justin, I'm sorry I hurt you," Lauren pleaded. Despite her loathing for this man, she had to make some effort as precious seconds ticked by. "Please forgive me. I can't change the past, but Ruthie is innocent. She didn't—"

"She looks just like Patty. Is she hers?"

Is he unhinged? she thought. *He knows Patty's baby couldn't be as old as Ruthie. And surely he heard that her baby died?* But not wanting to anger Justin, all she said was, "No, Patty's baby died with her. Ruthie has just turned five."

"You're lying." Justin hit her viciously across the face.

"Justin, leave her alone."

So, my father has finally stood up for me, his daughter. It has taken him long enough.

"What? Suddenly playing the caring father, are you, William? Go on, admit it. Lauren was only ever just another asset to you, something to sell. You never cared for her, you cold-blooded old—"

"I love my daughter. I have always loved her. I made mistakes. But the past is the past. Besides, Lauren isn't stupid. Think about it. She wouldn't have come here alone. There must be others on their way."

"Sheriff Dillon is rounding up a party of men and following me here. He won't be long now. If you just tell me where Ruthie is, I won't say a word about you to him, Justin." Lauren knew she was stretching the truth a little, but she hoped that Bart would have persuaded the sheriff to help.

"Shut up," Justin snarled, pulling a pistol from his pocket. He waved it about in the air. Her father began to move, but Justin leveled the gun at him: "Don't take another step."

William held his hands up and, using a reasoning tone, he spoke softly: "Put the gun away, Justin, and think straight. Your new wife is at home waiting for you. I am expected at a friend's house in Charlottesville for Christmas dinner. Tell Lauren where the girl is, whoever she is, and let's all get out of this gloomy mausoleum."

"Rose, my wife... She was another of your bright ideas, William. Mother of Creation, but that woman is a nag! She never stops twittering on and on about this and that. She spends money like water. Why did I ever marry her?"

Lauren inched forward out of her chair. If Justin and her father kept talking, she could use the element of surprise. A poker stood beside the fireplace. If she moved another few inches, she would reach it. But, as she rose to her feet and attempted to grab it, her shoe caught in the plush carpet and she stumbled.

Justin pivoted and fired in her direction at the same time as her father jumped toward her. He slumped to the floor with a thud.

"Father!" The scream tore from her as she stretched out toward him.

Another shot rang out behind her, and a bullet hit her in the upper arm, sending agonizing pain shooting through her. Lauren cried out as a third shot rent the air. She turned just in time to see Justin, still clutching the gun, flying backward through the window; glass shattered everywhere. The icy gale that swept in through the remaining shards brought thick, swirling snowflakes with it.

CHAPTER 83

Lauren crawled to where her father lay. The plush blue carpet was turning red beneath him. "Oh my God!" She couldn't stem the bleeding from her father, her hands turning crimson. "Someone help me! Please! Help me!" Her cries echoed around the room but there was no one there to hear them.

"Lauren, I'm sorry. I love…"

"Shush now, everything will be all right, Father."

Somehow Lauren managed to get to her feet. She went over to the sofa, and with one arm, dragged a dustcover from it to put over her father. She kneeled down beside him. He was breathing, but so cold, and the color was draining from his face. "The sheriff will be here soon, Father." Lauren stroked his hair. "He'll know what to do. Just stay with me." But as Lauren held his hand, she felt it go limp, and she saw the light flicker in his eyes before they darkened and his breathing stopped. "Father?" she whispered.

Lauren closed her father's eyes, her tears raining on his face, before she pulled the dustcover over it. She knew she couldn't stay. Somehow she had to find Ruthie, although she had no idea where Justin had hidden her.

Staggering to her feet again, she fought the weakness in her legs. Grasping bits of furniture, she pulled herself through the study and into the hall. "Ruthie, where are you? Can you hear me?" she called, as loudly as she could. "Please, Ruthie, you can come out now. There's no one here to hurt you. Everything is going to be okay." Her legs gave way under her, so she crawled across the marble floor to the base of the great staircase. "The bad man has gone, Ruthie. It's safe now," she managed to croak into the silence.

Lauren couldn't fight the dizziness that swirled in her head any longer. The marble floor was so cool under her face, but she couldn't understand why she felt so hot. She tried to keep her eyes open but failed. Her eyelids felt like lead and she was powerless to keep her eyes from closing.

*

She woke to the feel of a hand grasping hers. A child's hand was pushing the hair out of her eyes. "Wake up, Miss Lauren. Please wake up. I's scared," came a small, frightened voice.

"Ruthie?" Lauren whispered, forcing her eyes open. She thought she could make out the child's golden hair, which seemed to be swimming in and out of focus.

"Miss Lauren, you's awake." The little girl pushed closer and pain seared through Lauren's shoulder.

"Ruthie, are you hurt?"

The child shook her head, her eyes wide. She stuck her fingers in her mouth.

She must be terrified. At that moment, she heard shouts and sounds from outside. She recognized one of the voices as Bart's. Someone was rattling and banging on the door.

"Ruthie, can you tell Bart to use the back door."

Ruthie shook her head, moving closer to Lauren.

"Sweetheart, it's Bart. He's looking for you. He loves you, precious."

The little girl looked in the door's direction, but stayed where she was.

"Please, Ruthie, I need Bart's help. Will you be a good girl and help me?"

The child nodded, getting up and running over to the door. Ruthie shouted at Bart to use the back door before running back to sit with Lauren. A couple of seconds passed and the last thing Lauren heard was Bart's voice saying, "Ruthie! Oh, am I glad to see you!"

CHAPTER 84

December 23, 1933

Lauren lay in bed, her arm and shoulder bandaged. The doctor said she'd been lucky, it was a through and through, meaning the bullet had gone straight through her arm. It would take a while for the wound to heal, but the injury wasn't serious.

She gazed out the window, not seeing the dull gray winter sky, the barren limbs of the apple and peach trees swaying in the wind, or the fresh blanket of snow. Instead, she was back in her father's study again, reliving all that had happened that terrible night.

Could I have done anything differently? Father died trying to protect me. His last words were that he loved me. Why couldn't he have shown that before? What went so wrong in his life that he had to make the choices he did? The questions assaulted her, bringing her to tears. She closed her eyes, seeing Patty's face, wishing the young girl hadn't had such a tragic end. If she was here, she'd have been relieved to learn Justin was dead, unable to hurt her again. She couldn't feel anything about Justin's death. He'd threatened Ruthie, scared everyone at the orphanage, and killed her father.

"Miss Lauren, the sheriff's here," said Becky, entering the room. "Shall I send him up?"

"Yes, thank you, Becky." Lauren pulled the covers up. She should get up, but Becky had warned her she'd cut the legs out from under her if she tried to do anything but rest.

Sheriff Dillon didn't know where to put his eyes. He shifted from one foot to another, so obviously uncomfortable that Lauren felt sorry for him.

"Sheriff, sit down and stop putting both of us on edge. Leave the door open if you feel more comfortable. Or do you want me to call Becky to join us?"

"Might be best, Miss Lauren." He went to the door and called for Becky.

Lauren's stomach heaved. *I was joking. What's he going to tell me? My father's dead. How much worse can this get?*

Becky brought two cups of chicory coffee with her, giving one to Lauren and one to the sheriff. "Sorry, Lauren, we've run out of the real stuff," she said with a smile.

Lauren drank, for something to do, ignoring the bitter taste. She wished she could postpone whatever bad news the sheriff had.

"Miss Lauren, I know how much you loved—"

"Sheriff, please, just tell me. I know Father is dead, so what is it?"

Sheriff Dillon stood up and went over to the window. He stood with his back to it. "Your father and Mr. Prendergast were both being investigated for fraud and other offenses. There is some proof they were involved in illegal activities—bootlegging, tax evasion, and other such things."

"Bootlegging? My father didn't have a still up on the mountain, Sheriff."

"No, Miss Lauren, he was part of a group of men who were funding the operation. Someone else drove containers of whiskey to the relevant places."

"The cash." Her words came out as a strangled cry of frustration. How had she been so naive? Trembling, she met the sheriff's gaze. "Nanny said it was unusual that Father had a supply of cash. Mrs. Prendergast made a joke about whiskey once. My father and

Justin became quite uncomfortable. Why didn't I suspect they were involved in something?"

"Miss Lauren, your father—well—he always acted like a gentleman and he looked like one too."

Lauren stared at him. *Can he hear himself?* Just because her father wore nice clothes, lived in a large house, and drove fast cars, he couldn't be anything but a gentleman, could he? "You didn't come all this way to tell me that, did you, Sheriff?"

"Partly. I wanted to let you know that you are free from suspicion. It's obvious that Justin Prendergast shot your father, and you, before he turned the gun on himself. It's Christmas Day on Monday but by Tuesday the news will be in all the papers. 'Virginia State has its very own Al Capone'—I can just picture the headlines."

Lauren winced. She'd read about the gangster Capone and his shady dealings, including the numbers killed and threatened by his mob. *My father couldn't have been that bad, could he?*

The sheriff didn't notice her reaction. "Rosehall has been seized by the government because there are taxes due. I'm afraid you can't go back to the estate. The house has been sealed."

"I wouldn't go back there anyway, Sheriff. There is nothing there for me anymore." Lauren couldn't believe her voice sounded so level. Her insides were quivering, a feeling of panic threatening to overwhelm her.

"I best get off then. I just wanted to tell you in person, Miss Lauren. I imagine the next few weeks will be difficult."

"They will, but not for the reasons you think. We have nineteen orphans to feed. It's Christmas and we haven't enough food to feed a mangy cat, never mind put on a show." Lauren glanced over at Becky. The two of them, with Norma, had stayed up night after night, knitting and sewing, before Ruthie was taken. They'd wanted to make cloth dolls for the girls. Bart, Big Will, and Earl had worked on wooden toys for the boys. Compared with last year, it would be rather miserable.

"I may be able to help there. I caught some poachers and well…" The sheriff pulled at his collar, his cheeks flushing. "Thing is, them turkeys goin' to go off and you got all these kids to feed."

Becky, in a rare show, wrapped her arms around the sheriff, making him flush. "You *do* care!"

"Becky Tennant, you get your hands off me! I'm trying to say something."

Becky winked at Lauren. "Sorry, Sheriff, I couldn't help it."

He looked even more flustered. "Miss Lauren, I wanted to say I'm sorry."

"You aren't responsible, Sheriff."

"No, but I wasn't impressed when you left your home and came here. I should have been more supportive. Should have believed you'd become the woman your mama would want you to be. You might not have much over here, Lauren Greenwood, but these kids have something special: they have you. I'll see myself out."

He was gone before she could respond.

"Miss Lauren, I'm so sorry about Rosehall," Becky said. "I know how much you loved your home."

"A home is where your loved ones live. That's here, Becky. Now, do you mind if I get some rest? My arm is paining me."

"I'll make up some feverfew tea. That will kill the pain and help you sleep."

"Thank you. And, Becky, are the toys finished?" She couldn't bear the thought of some kids going empty-handed on Christmas Day.

"Just about, Miss Lauren. Every child will have somethin', no matter how small."

"And the tree?"

"Bart is takin' some of the older children up to the meadow to choose one today. We'll decorate it tomorrow."

At least we have the decorations from last year, Lauren thought.

Becky turned to leave but then stopped, first giving Lauren a hug. As she departed, Lauren closed her eyes, picturing happier days at Rosehall. In her mind she could see a shadowy figure watching as she placed the angel at the top of the sparkling Christmas tree. Her father had held her up while Nanny and this woman had clapped. She figured it was her mama.

*

Giggles coming from downstairs woke Lauren. Her throat felt dry and scratchy from thirst. She got up, swaying a little as she put her feet to the floor. She pulled her dress on, taking deep breaths as the pain throbbed in her arm. She gave up trying to close the buttons.

Walking down the stairs, she placed one hand on the wall so she wouldn't fall. The voices grew louder and the scent of cedar leaves filled the air, its fragrance dominating the smell of cinnamon and ginger coming from the kitchen.

"Miss Lauren, look. It's huge!" said Cal, catching sight of her on the stairs. "We picked out the biggest one we could find."

Smiling, Lauren gazed at the large tree, pieces of snow still clinging to some of the bushier branches. The smell tickled her nose, reminding her of previous happy Christmases at Rosehall. But she cleared those images—this was a special day for the children, not one to dwell on sadness. She watched as they set the tree in position, noting that Bart had fixed a plank to its base to help it stand properly. "You sure did. I don't know if it will fit, the ceiling might not be high enough," Lauren teased as they tested it. There was less than an inch between the top branches and the high ceiling.

"It's okay, we measured it." Cal beamed at her. He now held his head up straight and laughed readily. As Lauren ruffled his hair, she mused on how he was almost unrecognizable from the boy she had saved from the angry baker.

"Miss Lauren, are you still sick?" Lottie asked. "Your face looks like the snow before we walk in it."

"I'm fine, don't you worry about me, Lottie." She drew the young auburn-haired child to her side. "What have you been up to and where's your brother?"

The little girl rolled her eyes dramatically. "Cleanin'! Becky has everyone doin' chores. Don't she know it's Christmas?"

"Well, it's not Christmas just yet, precious." Lauren looked around her. Apart from some scattered needles from the tree dusting the ground, the place did look good. The windows glistened and there wasn't a cobweb or dead fly to be seen. The floorboards shone and Becky and Norma had laundered the quilts they used to cover up the old sofa. Feeling weak, Lauren sat down. Ruthie climbed up, careful not to touch her arm. The child hadn't said a word.

"Ruthie, are you looking forward to Father Christmas?"

The little girl shrugged her shoulders.

"What's wrong, precious?"

"I thought you was dead. You left me and went to Mama to become an angel. I was sad."

"Miss Lauren isn't an angel. She's right here, look." Lottie leaned across Lauren to take Ruthie's hand and pushed it into Lauren's. "See, she's real. Heaven isn't ready for Miss Lauren, we need her too much. That's what Becky said."

Lauren's eyes watered as she looked up to see Becky wiping her own eyes with her apron.

Bart coughed as he nailed the tree to the floor. "We got ourselves enough accidents around here lately, we don't need no tree fallin' over," he said, gruffly.

"Ruthie, sweetheart," said Lauren, "please smile. The nasty man has gone away and won't come back. Everyone is safe and it's Christmas."

"You sure you're not going to leave me?" The girl twisted her hands in front of her chest, and Lottie went to sit by her side and put her arms around her.

"Leave? Never. I love you to the moon and back."

"How much is that? Is it this much?" Ruthie held out her hands, a little gap between them.

"No, precious. You know on the top of the mountain, where the moon is trying to peek out from behind a cloud? I love you all the way up there and back."

Ruthie stared at Lauren. "That's a whole lot of love."

"Sure is."

Ruthie came closer and laid her head on Lauren's chest. "I loves you, Miss Lauren. My smile is goin' to be the best one ever." Ruthie took Lauren's head in both hands and kissed her on the forehead. "You rest now. I'll ask Becky to give you a cookie."

Ruthie almost fell in her haste to climb off the sofa, her leg knocking against Lauren's shoulder. Lauren gritted her teeth, so she wouldn't cry out, and Ruthie looked at her and smiled. "To the moon and back," she whispered before running into the kitchen, calling for a cookie. Lottie followed her.

"You're one special lady, Miss Lauren."

"Bart, will you please call me Lauren. Nobody calls you Mr. Bart."

CHAPTER 85

Christmas Eve, 1933

A fresh fall of snow overnight had the children racing outside in the morning to build a snowman on the lawn in front of the house. Their laugher rang out, seeming to echo off the mountains around them, and Lauren wished that she could join in. Inside, strings of popcorn made by the children adorned the room, even if the boys had eaten more corn than they put on the decorations.

The scent of cinnamon, cloves, and nutmeg drifted around the house as Becky and Norma baked cookies and pies in the kitchen. Lauren was allowed to stir the apple sauce with her good hand.

Once the cookies were in the oven, they all sat at the table with a cup of rich dark coffee. It was a real treat as they only had enough coffee left for one more pot the next day. Afterwards, Lauren looked out the window at the mountain, which looked blue in the wintery sunlight. As she took in the view, she thought of Nanny: *I wonder if she's heard about Father and Justin?* Lauren shivered.

"Are you gettin' a chill? You should go back to bed," Becky ordered.

"I can't stay in bed forever, Becky. I want to be part of the Christmas joy. Although a funny Christmas it's going to be, with so little in the house. The children will be disappointed tomorrow."

"Lauren Greenwood, you stop that at once! Those children are blessed to have a roof over their heads and food in their bellies. So what if they don't get the best toys or have new clothes? They're alive and so are we. You just count your blessings, you hear?"

"Yes, Nanny Becky!"

Ruthie and Lottie, holding hands, ran in and asked for help with their snowman's face.

"Girls, use small stones for his eyes and a stick for a nose. You can make a smile out of small stones too," Becky replied.

"He needs to keep warm, Becky, can we have a scarf?" Ruthie asked, holding Lottie's hand.

"Yes, please, Becky." Lottie's voice shook with the cold. "He will get awful cold without it. I was goin' to give him mine, but Ruthie said not to."

"Ruthie was right, can't have you gettin' a chill before Christmas, darling." Becky planted a kiss on Lottie's auburn curls.

Lauren found the old scarf belonging to Nanny. It still smelled faintly of the old woman and she gave it to the girls knowing Nanny would approve.

The turkeys donated by the sheriff were dressed and ready for roasting. Ginny Dobbs, the hairdresser, had sent out a small box of potatoes, yams, and squash with a note wishing Lauren a fast recovery. Mrs. Hillman had sent over some English peas, a small bag of flour, and a pound of coffee with a note. Lauren opened it: *Thought you might prefer coffee to candy. X*

"May the children come in now and put the decorations on the tree, please, Becky?" asked Lauren.

"Who's the child, Miss Lauren?"

"*Lauren*. I'm not going to answer to Miss Lauren anymore. That ended with Rosehall."

Becky opened her mouth, but immediately closed it again. She nodded and, taking a chair, stood up on it and pulled down some boxes from on top of the kitchen cabinets.

"There you go, Lauren. I'll get the kids in to help you."

Lauren smiled, feeling a little hope. She picked out some of the decorations they'd saved from Rosehall. A silver bell shimmered in the light—Nanny's gift the Christmas after Mama had died. She could still hear Nanny's voice: *"Every time a bell rings, an angel gets his wings."*

The bell tinkled in her hand.

"That's pretty." Ruthie and Lottie stood beside her, staring at the bell.

"It is. Do you want to put it on the tree?"

Both girls jumped up and down, screaming, "Yes!"

Ruthie took a step back. "Give it to Lottie to do, she's smaller than me."

Lauren handed it to Lottie.

"Can you help me, Ruthie?" she asked, holding out her hand.

Ruthie led Lottie over to the tree and together, they put the bell on the highest branch they could reach. It rang again. To Lauren, it seemed like Nanny was a part of their Christmas.

Fred surprised them with some carved wood figures for the Nativity.

"This is what you spent your time doin'?" Becky ruffled his hair. "They're beautiful."

"Thanks. I reckon you do so much for us, I should make something for you."

Becky couldn't speak, her eyes watering as she turned a sob into a cough.

"Don't look so worried, Fred. Becky's crying cause she's happy."

"Girls! I'll never understand them," he said gruffly.

"It's good to learn that lesson when you are a young'un," Bart said, earning him a playful smack from his wife.

Norma placed the wooden figures in the cardboard box they'd decorated for the crib. Baby Jesus wouldn't go in until the morning.

"Pity we don't have electric lights. I saw them in the catalog, they'd look lovely on the tree." Lauren gazed at the tree now fully decorated.

"Wasn't one fire enough for you?" Becky teased.

*

The children spent the rest of the day cutting out decorations for the tree. Fred drew shapes for the younger ones and Carly helped Ruthie, Bean, and Lottie finish their paper chains, coloring them with crayons.

Becky and Norma punched little holes into some cookies, then threaded string through, and tied them to the tree. The children helped themselves from a plate of cookies on the kitchen table so no one was tempted to try to climb the tree. Lauren savored a mouthful of cinnamon bun—the sweet chunks of apple dipped in cinnamon surrounded by butter-rich dough was her absolute favorite.

The day flew past with relatively few squabbles. The children were washed and dressed in night clothes in record time, because Lauren had promised them they could listen to the *Children's Christmas Show* on the radio. Gathering around the living room in front of the fire, they listened intently to the program. Bean sat on Bart's lap, Clarissa sitting beside him, Norma on the other side. Lauren sat on the couch, Ruthie beside her, holding Lottie's hand as "Jingle Bells" played out.

Then a voice boomed, making the children jump: "Have you been good, boys and girls?"

The children shouted, "Yes!"

"It's Santa's elves. They listenin' to us," Cal said, pointing at the radio. "Can you hear 'em workin' in the background? They're hammerin' and sawin'."

"Does that mean they're still makin' toys? Is it not too late?" Shelley shrieked.

Cal retorted, "Of course not. Santa's magic."

Lauren saw Bean frowning before climbing up on Bart's lap to whisper in his ear. He whispered back and she was all smiles.

The star-struck children listened as the Elf described packing up Santa's sleigh. "Dancer, stop eating all those carrots. You will have cookies later. Excuse me, children, but the reindeer are a bit too excited. Can you shout out their names?"

"Cupid, Comet, Blitzen," Shelley roared.

"Prancer, Vixen and Rudolph," Carly added.

"Dasher and… oh, what's the other ones?" Shelley stared at Becky.

"Ask Lauren," she responded.

"Donner and Dancer."

"Yeah, we got 'em all!" Ruthie shouted. "Miss Norma, you got nine carrots? You can't not give one to the reindeer. They all work hard but everyone only remembers Rudolph."

"I'll give them cookies. They prefer those," Norma replied with a wink at Bart.

CHAPTER 86

Christmas Day, 1933

"Miss Lauren, this is the day of our party, isn't it? You said we would have one on Christmas."

Lauren was still in bed when Ruthie raced into the room, hopping with excitement. She'd recovered from her ordeal now and Lauren grimaced as the child threw herself on the bed, in the process banging into her arm. Becky pulled her back gently with a glance of apology at Lauren.

"Yes, Ruthie, I did…" Lauren looked at Becky.

"Miss Lauren, you should be smiling. It's Christmas."

"Yes, Ruthie, I'm just waking up. It's early."

"All the children have been up for ages. We couldn't wait for you to get up, but Becky told us to have patience."

Lauren scrambled awkwardly out of bed, pulling a robe around her shoulders as Becky grinned at her. "You shouldn't have let me sleep in."

"Why change the habit of a lifetime?" Becky teased.

"Somebody left a sack at the front door," Ruthie said. "Do you think it was Father Christmas?"

"Maybe, Ruthie."

The little girl's eyes sparkled with excitement. "Hurry up, Miss Lauren."

Lauren didn't bother to brush her hair. She'd do it later when the children had their gifts—what little there was for them.

Ruthie took her good hand and walked her slowly down the stairs, the scent of the Christmas tree competing with the smell of frying bacon and freshly baked cinnamon rolls. Downstairs, each child ran to find a parcel with their name. The sack Ruthie had mentioned was now sitting under the Christmas tree.

"Who's the sack from?" Lauren whispered to Becky, wondering what the child was talking about.

"I thought it was you plannin' a surprise."

"No, I've never seen it before. Why didn't you open it, Becky?"

"I was waitin' for you, Lauren."

"Go on, open it."

"You open it. I ain't touching it first."

Lauren approached the sack, her mouth dry. *What if it's something nasty?* Taking a deep breath, she opened it and found some envelopes inside. One was addressed to Becky, in handwriting she didn't recognize. She gave it to her before taking out some other presents.

She handed out the gifts to the children, with one eye on Becky, who seemed to be struck dumb at the contents of her envelope. Then she saw the tears—Becky never cried. Alarmed, she moved to her friend's side.

"What is it? Why are you so upset?" she said, slinging her good arm around her.

"It's two tickets and a note to say dinner is paid for."

"To where?"

"To a movie theater in Charlottesville with dinner at a restaurant nearby. I've never eaten anywhere but at home. Lauren, you did this, didn't you? Nobody knew but you. You shouldn't have wasted your money on me."

"I didn't do it. I didn't buy the tickets. But remember that man who put an ad about Christmas in the paper? I did write and ask him to give them to you though."

"You did?"

Lauren nodded, beaming from ear to ear.

Becky wiped a tear from her cheek. "He picked me. Why would he do that?"

"Because you are a very special lady." Lauren could barely see through her own tears. She looked down as someone grabbed her skirt and pulled it. Ruthie looked up, her eyes wide with wonder.

"Ruthie, what's wrong?"

"Why are you and Becky crying? Do we have to leave?" the little girl asked in a quiet voice.

"No, darling. We're happy, not sad. What do you have there?"

"It's a doll, Miss Lauren. See?" Ruthie held out the cloth doll that Lauren had made.

"So it is. What are you going to call her?"

"Christel. That way I always remember I got it at Christmas. I loves her."

"Pleased to meet you, Christel."

Ruthie grinned as she cuddled the doll.

"What was in your other present?"

"Another doll. She's pretty, too, and I know I am lucky to get two, but I like this one best."

Lauren recognized the other doll from a picture in Sears Catalog. Trust Ruthie to prefer the handmade option.

She bent down to hug the child. "You are a special little girl. Never forget it."

"I won't, Miss Lauren. What present did you get?"

"I don't know, I didn't open it yet."

"You didn't? You got to open your presents! Do it now."

Lauren did as she was told and picked up the envelope, opening it, trying to read the letter, but the words danced in front of her eyes.

Ruthie sighed with disappointment. "You got a letter. A doll is better. Why would anyone give someone a letter as a present?"

But Lauren barely heard the child. She started reading and then re-reading, but the words wouldn't sink in.

Becky came to her side. "What is it? Your face is all screwed up. I can't tell if you are happy or sad."

"I'm happy, Becky. Do you remember Mary and me talking about the Cullens in New York? Well, it says here that Mr. Cullen and his friend Seamus Murphy both got jobs in the construction industry. They sent us this." She held up a ten-dollar note. "They wanted to buy Christmas dinner for us, just like I did for them back in nineteen thirty. Mary must have told them about the orphanage and sent them our address."

"That's wonderful, Lauren. Isn't it nice that things worked out well for them? Mary told me the Cullen family really suffered."

Lauren closed her eyes for a moment, remembering Maggie and Biddy. In her mind, she sent them her love and resolved to write back first thing tomorrow morning.

A knock at the door intruded on her thoughts. Opening it and finding Sam waiting on the other side, she couldn't help running into his outstretched arms. He picked her up and swung her around. She ignored the pain in her arm.

"It's so good to see you, Miss Lauren."

"Sam! Oh, my goodness, what are you doing here?"

"I heard you needed some help, miss. I was always good with my hands. And my new boss, she's ever so demandin'."

"She should appreciate you. Oh, Sam, I've missed you. How's Old Sally? How's—"

Her words faltered as Sam moved to one side.

"*Nanny*," she uttered in a whisper, barely able to believe her eyes.

"Lauren, child, it's so good to see you."

"*You came back.*" She couldn't move, fearing that Nanny was a figment of her imagination. Yet here she was, in the flesh, talking to her. She ran forward, her eyes blurring with tears as she hugged her. Nanny gripped her fiercely. Lauren ignored the piercing pain in her arm.

"I never went far. I had to hide from your father and Justin, but I always kept an eye out for how you were doing. You've made me so proud, Lauren."

"Oh, Nanny, I can't believe it! Sam… and now you. This is the best Christmas ever." *If Patty had been here to enjoy it, it would have been even better.*

Nanny squeezed her hand, her eyes sparkling with tears. Before she got to respond, Ruthie intervened.

"Are you, Mrs. Claus?" Ruthie asked, as she pulled at Nanny's coat.

"No, sweetheart. I'm Nanny Kat. Who are you?"

"I'm Ruthie. You want to come inside the house? It's warmer in here. You too, Mister Sam."

Ruthie led Nanny by the hand into the house, while Lauren lingered outside with Sam.

"I tried to find you and Old Sally when I discovered Father had closed Rosehall. There was no trace of either of you."

"Nanny wanted it that way. She took us back to her friend's place, where she was staying. Ole Sally don't know herself now. She got a set of rooms all for herself over Charlottesville way. You will have to come and see her. Let her show off her nice bed and a sofa with her own fire. She feels like a queen." Sam hesitated outside the door of the house. "Mind if I take a moment, Miss Lauren? I'd like to pay my respects to Patty."

"Of course. Just come in when you are ready."

She watched as Sam walked down through the yard and into the orchard, heading for the lake. His large footprints were soon covered over with the falling snow, and she shivered as she went back indoors.

Lauren sneaked upstairs to fix her hair, change into a dress, and take a few minutes to compose herself. She heard the Hillmans' truck arrive, followed by the squeals of the children greeting Ellie-Mae and Dalton.

Walking down the stairs, Lauren bumped into Ellie-Mae, who was en route to find her.

"Miss Lauren, Mama says you got hurt. Are you okay?" Ellie-Mae tugged on Lauren's dress.

"Yes, darling. I'm fine. You look pretty."

The Hillmans had done wonders with both children. Ellie-Mae wore her hair up off her face, something that would never have happened a year ago. Dalton was on his hands and knees, giving one of the younger boys a ride around the kitchen.

"Dalton had to take Lottie on his back as Lottie kept trying to climb up on Shadow," Elllie-Mae explained. "The dog doesn't like being a horse."

Shadow barked in response to Ellie-Mae's comment. "See, he's agreeing with me. Why you crying, Miss Lauren?"

"I'm so happy, Ellie-Mae. Everyone I love is here—well, apart from Mary and Jed. I'm a lucky woman." She whispered a "thank you" to her departed father. In the end, his love for her had saved her life and enabled her to have this joyous time.

Ellie-Mae gave her a quick hug before squeezing in between the two Hillmans, a huge smile on her face.

Becky was hugging Nanny as if she'd never let her go, tears streaming down her face. Lauren hurried over.

"I was just telling Becky that a friend of mine was looking into the story of her brothers and her ma," Nanny told Lauren. "He's heard rumors about the Colony. Maybe he can find out what happened to them all."

"I hope so, for Becky's sake. Who is this friend? How did you get here, Nanny? Did Sam bring you?"

"No, I did."

Lauren gasped as Edward Belmont walked in the door, holding his hat in his hands and looking rather uneasy. "May I come in?"

Lauren couldn't answer. What was he doing here? He had printed so much about her father, none of it flattering, but all of it true.

"Of course you can, Edward," said Nanny with a smile. "Lauren, it's Edward who has kept me informed of what was happening with you."

"You did? Why?"

"I guess I figured I had misjudged you, and then when you left your home and moved out here, I knew that I had."

Lauren tried to keep her smile in place but she struggled to catch her breath.

"You've done great work with these children," he continued.

Becky glanced from the sack on the floor to Edward Belmont's face. "You brought this?" she whispered, not wanting the children to hear her. "You're Mr. Virdot?"

"No. Just like the article said, Mr. Virdot's a man over in Richmond. I may not have forwarded your letter onto him though. I figured he might have had enough requests to deal with over there."

"So, you read all the letters that were sent in to the newspaper and Lauren's was one you chose?"

"Guilty as charged."

Nanny stepped forward. "Edward has been rather busy, fighting for the victims of people like your father and Prendergast. I consider him a member of my family."

"Well then, it looks like you just inherited nineteen orphans, Becky, the Leroys, and me," Lauren said with a smile, and this time it was genuine.

She turned to pick up the gift she had wrapped for her friend. "Thank you for everything you have done for me, Becky. You are the best friend anyone could wish for."

Becky opened the package. The wooden shingle said:

Hope House
Proprietors: Lauren Greenwood and Becky Tennant

"Big Will made it for me. Do you like it?"

"I love it," she whispered, tracing the letters with her fingers.

"Big Will told me he's got a replacement ready. The new one reads 'Becky Strauss'."

Becky turned scarlet, her eyes almost popping out of their sockets. "He got no right sayin' stuff like that. Don't you be listenin' to that man."

"What man?"

They both turned as Big Will walked in, followed by the Leroy family. Lauren distributed their gifts, while Big Will picked Becky up and squeezed her.

"When you going to put me out of my misery and marry me, my mountain girl?"

"You put me down this second, d'ya hear me?"

The children giggled as Big Will carried Becky out to the kitchen.

"This is the best Christmas ever, isn't it, Miss Lauren?" Ruthie was standing beside her.

"That it is, Ruthie, that it is." She cuddled the little girl as they all stared at the Christmas tree. Lottie's angel hung on top of the tree and cinnamon and gingerbread cookies in all different shapes hung on the branches, along with strings of popcorn scalloping the edges. Bart had fashioned some holders, Norma lit some candles, and the children cheered.

Ruthie and Lottie started to sing the words of "Away in a Manger" and soon everyone was singing along.

"*Away in a manger, no crib for His bed…*"

A LETTER FROM RACHEL

Thank you so much for reading *A Home for Unloved Orphans*. I cried and laughed while writing this book. I wanted to strangle Justin and Jackson and to wrap the little ones up in cotton wool so nothing would harm them again. I hope you loved the story. If you did enjoy it, and want to keep up to date with all my latest releases, just sign up at the following link. Your email address will never be shared and you can unsubscribe at any time.

www.bookouture.com/Rachel-Wesson

Although Delgany is a fictional town, much of what I wrote about the treatment of children is true. I'm Irish and grew up with horror stories of how children were treated in some of the religious orphanages in Ireland. I've since found out that children all over the world were schooled and "cared for" in similar harsh environments. It's a subject close to my heart as my father and his siblings narrowly avoided being sent to such a place after their father's death in 1951 left the family penniless. His uncle, a priest, wanted the boys admitted to a rather infamous Industrial School in Dublin, for no other reason than they were now "orphans". But for the strength of my grandmother, their story could have been similar to that of Cal or Dalton. The first time I saw my father cry was when the story of this particular school was told on RTÉ—the Irish national television station.

This book was also partly inspired by a book I read called *A Secret Gift* by Ted Gup. In the winter of 1933, Ted's grandfather decided to give a Christmas gift to some of his friends, neighbors, and fellow citizens, but he wanted the gift to be anonymous. He opened a checking account in the name of 'B. Virdot' and issued fifteen checks in the sum of $5 to fifteen people. The people who received the checks never knew his real name.

Ted found the newspaper ad and some letters from the recipients of the gift. He went on to meet family members of the original recipients and found out how the gift of $5 impacted their lives. It is hard to believe, especially today, what that gift meant to those people. Even the ones who didn't qualify got something out of the process. For many, it was the first time they articulated the impact of the Great Depression on their families. Most of the people were not shareholders or bankers or those you read about in history books relating to this era. They were ordinary people trying to keep their families fed, housed, and clothed in a time when they didn't know where the next meal was coming from.

One of the best parts of writing comes from reading the reactions from readers. Did the book make you smile or laugh, did it make you cry, were you ready to murder Justin and Lauren's father? What about Jackson? Did you fall in love with Cal, Ellie-Mae, Ruthie or little Lottie? If you enjoyed the story, I would absolutely love it if you could leave a short review. I enjoy interacting with readers so please do reach out to me. I am so grateful to everyone who buys and reads my books, allowing me to have the career I adore.

I hope you loved the characters in this book as Lauren, Becky, and the orphans have many more adventures ahead of them.

Thank you for reading.
Love, Rachel x

@authorrachelwesson

@wessonwrites

rachelwesson.com

ACKNOWLEDGMENTS

This is the first book I have written for Bookouture and it wouldn't be the same book without the incredible insight and support of my editor Christina Demosthenous. She has the patience of Job, the insight of King Solomon, and a fabulous sense of humor.

I'd also like to thank all readers of my earlier books, who gave me the encouragement to pursue my dreams. Marlene, the Janets, Meisje, Robin, and so many more. I am so grateful for your help and support.

Printed in Great Britain
by Amazon